LIVE LIKE LEGENDS

ALLIE SHANTE

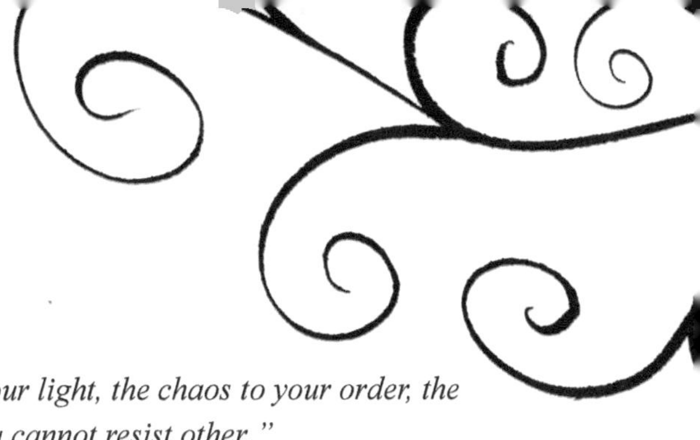

To that young thirteen year old girl who had a dream to write a story
that she was proud of…
I hope you're proud of me.

To anyone who needs to hear that they're strong, capable and
something to admire. Remember you are not weak and having
someone stand beside you when you're down can give you strength
you never thought possible.
Your light can be just as powerful as your darkness if you let it.

CONTENTS

PART THREE

Live Like Legends is the third and last book.
Reading Living Legend & Legendary is detrimental in how this story
is told. Make sure to get the full story so that you can enjoy without
any confusing chaos.

Live Like Legends has some content warnings that show up at certain
parts to help aid you while you read. It is up to you whether you read
them or not, or simply go in blind! The full list is on my website.

PROLOGUE

A LONG TIME AGO...

I was different, much more hard-headed. I had the kind of confidence that others envied, and I thrived off of it. There was so much talk about my achievements and my skills, but I didn't care much for the words of anyone else but hers. She was the most beautiful person I'd ever seen and just my luck, she wanted absolutely nothing to do with me. I was nice enough and she was cordial to me, but if she even caught a whiff of me flirting with her the conversation would be over. Jonah had continuously told me that there was someone else and I should have been fine with the hand of friendship she extended to me.

Eventually that's exactly what I did. I was a sentry, and she was a messenger. She had this eagerness to train and fight, but once you were settled into your chosen field, that was it. There was no changing that. I would secretly train with her, not because I found myself constantly wanting to be near her, but because I believed that if given the opportunity, she would have passed the test of a sentry angel with flying colors. I could always feel us getting closer, but there was always someone else. She kept them a secret and I respected that—begrudgingly so, but I didn't push.

I remember that baby being born. There was so much talk on both sides and while I didn't interact with the happy couple, I saw what this could mean for the colliding of entities. I remember Moira hoping that this could be the first step in the right direction for all our kinds. I knew that Jonah's father was angry at her, I knew he was jealous of how beloved Moira was. Hell, I loved her myself. She was best friends with the girl I loved, even though I would hardly admit that to myself at the time. Then everything fell apart. That baby was gone. Everyone was outraged and Isaac Zuriel was one hell of a tyrant, using it to his advantage.

Up until then, I had always shrugged off his threats and angry tones. I was a kid; I never really looked at the bigger picture until it was right in front of my face. This man wanted me to fight my friends and stand up against a group of individuals that had done nothing. I couldn't believe for a second that Natalia's mother would harm any living soul, especially something so innocent. Jonah was so scared of his own father back then; he was in so deep with eventually taking over that there was no getting through to him.

I said no. His father told me, *"you either fight with us, Mr. Cassial or you never set foot on this foundation again."*

I'd built so many memories at The Skies, it was like my second home, but whatever this man was turning it into wasn't my home anymore. So, I left it behind. I left my best friend. I left my rising status. And I'd left her.

I left Moira to fight on her own. I didn't think to go back and fight for the other side. For the first time in my entire life since handling the hilt of a sword, I just didn't see the point in the fighting.

Then everything was silent for a while. Years passed, my parents passed on and at some point, I ran into your mother again. So much had happened that I hadn't been around for, but for some reason as we spoke, it was like no time had passed at all. At one time there was someone else that kept us apart, but now there was no one in the way. He had died in that fight, and she made it very clear that she only wanted my friendship. That friendship turned into holding hands and cuddling on my couch. It turned into reconnecting with Jonah and his new wife, Amelia. Even Moira gave me another chance to make amends. Jonah never spoke about The Skies when we would spend time together, so we all let it be. I could feel my life coming back together.

Soon that friendship I wanted to maintain with her became something else. Slowly she started to let me kiss her and then we became this inseparable pair. She was mine, even if she continuously claimed she was out of my league.

Then I married her.

Next thing I knew…she told me we were having a baby boy.

She had her secrets though and one-night things that happened during that war came out, how she lost her first love was revealed to me and how she still carried a piece of him with her—magic that he'd transferred from himself to her. On that very long night, I knew I would do anything for both of you.

While I was away Jonah's father had made it so that any show of Enchanter magic outside of Oculus, especially the magic that they had deemed threatening and unworthy would be dealt with in the harshest form—torture and death being his two options. Lilith may have been trapped in Purgatory, but he was no better than her. I had tried to get Jonah to reason with his father, but he never would. Isaac Zuriel never truly liked my friendship with his son in the first place so he would know where the resistant attitude came from.

Then as it always seemed to do, things fell apart. All of us were spending time as friends and you were just the cutest thing. Your wings were coming in and you were so adventurous and had this thirst for knowledge even at such a young age. Jonah and Amelia had gone off by themselves for a moment and we took our eyes off you for just a second, but that was all it took. You got too close to the edge of a steep hill that you shouldn't have even been near. And you…you fell.

We ran to get you and my heart stopped in my chest seeing you on the ground, crumpled up and lifeless. You were bleeding from the back of your head and there was so much blood that I couldn't think straight. The best infirmary in the realms was at The Skies, but we didn't want to fly with you in that condition and portal usage was something we were all so rusty at, thanks to Isaac banning it, that it was like our hands were tied. She…your mother…she was breathing so hard, she looked like she wanted to scream. She brought her eyes up to mine and I knew what she was telling me what she had to do. She loved you far too much to let you go.

We nodded at each other, and I looked around to make sure no one was watching. She placed her hands on your body and closed her eyes. There were these lights that lit up her fingers, but it wasn't an angelic light. The colors were a green shade, mixed with a white that I was mesmerized by. Her brow was furrowed, she was concentrating so hard, and it was like the light was scanning your body and then eventually it was gone. She opened her eyes, and they were glassy as if she was so afraid it wouldn't work that tears had started to form.

Your eyes blinked once, twice, and then those brown eyes that looked so much like hers were looking back at me. Your mother let out this nervous laugh, like she was even surprised it worked at all, but then she grabbed you and hugged you.

Almost losing you was the worst thing I could have imagined. But then I lost something else.

Someone was watching that day. Someone saw what your mother did and ran straight to Jonah's father, but she never told me who. I had to find out the hard way and hope that you didn't suffer from all the rage I held in for the first few years without her.

She didn't want you to seek revenge for it. She didn't want you to spend your whole life fighting for her when you could try to make this place something better for when your time came to make decisions and be the kind of angel we always knew you'd be. Your mother believed that angels did not have the right to dictate Enchanter powers, so she made sure the gift—the power—she was given by her first love remained in someone good, someone she loved with all her heart.

Before they came for her, she made me promise her something.

"I don't want him to remember this, Maurice, please. Make him forget. If he wants to fight, don't let him fight for me. I won't be his burden to bear or the reason he doesn't live the life he deserves. Let him fight for something all on his own. Love him for both of us, he's the best piece of both our hearts."

I did what she asked. I went to the only person I knew that could do what she'd wanted.

You begged for your mother so many times. You didn't understand, but then Moira touched your forehead with tears in her eyes and took away your pain. Your mother was a fleeting memory and everything about the day you watched them take her from our home was gone. Moira didn't take everything, but she removed enough to where you didn't linger on those memories. I kept my answers to you short and concise, letting you believe she'd simply just left us. I did it all for the sake of a woman who still has a hold on me even after all these years.

I kept that promise for her, for my Scarlett, even though I knew what it might mean when the day came for you to find out the truth.

Your mother loved you.

She died loving you.

PART ONE

"It's never too late to be what you might have been."

Death.

Experiencing it was one thing, but having lived *through* it was something entirely different. I had seen it firsthand, watched the light leave creatures' eyes as they took their final piece of my torture and then succumbed to their wounds. It always seemed to happen so fast even when I was trying to make it last and give the crowds something to salivate over. My own death—the thing that still haunted me daily—was a constant slow-motion rendition of everything playing in my head. I wondered if this happened to every single entity that ever got resurrected.

Did they also have memories of their deaths?

Was the last visual they saw a person they loved? That's how it was for me and despite a dagger to the stomach being a painful way to go, seeing the angel that owned your heart crying over you was worse. Much, much worse.

I'd had that same thought pass through my mind right before I passed out in Nicholas's bed. I'd been staying in his room ever since I got discharged from the infirmary, well, more like Nick *told* me I was staying with him, and I wasn't about to argue if I could have him all to myself. It had been nearly two weeks now and Nicholas Cassial had doted on me continuously, but my answers to him were always the same.

I felt fine. No, I was better than fine. I felt *balanced*.

It was an odd thing to admit, but it was the truth. I wasn't about to go into details about something I didn't quite understand yet. I hadn't really had enough time to process it since getting swept away and, yet again, being on lockdown at The Skies. Elise had chosen to stay at Oculus with Natalia and Xander, stating in the nicest way possible that 'she would rather gouge out both her eyeballs with one of Reese's arrows than be stuck in this fortress of ineptitude again.' Garrett and Beetee had remained in Oculus with her, even though Beetee herself didn't have any choice in the matter if Elise had anything to say about it. I hadn't seen much of them if I really thought about it; everything had moved so fast once the dust seemed to settle.

Nick had sat me down the night we settled into his room and told me about Beetee. I had let him speak without interruption, but I knew that he was looking for some kind of reaction out of me. I had simply nodded and told him that I wasn't all that surprised. I had a feeling her snake shifting abilities weren't the only thing intriguing about her. I knew Nick assumed Beetee and I would have some sort of weird connection since we were both hybrids, but things were a big, jumbled mess now. I couldn't even begin to imagine how that conversation would even begin.

I loved Nick with all my heart, but he wasn't the person I wanted to talk to about what I was feeling. I needed to speak to someone who understood magic, dark or light, the way he couldn't. I had no idea if his newfound powers, his whole necromancy moment, was the reason my insides felt the way they did. My dagger had always been my main source of everything and now that was gone. I wanted to talk to Natalia, but I learned she only ever came to The Skies for short periods, likely trying to avoid Ariel at all costs. I didn't blame her. My insides didn't seem to be battling for dominance any longer, so I wouldn't ponder on this odd sense of peace in my...*soul*? For now, I was the best I could be.

The minute the word, *fine*, left my lips, Nick would look at me with that raised eyebrow expression of his that screamed skepticism, but he'd eventually concede because arguing with me never ended well for him. Okay, arguing with me *did* end well for him during our little fight in the training room, but that was much different. I had dealt with his many, many versions of "I'm fine" while we were in Purgatory so he could deal with mine.

He had stomped past my room in the infirmary after I'd told him to go talk to Natalia about what had happened in Purgatory and what he had done, but somewhere in between, leaving my room and whisking me away to his, something threw him off. Nicholas was so set in his ways that getting anything out of him was like cutting through thigh muscle. That shit was thick and tough, no matter how sharp the blade.

I wasn't a complete idiot and could figure out that it had something to do with how he came to have resurrection powers. I was cuddled up against his chest, when he leaned into me, speaking right into my hair and told me everything. What I was not prepared for was for him to tell me that it had anything to do with his mother. My heart nearly broke the moment he uttered the words that she had died, his voice cracking just a tiny bit.

There were times when his voice was tight like he was holding in anger and times when it was soft like he was trying not to cry. He'd told me how he was surprised about Natalia's mother, but that Natalia herself would be more upset about that part than he was. The air felt different when he was done speaking and I realized I had been holding my breath for too long when my chest felt tight.

I figured he hadn't wanted me to say anything about his confession, but I did say the only thing that mattered. I said I was sorry. There was so much he knew and still so much he didn't. Even the smallest missing details could seem major for a revelation like that.

His response was just to hold me tighter and kiss my hair, leaning further towards me and angling my chin so that I was looking at him.

Even in the darkness of his room, his features were always something I could make out. His lips met mine and it was quick and chaste, but it was enough. He'd put on a good front pretending to act like the information didn't affect him, but the realization that after all that time in Purgatory, he hadn't once decided to go home and see his father. It had me concerned for lack of a better word. Maurice Cassial was clearly giving his son space, which was fair, but at some point, someone would have to cave. I had a much better chance of convincing the younger Cassial.

At least that's what I'd thought. I hadn't anticipated him being so fucking good at redirecting the conversation to more physical pursuits or finding some reason to leave and dodge talking, which is exactly what he'd done early this morning before the sun came up. His excuse: sentry angel stuff—whatever the fuck that meant. That was also what he'd said yesterday, but today I had been too fucking tired to argue with him. It was as if he had said what was needed and was moving on, which included leaving his father behind.

The moment the topic was brought up, he would look annoyed and claim there was nothing left to say. That was true, there was nothing left to say—*to me*—but to his father, there was still so much more. When Nick and I were so close, snuggled up together, whether it be day or night, I felt warmer, like his light and whatever light I had mingled and coexisted together. I could feel at times that his light would waver like something that used to light it up just a little brighter was gone, same as the light in his eyes would dim when any mention of his father was brought up. There was some darkness there, always letting me know that he wasn't cured of his internal pain, but I would honestly be more concerned if it didn't linger just a bit. It was a part of him now, but he was working through it, and I had never been prouder of him.

He was hurt, but I'd told him so many times in Purgatory that letting it out was a lot better than keeping it in. I couldn't help him through *this* conversation like I'd done before. What I *could* do was incessantly annoy him about it to the point that maybe he would rather go home than stay quiet, not that my plan was working out well for me.

My overworked mind was rivaling what should have been restful sleep when I felt a surprising but not unpleasant feeling between my legs. My panties were being moved to the side and a cloud of warm breath hit my pussy. I felt my stomach tighten but I kept my eyes closed. I felt kisses being placed along my inner thighs and then one kiss right at my clit. Something wet that felt like a tongue flicked against the sensitive bundle and I clenched the comforter in my hand. I hadn't had a dream like this in a minute and with everything going on, I severely needed it. The tongue took one long lick and then another, eventually hyper focusing on my clit like it was on a mission to give me the best fucking orgasm. I reached up and held onto the pillow behind my head, letting out a moan into what I assumed was an empty room.

I felt hands wrap around my thighs and push my legs up and apart a little more. One of the hands glided towards the inside of my thigh, between my legs and a finger slid down my wet slit. That finger gently circled my entrance and then slid inside. My body responded in this way like I knew the hand those fingers were attached to. The finger curled, massaging that part of me that made my toes curl, and matched with the way it moved in time with the skilled tongue had me wanting to scream.

I pressed my lips together before parting them, blowing out a breath and whimpering, "more."

I heard a groan, and it sounded familiar, like I'd heard it muffled against my ear recently. I still had my eyes closed and my mind was foggy from sleep, but I turned my head seeing the tiny bits of light from behind my eyelids. I slowly started to open my eyes, slightly disappointed that this dream was over, when I felt two fingers slide inside of me and a mouth clamp around my clit. I bit my bottom lip as my eyes flew open, the window in the bedroom shining light on the large lump that was shrouded in covers as I looked down the bed.

This wasn't a dream at all, and I knew exactly whose fingers those were. I must have been in a deep sleep to not be aware of that tongue and who it belonged to. His other hand worked its way up my body, pushing the t-shirt of his I wore further up. The warmth of his skin sent tingles throughout my own. I slipped my hand under the covers and down my stomach until I felt his mess of hair. I grasped as many of the strands as I could, pressing his face further between my thighs. His growl of approval had me thrusting my pelvis up against him, wanting more of what he could give me. He pressed a third finger inside, keeping up the rhythm his tongue created along my clit.

"Fuck, Nick. That's so good, so fucking good," I felt my thighs tighten as his fingertips kept rubbing that perfect spot over and over again. My heart thundered in my chest from the way he sucked my clit into his mouth and then flicked his tongue over it, just to bring it back into his mouth again. I pushed my body into the comforter trying to hold out and make this last, but *fuck*, he was good at this. My orgasm slammed into me so hard I had to close my eyes again, so I could hopefully regain some composure. His mouth and fingers left me, not before he planted a soft kiss to my pussy while both his hands trailed their way up my body.

He tickled me as he traveled towards my face. I giggled, searching for him under the covers, but he swerved out of the way, continuing to torment me. He eventually let up, shoving the covers away from his head with a smirk on his face. His hair was a mess and his mouth glistened slightly, still coated in my arousal. His smirk melted into an adoring expression that was only reserved for me when he nuzzled his nose alongside my own. "There she is."

"Hi," I answered, leaning up to kiss him. I tasted myself and it caused me to wiggle the lower half of my body against him. Nick pulled away, burying his face into my neck, planting kisses that heated my skin to an unhealthy temperature. His hand toyed with the hem of my shirt and dragged it up, so that he could touch more of my skin, eventually palming one of my breasts. As if on instinct, I lifted my legs so that my knees were bent near his sides. "Nick, we need to talk."

He removed his hand from my chest and back down to where my panties were. Hooking his fingers into them, he deftly slid them down, removing them from one of my legs but not bothering with the other. "Mmhmm." His voice was muffled as he continued to move in a way that we both knew so well. Before I could blink, he had his pants down enough to slide his cock against me.

"Nick," I said, trying to sound stern, but it only came out like a desperate plea when a moan escaped right after it as he pushed inside of me with ease. "Oh, god."

He continued to rock into me, his rhythm almost lazy, but it was still meticulous like he knew exactly what I liked and what felt good for both of us. He pressed his forehead to mine, his breath mingling with mine as he grabbed the side of my face gently, grazing his thumb along my cheek. He pushed his hips against me, and I swallowed hard, trying to remember myself and get my shit together.

"Nick."

His eyes were closed when he answered me, "yes?"

"T-talk. You a-and m-me." My words were coming out stuttered as he kept thrusting into me over and over again.

He nodded, but not in a way that told me he was understanding but more like he was distracted by what we were doing to really give me all of his attention. "Talk. *Fuck*. Okay, right." He kept his one hand on my face and moved his other one to my thigh, bringing it up higher. The movement now caused me to feel his cock deeper and nearly had me screaming.

I licked my lips, gathering my thoughts. This wasn't the best time to say any of this, but there *never* seemed to be a right time with this man. "We really need to....*fuck*...talk about your, *yes, right there*."

My words were lost when he took the one hand that was still wrapped around my thigh and started rubbing his fingers along my clit. My orgasm had been starting to creep up on me, but right then I felt myself starting to come. He pulled me in for a deep kiss that had me needing oxygen. My breathing started to even out as he started to pull out, which had me feeling like my opportunity to question him was among us. That was short-lived, when he lifted himself up, grabbing me and flipping me over in one fluid motion so I was on my hands and knees in front of him.

I blew my hair out of my face as he tugged on my panties that hung off my other leg, chucking them onto the floor. He smoothed my shirt out of the way, so he had a full view of my lower back and ass. I looked over my shoulder watching him. Nick spread his whole hand out, palming each cheek. He pressed one of his fingers inside of me, then took it out, putting it in his mouth to taste me again. A satisfied groan left his throat. "You're so fucking perfect, needy one." He grabbed his cock, teasing my pussy as he worked himself over my clit and then up to where I wanted him most. I felt him push inside of me, inch by inch, wanting me to feel all of him and all I wanted to do was bury my face in a pillow and take it. He pulled out all the way to the tip and then drove himself back in with no hesitation, starting to create a less casual rhythm than before.

I would regret this...I really, *really* fucking knew I would, but in the long run this would be good for him. At least that's what I hoped for.

"I really think...*oh, fuck*, we need to talk about your...*fuck*, your dad." I almost felt myself cringe when the words left my lips. Out of all the times I'd brought up what happened in Purgatory and his conversation with his father, I'd never brought it up during sex. It was a risk, but I loved a little risk.

Nick slowed his movements, but he didn't necessarily stop. I could feel the pressure his fingertips were applying to my hips, while he took in my words as if he was making sure I had actually said what he thought I'd said. "Did you really just bring up my father?"

"Umm, well..." I started, bringing my bottom lip into my mouth as his hips moved slowly, "yes."

"Why in the fuck did you think right now was the best time for that?" He brought his hand towards the middle of my back and pushed me down, so that my ass was propped up more and I instinctively turned my face so my cheek could rest against the pillow. His cock was still moving inside of me, and I could feel his motions becoming quicker and more persistent.

"You really haven't... *yes, don't stop*, left me with any other options," I replied in between the moments of pure pleasure he was still bestowing upon me.

Nick held my hips and moved me with him, harder and rougher, as if he was unloading all of his frustrations towards the situation I was trying to mend. My ass hit his pelvis over and over again, but he didn't let up. "I don't want to talk about my father while I'm fucking you. All you should be thinking about is how good my cock feels inside that pretty pussy of yours." His palm landed right on my ass with a loud smack. I nearly yelped in surprise and the stinging quickly dissolved into more need that caused my thighs to tremble.

I started to speak again, but another smack landed on my other cheek and the words got caught in my throat. His bed was starting to shake, and my orgasm was brewing, I could feel it…yet again. I planted my hands on either side of my head, pushing myself up so I could look at him over my shoulder.

"But Nick, I think…"

He reached out and grabbed my hair, pulling me up so that my back was to his front. He leaned down enough so that his mouth grazed the shell of my ear. "*I* think *you* should focus on coming, like my good girl." He put his hand between my legs and rapidly began to rub my clit. He was completely obliterating any sort of coherent thoughts I could have, but there was always this tiny piece of reality that settled in the forefront of my mind. No matter how good his dick was, he couldn't just make me forget.

"*Fuck, fuck, Nick*, I just seriously think…"

Nick held me in place as he pounded into me in short rapid thrust, wrapping his large hand around my throat and tilting my head up. "Just come for me and we can talk about whatever you want, baby."

"We both know you're lying, Nicholas," I taunted, reaching around, and grabbing the hand that was clasping my throat. He moved harder, but when he looked down at me, he was smirking. It was that look of adoration again with just a hint of annoyance. "But, fuck, I really want you to make me come." His fingers pressed on my clit as they continued to rub, and I felt my orgasm barrel through.

"That's it. That's my good girl," he praised as I held his hand against the soft skin of my throat. I let my orgasm continue to come in waves and I heard him groan behind me almost like he was in some sort of pain, but I was too far in my sex fog to determine the cause. He pumped into me a few more times before he released all that he had inside of me, resting his head on top of mine and breathing heavily.

I released his hand which he swiftly removed from my sight…which was odd. He bent down to kiss my hair, my neck and both my shoulders, mumbling an *I love you* with each kiss. I felt his cock leave me, each and every time making me realize how full he made me feel. He walked back on his knees, pulling his pants back up. Nick shimmied off the bed and headed for his bathroom. I settled back on the bed, searching for my panties somewhere in the giant heap of fucked up sheets and comforter. Once I'd found them, I dragged them up my legs and sat cross legged on top of the sheets.

Nick emerged from his bathroom, immediately heading for his dresser. I narrowed my eyes directly at his back, knowing that he could feel my stare.

"Nicholas?"

"Yeah?" He answered, searching in one of his drawers. He pulled out a fresh shirt, throwing it on top of the wooden piece of furniture and started to remove the current shirt he was wearing.

I cleared my throat and started to mimic him, "'just come for me and we can talk about whatever you want, baby.' Sound familiar?"

I noticed his shoulders tense and his impressive back muscles pulled together. He finished getting dressed before turning to look at me. "There really isn't anything to talk about. I told you everything he said to me, so I don't really understand why you keep pushing. There isn't anything for me to say to him."

I scoffed, "I'm not pushing. I'm trying to understand." I wagged my finger in his direction. "That's a load of bullshit by the way. From what you told me you didn't say much to him at all. I have a really distinct feeling you heard him speak, said some version of *what the fuck, dad* or *how could you*, and stormed out." I raised an eyebrow expecting him to try to tell me I was wrong.

Nick looked away from me, giving me my answer.

"Ugh, Nick, I'm not trying to…"

"He kept so much shit from me, he fucking withheld things from me about my own mother! The man lied to me, Dani!" He shouted, slamming the still open drawer shut. Ah, there it was.

I let out a heavy sigh and moved off the bed. I padded over to where he stood, wrapping my arms around him, and tilting my face up so I could see him. At first, he didn't move, he just let me hold him, but with every passing second his tension melted away and he placed both his hands on either side of my face. I stood on the tips of my toes and kissed his lips. "Maybe I do push a little, but that's because I care. You have every right to be upset but maybe some time has passed that you can try to look at it from his point of view. He is still your dad, babe."

He nodded, but it was the same nod as before. The nod that told me he was distracted and only doing it for the benefit of the moment. He moved his hand to the back of head, threading his fingers into my hair and pulled me towards him, kissing my forehead.

He gave me the answer he always ended up on. "Yeah, okay."

"Nick."

"I'll think about it, how's that?"

I kissed his nose, mumbling a *fine* against his skin. "Can I go with you?"

He raised one of his eyebrows. "Go where?"

I took a step back and nodded over to his door. "Wherever you're going. I'm quite literally a prisoner in your room, Nicholas."

He ran a frustrated hand through his hair. "Don't be dramatic, you are not a…"

"I promise you I can be dramatic when I need to, but right now I'm speaking only the truth. The only outside knowledge I get is from you reporting on life beyond that door. We've been out of your room once and that's only because it was pitch black outside and I'd begged you for twenty-four hours straight. Not to mention every time I tried to bring up your dad you kept trying to kiss me, mister master deflector."

Nick closed his eyes, tilting his head towards the ceiling. He hadn't bound me to his bedroom or threatened me into remaining here under his watch, but after the first two days of living in his room, he'd come back from his first of many Ariel meetings and told me—in so many words—that the red-headed angel was still not my biggest fan and that he was severely unimpressed, but also not surprised with the fact that Lilith was still out there. Nick had thought it was best I didn't try to move about The Skies—unless he was with me, and it was the fucking witching hour— in hopes that I wouldn't run into Ariel or any of the other sentries he had gotten to follow his lead of tyrannical insanity. I'd wanted to let things cool down but after about three days of his insanely boring four walls, I'd wanted a change.

"I can handle Ariel, you know."

He shook his head. "I know you can handle yourself. You are probably one of the most capable creatures I know." He sent a small smile in my direction, "I just…with everything that happened…Ariel can be a triggering individual." Nicholas had a good heart, a heart he had ultimately given to me, and I had a feeling that was holding me back from simply walking out of this room during all hours of the day.

"I'm well aware or did you think I forgot about the time you almost pounded his face in because he insinuated you made all your choices because I seduced you."

He narrowed his eyes at me, but there was a glint of playfulness.

"You also almost beat him up because he talked shit about your dad. I'm pretty sure *that* Nicholas would give his old man a chance."

The playfulness was gone, and it looked like he was lost for a moment remembering a time when he held his father on a pedestal. He licked his lips, taking one step towards me. He kissed my forehead again. "I said I would think about it."

I placed my hands on my hips, blowing a loose curl from my face. "And I've said to *you* before that I can control myself. If you want me to believe you, you will need to believe me." I didn't have my dagger anymore and that in itself had me feeling like I was just an ordinary demon. I felt like something Ariel shouldn't be worried about, although there was a nagging feeling telling me that was a complete lie and that I should quit while I'm ahead.

"You need to just lay low, alright. We don't need anything leading Lilith or Dimitri to believe you're alive. Until I can get Ariel to simmer down and not look at you like…" he hesitated, rubbing his lips together. The sun was starting to shine through his window more, casting a light on his face and that distinctive scar under his eye.

"A monster," I finished for him. "I know you don't think I'm anything like that Nick, but the longer you hide me away in here, the more you are giving into whatever Ariel thinks. I can be a lot more helpful out there than I will be in here, or at least I won't understand how helpful I *can* be unless you let me out so I can talk to Natalia."

Nick gave me a sympathetic look, almost like he wanted to keep me in this bubble to shield me from the realms. It was sweet but suffocating. "Just relax. I'll be back with some food, and I'll take you for a midnight walk through The Skies again later tonight." He sounded like he wanted that moment to hold me over for the time being and all I could do was roll my eyes. He grabbed his sword from where it leaned next to his dresser.

I caught a small glimpse of his hand, the one he had pulled back from around my throat far too quickly. I thought I saw a pink handprint on his skin, almost like a surface level burn. "Nick, what's on your hand?"

He tensed for a moment, but rallied, placing the hand in question into his pants pocket. He took one of my hands in his free one and kissed it. "I'm going to be late, but I'll be back soon. I love you."

He had given me one last forehead kiss and was out the door before I could figure out what the fuck just happened.

I walked over to his dresser and leaned down, opening up one of the drawers that had my clothes in it. Pulling out what I wanted, I headed towards the bathroom. I turned the knob for the shower, running my hand under the water while I waited for it to get hot.

Nicholas had told me to stay put.

I told him to talk to his dad.

I laughed to myself, shaking my head. I guess neither one of us was getting our wish. I had sat in this room and played house with him, waiting for way too long. I removed my clothes and stepped into the shower knowing he would be less than thrilled. My handsome angel should know by now that his authoritative tone only worked when he planned to get me naked and use that mouth for better things.

I rubbed my hand as Reese and I walked down the hall. It didn't hurt, well, it didn't hurt *now*. The moment I felt the heat from her palm sink into my skin, I wanted to immediately pull away, but in a moment like the one we had, it was extremely hard to want to do anything but let her do whatever she wanted.

This wasn't the first time it had happened, but this *was* the first time she'd started to notice. The burn was never bad enough to leave a scar, so the evidence wasn't there too long to rouse any sort of suspicion. I should have been one hundred percent concerned with why it was happening in the first place, but I was honestly rattled by the idea that I didn't have an answer to that very question if she were to find out and question it herself.

"You good?" Reese asked, waving his hand in front of my face as we walked. I was walking, but he walked with a slight limp given the damage he took to his leg during our fight in Purgatory. It wasn't noticeable anymore unless you really paid attention. His wings had survived without much of an issue, but from what he'd told me about his continuous visits to the infirmary, his leg needed more time.

I shooed him away, placing both my hands in my pockets. "Yes, why?"

"You have that preoccupied look on your face. The one where you would rather be anywhere else, but you also have a job to do so you have to look like you care."

"I don't look like that."

Reese scoffed. "Yes, you do. I would think shacking up with your girlfriend would make you a little less like you have stick up your ass."

I rolled my eyes. "Having Ariel second guessing and undermining everything I have to say allows me to have this look on my face," I bit the inside of my cheek. "She's also not my girlfriend."

My best friend stopped, grabbing my elbow. We were a few steps from the briefing room doors and all I wanted to do was go inside and yet again have my ass chewed out for things I couldn't control, while actively avoiding this conversation.

"Excuse me?"

"What is the problem now?" I said, annoyed.

"Let me try to understand this…you went all the way to Purgatory for her, yet you haven't asked her to be your girlfriend?" Reese's hazel eyes narrowed as if he was truly trying to break down the very words he spoke.

"Oh, I'm so sorry, my first thought when coming back to Heaven's Gate wasn't to lock down my relationship."

Reese shrugged. "I mean she did basically die, so wouldn't you want to make the most out of her newly resurrected status." Then he smirked. "I mean, besides having more sex than I think you've ever had in your twenty-four years of life."

I let out a small chuckle, but then there was a sharp tug at my chest at his mention of my age. My birthday had been during the time I'd spent away from Dani, those months we didn't speak. My mind drifted slightly to the tiny party my father threw for me. I was never one for big ordeals, especially for my birthday, so it was small and intimate. It took my mind off of the darkness I was harboring, and I felt lighter even if it was only for a few hours. Maurice Cassial didn't always know everything that was going on with me, but he somehow knew how to make me feel just a little bit better with the simplest things.

I shook my head letting the happy memory fall away. I realized I had yet to even tell him all the details of my time in Purgatory, all the dark things my mind still toyed with every now and again. None of that seemed even half as important as finding out my mother hadn't just up and left us like he let me believe or that somehow, I gained additional powers I still didn't quite understand from a woman I would never know.

As if he could read my mind, Reese said, "he asked about you."

I turned for us to start walking again. "Who?"

"Don't play dumb, Nick. He just wanted to know how you were doing, that's all."

"Did you tell him I was just fucking fine?"

Reese rubbed between his eyebrows with his index and middle finger. "Yes, although I did leave out the hostility."

"Great. Is he doing fine?" Once we got to the doors, two sentries were stationed outside as Ariel had now permitted. They were literally in every single briefing room, lounge area, the cafeteria and the outside of the Divine Library. I swore even the storage closets had security.

The sentries nodded at us, remembering us from the last ten times we'd been here.

"Yes, he's fine, except for the fact that his son refuses to see or speak to him. You told me what happened, and I understand you're upset but..."

"Good, let's move on." I had told Reese as much as he needed to know and the look of sympathy in his eyes had me regretting opening my mouth at all. Despite his lack of words when I'd finished relaying my newly found past, Reese had just sat in silence with me, realizing that right then I didn't want pity or comforting words. Now that some time had passed, it was like he and Dani had some sort of mutual agreement when it came to getting me to finally talk to my father.

The sound of hinges unlocking and the door creaking open filled my ears as I cut him off. I heard Reese let out a sigh. The sentries moved to the side so we could step over the threshold and see Ariel in all his unearned glory.

His red hair was tucked behind his ears and hit right at his earlobes. His teal suit looked freshly washed and ironed. He was speaking to angels who looked like messengers when the doors closed behind us. Ariel leaned against the long table, but straightened when he noticed us. He spoke a few more words to the others, gave a cheeky laugh which they reciprocated, then sent them on their way.

The angels gave Reese and I small smiles before they left. It always felt as if people wanted to say so much more, but with Ariel around it was hard to speak your mind without being reprimanded for having a personal thought.

"On time yet again. I'm delighted you boys are following the rules," Ariel said, giving two small claps.

Reese laughed. "Let's not pretend like you aren't making us come here to keep an eye on us."

"All I want is everyone's safety, Mr. Diniel. It is quite simple."

I pulled out a chair, removing my sword from behind my back and sat down. "We've already told you Lilith thinks she's dead. I hardly think she's coming to search for her."

"You've yet to explain to me how it is that Lilith would have this idea of her demise to begin with," Ariel pushed, pulling out the chair next to me and sitting way too close for my liking. He had this way of trying to be intimidating, which almost had me laughing. Dani was way more intimidating than this guy.

I watched as Reese leaned against the side of my chair. He cocked his head to the side. "That part doesn't matter. What *should* matter is that Heaven's Gate is safe, and you can keep going on your perfect little hunt for Jonah's magic."

Ariel flicked his eyes up to Reese who made sure to stand his ground. "Ah of course you also have some loyalty to the Soul Seether just like your charming friend here." He motioned towards me.

I felt my hands clench around the arm rests. "She hasn't done anything worth your attention since she's been here so just back off.

Maybe, I don't know, everyone wouldn't feel like she's some kind of pariah if you just stop trying to scare them into thinking she's the villain."

Ariel shook his head. "Nicholas, I've heard your request over and over and I honestly don't think bringing her into our society like it's normal is something the people are willing to do."

Reese leaned down a little, getting into Ariel's space. "Have you even considered asking them?"

"I have bigger issues to focus on than what you want for the girl you like. I've allowed her to stay under the conditions I've told you. I've also allowed your other trespassing friends to remain as well. I am not an idiot; I am well aware that opening a portal to Purgatory is ill form at the moment. I am generous if nothing else for providing everyone with a place here." Ariel held his hands up as if he was the victim here and we were berating him.

"Under your conditions!" I nearly growled, hearing the wood of the armrests whine under my hold on them. "Your conditions are wanting to keep her locked up. The rest of them would rather stay with Natalia than be anywhere near here. She's trading one prison for another and it's not smart to think that she won't grow tired of that." I only spoke the truth since she had pretty much told me as much earlier.

Ariel simply smirked. "Well, that must mean you need to have a better handle on her now doesn't it, Nicholas. You spent all this time defying everyone just to be with her and what…you can't deal with her anymore. If *you* would still like a place here, you will keep her away." He swatted his hand towards me, communicating that he was done with this part of the conversation. "I have more pressing matters with Jonah's magic. I did task you with helping with the search, speaking to those who could be useful."

Reese nodded. "We did all those things and came up with nothing. You think maybe Jonah's powers simply don't want to be found by *you* specifically. It would explain a lot."

The executive gave him a tight-lipped smile. "The magic doesn't work like that, I assure you. Jonah was secretive about many things, so it just takes time to figure that out. Jonah's father's power went immediately to his son without hesitation. Without an heir, well, he seems to have hidden it away as if it's some sort of game." Ariel made a disgusted noise before turning to me expectantly. "I asked you to question your father, so did that bring anything new?"

Ariel had told me to ask my father questions about Jonah and where he would suspect the magic was. We'd had small conversations about Jonah's magic here and there after his death, but nothing jumped out at me that made me think he knew anything about where Jonah would have hidden it. I wasn't about to explain to Ariel all the reasons why I wasn't on speaking terms with my father right now so I said the only thing I could. "It didn't."

Reese let out a deep sigh as if he was annoyed by my answer.

"Damn, well then we will have to move forward with the ceremony and celebration as I had planned." Ariel nodded more to himself as he got up from his chair. He rubbed a hand down both his velvet lapels and turned to us. "Jonah's magic simply doesn't need to be found. I have waited too long and so have the people of Heaven's Gate. They need a leader and maybe then once the power is settled and I have leverage, then I can see about letting your precious Soul Seether out…under supervision of course."

"Woah, you can't be serious. Does no one get a vote on this?" Reese asked, his hazel eyes wide.

Ariel chuckled almost as if the question was absurd. "Of course not. As much as I didn't care much for Jonah's father, the man did believe in a strong leadership. I would like to continue that."

"I think you are confusing democracy with dictatorship." I spat out.

"Call it what you like, but in a few weeks you all will officially answer to me. It is a fact, Mr. Cassial. One that you should get behind quickly or your hand will be forced."

I shot up from my chair, walking up to him and sticking my finger into his chest. "I do all these things you asked because it's easier than arguing half the time, but you can't *force* me to do anything. The last time we spoke, and you acted like this, I told you that you don't deserve this, this position isn't yours and it never will be. No ceremony will ever make me answer to you the way I did with Jonah."

Ariel let his green eyes take me in. He let out one cool breath, removing my finger from his jacket. "You know your father tried to get out of his duty and well, he never stepped foot on these grounds for a very long time after that."

His words brought me back to my father's story, his truth about the past. His truth about all the things he'd let fall away for the sake of my mother's wishes. Why did every fucking thing come back to that man? No matter what I did to try not to think about him, he still seemed to invade my life at every turn.

I opened my mouth to argue but a loud grunt and then a crash caught all of our attention.

"The fuck was that?" Reese said, swiveling his head towards the door.

I reached for my sword, taking a small step forward.

Ariel stood behind us, like he automatically assumed we would protect him, when in reality all I wanted to do was throw him at whatever was waiting on the other side. If I knew myself at all, I would likely fight to protect him, but it was an intrusive thought that I knew Reese was likely thinking as well.

Another thump and panting, then a muffled *they are in there*.

I made a move to step closer when I smelled it. The one smell that could calm me, but in this very moment, frustrated the fuck out of me.

The door opened with a dramatic flourish slamming against the stone wall. Dani stepped over the sentry on the floor and strutted into the room with all the confidence in the realm.

"Thank you," she said as the sentry scurried backwards, attempting to pick up his lost sword but failing multiple times. Dani eyed all of us, but her brown eyes landed on mine with such intensity I knew she was silently telling me that I should have seen this coming.

"Nicholas! What is the meaning of this!?" Ariel sputtered. "Where are the guards! Any of them!"

Dani walked over to me, and I kept her eye contact, but I only broke it to look over her head at Reese. He ducked his head out the door and looked down the hall. He let out a small chuckle. "Yeah, I think they are a little out of it at the moment. Nice job for what it's worth." He gave

Dani a thumbs up, but quickly stopped when he looked behind me at most likely a disgruntled Ariel.

"What did you do?" I asked the no nonsense hybrid I just so happened to be in love with.

Her curls bounced as she got on the tips of her toes to peck my lips. "I found you."

3
DANI

He had this look of shock on his face that had me wanting to burst into a fit of laughter, but I refrained for the sake of his very unimpressed leader. Ariel's face was turning redder by the minute and there was a moment where I thought he might combust.

It didn't take me long to find Nicholas, but my time would have been cut in half if I hadn't been stopped every few steps by a power-hungry angel who thought I was some sort of threat. It was as if each one knew who I was, but wanted to test their luck with how far they would get in a fight with me. I had to admit I thoroughly enjoyed the interactions as negative as they were. Each one gave me a different direction which finally led me here.

"Lucky you. You found a girl who is willing to tear down at least ten sentries for you," Reese said, rapping his knuckles against the doorframe.

"Ten is an understatement and a little insulting," I added, running my hand through my surprised angel's hair. He grabbed my hand and squeezed it with his own.

"Dani, I told you…"

"I told *you* I wouldn't sit idly by anymore, did I not?" I interrupted, yanking my hand away from him.

Ariel rushed around him so that he was nearly in between us. "I don't give you many jobs Mr. Cassial but keeping her in line was one of them and you can't even do that. You want me to trust her and allow her freedom here? The minute she is given access without supervision she goes and does this." The executive motioned towards the door.

"If your sentries had been more forthcoming, it wouldn't have come to that," I stated, shrugging. "No one is seriously hurt, so thank your angelic stars for that."

Ariel swiped a hand over his forehead, exasperated. "I think it best if you handle yourself in the Ethereal Bastille for now." He gripped my forearm with a force I didn't know he had.

Before I could shout about the unwelcome touch, Nick did it for me.

"Get your hands off of her." He roughly grabbed Ariel's wrist and threw it back, simultaneously pulling me over to him so that I was out of his leader's reach.

"Mr. Cassial, I beg your pardon?"

"You can yell and scream at *me*, but do *not fucking* touch her." He kept a hand near my side. It felt like he was saying that he couldn't hold me back, but he could at least let me know that he was here.

The sound of footsteps and clanging weapons sounded outside the door.

"I should yell and scream at you since you want to act like a petulant child, but maybe it's best if you yourself go into the Ethereal Bastille to cool off. How does that sound?"

"Ariel you can't be fucking serious!" Reese yelled over the sentries that barreled through the door. They all looked to Ariel for their instructions and quicker than I expected he nodded over to Nicholas. The sentries all seemed to hesitate for a moment as if they didn't know if he actually meant to seize Nick.

"Do it now!" Ariel commanded, pointing straight at Nick. My raven-haired angel's mouth gaped open. Reese mirrored that expression from across the room. The sentries charged forward, but they wouldn't get much farther if they were aiming for what was mine.

I let shadows stream from my fingertips and towards the floor. Tendrils escaped from the stones, whipping and winding back and forth. They wrapped themselves around their weapons, tossing them aside. The shadows aimed for legs and arms, slithering around necks and squeezing so hard, any sort of circulation would have been nearly impossible. I flung my hand left and right, watching bodies get thrown towards the walls.

Reese ducked down, letting a body fly past him and into the stone interior.

I had a shadow slam the door shut, sealing the edges so we wouldn't be interrupted. I looked over my shoulder quickly, my eyes connecting with Nick's. He quickly assessed my damage and his face all but said *impressive, but was this necessary?*

"This! Mr. Cassial! This is…"

I put a hand up to stop him. "If you want me to say sorry for hurting your little worker angels then I'm sorry. Next time please let them know that telling me what I want to know and politely stepping out of my way is the best course of action." Ariel opened his mouth, but I lightly pressed a finger to his lips, telling him that I wasn't finished. "I'm on your side here. I clearly always have been, I just don't want to be confined to Nicholas's room any longer, no matter how satisfying the sex has been."

Reese let out a choked laugh in the otherwise quiet room.

"The one thing you should understand about demons is that the more you try to confine us, control us, the more unreliable we can become. You show me you can trust me, and I won't be a problem, I assure you."

Ariel took a step back and straightened his jacket. "Hand over your dagger if you want me to trust in you so much, Soul Seether."

I felt my eyebrows pull together. There was always this phantom hold that my dagger had over me even knowing that it was no longer in existence. The very mention of it made my fingers twitch. I wanted to summon it and make him wish he'd never asked for it, but I couldn't. A piece of myself was gone and I didn't know how to fix it.

"I can't."

Ariel rolled his eyes, putting his hand out between us with his palm facing upwards. "Hand it over. I have no patience at the moment."

"I don't have it. That's the truth," I answered, crossing my arms over my chest.

The sentries were coming around, picking themselves up from the ground. They shook their heads and began to rally, seemingly trying to figure out what the fuck just happened to them.

Ariel raised a suspicious eyebrow at me. "Would this have anything to do with you being dead in the eyes of the Queen of Darkness?"

I licked my lips. "Perhaps."

"You wouldn't mind explaining that since your two companions seem to keep a tight lip about that part of your time in Purgatory, would you?" Ariel spoke to me as if we were friends, but the sharpness of his tone told me otherwise.

I gave him a small smile. "If they didn't tell you anything, then I think it is highly unlikely that I will either."

Ariel's lip curled up as he turned away from me. "Mr. Diniel?"

Reese blinked over to him. I watched his Adam's apple bob up and down as he swallowed. "Yes?"

"You are still in contact with our High Priestess?"

Reese moved his eyes quickly over to me and Nick before returning to Ariel. "I am."

"You and Mr. Cassial will make sure the High Priestess helps our dear Soul Seether."

I stalked over to the red headed executive. "Excuse me, I'm right here. You want Natalia to help me with what exactly?" I noticed smoke seeping from the ends of my hair, and I tried to bat it away. The smoke wasn't the only thing I noticed though, there were tiny sparks of light that came with it. I wasn't used to that.

Ariel reached out, touching the light spark and it illuminated for just a moment before dispersing. I heard Nicholas's loud huff at Ariel's proximity to me, but he stayed put. "Dani, correct?"

I narrowed my eyes at him, but I nodded.

Ariel's lips pulled into a sly smile. "Well, Dani, you want freedom to roam and not be watched with such scrutiny…then fine. I plan to consider the good your hybrid status could mean for us at Heaven's Gate as a defense. I am well aware that you are a novice in understanding this combined power of yours, but I trust your established relationship with Natalia will do wonders."

"You want Natalia to teach her how to use both?" Reese asked, each word coming out cautiously.

I didn't let Ariel answer that before I asked my own question. "Heaven's Gate's defense? You want me to *work* for you?"

"You are the reason this entire mess is happening. Lilith wanted you here. You are the reason these two gallivanted off to Purgatory and put yet another potential target on us, I mean who knows who or what you angered there. The least you can do is offer your help and hybrid services to a place that you wish to see freely. Without your dagger and despite your withholding of information, I'm sure there is still some great use for you."

"You are fucking insane if you think I'll let you have any say on what I do or how I use whatever powers I have," I spat out.

Ariel's shoulders lifted in a soft laugh. "Alright, Soul Seether, have it your way." He pointed to both Nicholas and Reese. "Seize them." The sentries started to make their way to Nick and Reese, who began to back away from the throngs of angels.

"No! Stop!" My hands turned to fists as smoke started to envelope the room, but I was halted by the executive's voice.

Ariel tsked. "This time I wouldn't if I were you. You help Mr. Cassial and Mr. Diniel, but what about your friends in Oculus? They are of no use to me so disposing of them would be nothing at all. Your self-righteous behavior does not save everyone I'm afraid."

I had a lot of power but being in two places at once wasn't one of them, so it hurt to know he had a point. My shadows were inches away from their victims, but they began to retreat, the tiny light sparks within them doing the same.

Ariel put his hand up to stop the sentries and continued, "you want to show the people of Heaven's Gate that they don't need to fear you so much, that they should want to work with you and trust your aide, well then obliterating so many angels all because you didn't want to accept my extended helping hand just isn't a good look now, is it?" He smiled with all his teeth, but it wasn't a pleasant smile. It was menacing and manipulative.

"You are fucking rotten. The people will see right through you," I said, letting the shadows melt into my skin.

"They need something to hold onto, now more than ever. The ceremony and with your now delightful help, they will see that I only have their best interests at heart." Ariel grabbed my hand and placed his other one on top of it. The gesture was meant to be tender, but all I felt was cold, icy skin. "I think you should head to Oculus and begin your training at once, no time like the present."

I was pulled away from the cold feeling in moments and a strong, warm chest was at my back. I felt his thundering heart and it mirrored my own.

"I think I made it clear that you don't *touch* her," Nick warned, his voice low and authoritative. I wanted to fight back, but with everything I'd been through, everything I'd fought to keep, I didn't want any threat Ariel threw at me to potentially have merit and it was all taken away.

Reese looked at me, mouthing, "are you okay?"

I nodded, letting my body fold into Nick's as he turned me around.

"Keep me informed, would you Mr. Cassial? Your father must be so proud of all you've accomplished."

Nick stopped, throwing a stone cold look over his shoulder. "You do know that you will *never* be Jonah."

Ariel's laugh came out hollow. "Ah, well, Jonah is dead. I am all they have."

I watched as Nick frustratingly yanked out his portal key once we got further away from The Skies and closer to the woods. The sentry angels kept a close eye on us as we walked out; none of them making eye contact with Nick or Reese. I liked to think if they thought they had a choice in the matter, they wouldn't be siding with that red-headed idiot.

Nick looked back at the castle-like structure with as much disdain as his face could muster and I caught myself nearly giggling. My blood was boiling over what happened in there, but I didn't want to let it fester so much that it took away the happiness I felt since we were finally getting out of here. Ariel's manipulative offer felt like selling my soul all over again, but at least this time, maybe some good would come out of the arrangement.

I would find a way around Ariel, but I had to get a hold on this odd thing I felt inside of myself. If the angelic executive could see the light that I was beginning to wield then it was probably time I learned—or attempted to learn—how to manage it. I noticed Nick's hand shaking as he tried to make a circle with the key. It took him a few tries but eventually the telltale light from the portal shined. I let Reese go first, so I could grab Nick's hand and stepped in behind him.

We ended up in the middle of all the shops. The woman who could make the smell of chocolate from her little bakery was to the left and the apothecary was to my right. Before I could look away from that direction, I caught sight of Natalia headed towards us. I started to open my mouth to speak but she had her arms around me in minutes. Hugs didn't bother me, but this kind of hug wasn't one I was used to. It wasn't quick and sweet, like a general greeting, but it was more like the kind where you wanted to let the other person know you cared with your entire soul. It was odd that the first instinct I had was to hug her back with the same level of affection.

After some time, she let me go, holding me out in front of her so she could inspect me from head to toe. "Are you alright?" That voice of hers, the light musicality of it, washed over me with a sense of friendly security, like I knew I was amongst friends.

I nodded, but also shrugged at the same time. "More or less."

She looked over to both Reese and Nick, who flanked my sides. Her honey-colored eyes were lined with silver and her cheeks were dusted with the same color, making her dark skin glow beautifully. Her dark hair was made up in a collection of braids that flowed past her chest, with various pieces of jewelry decorated within each one.

Reese rubbed the back of his neck. "Ariel is a piece of work, let's just put it like that."

"That's a fucking understatement," Nick muttered, rubbing at his temple.

Natalia pressed her lips together. "Well, then I guess we have much to discuss. It is good to see you though. Your presence has been missed."

Reese started walking backwards past her. "You can thank Ariel for that. Although, I guess you can also thank him for having her back."

One of the High Priestess's neatly arched eyebrows raised. "Much to discuss indeed." She reached over to stop Nick from walking around her. She looked at him, directly in his eyes, as if she was searching for something.

His facial expression quickly morphed into one of understanding. "I'm okay. Good days and bad days, but I'm okay." He looked back at me, giving me a small smile that made my stomach flip. "She takes care of me."

Natalia delicately placed a few of her ring-covered fingers at his cheek. "Good. Very good."

Nick gripped her hand and placed it back at her side. He cleared his throat and asked, "he's not here, is he?"

I sucked in a deep breath, knowing exactly who he was referring to. Natalia, who had likely been trained to control her expressions, was failing in this moment, which told me she knew who *he* was as well.

She brushed her braids over her shoulder, showing off her multiple earrings. "No, not today."

Nick didn't say anything else; he simply continued walking as if that was answer enough.

Natalia stuck her tongue into her cheek, her eyebrows pulling together. She shook her head and arranged her expression into one of content. She reached her hand out to me, and I took it happily, sliding my palm up so that I could grip the inside of her elbow instead.

The apothecary looked the same as always when we passed it, but there was always something different about seeing something again after thinking that you might not ever get to lay your eyes on it again. You appreciate the things you once thought so simple—not that they are a big deal now—but your eyes tend to pay more attention. All the smells of Oculus were so much more intense, and I noticed more laughter than I had before.

We came up to a large house, well it was more like a mansion, once we cleared the dirt walkway past some gorgeous weeping willows. The smell of fresh flowers hit me instantly and I looked around noticing them everywhere. The dirt at my feet turned into a stone pathway which expanded toward an eggshell-colored three-story building. The exterior seemed to twinkle in the sunlight as if without words, telling you this place was magic.

The left side had one large veranda on the ground level with multiple rounded archways. Various colors of foxglove cascaded from plant hangers that were attached to the top of each archway. Another balcony was right above it with the same decoration and behind it sat two large glass doors, a large purple curtain covering it from the inside. The top floor had no balcony, just a section of hexagonal windows with drawings carved into the exterior surrounding them. I tilted my head back so that I could see the very top which looked like it had an expansive roof surrounded by a railing.

Stairs greeted us, along with a stone-faced Zane, who stood under a monstrous bell-shaped archway that was covered in green vines.

"Long time no see, buddy," Reese punched Zane in the shoulder, and I pressed my lips together so I wouldn't laugh too loudly. Zane's eyes turned into slits at the blonde angel, who simply put his hands up in surrender. "Okay, fine. We still aren't there yet. I'm a patient man."

I could have sworn I caught the large Enchanter rolling his eyes with a huff, but I couldn't be too sure. Nick hadn't moved from his place at the top of the stairs. His eyes roamed around what he could see. "You live here?"

Natalia chuckled. "Yes."

"By yourself?" I chimed in, knowing full well this place had multiple bedrooms.

The High Priestess unlatched her arm from me and walked over so she could stand next to Zane. "Not always." Her tone was a bit defeated, letting me know that she likely used to stay here with Isabel. She continued, "I have so much space, I like to let my people stay if they need it. I like the company. It can be surprisingly lonely leading so many people, but never really being able to *know* them. I can't really be of any use to them if they can't find me accessible."

Zane cleared his throat. "Accessibility can breed dangerous creatures, but no one listens to me."

Natalia looked up at her bodyguard and gave him a small smile. She raised her hand, patting his cheek softly.

I ran my fingers along the archway. "You sound like Beetee."

Natalia motioned for us to follow her inside, Zane walking past her to open the door before she could. "Ah your little pink haired friend is quite a delight."

Reese followed after her, but I grabbed Nick's arm before he could walk through the threshold. He gave me a look of confusion as he gazed down at me. I looked past his arm to make sure we were alone before I spoke, "you aren't letting Ariel get to you, right?"

His brown eyes narrowed. "No, why would I?"

I nearly snorted. "You practically growled at the man for coming into physical contact with me."

He nervously readjusted his sword at his back. "That's different."

I tilted my head to the side, waiting.

He groaned. "I don't like the guy, for one. Secondly, I…you…ugh." He fumbled over his words in an adorable way. I blinked, patiently assessing him. He scrubbed a hand down his face. His voice was a little lower when he opened his mouth next. "The fact that he's a fucking ass makes me even more angry that he touched you at all. You're mine, okay. I would have cracked my fist against his face if he would have tried to put his hands on you again. I would let him cast me out of The Skies just to keep you safe."

I bit my bottom lip, mischievously. "Very possessively sweet. Don't think that being in the presence of our friends means I won't drag you to the woods and rip your clothes off, Mr. Cassial." I lifted myself up onto my toes and kissed him. "I *do* expect you to hold up your end of our conversation though."

He kissed my nose. "What conversation would that be?"

"About a certain father of yours…"

He took a tiny step back. "I told you I would think about it."

"I know, but I don't want you to backtrack on all the progress you've made since Purgatory." I stepped up to him, so that we were back in each other's space again. "I took some of your darkness, sure. You still have some lingering and you always will. I just don't want it to start feeding on…"

Nick placed his hands on either side of my cheeks, stopping me from finishing. "Dani, I'm fine. I have you and your support, so that's all I need. Your caring makes me love you probably more than I already do, but right now my dad is the last thing I want or need to think about. He knows I'm alive and well, so that has to be good enough for now."

I flattened my palms over his hands, pulling them off my face. "Yes, but he doesn't know all the things you've been through…"

Reese's voice rang out, interrupting us. "You've spent every fucking day together since we got back. You can survive out of your fucking love bubble without imploding for an hour." We both looked over at him to see the blonde angel motioning for us to come inside.

Nick gave me a sympathetic look, before heading towards his best friend, but I grabbed his hand pulling it towards my face. It was the same hand I'd noticed earlier. The top of his hand was less red than before, but I could tell the top layer had been slightly burned. "Nick, what the hell is…"

He yanked himself free and pointed a thumb over his shoulder. "Nothing. Come on, they're waiting."

I chewed on my bottom lip before following him. Nicholas was hiding something from me, but I didn't exactly know where to place *this* on the list of things to be dealt with.

4
NICK

The inside of Natalia's home was massive, yet it still gave off the warmth of a smaller more intimate residence. The inside was colored light pink and beige. Large columns flanked a grand staircase that resided in the middle of the foyer. The stairs were graced with a cream-colored runner that looked soft enough to sleep on. Lights twinkled from above us, intricately placed so that the light was even on all ends of the room.

I twirled around, trying not to miss a single thing. "This is incredible."

Natalia giggled. "Thank you. I like it very much. I redecorated a bit after my mother passed, but most of it is still her original designs."

Enchanters passed by us, as if we were invisible. They moved at a speed I didn't think angelically possible, but I assumed they worked here, so I could get behind getting the job done. Reese had wandered in another direction, and I really wanted to see what else this place had to offer, but I could feel Dani's eyes on me. I glanced over to her, which confirmed my suspicions. Her eyes looked me up and down, but it wasn't in the way I liked; it wasn't in the way that told me she was very eager to have my hands on her or for me to be inside of her.

No, this look had skepticism written all over it. I didn't know how to explain to the woman that happened to have my entire heart in a choke-hold that she occasionally burned me during sex. It could happen other times, I'm sure, but for now that particular new Dani feature had only happened during intimate times. That was partly why she was staring me down, but the other reason was for me to deal with on my own. My father had to go to the back of my mind, especially with Ariel now on more of a power trip than I originally thought.

I looked away from Dani when Natalia stopped an Enchanter in their tracks. "Where are you taking that?" Natalia pointed to whatever was in the girl's hand.

The girl's voice was shaky and timid as she looked up at her queen. "Um, you told us to give them whatever they needed."

The High Priestess gave her a tight-lipped smile before gently removing whatever she had from her hands. I heard the slosh of liquid, craning my neck to finally see a bottle of alcohol. "You are not in trouble Sarah, please go back to your duties."

The Enchanter quickly bowed her head, looking around at us and then darted off. Zane walked over to her, grabbing the bottle and huffed. The large Enchanter began to read the bottle's label. "At least she picked a good one."

Dani chuckled. "Oh, did you just make a joke, tough guy."

Zane raised an eyebrow at her but turned to Natalia. "I'll return this to the kitchen."

"Elise?" I questioned, smirking.

Natalia fluffed out her long, maroon colored dress. "She hasn't changed, that I can assure you." She turned around, walking up the stairs. "Come, we have much to discuss it seems and I'm sure a nice little reunion is well overdue."

Once we were at the top of the stairs, we followed Natalia past a few doors until we got to a large room that held multiple couches, a day bed and bookcases that looked as if they had never seen a days' worth of dust. The ground was covered in oakwood and a glass coffee table was placed in the middle of the room atop a rectangular lilac rug with silver tassels. I was so busy surveying the room that I hardly noticed who was in it.

Beetee sprang up from her place on one of the couches and ran over to me. She embraced me in a hug that almost sent me into the wall. I laughed as she held onto me but hugged her back. Over her shoulder I saw Elise sprawled out on another couch and Garrett looking out one of the windows near the side of the room.

The pink-haired demon let me go, pulling back to look at me. "Sorry for the abrupt approach."

I shrugged. "It's okay. I'm happy you're healed."

Beetee tucked a piece of her hair behind her ear. "For the most part. I j—." She stopped when she locked eyes with something behind me. I swiveled my head to follow her lilac eyes and found Dani watching her as well.

Add this to the list of things that needed to be resolved before Ariel crowned himself leader of his realm.

Beetee rubbed at the back of her neck, her brown skin growing red as she shuffled from foot to foot. "It's really good to see you again, Soul Seether."

Dani squinted at her, but then she started rubbing at the back of her neck as well. Was she nervous? "I thought we discussed this whole Soul Seether thing. Dani is perfectly fine."

Beetee nodded quickly. "Of course, right I forgot. I should have remembered, I'm sorry. Like seriously, I am so, so…"

"Hey, I think she gets it." I placed my hand on her arm, ceasing her rambling. She winced as if she had severely fucked up.

Dani shook her head, making her way over to us. "The constant apology is going to get really annoying, so let's cut that off. Actually, without a certain weapon, I don't even know if Soul Seether is correct anymore." She ruffled her curls with her fingers, her eyes flicking to mine so quickly that if I hadn't been looking at her, I would have missed it. "We should talk soon….about…things."

I could see that Beetee was chewing on the inside of her cheek, more redness blotching her golden brown skin. Her bright yellow dress made the discoloration even more apparent. "Yes, we should."

"Finally, the gangs all here," Reese announced, strolling in with an apple in his hand. He brought it to his mouth, taking a large bite. He lifted his chin towards Beetee. "What's up, reptile queen."

Beetee rolled her eyes. "That's still an awful name."

"Accurate, but yes I agree, awful," Elise piped up from her place on the couch. She had her arm flung over her face, so she hid her eyes. Dani shuffled over to her, lifting her foot and kicking Elise's thigh.

"Fuck what the hell…"

"Look alive, you asshole." Dani laughed as she walked over to the purple curtains that cover two large glass double doors. She grabbed the curtains and pulled them apart, making sure each side was equally open. Sunlight shined into the room, making everything look more alive. "Much better."

"Oh, for fucks sake." Elise grabbed one of the throw blankets from behind the couch and moved it over her eyes. "Can I not have my raging hangover in fucking peace? I'm very happy to see that Nicholas hasn't ripped you in half with his massive cock already, but like can we move this little meeting until tomorrow?"

"Hangover? They were just about to bring you more alcohol from downstairs," I pointed out, ignoring her comment. Elise threw the blanket down and gave me a death glare.

"Also, Nick has an average sized dick, it's not massive," Reese joked, slapping me on the back. I heard Dani snort from where she was standing near Natalia.

Elise hummed. "You would know that how?" She placed her fist under her chin, her eyebrows raised, challenging my best friend.

Reese opened his mouth to continue this usually normal back and forth of theirs, but we all heard Garrett clear his throat. "I think we should be getting around to talking about what we are here for."

He was likely around my father's age, but he looked as if he had aged more in two weeks than any normal entity should. I couldn't possibly understand what he was going through, and I hadn't been around the past few weeks to ask him. His voice was the same deep fatherly tone that had us all standing up straight and taking a seat wherever we could find it.

I opened my mouth to say anything, something of merit at this point and time, but he just patted me on the shoulder and pulled me in for a quick hug before settling himself into one of the armchairs. The talk would have to wait.

My eyes quickly searched the room before I found Dani who patted the spot next to her on the couch opposite Elise and Beetee. Natalia chose to stand, leaning her back against one of the bookshelves, while Reese made himself comfortable on one of the couches armrests.

"So, they let you out?" Elise asked as she leaned forward.

"Well…" Dani started.

"Or did you escape? Personally, I prefer knowing you pulled a fast one on that red head buffoon."

Escape always sounded like an intense word. "It's not like she was in a prison, Elise."

The grumpy demon fluttered her eyelashes at me. "Oh, yeah, I'm sure being secluded in your bedroom is just a dream, isn't it Nicholas."

I rolled my eyes and felt Dani's hand land on my thigh. She squeezed and I placed my own hand over hers, not really understanding what she was doing, but any reason to touch her was enough of a reason for me.

"He let me out," Dani blurted quickly.

Beetee cocked her head to the side. "I haven't really met the man before, except for super quickly when he scowled at me, but he doesn't seem like the type to let you out. It's just so simple."

I peeked over at Garrett who was running his index finger across his chin, almost in thought. Elise scoffed. "Ariel is a simple man with less than half a brain cell, but there is no way in fuck he just let you out."

"From what Reese said, he was very adamant on you, oh how did he put it…" Garrett rubbed his lips together. "Staying put and knowing your place."

I had to remove my hand from Dani's, or I would have crushed hers. My hand automatically wanted to curl into a fist thinking about all the things Ariel had said under his breath or even in a leveled tone to my face.

Dani nearly growled with frustration. She ripped her hand from my leg and shoved both hands into her curls. She moved the majority of her hair to one side and shot up from the couch. "He let me out under *stipulations*." She walked towards the back of the couch, placing her hands on it so she could lean forward. "That smug faced fuck let me out on the conditions of working for him." Her cheeks were red and so was her chest.

Natalia's eyebrows raised as she motioned for Beetee to scoot over on the couch. "Let's start from the beginning."

Dani, Reese and I all explained what happened, each of us occasionally interrupting the other. Reese balanced his apple core between his hands as the room went silent once we finished.

Elise tapped her fingers against the glass coffee table. Beetee chewed on her bottom lip, twirling her pink hair around her finger.

Garrett cleared his throat. "So, he wants you to learn how to be a full hybrid and harness it, so he can weaponize you? Does he plan to make you go to Purgatory once you've figured it out?" There was a tiny sliver of hope in his voice, likely the idea of going back and collecting his family. It wasn't something I would ever say to him out loud, but as much as I cared for Garrett and his family, I wouldn't throw Dani into something she wasn't ready for and potentially lose her.

"I don't know," Dani answered, shrugging.

"I have every faith that you can develop them equally, but it does seem a bit presumptuous that he thinks I can manage to teach you anything about that. Does he even understand that learning all of this might take you a while?" Natalia said, her eyes narrowing in confusion.

"I don't know," Dani repeated.

"I guess it's nice that you get to spend so much time in Oculus. Are you going to stay here forever and just be like some kind of hybrid sentry angel, always on alert just in case Lilith catches wind that you're alive?" Beetee asked, her voice a bit softer than everyone else's.

"Ugh! I don't—" Dani's words were cut off by a loud crash, followed by shattering glass. Everyone shot up from their seats watching as the light from the large glass doors hit the cluster of glass shards, decorating the room in twinkling colors.

"Did you just break my table?" Natalia asked under her breath towards the only person left sitting.

Elise still had her hand over the now destroyed coffee table. She unfurled the fist she made, ignoring Natalia and pointed her finger at me. "You let that overzealous piece of fucking shit force her hand by threatening *us*?!" Her voice got louder as she walked around the pile of glass and came up to me, her finger pushing into my chest. "You take your pretty ass right back to Heaven's Gate and you tell that mother-fucker that if he wants to fucking threaten me, then do it to my face. I mean come the fuck on?! Where are your balls?" She looked from me to Reese, who stepped up next to me.

"I didn't *let* anything happen. If you haven't realized, Ariel is a little bit out of fucking control and trying to maintain some level of truth while also keeping a load of information away from him is really fucking exhausting." I ran a hand through my hair, watching as her facial expression never wavered.

"Am I supposed to be sympathetic to you, Nicholas?" Elise raised one of her dark eyebrows.

"Okay tiny psycho what did you want us to do, fight him? Shit doesn't work like that here," Reese explained.

Elise laughed, "oh, and what does? Bending over and taking it?" Beetee let out a small cough at Elise's blunt comment as she walked past us to the entrance door.

Garrett clearly had all the confidence in the world when he came over and pushed Elise away from us. Her eyes glowed a tiny red before turning back to their gray coloring. "I think everyone here needs a minute. Ariel seems like a piece of work, but maybe the best course of action is letting him think he's gotten away with something. Those kinds of men always need to feel like they have the upper hand."

Elise rolled her shoulders and her eyes. "Whatever. At least you're smart enough to keep your newfound resurrection powers to yourself because I can already tell he's probably asked about the fucked-up mess that was Purgatory. Nosey little shit." She reached out and lightly slapped my face. "If I see Ariel, I'll force feed him his own dick, got it?" If all of this was her way to saying, *I care about Dani, so don't let your leader fuck with her*, then she was doing an excellent job. She turned around to the sound of the door opening and Zane rushing inside with Beetee trailing behind him.

"Zane, we're fine. Just a little err…mishap." Natalia started picking up more pieces of glass from the floor, but Zane stopped her before she could even attempt to accidentally cut herself.

"Mishap, mmhmm," he muttered, keeping his eyes clearly on Elise.

"About your powers…" Garrett began, rubbing his hands together. I licked my bottom lip and shook my head. For now, my resurrection powers were off the table, they'd given me Dani back and I was grateful for them, but I honestly didn't want to think anymore about them.

"We really don't have to talk about that. You have a lot of things going on already, my issues aren't your problem."

Garrett nodded as if he understood, but he still pressed. "There aren't many out there with these kinds of powers and if you did ever want to understand it, I'm here. The distraction might be, well…" His voice trailed off as he looked towards the window he was previously at.

I gave him the best smile I could. This man made me miss my father and I knew that what he was feeling would be my own father's exact same feelings if it were me stuck in another realm. Our issues seemed so trivial next to Garrett's, but on the other hand, I spent almost fifteen years thinking there weren't any issues at all. If I spoke about the powers then everything else would come up and personally, I wasn't ready for that. His shoulders were too heavy with his own burdens and my own would not be adding to it.

"I think for now my plate is full dealing with Dani's—" I turned to look over to her, but she was nowhere to be found. She must have slipped out while Elise was on her tirade, because the room wasn't big enough for me to just miss…

That's when I found her. She had opened the doors and was outside on the balcony. She was hanging out near the railing with her back to me. The sunlight framed her so perfectly I could have just stared at her for hours; there was no doubt in my mind that she deserved anything and everything that the realms had to offer. If I didn't know what was going on with her, I would think she was so calm and serene from where I stood. my heart hurt, knowing how much she was dealing with it and how there wasn't much I could do about it. Loving her just didn't seem like enough sometimes.

I gave Garrett one more smile, which he reciprocated, but his particular smile told me that our conversation wasn't over. I started to make my way over to Dani, but Natalia stepped in front of me. Her honey-colored eyes were soft as she looked over her shoulder at the balcony. "You've spent a lot of time with her, Nicholas. Maybe let me give it a try, hmm?"

5
DANI

I desperately tried to let every ounce of tension leave my body the minute I got outside. I'd slipped away from Nick and managed to escape to the balcony with no issues, but regardless of how many people were around, it was never enough. So many questions that I didn't know the answers to. I understood that they were curious but, fuck, I'd never been so agitated in such a short amount of time. My fingers tightened around the railing as I closed my eyes, mentally counting to whatever number I could before I felt a hand on my shoulder.

"It's a little much in there." Natalia gave me a small smile when I looked up at her.

"Isn't it always?" I volleyed back, chuckling to myself.

Natalia turned around so that her back was against the railing. "Now that we are away from everyone else, would you like to tell me how you are really feeling?"

I pressed my lips together, mulling over my thoughts. I wanted to sound sure of myself with whatever I said, but that was proving harder than I imagined. "I guess I'm fine, but then again, I'm not. Does that make sense?"

She nodded, never keeping her eyes off me. "You did die and then came back to life, so I would think it odd if you didn't feel something exactly like that."

I nodded solemnly. "I think I just don't understand what that means for me now. On the outside, I'm perfectly some version of my normal self, but on the inside…"

"Things are a little off?" She inquired, raising an eyebrow.

I scrunched my mouth to the side. "Actually, no. It's not like that at all." I raised both my eyebrows at her, hoping my point was clear as day.

Natalia twisted her body so she could lean one of her arms on the railing. Her eyes left my face and looked out over the trees and floral arrangements that were scattered around us. "Ah, so you feel like everything is much more balanced within yourself. The dark and the light."

It wasn't really a question; there was no inflection in her voice.

Instead of answering her, I followed her gaze, watching the wind take hold of the foliage that fell from various tree branches.

After a moment, the High Priestess spoke again. "I'm going to take a wild guess and say you haven't told Nicholas about your internal balancing act?"

I rolled my eyes, taking a glance over my shoulder. I found my angel easily. Fuck, he was handsome. He was also an overprotective, grudge holding deflector, but I loved him. "I haven't lied to him, okay. I am actually *fine*. I didn't want to burden him with something he can't fix or change. We both know he would try." I caught myself smiling at that last part. Nick put his whole heart into everything he attempted, even when he knew it was a losing battle. There was a tiny part of him that thought there could be a chance. "Despite Ariel's horrendous fucking attitude, this is kind of what I wanted."

"You *want* to work for Ariel?" Natalia sounded appalled at my words.

I nearly choked. "No. Fuck, no, I don't want to work for that piece of shit, but I wanted to figure this out. I wanted your help, and I wasn't going to see you anytime soon otherwise. Without my dagger, it's all just kind of swirling around inside of me, which is fine, but now there are two different kinds of powers. They are trying to find a way to connect but they can't. Maybe I won't let them, I don't know." I shook my head, feeling frustrated. "I can find a way around his threats and probably find a way out of his grasp, but I need this handled. You are the best, are you not?"

Natalia laughed and it was musical the way it settled into my ears. I'd missed it. "I'm no miracle worker, Dani. I've never tugged on the powers of angels, nor have I touched the power of the darkness, but I do have a place where we can experiment with both and hopefully get you into a position where you can use them both safely and confidently."

I gave her the most genuine smile I could muster up and she awarded me with a look that told me she saw right through my efforts. I wanted to figure this out and I wanted to do it safely. The dark was all I'd ever known; I was safe there.

I could be safe in the light as well, couldn't I?

I noticed Natalia chewing on her bottom lip and my eyebrows pulled inward. "What is it?"

"I know you don't think he'll understand, but Nicholas might be your biggest asset."

I kicked at the stone flooring. "How do you mean?"

"You want to connect with your light? Maybe you should confide in someone that already understands their own completely. Consensually feed off of it, so that you get the hang of yours. Light calls to light and all that. I can only do so much, but you do have to want to get along with it, meld both powers together from within yourself. Just because they feel balanced doesn't mean the execution will be as such."

I wasn't a damsel in distress, and I didn't like the idea of not being able to help myself if needed. This feeling of confused helplessness was new for me, and I hated it. Lilith or Dimitri may not stay dormant forever and I wanted to be at my strongest if it ever came to a fight that needed me at my absolute best. Nick's light was his own and I *did* feel comfort in his warmth and body. If he put all his efforts into me, using his light to help my own, well then what did that mean for him? Just because he was back in Heaven's Gate didn't mean that he couldn't be weakened yet again by all the things he wasn't saying…or doing. He might have forgiven himself for what happened with Jonah, but Nicholas Cassial, like his own father, had layers to him. Nick could lay some things to rest, while other things needed more time.

"I think he would understand just perfectly. I think he would listen and give me numerous amounts of advice and make some sort of ten-point plan on how to do things." I was making a small joke, but damn it, if it actually wasn't the truth. I let go of the railing and ran my hands through my curls, catching one of my fingers on a knot. "Nick has a ton on his plate. He has spent way too much fucking time making me the priority. I mean I love being waited on hand and foot, not to mention the daily orgasms were something to get used to, but he…"

"He *should* wait on you constantly. The guy did stab you to fucking death." Elise sauntered over, standing next to Natalia with a cheeky smile.

"He did bring her back though." Beetee lightly shoved Elise's shoulder before joining our huddle. She gave me a tentative smile. We really did need to talk soon. Neither of us understood what being a hybrid meant and both of us had only ever known Purgatory.

Elise scoffed. "The guy got stupid lucky on that one. I am kind of impressed now though. He is way more than just a handsome angel with a sword up his ass. Now, he's a handsome angel with a sword up his ass that just happens to have necromancy powers."

"Those powers get heavily avoided, as do many things when it comes to Nicholas," I admitted, taking a deep breath.

Natalia stepped away from the railing, her jewelry glittering in the sun. "Perhaps him spending some time here alongside Garrett will help with that. At least with his powers, even if he never uses them again."

"Garrett's been having a rough time, we both are, but I know my moms can handle themselves. His children and wife, they were in hiding for a reason, but now…" Beetee shook her head, her eyes a little on the verge of tears.

Elise stalked over and took her chin in her hand. "They'll be okay, so stop. I'm not all worried about Axel because that fucking dog knows how to handle himself and he knows how to protect what needs protecting. For some reason, he loves those fucking kids and Leah, so when I say don't fucking worry, I mean it." She released the pink-haired demon's chin prepared to walk away, but Beetee wrapped her arms around her, holding her in a tight hug.

"Thanks Ellie. I needed that."

Elise stiffened, making a disgruntled noise before grasping Beetee's wrists from around her back and shoving her off. "Yeah, okay. Don't ever do that again."

"Did Axel learn how to protect what needs protecting from his devoted dog mom?" I joked, poking her in the side.

Elise gave me a sour look. "Did Nicholas ever figure out his daddy issues?"

I narrowed my eyes at her, almost wanting to cease this conversation before he came out here and heard us. Beetee huffed. "Ellie, you can't just say things like that."

Elise scoffed. "Why the hell not? The man comes here like every other day. I'm allowed to be on the edge of my seat in this father, son shit show."

I blinked over to Natalia. "Maurice comes here often?"

The High Priestess nodded. "He comes to see me or Zane. Sometimes he comes alone, sometimes he brings Daya or Alex."

"As much as he loves Reese, he is a little disappointed when he doesn't see Nick. He asks about him a lot, just wanting to know how he's doing. He asks about you as well." Beetee pointed out, nervously fiddling with one of her earrings.

My heart faltered a little knowing that Maurice Cassial wondered about my well-being. I assumed being in love with his son had something to do with that.

"I kind of feel bad for the guy and yes, I feel disgusting saying that." Elise shook her shoulders as a shiver climbed up her spine.

"Maurice told me the entire story. I knew my mother and Nick's were close, I mean she spoke about her sometimes, but I just didn't… I had no idea that my mother was the one who…"

A deep voice came from the open doors, and I closed my eyes, internally knowing this was going to happen. Nick leaned against the threshold, looking down at the ground. "I don't blame you, if that's what you're thinking. The minute he told me what your mother did, I didn't blame you at all." He pushed away from the door and walked over to us. He had his hands in his pockets, playing like he was nonchalant, but I knew he was tense and would rather not be having this conversation.

Natalia gave him an apologetic smile. "I know, I just wish that I would have known sooner, so that I could have made better sense of it all."

Nick shrugged. "I wish my father would have told me sooner, so I guess we are both shit out of luck."

Natalia opened her mouth and then promptly closed it, seemingly lost on what words she wanted to speak next.

The silence that followed was thick and I almost couldn't breathe from the way it suffocated me. The fresh air wasn't enough to thin it out. I cleared my throat, catching his attention. "Why don't we start that training?"

Natalia rallied, her expression morphing from concerned to determined. "Of course, I'll get Zane." Beetee and Elise followed behind her, not before Elise started walking backwards and giving me an awkward smile. She pulled at the collar of shirt, silently saying *well that was fucking awkward.*

Nicholas placed his hand out for me to take it, his open palm looked as inviting as ever. "Let's go."

I took his hand, the warmth enveloping me like it always had. He kissed my knuckles before pulling me in the direction of everyone else. There was a tingly sensation in my body, almost like contentment. I also felt sadness there, my darkness mingling with the dark that still lived inside of him. As much as Nick didn't want to admit it, his father was a piece of his light. Until he had that piece back, I wanted him to keep as much as he had to himself.

We traveled back downstairs, turning right as we got to the bottom of the large staircase. I wasn't nearly as stunned as I thought I'd be when Zane opened another set of doors, where another set of stairs awaited us. The walls lit up the minute we descended towards the next floor, twinkling with each step we took.

The bottom was covered in multicolored stones, but they didn't kick up dirt each time any of us moved. Despite moving further down into her home, the amount of effort to keep things clean was maintained wherever we went. I admired that kind of time and motivation. I could imagine that her bedroom had the same meticulous touches her entire home did.

"Right through here." Zane opened two large wooden doors that had silver sparkles etched into the trimming. Beyond the doors lay a room that was double the size of any training room at The Skies. There were mirrors on either side, expanding the length of the walls. Towels hung on racks near the back and there were two benches that connected to the wall on either side of the door.

"Now this is a training room," Reese said, spinning around so that he took it in.

"I didn't know you trained. Like this kind of training," I pointed out, looking over at the High Priestess.

She chuckled and shook her head. "Oh, I don't. This is for Zane and the others that watch over me. I expanded it a bit more after my mother passed. Zane doesn't ask for much, but he did want a larger space for his men and women to learn better skills and whatnot." Natalia winked over at her bodyguard who simply huffed, but he looked like he wanted to smirk over at her.

Nick removed his sword from around his back, setting it against the wall. "So, where do we start?"

"Yes, witch, please tell us how you plan to fix this," Elise deadpanned.

Beetee let out the loudest sigh of embarrassed annoyance, while

Natalia only smiled. "I can't *fix* anything, but I can attempt to help as I've said." She faced me, gaining my attention. "You want to understand how to use both?"

I nodded.

"Good, well, first I think it's best if you simply show me what you can do for now."

I clenched and unclenched my fists. "We are all well aware of what I can do."

Natalia placed her hand on my shoulder. "I know, Dani. All I'm asking is that I see it without any threats, without any distractions. I'll be able to assess from there and decide where we take this."

I opened my mouth to speak but she had already turned away and was walking over to Zane and Garrett. I had never been shy about my powers, nor had I ever not thrilled at the notion that had people watching me…perform, for a lack of a better word.

This felt different. It felt like a step in a monumental direction for me and there would be so many people by my side, but what if it amounted to nothing? I shook away the thought, knowing that if it festered, this place would be filled with smoke that would nearly suffocate all of them.

"Don't think about holding back," Elise said, as she leaned against the mirror near Beetee. Her gray eyes bore into my brown ones as if she could read my mind.

"I'm not. I mean I don't—"

Natalia cut me off. "She isn't wrong. I promise you; I can handle whatever you unleash, just be yourself."

That was a new one. Be myself. I was trying to, but it was hard when I had no clue who the fuck that was.

I closed my eyes, tilting my head from side to side. The darkness came so naturally. It flowed into my veins like an old friend, like an essence that embodied my entire being. I almost shivered with the way it threaded itself inside of me as if it wasn't sharing me with something else. I opened my eyes, my surroundings looking muted. I felt the smoke revolving around my arms and fingertips. I looked down at my hand, a ball of black wispy smoke developing. It vibrated and grew bigger with every breath I took.

I saw the tail end of smoke wisps in my vision, the darkness starting to move all around me. There could be no room for the light, because this was what I was. I heard Zane's voice.

"Your Highness, do you want me to…"

Natalia quickly stopped him. "No. Do nothing. She is okay."

"But your Highness…" Zane's voice was wary.

I heard the sound of footsteps behind me, but they didn't sound too close. I felt an immediate pain in my back as a large source of power hit my back. I spun around to the remnants of teal light and Natalia standing a few feet away from me, another teal ball of light settled in her hand. She reared her hand back and thrust it at me. I blocked it with my own powers. The black smoke connected with the teal light, both powers fighting against each other until they were snuffed out in between us.

Natalia didn't let up. She shot different colored magic at me, over and over. It was exhausting and I could feel myself getting more and more aggravated. The High Priestess would either take a few steps to one side or the other, but it was as if she had no care in the world how long this lasted.

"This can stop now, Natalia," I said, my voice clearly over this.

"We could." She shrugged. "We both know that you are holding back for my sake, and I don't appreciate that one bit. Dagger or no dagger I think everyone here can agree that you aren't this…. *incapable*." She said that last word in a mocking tone, as if she was better than me.

"*Incapable?*" I repeated, the word rolling off my tongue with disgust.

"Oh, did I stutter?" Natalia snarked, teal and pink light traveled down her arms and enveloped her hands. It felt like she was getting ready for me to erupt, but I wanted to keep myself in check. I should want to do that, right?

Pink light flew by my face, hitting my hair. She brought her arm back and flung another colorful light ball in my direction. I grabbed hold of it, feeling it pulse in my grip and started to squeeze. The light flickered and then started to dim, darkening more and more until it molded itself with my own darkness. The smoke grew bigger and all I wanted to do was prove her wrong.

I allowed my shadows to travel away from me, barreling towards her. Large clumps of smoke following behind, her magic trapped within my own. Natalia barely moved before it all got inches before her, but then she held up both her hands and everything I threw out was encapsulated in some type of translucent bubble that sparked with colorful light. The High Priestess moved her hands, making a flinging motion so that the bubble holding the dark power was thrust towards the wall, exploding as if none of it ever happened.

I went to let out more, but she pointed a finger at me and my whole body felt as if it was being wrapped up with my wrists plastered to my sides. The magical rope she cinched around me pinched as it tightened each time I squirmed.

"Let me go," I demanded.

"Free yourself."

I tried to wiggle myself out, but nothing worked. The rope circled around my elbows, slowly. I let my shadows slither around the ropes, hoping to remove them. Natalia was in front of me, grasping the shadows and they whined as she snuffed them out.

"Not like that. Use the light before the rope gets too high, Soul Seether," she hissed, nodding at me before taking a few steps back.

"Natalia, you aren't going to just leave her to…" Reese started, but he let the sentence trail off when it seemed like no one was going to do anything until I at least tried.

The rope climbed up my biceps, snaking around my shoulders. I willed whatever light I had in my semi-panicked state. The shadows screamed at me to fix this, to help me. I batted them away in my mind and only pleaded for the light. That light that appeared so dim before was a tiny bit brighter and peered back at me like it was happy I was noticing it for the first time.

It tried to speak to me in a language I didn't understand, but it wasn't words. It was speaking with feelings and emotions that I'd never noticed. I could feel the warmth trying to seek me out and fill my insides, but the darkness was barking back at it, not wanting to share space within me. I needed a balance to make this work and neither power wanted to play nice.

The ropes touched my neck, threading around my throat.

I saw tiny light sparks flicker at the tips of my hair and at my finger-tips, the idea of my imminent danger too much for it. I wanted to trust it, I wanted it to trust me as well, but it couldn't be at its maximum power without my willingness to trust it fully and put the dark aside to give it room to grow.

The rope constricted around my throat, and I started coughing. I wanted Natalia to let me go, but I knew she wouldn't. I tried again, reaching for the light I knew was there. I strived to push the dark back and make the light feel comfortable and wanted. I saw the light sparks again and they started to flourish just a tiny bit more. My vision was less muted now and it started to blur from my lack of oxygen. I started to teeter back and forth on my feet, trying to suck in air but to no avail.

Natalia's magic touched my jaw and was just at my chin, a large shot of golden light struck me. Air filled my lungs instantly and I fell into a coughing fit when I landed on the ground. I looked around to see my raven-haired angel standing near me and his palm was bright, steadily going back to its normal color.

He heaved in breath after breath as if he had run a mile.

"Pretty boy can't even follow directions. The point was to let her help herself." Elise rolled her eyes.

Garrett came down to kneel beside me. "Are you alright?"

I nodded, knowing that my pride hurt more than anything physical ever could.

Reese and Beetee both started to walk up to Nick, but Natalia stopped them both. Nick came down to my level, tucking my hair behind my ear as I looked up at him. "I'm sorry, I just…you—" His brown eyes assessed me quickly and then they settled on my face. "I don't like seeing you like that."

I took his hand in mine, patting it softly. For Nick, it was about my safety, no matter how many friends surrounded us. My pride would recover. "I know."

6

NICK

I leaned outside the door to my bathroom, listening to the shower running on the other side. We didn't talk much when we came back but she did hold my hand the entire time until both our palms were sweaty, so I called that a win. Reese and I had planned to meet later, while Natalia gave me a hopeful smile on our way out. She'd said for now, she had as much as she could go off of and this kind of thing was one part power development and one part revolving around what motivates those powers.

Something inside of me wanted to let her do what she had to, let her help herself. There was another part of me, a much larger part that nearly combusted at the thought of seeing her in any pain. I honestly didn't care if it was for training purposes or not.

It made my chest swell with pride to see the tiny bits of light that she tried to release and even though I knew she couldn't hear me, I mentally kept thinking *you can do this*. My heart did stutter though when her darkness kept popping up, but not in a way where it didn't belong there. I had no idea whether she noticed it or not, but from where I stood there was an inner turmoil going on in the middle of that room. The darkness and the light weren't really fighting each other, but it looked as if they were both trying to grab her attention even though her entire existence had been dedicated to only one. Splitting her affection had never been an option.

Growing up, angelic light wasn't something that just forced its way out of your fingertips. I had developed it over time and watched my dad and so many others before me use theirs, in hopes that I would mimic them in some way.

I tilted my head back against the wall and closed my eyes. I thought back to when my father would watch me try to control my own light in my palm, while I watched it mold and move. It grew in size the harder I focused and most times I would get embarrassed that it wasn't good enough so I would snuff it out before anyone could see how mediocre I thought mine was. My father would sit next to me on the edge of my bed and bring up his own light, so confident and mesmerizing.

He would say, "open your hand and let it out."

I would hesitate but did as he asked. My light so tiny, yet so powerful would emerge.

He would bring his own light near mine and my eyes would light up as they intertwined, causing the whole room to seem as if it was set ablaze. I wasn't in my head in those moments. I was proud that I could be a part of something that was so much bigger than myself.

My father would close my hand with his own and kiss my head, mumbling into my hair. "One day your light will be just as big as that all on your own, but sometimes it's okay to get a little help." I'd shrug him off but keep his words with me, even now they still lingered.

My light only ever grew after each of those moments and even now I still surprised myself with what I could do. I was still getting to know myself and I wanted to give Dani the same grace. She could feel both powers, but that didn't necessarily mean she could perform a seamless balancing act without fuck ups. I, of all people, knew angelic light wanted nourishment and dedication. It wasn't jealous or fragile, but perhaps it wasn't all that different from the darkness in some way.

I'd never truly asked Dani about it; she'd always said she was fine in that way that honestly had me wanting to believe her. She wanted to protect me just as much as I wanted to shield her from the world, but of course, my girl quite literally gave me a proverbial middle finger while simultaneously swooning over my protective nature.

My eyes popped open when I heard my name. I quickly opened the door, the steam from the shower dissipating once I let some of the outside air in. I noticed her silhouette in the shower and tried to rid my brain of the thoughts of her naked and drenched in soap.

"Yeah?" I answered, clearly ready to do whatever she asked.

The shower door rattled open, her face coming into view. Her curls were soaking wet, glistening from the water that dripped off the ends. One of her eyebrows was raised in a way that told me she was about to be incredibly cheeky, and I was never prepared for it. She tapped her fingertips along the glass of the shower door, letting out a huff. "Are you getting in or not?"

"I thought you would rather…"

She shushed me. "Always so sweet, but who cares what you *thought*. I'm asking you, are you coming into the shower with me or not? Choose wisely, Mr. Cassial."

I closed the door without another thought. My clothes were off in seconds, and I fumbled into the shower with her, the sound of her intoxicating laughter filling my ears. I bent down to kiss her, her lips wet and slippery. The shitty lighting in my bathroom still didn't dull the way every part of her brown skin glowed and I could have kissed every single inch of her body. She lightly pushed me away, reaching down and picking up a bottle of conditioner. I looked at the opal-colored bottle that I'd gotten at one of the village's markets the day after she started staying with me.

I thought she'd like the scent—cinnamon— and from the amount of liquid that remained, I was correct.

"We can talk about what happened, but you have to be of some use in the meantime." She turned around, moving all her hair to her back. I smiled to myself as I squirted the product into my hand. I started to work it into her hair from the ends, easing my fingers through every tangle I got caught on.

I cleared my throat as I continued taking my fingers through her hair. "I am sorry."

Her shoulders moved while she laughed. "It was probably one of *the* most unsurprising things you've done."

"That's not fair. You were nearly choking, Dani." I reached the middle of her hair, which was the thickest, so I started to move slower as I worked.

She tilted her head back a little, eyeing me from over her shoulder. "Nick, it was Natalia. We aren't dealing with Lilith or Satan forbid, Dimitri. I would love for your faith in me to last a little longer than five minutes."

I paused, wrapping her hair in my fist and pulling her head back. She stared at me with those innocent eyes that I knew were anything but. "I have all the faith in you Dani. Don't ever think that I don't, got it?"

She gave me a smile that made my chest thump, even with her looking at me upside down. "Fuck you're hot when you're feisty."

I let go of her, feeling myself getting hard and started to condition her curls again. My fingers began to slip through her hair with ease, silently showing me that I had done a solid job. "I have to keep up with you somehow, don't I?"

She hummed. "So does this mean you'll keep your light to yourself?'

I reached out and let the shower water rinse off my hand. She took that as her cue that I was done, moving her hair to one side and turning around. I couldn't help but move my eyes down her body. "Absolutely not."

Her mouth dropped open slightly in shock. "You are unbelievable."

I walked forward causing her to back up so that her spine was against the wall, and I crowded her so the water from the showerhead ran down my back. She had this nervous look about her, but she was never afraid of me. I think despite the level of the conversation, she was still turned on.

"I love you. I'll admit I might have been a bit too hasty this time and like I've said before I'm sorry. I don't want to fight your battles, Dani. I do, however, like knowing you want me involved in those battles, right alongside you. I actually have an affinity for watching you win, but sometimes I like knowing we won together." I placed both my hands on either side of her head and rested my forehead against hers.

She moved her head to the side, examining my arm. Her brown eyes zeroed in on the faint scars left by Dimitri's nails. "The last time you fought with me, you…it…" She tentatively touched her fingertips to my arm as if the wound still ached. There were times when I noticed my arm and my blood raged when Dimitri's face would appear, perfectly clear in my thoughts. That darkness that would also linger inside of me would build but then I thought about all the progress I'd made since we got back, the lack of nightmares and panic attacks I'd had, and my light would win out in the end. She had so much to do with that.

"Every day gets a little better, I promise. I'm never going to be one hundred percent perfect, but I'm working on it. I don't regret ever fighting next to you and I never will. This isn't about me though, it's about you." The shower was steaming again, and I ran a hand through my wet hair, placing it on her cheek, so my thumb could caress her face. "I'm not going anywhere, Dani. If Lilith or fucking Dimitri find out about you and come here, I'm right here. I want you to be ready, but I also want you to know I'm here even if you falter."

"And what if *you* falter and I'm not any good for either of us?"

I kissed her forehead. "I've already done that. I thought letting the darkness suffocate me was a good idea. I thought stabbing you was an even better one. I've faltered, baby, believe me."

"Yeah well, what happened wasn't ideal, but it led me to this very odd balance." She chuckled, looking down at where her stab wound should have been. It disappeared the minute I brought her back. It was like those moments where I thought I'd lost her, the moments where I would have done anything to rewind time hadn't happened. "Now I suppose we just exist together. Two very overprotective entities."

I gave her a small smile, rubbing my nose against hers. "You and me."

She spun us around, so that she could let the water run down her hair, removing the conditioner. She ran her fingers through her mass of curls, scrunching out the water. Her eyes narrowed as she looked at me. "Honesty is a main priority, yes?"

I reached for some soap and started to wash my own body. "Yeah, of course."

She ripped the soap out of my grasp, pointing at where the red had started to fade significantly at the top of my hand. "Then what the fuck is that?" Her tone was nearly lethal and I really, *really*, didn't want to talk about this right now.

I clasped my hand around hers tighter as I pulled her into me. She let out a small gasp of surprise at our sudden closeness. "How about we talk about this…afterwards." I bent down to kiss her, practically hearing her heartbeat thud from within her chest.

She let her lips graze my own. "I'm not being swayed by your cock this time, Nicholas." She pressed her hand against my face, pushing me away.

I groaned, absentmindedly stroking the top of my hand, drawing attention to it. I stopped the minute her brown eyes flew over to it. "It's really nothing."

"How come I don't believe you?" She rolled her eyes, reaching around me to turn off the water.

I watched her reach for the towel she'd slung over the shower wall, wrapping it around her body. I sighed, a bit saddened that I wasn't freely viewing her gorgeous body anymore, but more so, I was considering all the outcomes from telling her the truth.

"You." I admitted, stepping out after her.

Her eyes narrowed with confusion as she grabbed another towel from my neatly folded stack shelved above my toilet. "Huh?"

I tucked the excess part of the towel away once it was securely around my waist. "You caused it."

She pointed her index finger towards my hand. "I burned your hand?" It was almost like I could hear the cogs and wheels turning in her head.

"Yes, but it doesn't hurt for long and it normally goes away in a few hours or a day."

"Nick, what the fuck!"

"I said it's fine! What are you upset about!?" My tone wasn't serious, which was clearly the opposite reaction she wanted from me.

She ran her hand roughly though her wet curls. "I've been randomly burning you and you've just kept it to yourself. Who does that?"

I let out a laugh with no humor laced in it whatsoever. "Someone who didn't know what the fuck was going on, so he kept it to himself so he could figure shit out, while making sure the person he cared about the most was okay, like a good boyfr—" I stopped myself before I could finish, looking at the floor. We hadn't had that conversation yet and with everything else going on, it was just never a solid time to bring it up. I didn't know if Dani had ever had boyfriends before; she'd told me she'd never been in love or had someone say it to her, but that didn't mean she'd never been in a committed relationship of any kind.

I *wanted* to be her boyfriend, but I didn't want that to happen while also mentioning that she nearly melted my flesh a number of times in the last few weeks.

She pulled her lips in, pressing them together as she let my last words fall away. I heard her feet pad along the floor before she was right in front of me. Her eyes looked softer when I gave her my full attention. "When?"

I tilted my head to the side, not understanding.

"When does it happen?"

I laughed again, but this time humor enveloped it fully. "Well, so far it's only happened when we…well when you…"

"Nick…"

"It's only happened when we're…well right when you…."

She sighed, annoyed. "Just spit it out!"

"It's when you come!"

She opened her mouth but closed it immediately. Her eyes widened in shock, but in a matter of seconds, her shoulders started to shake from laughing. "Wait, wait, fucking wait. That's why you acted so weird the morning you went to see Ariel. When I was holding your hand, you took it away so fast that I was confused. It was right after I…oh my god!" The side of her mouth scrunched up, her laughter ceasing instantly, as she brought her hand up and slapped the side of my head.

"What was that for?" I rubbed my head, knowing it didn't hurt one bit, but trying really hard not to chuckle over her frustration.

"You don't just keep that to yourself, Nicholas. No matter how it happened, I deserved to know. Despite what you say, I hurt you and I don't love that." She walked past me, opening the bathroom door, letting some of the cool air from the other room filter in.

I lifted my head towards the ceiling, hating that I made her feel this way. "I didn't think I'd be saying sorry this much today, but I'm sorry that I didn't tell you. I'm being honest when I say you didn't necessarily hurt me, and I mean…I'm not completely upset about how it happens." I smirked over at her, watching as she playfully shook her head at me.

"Natalia is probably right," she muttered more to herself than to me.

"What about Natalia?"

She tucked pieces of her hair behind her ear. "Ugh, she said you might be an asset to my whole situation. The internal turmoil."

I blinked, patiently waiting for her to continue.

"I told her that you had other things to deal with. You are working on a healthy mental state, you have your whole dad thing happening and I just didn't want to be a burden, nor do I need you to be all macho hero man because I would rather throw myself out your fucking window than be a damsel in distress." She started to chew on her thumbnail anxiously. "She *might* have mentioned something along the lines of light calls to light and all that nonsense."

One corner of my mouth tipped up, but I covered my lips with my hand, trying to seem nonchalant. "Hmm, so she thinks my help is needed?"

"She *suggested* it, but that doesn't mean I'm asking."

I shrugged. "My light seems to be mingling with yours, which would mean that in some odd way I'm actually burning myself. The burning could be morphed into something constructive if you let it."

"It's not funny."

"I'm not laughing. It's just an observation." I walked over to her, clasping my hands around her shoulders. "I am willing to provide you with any thread of light I have. I would love to be able to do that without having to get you naked and needy."

She scrunched her nose up at me. "We both know you don't mind."

"I do not. You could burn me anytime you want, and I wouldn't complain. I do want to give you the best advantage possible though, Dani. I am not asking you to give up this independence you have, but maybe your light would cooperate better if it knew you could trust it like you trust me." I lifted her chin with my finger, forcing her to look directly at me. "You completely let go when you orgasm, so we'll focus on that next time we see Natalia. Not the orgasm, but the letting go thing."

I heard my father's words echoing in my head.

One day your light will be just as big as that all on your own, but sometimes it's okay to get a little help. He'd meant it for my younger self to be able to reflect on it for when I got to adulthood, but maybe, it could be of use right now. "It's okay to get a little help, Dani. You took some of my darkness, remember, so how about you let me willingly give you some of my light."

She rubbed her lips together as if she was mulling this over. "You'll back off when I need you to?"

I groaned, but she stared at me with this look in her eyes that had me wanting to fold instantly. "*Only* when you really need me to. Otherwise, I'm at your side, soaking up how much of a badass you are."

"Compliments get you everywhere." She pecked my lips, seeming to concede for now. She leaned back a bit before I could kiss her again. "Do one thing for me please?"

I let out a steady breath, assuming she would say something like please, talk to your dad. I would do it, I promised her that, but I wasn't ready to face what that meant. The fact that I would have to discuss my mother was something that left a lump in my throat and a pained feeling in my chest. A feeling I didn't know existed, especially when it was over someone I could hardly remember.

"Talk to Garrett. Let him talk to you about anything. Your necromancy, his kids, whatever. You of all people should know what a relief it is to just talk to someone about how you feel."

She was my fiery hybrid with a heart as big as Heaven itself. I nodded, understanding every word she said. "Okay."

She kissed my nose. "Good boy."

I raised my eyebrows as she stuck her tongue between her teeth, giving me one of her various flirtatious expressions. "That is the first and last time you ever say that." I tucked my hand into the front of her towel, loosening it.

She bit her bottom lip, examining me. "Nick, the whole burning light thing…orgasms…"

I pulled her towel completely off, bending at my knees so that I could tuck my hands behind her thighs and pick her up. She wrapped her legs around my lower back, pushing her breasts against my chest. "That hasn't stopped me yet and it won't stop me now. If you burn me then you burn me. I'll heal."

7
DANI

I felt his legs unravel themselves from my own as he — very unsuccessfully — tried to not jostle me awake. His hands tentatively touched my arm as he leaned over, placing a gentle kiss to my temple. Despite his way of distracting me with his body, I couldn't help but attempt to focus on what he had told me earlier. The moment when I felt my stomach pull and my eyes tried to roll back in my head from the pleasure, I actually saw it. The light that evidently burned him exuded from my palm and singed his skin as I'd grabbed onto his bicep.

He had flinched but he seemed to be too engrossed in what we were doing to really feel the pain. The minute we flopped onto our backs, I'd rolled over to cuddle into his side and grazed my hand over where his skin was already beginning to redden and swell. I did feel closer to Nick while we were intimate, but there was something comforting about knowing I could be completely myself with someone. I could be wild and untamed for one minute, but all of a sudden, I could choose to be reserved and self-contained.

"Where are you going?" I asked, rolling over and catching a glimpse of his mildly stunned face. The dim moonlight that shone through his little window shaping his face.

"I told you I was meeting Reese."

"That you did, but it seems kind of late, doesn't it?"

He sat up, the covers falling off his stomach, giving me a very nice look at his abs. "His choice, not mine. I'm going to Natalia's though."

My eyebrows pulled together. "Won't you portaling yourself away to Oculus in the middle of the night be just another reason for Ariel to bitch at you even more."

He laughed that deep, throaty laugh of his. It was the kind of laugh that told me he thought what I said was actually funny and I prided myself on making him laugh like that at least once a day since we'd gotten back from Purgatory.

"Nowadays I think Ariel would bitch at me for breathing incorrectly." He ran a hand through his hair, leaving certain pieces in disarray at the top of his head. "I'm actually going to fly to Oculus, not portal."

It was my turn to sit up. "Do what you want, but can I ask why?"

He shrugged, sighing. "It helps me think, that's all."

I leaned into him, kissing his cheek. "Whatever relieves some of the pressure in that handsome head of yours." He turned to face me, and I tipped my head up to kiss his nose. "You know I would fucking murder the demons that torture your mind if I could, right?"

He kissed me softly, not rushing so that the moment felt like hours instead of seconds. "I know."

I slithered back into the covers and closed my eyes, feeling the bed dip when he kicked his legs over the side and got up. He tried to be as quiet as possible as he got himself dressed to leave. My eyes popped open when I heard him clear his throat.

"Do you want to come with me?"

I bit the inside of my cheek, attempting to keep my smile to myself. I shook my head. "You go. I'll be here when you get back."

He smirked at me from his place near the door. "Will I find you in a compromising position, like I did that one time?"

I pulled the comforter over my mouth, muffling my giggle. "Angel or not, we both know you thoroughly enjoyed finding me getting myself off. There are probably things I'll need from you Nicholas, but that's not always one of them." I rolled over so that I was facing the wall, but I knew he was narrowing his eyes at me. "And do not act like you didn't close the door and watch me finish, happier than ever."

"For the love of all that is ethereal, you are annoying." I heard him open up the door, the tiny creaking noise it made echoing as he was starting to close it.

"But…you love me."

The creaking stopped. "Yes, I love you. Always." I heard footsteps quickly before I felt a body looming over me. He grabbed my face, turning it so he could connect his mouth with mine, landing three solid kisses against my lips.

The door closed behind him and I stared up at the ceiling. When Nick was next to me, I fell asleep without issue, my body happily snuggled against his. When Nick was gone, sleep evaded me, not for my lack of trying. I used to be able to get to sleep just fine regardless of who I had in my bed, but things were different now. The ceiling started to blur as my tiredness began to take over.

Vivid images seared across my mind, blurring and then appearing in perfect color. These weren't the kind of dreams I liked as I tried to pull my eyes open. This wasn't like what Nick had described his nightmares as; this was strange, and it felt like it was pulsing into the fiber of my being. I didn't see all the bad things I'd done, the copious amounts of blood I'd spilled. I saw a face, a face of pure confidence and power. It was a face I never wanted to see again, yet here it was staring right at me as if he was in the room with me.

I was right there in his office, the same scene playing over and over.

The words were muddled as if the sound was distorted. The only thing that mattered at that moment were the actions and I was glued to where I stood, forced to watch. Dimitri sliced down Nick's arm with his elongated nails and blood leaked from my angel's arm. It looked like so much more than before. Thick, red liquid spilled out onto the demon's desk and the floor. This felt so much worse than when Lilith had infiltrated my mind. That felt real, but I knew it wasn't. I didn't know what this was at all, but I knew I hated every minute of it.

The scene replayed over and over. Dimitri would slice at his arm; blood would spill, and the Son of Hell would put his blood to his tongue and stare at me. Dimitri didn't have the means to slip into my mind, so this whole thing was my doing. Maybe I still somehow blamed myself for bringing him along and causing him unnecessary pain. I wanted this shit to stop. I felt my darkness wanting to unravel, but then right next to it, I felt the heat in my palms. It was foreign but not unwelcome. I screamed, but no sound came out, but then I jolted up from my place in bed.

My chest heaved, my skin feeling soaked in sweat. I looked around the room, making sure that I was back where I felt comfortable and safe. I ran a hand through my curls, moving most of them off my neck, so I could expose my skin to the cool air. I brought my knees up to my chest, looking over to the door, silently wishing to have Nick's comforting body next to me. My eyes looked up at the window and something in my gut told me things had to start moving quicker than I would have liked. There was a familiar darkness that seemed to ripple across the sky, clouding the moon and then it was gone, as if it was only meant for me to see and speculate on. I could only mark that as a bad sign, meaning that I wasn't as hidden here as my angel would have liked. I would keep my eyes open and alert from now on because for me to see that kind of visual dark power so casually only meant things weren't so forgiving back home—not that I thought they would be. As much as I enjoyed our little love bubble, I unfortunately needed to be the one to pop it and get back to what I did best.

I looked around the bed, a small gasp leaving me when my eyes connected with the small space next to my pillow. There was a handprint that matched my own burned into the mattress.

I brought my hand to my face, the moonlight from the window giving me a small amount of backlight. My small hand looked normal, a simple hand that used to wield a blade made just for me and created shadows at my will. Now there was no blade, but I had so much more than my shadows. I placed my hand in the space I'd burned through, and my chest swelled with a weird sort of pride at what I could do.

My light liked Nick, it wanted to protect him, just as much as it wanted to protect me. Intimate moments with Nick were just a small way for the light to grow and form a better connection with another source of light that was so readily available, but as much as I loved Nick, he couldn't be my only viable option. I put my hand out in front of my face and focused hard on whatever feeling I'd had before, pulled deeply from that place that haunted me. I wasn't afraid or scared, but to be vulnerable with Nick was one thing, but seeking that same vulnerability when it was just me, myself and I was daunting sometimes.

My palm burned, but it was a good burn. It was a burn that didn't settle in one place. I felt a warmth that I seemed to already know; it was like a solace I didn't know existed. Tiny sparks sprung from my fingertips and just as quickly as they came, they were gone. Disappointment didn't come because progress was all that mattered. Perhaps Nick's light *could* make me stronger, but I was already strong without him. I've always been strong without him. Ariel didn't need to make me protect people under the guise of his *'leadership'* because that's what I'd always planned to do. Light didn't suddenly make me good; it just made me more dangerous in the eyes of a fuck ton of people here. Whether I was deemed dead or alive, whether Dimitri or Lilith came roaming around, I *would* learn to trust any sort of power I had before I left the people I cared about defenseless. I would burn the realms down for any of them.

The resilient sparks from my fingers proved it. I wanted more than just sparks. I wanted a goddamn explosion.

8
NICK

I landed in Oculus with a kind of quiet surrounding me. The flight over here was helpful for my mind and thoughts. I liked the wind hitting my face and the feeling of limitless direction. I nearly flew right over my destination because I was so involved in my own thinking. I hated being away from Dani, no matter where I had to go and its importance, but I had promised Reese I would meet him, and the guy was still my best friend.

I was starting to understand that Dani, despite our connection and the love we both had for each other, needed her space. I fucking *hated* it, but I was slowly coming to terms with it. I had flown as close to Natalia's house as I could, realizing that no one could miss her giant home due to the small lights adorning the balconies and around the roof. Reese sat on the steps right outside, drumming his fingers on his knees.

He lifted his head up when he heard my footsteps, quickly hustling down the steps to meet me halfway. "So, how's the girlfriend?"

I rolled my eyes, not in the mood to correct him. "She's fine. Frustrated over something she doesn't even understand."

Reese hummed, nodding towards the house for me to follow him inside. "Putting all the things I've said about her aside, I do think Ariel, the whole Dimitri-Lilith combo and you know pretty much dying can be a mind fuck, so from where I'm standing, she's doing pretty okay."

"Did you just pay her a compliment?"

He made a shooing motion with his hand, dismissing my comment. "I never said I didn't like her, Nick. I just didn't trust her. Now well, you guys are like practically married so…"

"What the fuck, we aren't marri—" I was cut off by Natalia's lyrical voice from around the corner.

"Nicholas, just the person I wanted to see." She gave me a smile that warmed my insides and put me at ease. Both her biceps were decorated in gold jeweled bands and for the first time ever she wore a short dress. The royal blue color complimented her dark skin and long legs. I had to bump my shoulder against Reese's harder than I anticipated due to him staring at her for too long.

"Me?" I asked.

"Just checking in to see how you were doing. Yesterday was about Dani, yes, but I do like to make sure everyone else is thought about as well. Especially with what was said on the balcony about your…"

I cleared my throat, backing away from her and started rubbing the back of my neck. "Oh no, I'm all good. One day at a time and all that." I looked around the room, a thought brewing in my mind. "You both didn't want me to come here as some sort of family intervention. He isn't here, right?"

I wasn't ready for that. I missed my father; I could admit that. I could miss him and also want my distance at the same time; it didn't mean I loved him any less. I just needed to look at our relationship from this new viewpoint he'd finally shown me. I had no idea at this vantage point, the new view of my past—of my life—would give me vertigo.

I had made a lot of progress when it came to myself and maybe I could admit I wasn't strong enough at the moment to face the man I'd looked up to my entire fucking life. I could admit that I wasn't ready to hear him *really* talk about—*her*.

Natalia and Reese both looked at each other in slight confusion and then as if in sync, their faces morphed into mild disappointment and shook their heads. Reese stepped over to me and gripped my shoulder. "He's not here. We know you aren't ready for that, even if it would probably be for the fucking best."

The High Priestess shushed him as he patted my shoulder. I flinched just a little at the pressure of his fingers. Dani's newest burn spot was fresh, and the press of his fingertips just made it worse.

"You okay?" Reese asked, raising a blonde eyebrow at me.

I readjusted my jacket and tried to remain casual. I really, really, didn't want to explain this to them. I had told Dani we could let them in on things tomorrow, so I would uphold that statement, as much as Reese would have a field day with this kind of information.

I nodded, shrugging. "Never better."

"You don't sound like it." Elise stalked down the stairs, Beetee at her heels.

"Leave him alone, Ellie," Beetee scolded.

Elise scoffed, walking past us towards the veranda. "I'm allowed to make fucking statements. You all just hate it cause I'm right." Beetee mouthed an *I'm sorry* before following her.

"You actually enjoy spending so much time here?" I nodded toward the overtly grumpy demon.

Reese ran a hand through his blonde locks. "Enjoy, no. Would I rather be here than at The Skies, living under Ariel's thumb, fuck yes. Although, most of the time, I stay at your house." He had a laughing tone to his voice when he finished, but that quickly dissolved into an awkward silence.

I let out a joyless chuckle. "Right."

Natalia slipped her arm through mine and guided us towards where Beetee and Elise were settled. The hustle of Enchanter around her home was practically nonexistent, it was as if at a certain time of night, she simply wanted peace and if the High Priestess wants peace, she gets it.

A small silence hung in the air and then both Reese and Elise spoke at once.

"I overheard Ariel securing someone to babysit us."

"I'm going to head back to Purgatory."

Natalia, Beetee and I all let out one collective, "huh?"

Reese opened his mouth to speak, but Elise placed her hand at his mouth and pushed him away. "I'm going back to Purgatory. I'll use your key or get your majesty here to send me there, but either way I'm going."

Beetee's voice was small and laced with shock. "You never told me that."

"I decided today. Simple."

I pulled my eyebrows together. "No, not simple. You can't just make that decision."

"I just fucking did. What are you going to do, stop me? I would really like to see you try, although I don't think that would work out too well for you, pretty boy."

Natalia shook her head in disbelief. "I think you know I will not be opening a portal for you to go there."

Elise clucked her tongue, her gray eyes raging in annoyance before she peered over at me. Before I could answer, Reese beat me to it. "Just let the tiny psycho go. She wants to be on the front lines and destroy herself then so be it."

"Believe me, Blondie, no such thing will happen. I am *delighted* you are on my side for once. Maybe I'll start thinking about fewer ways to erase you from this realm from now on." She gave him a smile that showed all her teeth and held her hand out to me. "I don't have all day, Nicholas."

I grabbed her hand, shoving it away. "You are out of your fucking mind, if you think any of us are letting you do that."

"What are you even planning to accomplish, Ellie? You alone can't stop both Lilith and Dimitri."

Elise whipped her head towards the pink haired demon, who had more hurt and concern written on her face than anger. "It's insulting that you underestimate me." The look she gave her was one that told me they were having some sort of silent conversation that none of us were invited to.

"What about Dani?" I questioned, crossing my arms over my chest.

Elise stepped up to me with the kind of confidence that would suffocate someone who hadn't stood up to her before. She volleyed my own question back to me. "What *about* Dani?"

"I think he means, it's shitty how you want to completely leave her out of a fight she is pretty damn determined to participate in." Reese explained.

"Her determination to figure her powers out is due to this whole mess and you just want to go and be…" I added, my voice trailing off, but Natalia picked up where I left off.

"You want to go and be a hero." Natalia let out a small, satisfied laugh. The concerning nature of the situation no longer troubling her.

Elise turned her hands into fists at her sides. "No, you witch, that's not what I said."

"That is how it seems," Beetee offered, playing with the ends of her pink hair.

The grumpy demon threw her hands up. "I'm here *not* trying to deal with any of this shit anymore and you dumbasses are standing here telling me you don't want to just settle this?" She turned to look out towards the front yard, tapping her foot against the floor.

I let out a loud sigh. "No, fuck, Elise, your help is appreciated I promise." I slowly approached her, not wanting to increase her already boiling temper. "Dani tried to do whatever shit on her own in Purgatory before and look what happened. I'm not going to let that happen again, but I also won't let you have her make all this effort for nothing all because you're fucking impatient. Whether you like it or not, she's your fucking friend and you need to have some faith in her."

Everyone was watching us, but I focused all my attention on her. Elise tilted her head to the side and placed her hands on her hips. Her t-shirt rose up a bit as she lifted her shoulders in an overly exaggerated sigh. "I have faith in Dani believe me and the fact that you make it out like I've just forgotten seeing her dead body in Purgatory is fucking…" She pressed her lips together, halting her sentence. Elise closed her eyes, taking small, calculated breaths in and out. She opened her eyes and her gray irises flashed red for a small moment. "I don't think you quite understand how different Dani and I are. Purgatory—"

"What about Purgatory?" We all spotted Garrett as he walked out on the veranda. "Zane told me you all were out here. From the looks of it, it's not for pleasant conversation."

"It would be if tiny psycho over here wanted to play by the rules." Reese shook his head.

Garrett raised an eyebrow. "Elaboration seems necessary here."

Beetee answered. "Ellie wants to go to Purgatory to play hero and save us all because somehow that is so much better than admitting that she has a heart and cares…OW!"

Elise slapped the back of her head, groaning. "That's not what I fucking said!"

"Is it untrue though?" Natalia challenged, crossing her arms over her chest. Elise ran a hand down her face in frustration. I had a feeling if she could strangle all of us right here, right now, she would have.

Garrett cleared his throat, looking over at Natalia. "You plan to portal her to Purgatory?" His voice sounded hurt. It made sense since we had been continuously telling him we weren't going to just dive back into Purgatory, while Elise kept begrudgingly reassuring him Axel would make sure his family was safe.

Natalia walked up to him, tentatively touching his shoulder. "No, I'm not. Elise made a false assumption."

Elise growled in annoyance, but Natalia paid no mind. "Pretty boy here also refuses to be of assistance."

"I want to help, but not at the expense of everyone else, Elise." I touched the portal key that I'd tucked into my shirt. I snuck a look over at Garrett, who looked slightly more exhausted than usual. "You want to have this kind of discussion, make these kinds of decisions, then we *all* need to be here."

Everyone gave slow nods confirming that they agreed, or they were in their own worlds at this point. I felt Garrett's large presence before I'd turned to face him. "Your key can still get us back to Purgatory with no issue?"

I nodded, remembering that he had only been present when we were heading out of Purgatory. He licked his lips, placing a hand on my shoulder and nodded in understanding.

"Does anyone actually give a shit about what I was saying about Ariel earlier or are we all just ignoring that?" Reese said, but his voice was clouded by Garrett's.

The Enchanter's hold on my shoulder became a bit harsher and his fingers dug in deeper. "Please try to understand."

I tilted my head to the side, confused. It was like it happened in slow motion when his hand reached out towards my neck. His fingers trapped the chain of my portal key in their grasp, and he yanked. I hissed at the quick burn of the metal pulling at my skin as he ripped the key from my body, before he pushed me backwards into the railing

"Garrett, stop!" I yelled, gaining everyone's attention.

Natalia tried to step in front of him, but he used his elbow to shove her to the right. Reese ran over to catch her before she hit the ground, looking over at me in question.

"He has my key!"

Elise groaned. "Oh, for fucks sake." She darted out of the room with Beetee behind her. Natalia shooed us away from her as she followed after them with us on her heels. I heard a grunt as we turned the corner and saw Garrett on the floor with both his ankles tied up with Elise's tail.

We heard rushed footsteps from upstairs, telling me that Zane would be here in mere moments.

"Just give us back the key, Garrett. Please," Beetee begged. Her lilac-colored eyes looked more sad than angry.

"I'm sorry, I can't," Garrett refused, placing his hand on Elise's tail and pulling. Her grip on him was taunt and unmoving. "Let me go!"

"Give us the key and we will," Elise offered.

Garrett shook his head. I saw the chain of the portal key dangling out of his closed fist.

Natalia walked around us and towards his head. "Garrett, we will work together on this. This isn't the way to do this." The High Priestess knelt down and placed her hand over his fist.

"I can't do that, your Highness. I am sorry." He threw his palm out towards her, and a stream of colorful magic spewed out. It hit Natalia in the stomach, sending her flying backwards into one of the walls.

He directed his magic at Elise, causing her to lift her hands to block his magic. He grabbed hold of her tail and tiny sparks moved up her deadly appendage. A popping sound followed by her own yelp, had her releasing his legs.

"Garrett! Stop!" I ran over to him as he sprung up from the ground. His body ran right into Zane's.

The High Priestess's bodyguard looked flustered and pissed, if both emotions could be displayed at the same time. "What is the meaning of this?" He held onto both of Garrett's shoulders.

Garrett didn't speak, but he did pull his arm back and connect his fist to Zane's jaw. The bodyguard was thrown off, staggering back. Garrett kicked his foot out, colliding with Zane's stomach before trying to make his way to the front door. I caught up with him, pulling him back by one of his arms. He used that to his advantage and threw his arm forward, slamming me into the closed doors.

I groaned, this level of pain, not doing my fresh burn any favors.

Reese ran up to grab his other arm, but Garrett reared his arm back ready to throw a punch in his direction. A large burst of purple-teal magic struck Garrett's back. He clamped his teeth together and fell to the ground, on his hands and knees.

His head was lifted up by some invisible force and his eyes began to bug out and look around rapidly. His throat appeared as if something was cinched around it. Garrett let out harsh breaths, trying to consume as much air as he could. My mind traveled back to when I'd landed in Oculus, hoping to learn about Dani's past from Natalia. That's when I noticed the tiny blue sparks coming from his neck and looked past him, focusing on Zane.

The large Enchanter looked as if he was doing nothing at all, but I knew this magic was his. "Restrain him." Zane commanded. Other large Enchanters hustled over to Garrett, yanking him up and pulling him away from the door and over to The High Priestess.

Natalia held her stomach, leaning on Beetee for assistance. She didn't look upset, but more disappointed. Reese slapped his hand against my bicep, nodding at me as if confirming that I was okay. I gave him a nonchalant shrug and walked over to where they all surrounded Garrett. Zane had removed his magic as Garrett sucked in breath after breath.

Elise shoved in front of us and brought her fist to his face, shaking off her hand when his head was knocked back. "I applaud your effort to want to get your family back, but don't fuck with my tail or I will make it so the next time you see your loved ones they won't recognize your fucking face." She rolled her shoulders and stepped out of our way.

Garrett pulled against the other Enchanter hold on him. I looked to Natalia, just to confirm they had him. She gave me a small smile, pushing away from Beetee so she could stand on her own. "He can't move at the moment, and I've nullified his magic for now."

I flicked my eyes towards his closed fist, the portal key chain still hanging out. Through all of that, he never let it go. "Garrett…"

"Your majesty, we can throw him in the…" Zane offered, but Natalia shushed him.

"I am fine, Zane. Let him speak." The High Priestess inclined her head towards me. Her hair was done in multiple braids that started from the top of her head and ended in curled pieces; and they fell over her shoulders as she moved. "Go ahead, Nicholas."

They still had him on his knees, so I got down on mine. Garrett's head was slightly down, and his eyes were staring at the ground. His jaw ticked as if he was holding in so much that it was hard to just stay still. "Hey, Garrett, look at me."

He didn't acknowledge me, his eyes still fixated on the ground.

"Garrett, I need you to look at me."

Silence.

I closed my eyes and let out a few breaths. I could be gentle and give a little tough love when it was needed. I grabbed his face in my hands and lightly shook him. I forced his head up and forward. "Look. At. Me."

A few seconds went by before he did what I asked. I sucked in a breath when I saw that his golden eyes didn't have the same glow as before. They had dimmed and it looked as if tears could fall at any moment. Garrett wasn't a threat. He was a father that missed his kids. He missed his wife.

He missed his family.

"I understand why you did it. We will get them back to you, but we will do it the right way. I know it hurts but you are going to have to trust us." I removed one of my hands from his face and brought it over to his closed fist that was still holding my key. "You don't want this to be the story of how you saw your family again. Believe me when I tell you that you are already a hero in their eyes, so don't tarnish that."

The tears that had settled on his bottom lid started to fall. I peeked over at Natalia, who gave me a small smile before nodding over to Zane and the others. Garrett's body seemed to relax when the magic was removed, and his head tilted up towards the High Priestess. "I am so sorry, Your Majesty." His voice was cracked and small. "I just...I miss them...I..."

She grabbed his chin and patted his cheek with her other hand. "Never be sorry for loving someone that fiercely, alright."

I felt the chain of the portal key in my hand as he released it. I snuck a glance over to his palm and noticed the indention his hold had left. I looked down at the key to see that little spots of blood were on it. I placed my eyes back on his open palm to see that the indentions were deeper as if he had held on so tight, he had started to break skin.

He hadn't been prepared to let that key go without a fight.

"I didn't want to hurt anyone..." I looked over at him when I realized he was speaking to me. "I miss them." He felt the need to keep repeating this notion, as if he thought that if he stopped saying it, it would make it untrue.

I placed my key in my pocket and returned both my hands to the sides of his face. "We got you." I had to quickly regain my balance when he practically collapsed against me in a mess of tears. I remembered being in the same position with Dani holding me in Purgatory, where all I could do was cry and feel all the things I was harboring. I wasn't afraid to admit that I could one day be in that position yet again, crying into the arms of the girl I loved, but knowing I could hold it together for someone who needed me to be in a stronger position than them made me feel good.

It made me feel like myself again.

I didn't push him off to someone else; I wrapped my arms around his shoulders best I could and rubbed his back. "How about we go outside, sit down and you can tell me all about them."

It had been a little over an hour before Garrett started coming to the end of all his stories about his family. The way his eyes flickered with life when he was laughing over the past and even all the things they planned to do in the future made me smile. His voice was more put together and the only tears that left his eyes were happy ones from a fond memory or from his overbearing laughter.

Reese and I remained outside with him while the others cleared the mess inside. Zane kept a close eye on us from one of the windows, per Natalia's orders. Garrett spoke of how Elise was probably right, and Axel was guarding his family just fine. I would bet celestial coins on that, especially knowing that hellhound was immovable when it came to the people he cared about.

Garrett and I sat on one of the wooden benches that was placed near the tree lines, while Reese leaned up against a tree with his head tilted to the sky. The Enchanter cleared his throat when the silence of his finished stories wrapped around us. "Thank you for this. I thought talking about them would hurt, which it does, but in a way it doesn't. It feels good to speak about them even when the future is still so unknown."

My best friend let out a cough that wasn't a regular everyday cough. That was a cough that was directed at me and at Garrett's words. I gave him a knowing look and twisted my body so I could swing one of my legs over to the other side of the bench. "Um…you mentioned a day or so ago about my powers—"

"You want to learn to use them?"

"Oh, uh…no, well I don't think so. I just want to understand it."

Garrett scratched his chin. "I'm no history buff, Nicholas, but I can tell you that power was always very rare and kept tight within the world of Enchanters. Going off and marrying any other being that could somehow diminish that power line was unheard of. The fact that you even have it is astounding."

"Transference."

Garrett looked at me with raised eyebrows.

"That's how I got it. Natalia's mother took it from…my mother, who apparently got it from another Enchanter and gave it to me. I don't remember any of it."

Garrett slowly nodded and leaned over, placing his hand on my knee. "I was there when your father told us as much as he could muster about your mother. I can understand wanting to keep it together for the sake of your children but trust me when I say it's hard trying to be the strongest one." He jostled my knee so I would look at him. "Your mother keeping this power alive by holding it within herself and then giving it to you means a great deal to those of us who thought we were the only ones left. I would like to point out how it did come in handy when you needed it."

I ran a hand through my hair, blowing out a breath as a soft breeze blew in. "Yeah, I guess it did. I guess I just don't know what it means for me now."

Reese chimed in, "Nick, it doesn't have to mean anything. Or it can just mean that you have this thing that makes you slightly more interesting than we originally thought. If you never use it again, cool. If you do, great. The fact that you know you have it is a big step in itself."

"Did you just say something just a tiny bit profound?"

Reese placed a hand on his chest in faux shock. "I tend to do that every now and again, so fuck you."

Garrett chuckled. "The only thing you need to know is that the bigger and more powerful the entity, the more it will take from you. Necromancers have died giving too much. Consider this before attempting to be heroic, alright?"

I felt Reese push me over so I could make more room on the bench for him. I pointed my finger at him. "Weren't you saying something before?"

Reese narrowed his eyes at us. "Ah, now you guys give a flying fuck about what I have to say?"

I made a motion with my hand that told him to get over it and continue.

My best friend tucked a piece of his blonde locks behind his ear. "Ariel is likely sending someone to watch us."

"Like a babysitter?"

"Basically. Ideally, he can't be totally sure that we are here with Natalia, getting your Dani hybrid certified. It's just something I overheard; I could be wrong."

"Do you know who?" I inquired.

Reese shook his head. "Nope. Anyone who does Ariel's bidding like that can't be all that great anyway."

Garrett hummed. "Aren't you two doing Ariel's bidding?"

Reese and I looked at each other and started laughing. Garrett added to it with a loud thunderous laugh of his own. My laughter ceased when my eyes caught something in the sky. I shushed both of them and pointed towards the dark ripple that was longer than my eyes could make out. It wasn't there for long, but I couldn't unsee it.

"What the hell was that?" Reese asked.

I got up from the bench, feeling the need to get back to my girl. "No idea, but it can't be good."

The sun would be rising in a few hours, so I knew there were a few angels who would be getting up by now to shower and head to wherever they needed to be. The hallway was still quiet though as I walked, the sound of my own footsteps echoing.

It was odd, though. I felt like I was being watched.

I rounded a corner just to run into two sentries that I recognized, but not well enough to call them a friend. I said a low 'excuse me', but neither of them moved. I backed up, prepared to ask them what was going on, but a voice that had my shoulders tensing and fists curling had me backing up even more.

"Back from a little trip to Oculus?" Ariel said, stepping around the two sentries.

"Yes, is that a problem?"

He waved his hand at me. "No problem at all, as long as your time there is spent wisely. I would hate for all the effort that the little demon is putting in to go to waste."

I wanted to shove my fist down his throat, but I remained calm. "I assure you, we are doing what you asked. It's not something that can just be achieved overnight."

"Oh, I am well aware, Nicholas. I will do everything in my power to make sure that you are abiding by our agreement. If that means I need to take precautionary measures, then so be it."

Ariel is likely sending someone to watch us.

I swallowed the feeling of wanting to ask a million and one questions down. "You have every right to do that, just as long as you keep your end of this deal and let her be free to do as she pleases and not be a pariah."

"I can't help how people think of her Nicholas. I am no monster though, so of course I will uphold what I've said. I have much bigger things to grant my attention towards. These ceremonies take much preparation, and I would like for there to be no mishaps, distractions or rogue demons who don't know how to use their own powers."

I nearly rolled my eyes. "You're just done looking for Jonah's power?"

"No need to look for something that doesn't want to be found. I'm bored of it to be honest, and it would be nice to have that sort of power, but it isn't necessary for the people to see me as a leader." He walked over to me, placing his hands in his pants pockets as his green eyes bore into my brown ones. "Did you see the sky tonight, Nicholas?"

"I don't know what you mean?"

He snickered. "Of course you do. Oculus has a gorgeous view of the sky."

I narrowed my eyes at him. "It does."

He clucked his tongue. "The sky tonight let all of us know that something is coming and it will be here much sooner than you think." He motioned with one finger for his sentry angels to follow him as he walked around me. "And if you think that when it's time that I won't throw her into the fire along with the rest of you to maintain order…well then I would think again."

9

DANI

"Wait, I'm sorry, he punched Zane?" My voice cracked due to the laugh that came out. "And he almost punched you?" I pointed over to Reese who let us go ahead of him into Natalia's house.

The blonde angel shook his head. "No, I'm way too quick for that."

Nick rolled his eyes and shoved his friend. "Keep telling yourself that."

My forthcoming angel decided that the minute I woke up and started to get ready was the perfect time to clue me in on all the things that had happened prior. My eyes had widened a bit when he told me about Garrett's outburst. As out of character it seemed, it was something that didn't surprise me. Garrett was a good father that was without his family. They were a part of him and without them, it was like he didn't have much at all. Risking everything by taking Nick's key was the 'best' solution in his eyes. Desperation makes you do wild things.

I had rubbed my hands all along Nick's body, furiously asking if he was alright, which got me pushed against a wall and kissed very hard on the mouth. The story continued once we got to Oculus and in front of Reese who couldn't help providing us with a more colorful interpretation of what happened.

"Zane keeps his beady little eyes on him constantly now," Reese explained. "Natalia keeps telling him to back off, but the guy is a force to be reckoned with."

I tugged on Nick's arm, bumping against him. "And you talked to him?" The entire conversation about this whole mess had me wondering if he had taken what I'd suggested to heart.

He smiled down at me, nodding. "Yes, I did. Happy?"

I reached up and kissed his cheek. "Good boy."

I heard his groan of annoyance from his distaste at my form of praise. We made it to the doors of Natalia's personal training room and after what happened to me last night, I wanted to make today count. Everyone was already gathered and settled along the walls of the room, waiting. I had told Nick about what happened, especially when he noticed the hand sized burn into his sheets and mattress. He had mumbled that it was yet another piece of information to tell Natalia and the others, which I agreed with. Secrets were something neither of us were a fan of any longer, whether it be with each other or anyone else.

"All this time we've known each other, I've never asked…do you have wings? Like can you fly like most demons?" I swung my head over at the sound of Elise's voice and saw her engaged in a conversation with Beetee.

The pink haired demon wrinkled her nose. "Uhh, not that I know. I've never felt the urge to make something protrude from my back and it also sounds like it hurts so I don't think I would want to anyway."

"They are magic manifestations, Beetee, not actual appendages."

Beetee wrinkled her nose, again. "Yeah, well your tail is something you magically manifest and it still hurts like a bitch when something happens to it, so no thank you. I'll stick to shape shifting."

I received a quick wave from Beetee the minute she noticed me. It was a tiny bit awkward, especially with the way she was biting her bottom lip furiously. I was quickly reminded that we still needed to talk, but what I would say during that conversation was still lost on me. Listening to a sliver of what they spoke about just pushed my need to speak with her at the top of my list of priorities. Well, maybe not the *top*, but close enough.

Natalia placed herself at the center of the room, but before she could start with whatever she had planned, Nick and I both hustled over to her.

"There is something you need to know," I said, shuffling from one foot to the other.

"If it's about the sky last night, I saw it too."

I bit the inside of my cheek. "It's not that. Although, that's also a problem and unfortunately not the Lilith kind." I licked my lips before I continued, "so, you were right. Nick might be more of an asset to me when it comes to being more connected with my light. Well, actually it was apparent a while ago, because he actually decided to bring to my attention that I've been burning him with my light. It's likely our light put together, but it happens every time that we…or really when I—"

Nick let out an obnoxious cough. "We don't have to go into so much detail, Dani."

"Oh okay, well how else is she supposed to understand that my light powers become so powerful they burn you when you make me come, huh?" I waved my hands in the air, making more of a scene then necessary.

A loud laugh came from behind us. "I'm sorry, what the hell?" Reese asked between gasps of air. "That's a new one. Your light burns him because the dick is just that good." He couldn't get the last few words out without laughing.

I saw Nick shake his head and heard him blow air out of his nose with the way he was seething.

"I can honestly say, for you two horny idiots, that I am not surprised. You both can't seem to stop touching each other half the time, it's no doubt that level of intimacy could cause you to spontaneously combust."

We all looked over at Elise, but she was inspecting her fingernails as if what she said had no merit and was just a fleeting comment.

I turned my eyes away from Elise and over to Nick, who was already looking at me.

"It's not just the intimacy that makes it rage, is it?" Natalia asked, not seeming all that surprised by my comments.

I pulled my eyes away from him and locked eyes with her. "No."

I tried to sum up my feelings from last night and it wasn't the best idea going back to that memory of Dimitri. I told her about how I wanted to be able to help myself and not need Nick, even though his joy of being my catalyst was very cute. She listened to every word I said while each person around us seemed to be focusing all their attention on us as well. Zane even looked intrigued by my story, if intrigue was a facial expression he knew how to possess.

"Is Dimitri getting into your head like Lilith did?" Reese questioned. "You just said that the ripple in the sky was not a Lilith issue. Is the Son of Hell currently throwing a really big tantrum?"

I shook my head. "No, he can't. I have—had—a connection with Lilith, but I never had something like that with Dimitri. If I had money to bet, I would say a tantrum is correct." I frustratingly ran a hand through my curls. "I just felt a need to fight, but instead of my shadows doing the work...the light did instead. Trust me I'm still trying to comprehend."

The High Priestess placed a hand on my shoulder. "I think you are finally letting it in, which is a good thing."

"So, you just burned a handprint into your boyfriend's bed? Nice." Elise complimented, shrugging.

Nick put his hands up. "Okay, everybody can we just all come back to the point of why we are here. How are we getting her to harness both the uh...intimate part and the protective nature part?"

Natalia gave him a small chuckle. "I think I have an idea for that." She turned to Zane, who was standing so close to Garrett it made even me uncomfortable. "Go rally up some of your recruits for me, would you please?"

Zane swiftly dipped his head down, giving Garrett a *I swear, do not fuck with me* look and hustled out of the room.

Elise pushed out her bottom lip in a pout. "Awe, so you guys aren't going to demonstrate this burning light by having sex in front of us?"

I rolled my eyes. "Haha, no."

She stuck her tongue between her teeth and looked over at Nick. "Hmm, what a shame. From how pretty boy was dancing with you at Leviathan, he made it pretty clear he liked being watched."

"I never…" Nick started his cheeks turning a small shade of pink, but the sound of multiple footsteps interrupted him.

Five or six Enchanters walked in behind Zane in a single file line. They all stayed silent as they waited for his instruction. The men and women before us all had different tattoos decorating their skin and even though none of them were flexing, I was pretty sure they could throw around any of us. Not that I would give them the chance.

Reese pulled at the collar of his shirt as if he was stressed out. "Damn, they are more disciplined than us."

Garrett raised an eyebrow at him. "There are still some days that I wonder how you got into The Skies." His shoulders moved as he started to chuckle.

"That place doesn't have standards, I figured that out a while ago. Keep up." Elise rolled her eyes as she surveyed the Enchanter in front of us. "What is this all about, witch?"

Natalia let out a low sigh. "They are here to help with the issue at hand. Me simply throwing my magic at you isn't going to help it seems; you need something that feels like an actual threat. Something that causes you to trust yourself along with trusting one another. As much as the power is physical, this is still a mental diabolical in its own right. Like you said, when you saw that you'd burned through that mattress, you felt like you could burn the world…"

"In a good way." Nick chimed in, always looking for the best in me it seemed.

Natalia smirked, winking at him. "Yes, in a good way. You want that same feeling, do you not?"

I bit my lip, already getting antsy for that high again. "Fuck, yeah."

The High Priestess pushed her mass of braids over her shoulder and sauntered over to Zane. They both left the recruits in the middle of the room while Natalia also grabbed Garrett. She made sure they were all placed in the corner of the room while we all simply stared at one another.

Natalia's regal voice echoed. "Neither side is fighting to kill, but I'd never want you to hold back."

Nick and Reese looked at each other from across the room, when I noticed one of the Enchanters, a girl with freckles that littered her face, zeroed in on me.

"You heard your Queen." Zane's booming voice rang out and a bright blue ball of light flew from the freckled face girl's fingers straight into my stomach, flinging me against the wall.

"Woah, woah, fucking…" Reese shouted before he was slapped in the face by a spark of magic and then picked up by a gust of wind from nowhere and thrown against the other wall. He grunted and grabbed the side of his face.

I saw Nick running over to me and I wanted to shake my head, because no, I didn't need him as much as I appreciated his efforts. He didn't get within a foot of me before a rope of magic the color of ivy wrapped around his ankle and jerked him back. I looked over at Natalia who gave me the most nonchalant look back, as if saying *we shouldn't be surprised.*

The freckle faced girl came charging at me, but I pushed out my hand, releasing dark shadows towards her. She had electric pink sparks coming from her hand and she grabbed onto my shadows, wringing them out like a wet rag before discarding them. My mouth dropped open slightly and my shoulders tensed up when I heard a thud.

"Fuck, this is fucking bullshit," Elise yelled, another thud coming as her back hit the wall again. A male Enchanter with a shaved head besides the one long braid cascading down the middle of his head, pressed his body weight against her. She worked her tail out, preparing to slice it through the backs of his thighs, but another Enchanter came up and grabbed it, twisting it around their arm until she yelled out.

Beetee ran up behind them, jumping on their back and I had to blink twice before I realized that maybe she didn't need to shift into a full snake to produce snakelike elements. Two of her canines protruded like fangs as she sunk them into the Enchanter's neck. They howled in pain, releasing Elise's tail and giving her an opening to successfully cause the pain she was hoping for. The male Enchanter holding her up threw her to the ground, but not right before she was picked up by another and slammed into the ground again.

A bolt of magic came at me again, but I sprung up from the ground, swerving away from it. The freckled faced girl threw bolt after bolt, and I shot out multiple shadows, dodging them. I let my shadows slither on the ground as I spun around and evaded the grasp of an Enchanter. I kicked my foot out and connected the end of my boot with her stomach. My shadows wrapped around my target's feet right as she was running towards me, ceasing her movement.

The shadows moved quickly, but there was a spark in them as if they were their own little thunderstorm. I was so close to her, I reached out and grabbed her throat letting my well-known darkness begin to encapsulate her completely. She didn't look nervous or scared. She almost looked like this was what she was hoping for. Before her fingers could be completely taken over, she shot out bright white sparks from her fingers and removed my shadowy holds as if they were nothing.

My mouth dropped open in shock, but I was propelled to the side when a body threw itself against mine. I skidded across the floor, hissing in pain. I'd felt worse, but fuck did that hurt. I pushed myself off the ground, blowing curls out of my face, when a body came up behind me. My arms were yanked behind me, and the feeling of immobility started to make its way through my body.

"Let me go," I demanded.

The female Enchanter tsked. "We both know I can't do that."

I heard grunts and yelps of pain around me and there was this feeling of agonizing dread. What if I couldn't do this? What if I was only worth something when I was being lied to and thought I was something I wasn't?

Nick and Reese were thrown together, colliding shoulder to shoulder before they fell on the ground. Nick's sword clattered in one direction and Reese, even though his face looked pained, was already moving to use his bow again.

Puffs of dark magic became the focus of my attention. I looked down and saw it swirling and moving up my legs, wanting to help me. I tried to shift my weight, tried to move my knees but I couldn't. I looked over at Natalia who had this look in her honey-colored eyes, like she knew this would work but just needed me to do my fucking part.

The girl leaned down to my ear. "They want to become one so let them. Are you so afraid that the light will consume you, Soul Seether? It doesn't want to consume you; it just wants you to make space. So *let* it."

I let out a slow breath and closed my eyes. I felt the dark shadows wrap themselves further, but I let my own heartbeat thrum in my ears, I let the warmth that used to baffle me seek solace in my veins. I felt the dark and light caress each other like old friends, rather than mortal enemies. One was stronger than the other, but that was to be expected, but I felt them both...I was *aware* of them both. The darkness pushed further but it was followed by a golden light as I brought my head down and opened my eyes. They quickly moved around my body, progressing together seamlessly.

The light sparked and tiny flames surged against her magic. I heard a shriek from behind me and my body was suddenly free of her magical restraints. There was a soft glow in my palms as I spun around, looking down at my hands. Holy shit this felt...interesting. I wasn't used to it, but it was something I could see myself getting used to.

I shot out a rope of dark magic peppered with light, but she caught it. Her face was tense with pain, and I peered down to see the light was causing small burns as she held on. She threw my magic to the left, sending me flying over to where Nick was caught between two Enchanters. The impact of my body against his sent us both tumbling to the ground.

I grabbed the side of my head and looked around at all these people I'd surrounded myself with fighting. It wasn't for me, but it was for them. I could fight for them, but I could also fight and trust myself. I peeked over at Nick, who was looking down at my hands.

The glow was stuttering, and the shadows danced around it in small wisps.

I could fight for myself…with some help when it was needed.

"Always here when I need you aren't you?" I said, gaining a small smile from him.

"For you? Absolutely." He gripped my hand so tight, I swore he cut off my circulation.

There was déjà vu with this level of light running through my system. The last time I'd felt this kind of shock was when I'd gone rogue during the fight with the hellhounds outside of Leah and Garrett's home. This feeling was different now that I wasn't getting mentally fucked by Lilith or legitimately fucked by Nick. I was more aware of everything; every single fiber of my being felt his light and I could feel mine nearly squealing at the intrusion.

I trusted myself, but I also trusted *him*.

I ripped my hand away from his and pushed against the wall behind me, so I could stand up straight. I brought my hands together and felt a sudden surge of heat between them, along with my shadows that swirled around my hands, becoming larger by the second. I began to separate my fingers and it was nearly too bright for me to look at, but then it started to feel too much for me to even hold.

My hands shook and before I had a moment to think, everything that was in my grasp released itself from my palms. Dark shadows and bright light magic that had now morphed into mild flames was bouncing around the room.

"Everybody stop! Get down!" Zane yelled, his voice causing everyone to duck and search above their heads.

Reese made his way to the other corner near the entrance door, while Elise forced Beetee to huddle near her. I heard a whoosh and realized Nick had forced his wings out, covering me. I was proud of myself, slightly embarrassed and just a tiny bit turned on. None of which mattered if whatever I had created killed all of us.

My power was headed right for Natalia, but she lifted her hands, and a large gust of wind blew around the training room, tossing my curls around so that most of them kept falling into my eyesight. The power

I'd held was caught in her windstorm and sent sideways, a crashing sound making me flinch when I saw that it had created a rather large hole in the wall giving us a perfect view of the forest outside.

A silence came over the entire room as the dust from the now open wall space settled. Zane coughed, swatting the air and inspecting the damage. "And you thought this would be a good idea?" He was speaking to Natalia but stuck his head out the hole in the wall.

"I think it proved to work just fine."

"Work just…there is a hole in the—" Zane started, exasperated, but Natalia placed her index finger to her lips, shushing him. Garrett patted him on the back and started to pick up some of the bigger shards that had broken around the room.

"That can be fixed." She came over to me, placing both her hands on my shoulders. I heard a whoosh behind me, letting me know Nick had retracted his wings. "I never doubted you, but I think the next plan of action is getting it controlled."

Reese let out a cough as he leaned down to pick up pieces of the wall and chucking it back to the ground. "You were always meant to blow a hole through a wall? You see when I want to do destructive shit, everyone thinks it's fucking weird and says no."

"Oh, stop fucking whining, the fact that you think you need to ask permission to be destructive is pathetic, Blondie." Elise said annoyed. She nodded over to me. "I, for on, am mildly impressed. Next time try not to kill all the people that want to help you, but good job."

The freckle faced Enchanter inclined her head towards me and smiled as she gathered with the others towards the broken wall. The number of people that just trusted Natalia's judgment and plans without question was astonishing. I turned around to see Nick and him off guard when I ran and jumped onto him, wrapping my legs around his lower back.

"I did it," I said, my voice prouder than normal.

"Well, of course you did, and you added a dash of sass by breaking a wall."

I laughed and leaned down to kiss him. His lips were just as eager to get to mine. I pulled my face away from him to see an Enchanter with a look of shock come into the room and make their way over to Natalia. The High Priestess nodded in understanding and told the room that she would be back. My eyes followed her out, curious.

I found Nick's brown eyes still looking at me, his face a bit sweaty from the fighting. "I know it doesn't really matter, but are you proud of me?"

He touched his nose to mine. "Yes, but more importantly, are you proud of yourself?"

I leaped off his body and yanked on his shirt, bringing him down to the ground and on his back. I really didn't care about all the people or the gagging sounds Reese was making in the background. I straddled him, leaning down so my face was inches from his. "I'm very proud, baby."

"Good girl, as you should." He gave me a peck on my lips and I pressed my lower half down on his pelvis. I bit my lip feeling something else besides pride for me. I heard a low groan from him when I rubbed myself against him again.

"Oh, does my success turn you on, Mr. Cassial?"

He brought his hands up to settle at my waist. "Maybe a little."

My lips met his in a kiss that felt hotter than when my hands created their own little fire. I broke the kiss to lean towards his ear. "How about you show me how proud you are, hmm?"

A small, strained, *fuck* left his lips when I nipped his earlobe with my teeth.

The door opened and Natalia strolled back into the room, attracting everyone's attention immediately. "We have a guest everyone."

A girl with shiny dark hair that came in waves around her shoulders came through the doorway with a kind of confidence I knew well. She had a complexion that was a warm brown like mine and rectangular glasses that showcased the mass of freckles that decorated her nose. She was cute and if I wasn't so enamored with my angel, I probably would have hit on her. She'd only just walked into the room, but I could tell she wasn't an Enchanter, especially with the anxious look on Natalia's face.

Natalia motioned towards the new girl. "Everyone this is—"

Reese let out a strangled cough. "Oh fuck."

"Morgan?" Nick pushed me up so that he could sit up and look over his shoulder.

Natalia pulled her eyebrows inward. "Uh, yes. This is Morgan, she is going to be around for all of our sessions from now on."

Reese waved his hands in the air. "Wait, wait, you're the babysitter? Ariel's little spy."

Natalia tucked one of her braids behind her ear. "It seems that Ariel didn't want to intimidate us by sending a sentry to be on guard. I assume it's just to make sure Dani is here doing what he said, no harm in it."

"Intimidate us? Of course that's how you would fucking phrase it." Reese crossed his arms over his chest as he stared at Morgan. Clearly, he had some dislike for her that ran deeper than this moment.

Elise pushed past him. "Okay, who the fuck are you that gets Blondie so riled up?"

I felt Nick lift me off of him and head towards the others, placing his hand on my lower back so I could stand close to him.

When she spoke her voice came out like honey, but almost like honey that was too sweet to consume. "I'm not here to bother you Reese, I'm simply here to keep an eye on you all. Ariel thought that it made more sense since I'm a guardian. It's kind of my job to watch over things." She gave each of us her eyes, but those brown eyes of hers lingered too long on me, like she was sizing me up somehow. Her words were meant to be innocent and understanding, but they had a condescending tone that made me want to wring her neck.

"Did Ariel promise you a fucking promotion? We both know you aren't doing this for the well-being of this realm," Reese said, his tone accusatory..

I ruffled my curls, clearly confused. "I'm sorry, did you two used to date?"

"Or fuck?" Elise added. The sound of Beetee hissing at her friend from behind us would have made me laugh if I wasn't on edge.

Morgan laughed, but it was laced with arrogance and something else I couldn't place. "Oh, no to either of those questions, although, I'm sure he wishes." Reese sneered at her, but she simply pushed her hair over her shoulder, every shiny piece falling down her back. "Should we suppress their confusion, Nicholas?"

Nick pressed his fingers into my back, like I was the only thing anchoring him in place. I looked up at him, but his eyes were narrowed at her. "I would really rather not."

Elise circled around Nick's back and over to me, whispering loud enough for everyone to hear, "oh, so Blondie is *not* the one she used to fuck." I heard Nick's sharp intake of breath and nearly bit my own tongue.

Morgan's eyes went from Nick to Elise then onto me. She tilted her head to the side and scrunched up her nose in a way that told me she thought I was beneath her in some way. "Fucking makes things sound so impersonal, doesn't it?"

Natalia scratched her temple clearly wondering how this had even happened, but not wanting to interfere. Beetee and Garrett were smart enough to stay on the sidelines, while everyone else watched as Morgan bit her lip and stared at Nick. He kept his hand at my back but wiped his other one over his mouth. "Fine. Um, Morgan is my ex-girlfriend."

I didn't feel jealous. That was for people who didn't know how solid they were with someone else. Nick was mine and that was that. If I had to use my newfound powers to burn this girl from the inside out so she understood that, then so be it.

10
DANI

Natalia closed her eyes and looked as if she were mentally counting to five before she spoke again, "you two have had a previous relationship?"

Morgan shrugged as if it was obvious and batted her eyelashes over at Nick.

"Isn't that like some kind of conflict of interest?" Elise asked, turning her nose up at the angel.

Morgan rolled her eyes. "Not at all. We are all professionals here, well…" She looked Elise up and down, her eyes widening a tiny bit as if what she saw shocked her, "maybe not all of us, but what can you do."

I could hear the growl come from the back of Elise's throat and if I was being honest, I wanted to unleash my own growl.

"We are doing just fine as you can see, so really, your presence isn't needed. So can you go crawl back into whatever socially climbing angelic hole you came out of." Reese pointed his finger at her.

She swatted it away, looking uninterested. Morgan licked her lips and moved her glasses further up her nose, blowing out a breath as she was already annoyed with us. "I don't make the rules. If you have a problem with me being here then you can bring that up with Ariel, which we all know you won't since you're already treading on extremely thin ice with the man, or did you not stupidly go into Purgatory when he told you not to?"

"We had our reasons, so just back off, Morgan." Nick ran a hand through his hair.

She pushed out her bottom lip in a pout. "A lot of time may have passed but you're always one to play the hero." Her eyes slid over to me, and she smirked. "Although, your motivations could use some work."

I felt his fingers press harder into my back, but I hardly felt them anymore. "Excuse me?"

Morgan let out a small chuckle. "I don't recall stuttering."

I started to stand in front of Nick, when I felt his hand try to catch mine and pull me back, but I pushed it away. Morgan had an inch or so on me, but that didn't matter to me. She could have been ten feet tall, and I would still rearrange her fucking face. "It's kind of pathetic that you took this job just so you could throw yourself at a man that doesn't even want you."

She was so close to me I could have wrapped my hand around her hair and banged her head up against the wall. "Nick is just a fun little add on to what I'm doing here, not that I needed to explain myself to you at all. You should really be much nicer to me since I could go back and tell Ariel that you're just fucking around and then oh, well what happens to you then, hmm?" She tapped her chin in thought before laughing.

"Someone who actually enjoys doing Ariel's bidding is the worst kind of person and believe me, I'm the worst kind of person." Elise hissed.

Morgan let out a fake yawn and looked over at Natalia. "Wow, you guys get riled up all because I used to date this handsome thing over here. No wonder you let Lilith slip through your fingers, and you were so easily fooled by Markus. Way too busy focusing on the unimportant things." She tsked at each of us, her eyes settling yet again on Nick. "The company you keep can really drag you down. Sully your name. I'm pretty sure Jonah told you to work with them, not slum it with them permanently."

Without warning I grabbed her face and focused her attention back on me. "I'd watch my fucking mouth if I was you."

While most would be quivering and thinking of possible ways to get out of this situation, they'd placed themselves in, Morgan wasn't one of them. She grabbed my wrist and pushed me away from her. She knew she had the weight of Ariel over me and she looked as if I was an afterthought for her.

"You are really not as scary as they say, Soul Seether. You're actually kind of adorable, so I can see why he likes you so much." She reached out and wiped a small amount of dust from the shoulder of my jacket. "I would really hate for everything to go sideways for you and everyone else simply because you can't learn to follow a few rules. You were Lilith's little pet right, so you should be used to having a leash."

"I don't need a *fucking* leash, you fucking..." I felt the light dim inside of me and the darkness boiling. The soothing wisps of the dark graced my hand and fingertips, but then they were gone when a hand pulled me back a tiny bit. Nick's large hand wrapped around mine and he squeezed.

"She's really not worth it," he said, pleading in his voice for me to calm down.

One side of Morgan's mouth lifted up in a slight smile. "Ah, see even I know Nicholas is very good at telling people what to do. You should really listen to him." The innuendo of her comment wasn't lost on me.

"So, what.... you just plan on standing on the sidelines and ogling the pretty angel boy over here? Daydreaming about what you used to have until he came to his fucking senses," Elise asked, tilting her head to the side.

Morgan pressed her lips into a hard line and forced a smile. "Just keep doing what you're doing, although, you said you had it under control and from the looks of it…" She looked over our heads at the large hole in the wall, "you've seemed to misunderstand what under control actually means." She pointed from the hole to me. "That was you, wasn't it?"

I gave her a fake smile. "Sure was."

"Hmm, at least I can tell Ariel you've made some sort of progress, so give yourself a pat on the back. You might actually be useful after all."

"What the…" I started but she put her finger up to silence me.

"Ariel also wants help with his ceremony. It will be a big day for Heaven's Gate, so he wants every helping hand he can get."

"He wanted us to help Dani and her training. He wanted to make sure she was all set for when or if things as you so kindly put it, go side-ways." Nick furrowed his dark eyebrows. "What about what happened in the sky the other night, you can't tell me you and everyone else didn't see it."

Morgan sighed. "Of course, that still matters, but Reese can bring her here. As long as she still comes here and strengthens…whatever she is…then that ripple in the sky is taken care of. Any issues that come from the other side are her responsibility or did you already forget what you signed up for, Soul Seether?" She peered over at me with a raised eyebrow. "You both aren't needed. You and I can help Ariel with things and then we can come here and continue on as if nothing changes."

Reese let out a joyless laugh. "Ah, so alone time with a guy that dumped you is what you want?"

Morgan clucked her tongue. "I really don't have to explain myself to you. It isn't up for debate anyway; Ariel already approved of it. I'm just nice enough to bring you up to speed."

My jaw hurt from the amount of tension it held as I clamped my mouth shut. Every fiber of my being wanted to run my hand through her stomach, but then that death would have been too quick. I could have always taken her head in my hands quickly and put my thumbs into her eyes, so she would stop looking at what was mine. She wouldn't die immediately, that way she would be in pain, and I could take my time with bleeding her dry. I wanted so much to wield my dagger again and do the damage I wanted.

Nick knew what he signed up for when he decided that I was what he wanted. I cracked my neck at that fact. Purgatory was filled with the kinds of girls that would break your neck simply because you touched what was theirs or even insinuated you had any ownership to it, regardless of it being in the past. Morgan was different. I didn't need blood to prove my point.

I gave her a tiny smile. "It's fine. If Ariel wants to be a dick and think that anyone is going to bow down to him after that ceremony, then let him. Nick can tell me all about all the shitty design choices he's making when you bring him back to me."

Reese pulled his eyebrows in and both him and Nick spoke at the same time, "are you sure?"

I waved them off in nonchalance. "Mhmm, I'm sure Morgan is well aware that I'm the one in your bed every night." I looked casually over my shoulder at my very nervously confused angel, but then focused all my attention back on Morgan. "I trust that Morgan is smart enough to understand the rule of don't touch what isn't yours, right? Especially when the thing you are aching to touch has something much better to play with and occupy their time. That must have been something they ingrained in your brain at angelic primary school."

I heard Elise snicker behind me, but I kept my eyes fixed on the guardian angel before me.

Morgan pursed her lips and looked over my shoulder at Nick. Her mouth formed into a mischievous smile. "I would never. I do want to ask you one thing though?" She lifted one of her shoulders as if the question was going to be nothing of importance as she walked around us, surveying the room and the destruction I'd caused.

She said her next words slightly over her shoulder, like she couldn't fathom giving me her full attention. "Does he still do that thing with his tongue that I taught him?"

"Oh my," Natalia, who had remained quiet during the interaction, mumbled.

My hands balled into fists at my sides, but I rallied, like I always did. "He sure does. Maybe I should really be thanking *you* for my many, many orgasms, huh? Too bad your pussy wasn't good enough to keep him."

Reese's mouth dropped open and I saw Nick close his eyes, shaking his head towards the floor, but there was a hint of smile on his lips.

I had kept my cool, but I still wanted to light her ass on fire. I could feel my palms getting warm, but then small spurts of dark shadows appeared near my feet. I wanted it to stop because shooting Morgan right through that hole in the wall was the last thing I needed. I felt my feet wanting to move towards her and fuck her world up, but a flash of pink hair came across my vision.

Beetee yanked me in the other direction outside of the room. "Let's go somewhere to cool you off."

"I'm just fine, Beetee," I said for what felt like the tenth time. The pink-haired demon had whisked me away, up the stairs, down a hallway and into an empty bedroom.

She fiddled with the bottom of her dress as she paced in front of me. "I know, but I mean you could have done real damage to her."

"Coming from the girl who can shift into a snake and could do real damage to anyone that comes within two feet of your tail."

She placed her hands on her hips and faced me. "I don't love turning into a giant reptile. It's cool in theory, but I try to keep it as under wraps as I can."

"Hmph, well, your assistance is appreciated, but I wasn't actually going to throw her out the hole in the wall."

"I never said you were…"

I cut her off. "Yes, but I wanted to, and I would have loved to see her break all her bones when she landed on the ground and then I probably would have flown down to pick her up and let her fall back onto the ground just because it was really fun to watch the first time, but I did not. I'm already doing angelic things."

Beetee snorted. "Sure, if that's what you call it. Morgan is the kind of person who isn't going to go away just because you can meet her verbal sparring head on, you know."

I spun around the room, taking in the bright interior. "Well aware. Her confidence is commendable, but I also know that it burns her perfect exterior to know that I'm the one riding her ex-boyfriend's cock most nights."

Beetee's face turned a shade of red before she turned away to face the only window in the room.

"Is this your room?" I ran my hand along the orange comforter

"Oh yes, it is. Well, my room for now, since Natalia is nice enough to let me stay here. She told me I could decorate it anyway I wanted. She had some of the Enchanters come in and just kind of add in the details I wanted. Their magic is so cool." She sounded like a starstruck little kid; it was kind of adorable.

The sun was still out, so its glow made her golden-brown skin much more prominent. The end of her snake tattoo peeked out from the back of her dress and that brought me back to what she'd said earlier. "You intentionally try to hide the fact that you can shift?"

Beetee knotted her index fingers together. "Not so much hide, but I just never wanted to lose control, especially when I was younger. When I learned to control it more, I guess I still just wanted to be seen as remotely *normal*."

"Fun fact: you are not."

The pink haired demon rolled her eyes and let out an exhaustive sigh as she sat on her bed. "The anchoring tattoo on my back makes me aware constantly."

"Did your parents..." I spoke slowly, wondering if anything I was about to say might upset her. She looked over at me expectantly, "they didn't make you feel like you had to keep your shifting a secret, right?"

She shook her head vehemently. "Oh my gosh, no! They were protective like any parent would be, but shifting isn't unheard of in Purgatory, you know that. Usually if you can shift, one of your parents has to have that ability as well, so I always wondered since they told me pretty early on that they adopted me. They always answered my questions if I had any and well, I guess...I never asked the right ones."

I sat down next to her and placed my hand on her exposed knee. "You never felt like something was off?"

She rubbed her lips together in thought. "Not really. I was so busy making sure I didn't burst into snake mode in public while simultaneously going through puberty that I didn't notice."

I chuckled. "Sounds about right."

"Did you?"

I nodded, remembering all the times I'd felt like there was something missing or that something in me felt misplaced. I couldn't help but be envious that Beetee had never had those feelings, but then again, her hybrid status was different than mine. Lilith had made me what I was and pretended to nurture me as if I was always meant to be that way, Beetee had been born out of love, but hidden away never knowing that. We were vastly different, but I liked to think our hearts were always in the right places.

Her voice came out in a whisper. "Lilith must have really had her claws in you deep to make you believe something for so long." She pulled her bottom lip into her mouth with her teeth. "How did it feel?"

I raised an eyebrow at her. "How did what feel?"

She flipped her hands up, so we were both looking at her palms. "Being both, using both powers. Was it scary? Intense? Confusing?"

I placed my hands in hers. "All of the above. Like something I was always meant to do.

You could feel all those things too you know. I think your dark magic comes from your snake shifting, so we can focus on your light, see how to..."

Beetee put my hands back in my lap with a small smile. "Mm... I don't know. Maybe someday when I see my moms again. That's my priority. And of course, making sure you have all the support you can get and if being a snake is how I can do that right now then, I will."

I watched her lilac-colored eyes as they tried to hold back their sadness. "Okay, if not your hybrid abilities, then what about the Daya issue?"

"Nick's dad's girlfriend?"

I nodded, pulling at one of my curls to give my hands something to do. "She is your family even if I'm pretty sure she isn't fully aware of it yet."

Beetee's chest and neck started to gain a reddish color as if she was slightly embarrassed. "I'm awful. I want to speak to her, I do. I just…I don't want to take a step into Nick's house with talks of a family reunion when his own family is still rocky and misshapen. I don't want to create this bond with someone I've never known when the people I've known my whole life, the family I've known are still…" She sighed, "waiting for me to come back."

"You don't owe me an explanation, Beetee."

She tilted her head from side to side. "Oh, I know. I guess I just want my moms with me whenever we do speak, just to make the transition easier. They know the story. They made sure I stayed alive. I think Daya would like to know them just as much as she'll want to know me."

"I think regardless of moms or no moms, she'll be happy to know you're alive, even if it means she starts hysterically crying in disbelief. You want to support me, so I suppose I'll just have to do the same for you." I nudged her with my shoulder and watched as her eyes became brighter.

"One thing at a time, Dani." She nudged me back.

"Alright, reptile queen, as you wish."

"That is still an awful…" Beetee looked past me at her window. I followed her eyes and watched as the sky did the same thing as the night before, but this time it was more intense. The ripple stretched out further and wider. You couldn't see much but black, but a shiver went down my spine. The ripple stayed for a few more moments and then dispersed as if it wanted to make an impression.

Knock, Knock.

Beetee jumped at the sound, holding her hand against her chest. She shuffled to the door, opening it to reveal a very anxious Nicholas.

"Elise said this is where you would take her."

Beetee shrugged, moving out of the way so he could get a full view of me.

"And so, you found me." I turned to look out the window again. "Did you see the ripple?"

He started to rub the back of his neck. "Yeah, which means Ariel is going to be even more of an unnecessary prick. We should tread carefully."

I groaned as I got off Beetee's bed and walked over to him. I winked at the pink haired snake shifter, placing my hand on Nick's arm. "I'm going to work harder than ever to be able to be the best hybrid I can be and then once this whole darkness in the sky thing is taken care of, I can burn Ariel to a tiny little crisp."

Nick laughed, some of the tension leaving his body.

"Is she gone?"

His brown eyes flashed a panicked look but went back to normal. "Yeah."

I beamed at him. "Good and don't worry, I trust you with everything I have." His face took on a look of relief. My smile fell when I spoke again. "You should know though, if she ever talks to me like that again, I'll kill her."

Dani walked into my room and started changing her clothes as if nothing had transpired in the last thirty minutes. She would occasionally look at me, throughout her trips from my dresser to the bathroom, but other than that, there was silence. I didn't want to bother her until she spoke first, so I leaned against the wall near the door and watched her.

Her face was the picture of contentment, like she had had a normal day doing everyday things. For some reason I was prepared for the fight first, ask questions later attitude, but this—I didn't know how to handle this. All this did was tell me that years from now she would still find ways of surprising me.

Morgan Lakes wasn't somebody I'd thought I'd see anymore besides the obvious times I'd pass her at The Skies. We'd dated a little over four years ago, I'd all but forgotten about her. The relationship wasn't something I cherished, nor was it something I would classify as life changing. It was honestly the kind of relationship I *would* have seen myself in at nineteen. She was ambitious, to the point where her confidence boiled over into being underhanded and mean.

None of what she said earlier had surprised me, but it had floored me that her sweet girl mask had come off so quickly. I had wanted so much for my career and life back then that what she'd painted as the picture of my future with her was something worth salivating over. She was an attractive guardian angel, and I was my father's child, one of the best sentries and swordsmen. A perfect pair picked out of an angelic social magazine. I shook my head at the idea that I had, at one time, wanted a life with her; I had missed all the signs that I was just a good-looking trophy that Jonah was keen on.

Did I think I would have a future with a demon or a hybrid? No, but when I peeked through my lashes at her as she trudged around my room, well, she was really all I could ever consider wanting. And with whatever was going on in the sky had me sending Morgan back to being an afterthought and sending Dani to the forefront of my mind, where she belonged.

"How long did you date?"

I blinked over to her, narrowing my eyes, not understanding. "What?"

She tilted her head to the side, repeating herself. "How *long* did you date?

"Uh...almost two years."

She nodded once and clapped her hands together. "Was she just as *wonderful* as she was in Oculus?" The sarcasm in her tone was far from subtle.

I sighed. "Honestly, she was much more reserved about it back then."

"That's shocking. She spoke to all of us like she had some personal vendetta."

I pushed away from the wall. "She likes positions of power and being overtly close to Ariel gives her that. Her loyalty is fickle."

"No shit, babe."

"I wouldn't give her anymore of your energy, like I said before, she isn't worth it."

She rolled her eyes, turning around and walking over to my bed, but turning on her heels before she laid back on it. It was right then that I realized she had changed into one of my shirts and…that was about it. I had a number of things that turned me on, but this girl, wearing my shirt that hit right above her knees and nothing but probably panties on…*yeah*, that would do it.

"I wish she just hadn't been thrown in my face. I'm not blaming you but like fuck, I was riding a really big high and then bam! A surprise gets thrown my way in the form of some girl you used to fuck."

The words tumbled out before I got a chance to rephrase anything. "I also got blind sided by Dimitri, a guy *you* used to fuck."

Her mouth opened as she reared her head back, thrown off guard. I hadn't said it in a rude way, but what I'd said was still valid. "Okay, well, Dimitri and I never dated, it was just…"

"For fun and a good time, yes, you've told me. It doesn't make me feel any fucking better about knowing that he, at one point in time, had his hands all over you."

"I don't like knowing Morgan had her precious little princess hands all over you either." She clucked her tongue, raising an eyebrow at me. Her brown eyes weren't trying to get a rise out of me, but Dani had this way of protecting herself with these back-and-forth verbal altercations.

She wasn't upset, just territorial.

So was I.

"I'm not mad at you about Dimitri, you've had a past and so have I. I had no idea she would even show up. We've talked about the Dimitri thing and that's behind us. You said you trust me, so just trust that my hands would rather be on someone else." I smirked at her and she stuck her tongue in her cheek to hide her smile.

She fiddled with the end of my shirt she wore. "I'm not making excuses whatsoever or trying to find a loophole, but there is one solid difference between Dimitri and Morgan."

I took a step towards her as she continued, "yes, Dimitri and I were just fun, there were no real feelings involved, at least on my part. You and Morgan had an actual, legitimate relationship. I'm not jealous of her because I know what we've got, but things just run deeper between you...."

I took longer strides to get over to her, tipping her chin up with my fingers. "Okay, please stop. We *did* have a relationship, but that doesn't mean anything when I look at you. Morgan would have never taken care of me the way you did in Purgatory, that just isn't who she is." I stroked her cheek with my knuckles. "It is who *you* are though."

She slid her hands up my chest, taking hold of my shirt. "One last question."

"Hmm?"

She bit her lip as if she was reconsidering what she wanted to say. "Did you love her?"

I leaned my head down to rest on her forehead. "I thought I did, but it isn't the same as loving you. Frankly, it terrifies me how much I love you."

"I've never loved anyone before, so lucky you being the one and only, Mr. Cassial."

I kissed her forehead. "Despite everything, we both have a past. I don't think we should let it define us, no matter how uncomfortable it may be." I rubbed my nose against hers. "I think we have something fucking great, so I would rather not ruin it."

She leaned back, giving me a bemused look. "Funny you should say to not let the past define us. I would advise you to consider those words when you actually talk to your father." Her eyes turned softer and she leaned up, kissing my lips. "You never know, the past could be a good place to heal."

She was beautiful and wise. And annoying.

I placed my hands on her hips and squeezed. I inhaled her cinnamon scent as it wafted off of her hair. Some of her curls took on a life of their own as they darted in a different direction than the rest. She hummed as she stood on her tiptoes and ran her lips over mine again but not quite kissing me. "I like knowing you're all mine, you know that."

"Is that right?" I moved my lips back over hers and the urge to just kiss her was strong, but she was teasing me. I couldn't help knowing that I kind of liked it.

Her breath hit my skin as she moved her hands to hold onto my shirt tighter. "So, tell me, who do you belong to, Nicholas?" She yanked me closer to her, so that her tongue licked at my lips.

I sucked in a sharp breath before answering. "You."

"Correct." She let go of me and walked backwards to my bed. She sat down and leaned back, letting my shirt ride up her thighs as she scooted further back. "Now show me who belongs to *you*."

I raised one of my eyebrows at her but placed my knee on the bed so that I hovered over her. I placed my hand by her knee and slowly grazed my fingers along her brown skin, seeing the goosebumps rise. I tilted my head down to kiss right below her ear. My fingers teased at the edge of her panties. I moved over the fabric but never touched her directly, just lightly playing with her until she bit her lip to the point where it looked painful.

She started to grab my hand and forcibly maneuver me where she wanted, where I knew she was already getting wet. I threaded my fingers through hers, moving her hand away. My teeth tugged at her earlobe hard enough to elicit a whimper.

"You're such a needy girl, aren't you?" A muffled *please* left her lips. I removed my hand from hers and slipped it into her panties, rubbing my fingers against her clit. She moaned loudly at the way I touched her and made her feel. She let her legs spread out wider as I continued to play with her, eventually slipping one of my fingers inside, watching as she moved her hips so my finger could touch her in the right spot. She reached down to take hold of my hand, trying to make it so I pushed in another one of my fingers. "Your pussy is so impatient, so fucking needy."

Before she could answer me, I moved to kiss her, picking her up and carrying her so that her back was against the wall next to my door. She kissed me back, sticking her tongue into my mouth. I met her aggression with the same vigor, as she reached down and rubbed my achingly hard cock. She squeezed, sending a groan out of my mouth before I pulled away from her lips. I placed her back on her feet before getting down on my knees.

I slid my hands up her legs, hooking my fingers into her panties and pulled them down. I thumbed her clit as I brought one of her legs onto my shoulder, inclining my head so I could kiss the inside of her thigh, licking at her skin. She tasted like everything I'd ever want, and she was mine. She was my confidently sexy girl that I could please for hours and thrill at her look of disheveled satisfaction.

"Nick, please, put your *fucking* mouth on me."

I chuckled against her skin as I hoisted her other leg up, settling my palms under her ass to steady her before burying my face between her legs. Her hand went into my hair, pressing her fingers in my scalp as she let out a moan. My eyes nearly rolled back in my head from her taste and the way her thighs squeezed me as I flicked my tongue over her clit. I sucked it into my mouth before releasing it and letting my tongue lap at her continuously.

She tried to move her lower body around, but I held her in place, devouring her like I wanted. Her free hand slapped against the wall as her breathing became erratic. "Don't stop, please. Keep going, r-right there."

I noticed the slight hint of light coming from her hands, but the one hand she'd moved to my shoulder didn't give me the burning sensation like it did before. It hurt, but it was like there was something else keeping it from melting my skin off.

I stuck my tongue inside of her, letting her ride out her orgasm on my face. She pushed her pussy against my mouth, and I shot my eyes up to her as she came down from her high. Her chest rose and fell as she closed her eyes for a moment, opening them when I sat her legs down.

I gripped her chin when I rose from the floor, licking my lips and giving her a taste of herself when I kissed her. "Fuck, you're beautiful when you come."

Her face was flushed, her curls fell over one of her eyes in a messy way that made my chest nearly combust with pride knowing I made her feel and look this way. I wanted her to forget all about Morgan and anything else that plagued her mind enough to even cause an ounce of a doubt about where we stood.

Dani inspected my shoulder, seeing only tiny marks of charred residue, then looked over her shoulder. My wall had tiny burn marks, but nothing alarming. This whole thing with her just took time and I was happy to be the one to witness her progress firsthand.

She kissed me again, bringing my bottom lip into her mouth, biting down. "Then I beg you to please make it happen again."

I gripped the front of her throat, pushing her away before turning her around. She placed both her hands against the wall, while I undid my pants. I kicked them away and spread her legs apart with my foot, pushing her shirt up so I could get a clear view of her ass and waiting pussy that was practically dripping for me. I lifted my shirt, hearing a small gasp when I inserted the tip. I took a shallow breath, taking in how good she always felt, even if I wasn't all the way inside.

She pushed her ass back so she slid further along my cock, her perfect pussy wrapping around me like a fucking vice. "Your pussy was made for my cock, *right*?"

"Y-yes." Dani moved back harder and I watched, running my hands along her sides and upper thighs. Her curls fell around by the sides of her face and the ringlets and spirals bounced from her movements.

I spanked her hard. "Say it. All of it."

"Fuck, my pussy was made for your cock. Nick, *please*."

Fuck, the begging would be my undoing. "That's my good girl." I held her hips as I started to fuck her in a steady rhythm that had my pelvis meeting her ass at every thrust. I moved her with ease as if she was just letting me do what I pleased and she would enjoy it no matter what.

"Harder. Fuck me, harder." Her voice was strained and vibrated with the way her body bounced back against me.

I grabbed a fistful of her curls and yanked her head back. Her back arched and she stood on her tiptoes to hold herself steady. I brought my hand down on the flesh of her ass so hard, I felt her legs tense up as I increased my pace.

"Oh fuck, yes." Her mouth dropped open at the new angle and her pussy started to clench around me, making me hold her hair tighter and go even harder.

"Yeah, just like that, needy one?"

"Yes, just—just like that."

I turned her head so that I could kiss her, deep and passionately. The kind of kiss that would leave her head spinning. "You always feel so fucking good," *thrust*. "Every," *thrust*. "Single," *thrust*. "Time."

I released her hair and placed both my hands back on her hips. I fucked her hard, the fervent slapping of our skin made any other sound outside of the room nonexistent. Any problem we'd had didn't have place in our little bubble that we'd created to protect ourselves.

"Nick, right there, fuck. I'm…I'm..." She reached back to hold onto my forearm. I could feel the tiny sparks of heat from her palm.

I snaked my hand between her legs to find her clit when….

Knock, knock

"Nick, we have a problem."

I knew that voice and I had never wanted to physically assault the person on the other side of my door more than I did right now. Personal space and my best friend never went hand in hand.

Dani panted underneath me as she blew her hair out of her face to look over her shoulder. She raised her eyebrows and pressed her lips together in a guarded giggle. I let go of her body to run both hands down my face. I was sweaty and still very horny, yet I knew just staying quiet wouldn't make him go away.

Knock, knock

Fuck, fuck, fuck.

I was annoyed beyond belief. "What!"

"Nick! We know you're in there." My eyebrows furrowed, knowing that voice didn't sound like Reese at all. It sounded like Elise.

I swallowed down a groan as Dani moved her lower body, grinding along my cock that was still inside of her. If they would just give me five more minutes, I could easily continue fucking her until she…

Elise's raspy demanding voice sounded again. "Nick, I swear if you…"

"Okay, fuck. I'm coming." I pulled out of my enticing demon and searched around for my pants.

Dani let out a soft laugh. "We were both about to, but I fear we are left equally unsatisfied."

I tossed her panties over to her, letting out a fake laugh. "Excuse me, you came at least once."

"Hmm…only once, what a pity." She slowly—agonizingly—slid her panties back on, bending down in the right ways and moved her mass of curls over her shoulder.

I bit down on my tongue, two seconds away from telling both of them on the other side of the door to *fuck off*. I shooed Dani away from the door, pulling it open to see Reese and Elise standing side by side.

I propped my hand on the door frame. "What?"

"We," Reese motioned his index finger between the two of us, "have to go."

I squinted at him, not understanding. "Go where?"

My best friend cleared his throat. "In the words of our supposed leader 'did you and Mr. Cassial forget you also have a job still. Animus Seekings are still part of our society and I'm sure you wouldn't want to let your fellow angels do your jobs now would you?'"

"I'm pretty sure we don't go until next week."

Elise scoffed. "Well, it certainly doesn't look like he gives a shit."

I gave a quick glance over my shoulder where Dani stood and gave me a small apologetic shrug. I sighed, nodding. "Fine, I'll be there." I focused my attention on Elise. "Why are you here?"

She gave me tight lipped smile. "While you and Blondie here are gone, I'll be watching her."

"Pretty sure she can take care of herself."

She moved her gray eyes down my body and rolled her eyes. "This coming from the guy who harbored her in this room for weeks. Yes, Nicholas I am well aware she can do things herself, yet you have a mentally deranged ex-girlfriend floating around here somewhere, so I'm just making sure that bitch doesn't come around." She reached up and patted my face a little too hard. "Besides, that witch is getting on my last nerve with her rules, so it called for a change of scenery."

Dani giggled and circled around me, so she was now in view of them. "It is her house, Elise. Although, you are very sweet for wanting to keep me company. That charred heart is just coming alive piece by deathly piece."

Elise made a gagging sound while putting up her middle finger.

Reese picked at my shoulder, pulling at the tiny, burned pieces. "Get into a fire fight?"

Dani covered her mouth to keep from laughing. Elise took a step into the room, fingering the bottom of my shirt that Dani wore. "No fire, Blondie," she sniffed the air. "Just fucking. Like I said, horny idiots."

I turned around, ignoring them and grabbing my jacket. Reese whistled. "Wait, so did we interrupt…"

I pushed my hand into his face and shoved him back. "Yes, you fucking did." I grabbed the door handle and looked over my shoulder at the two demons, particularly at Elise. "Take care of her."

Elise rolled her eyes. "I like to think I've been doing that for a while now."

"I'm so very happy you two could join us." Ariel said, placing his hands on both our shoulders.

I shrugged him off, walking around him to get near more crowds of angels. I could feel people looking at me as if they wanted to ask a million and one questions about Dani. There were only a handful that actually came up to me and spoke about her. Most people wanted to speak *about* me, ask me about Purgatory and Lilith. It was like they were more invested in what I had to say and what I was planning to do when it came to next steps, rather than anything Ariel had to say.

I had concluded that these people, the majority of them at least, were playing a part when it came to Ariel's personal brand of leadership. They didn't actually think he was the best or worthy, they were just all he had. The worst part about it was that he knew that.

"Nicholas, as I told Mr. Diniel, you have a job still. Despite you pretending like you can do whatever you like and gallivanting off to play hero, you are still just a simple sentry who made an oath to be here and perform your duties. Or would you like to look all of your fellow angels in the eye and tell them why you think you are so special that you should be exempt?"

I turned around to see the red-headed angel brushing his hands down the lapels of his jacket. Reese was signaling for me to stand down, like making a scene wouldn't help. I felt my fist itching to connect with his jaw and maybe someday it would.

"No, that's okay. I'm here, aren't I?"

"That you are. I also look forward to you assisting Miss. Lakes with some ceremony proceedings. She told me that demon of yours is coming along nicely. Walls breaking and whatnot. I am quite impressed. I do hope Morgan wasn't a shock, I can't be there to make sure you aren't going to pull one of your little stunts, so I had to take some precautions." I started to walk past him, but he caught my arm. "I stopped by your house to say hello to your father earlier today. I invited him to the ceremony and from the way he acted it was like he hadn't spoken to his son in weeks, which tells me that when I asked you to speak to your father about Jonah's powers, you did not. How you and that demon act reflects on both of you…I would advise you to not lie to me again."

The mention of my father made my chest tight, and I immediately started taking small breaths in and out. Ariel didn't even like my father, so that was just out of pure spite, wanting him to see everything he had *achieved*. I wish I could have been there and laughed at Ariel's farce of a power play with my father. I wish I could sit on the couch and talk about our day like we'd been doing for years. I wish there wasn't this cloud of information withholding over our heads. I wish simply forgiving him and moving all of it aside was easier said than done. I closed my eyes for a moment and swallowed, my skin feeling a tiny bit clammy from the minor panicked moment I'd had.

I took my hand and physically removed his hold on me. "She has a name, you know."

Ariel nodded, giving his attention to someone else in the distance.

"I'm sure she does. When she proves her usefulness, I'll make sure to care to learn it."

I ran a hand through my hair, pulling so hard it hurt my scalp. I sucked in a deep breath, letting it out slowly.

Reese came over, placing his hand on my back. "Hey, do we need to do those exercise things that the angels at the infirmary told you about? Focus on a spot or counting backwards, I can't remember which one works better."

I shook my head, appreciating his helpful nature. "No, no, I got it. He just…he's…"

"A dick."

I ran my hand along the back of my neck, feeling the tiny beads of sweat. "That's putting it nicely. His sole purpose is getting under my skin."

"Nick." Reese lightly hit my chest with his knuckles. I gave his hazel eyes my attention. "I promise you that one day he will say something that will make punching him in his face so fucking worth it and I won't hold you back. I might want to punch him as well, but I'll refrain because it will be your moment."

I laughed, feeling the tension in my entire body start to fall away. "You'll make sure she's all good, right?"

"Who?"

"Dani."

Reese looked at me confused as he put his blonde hair into a high bun. I waited for the moment of his understanding, when his eyes widened, and he nodded. "Obviously. You keep your wits about you with Morgan and the tiny psycho and I will make sure that your girlfriend is being her best hybrid self during the few hours you're gone." One of the executives that recently got appointed to Ariel's old position stood in front of all of us. "You may not think so, but I do like her, not like *that*, but like for you. I did always tell you that you needed someone with more edge."

I nudged his shoulder. "She's not my girlfri…"

Reese shushed me. "Yes, she is."

Elise looked out the window and up at the sky, inspecting. Her grey eyes darted from left to right as if she was waiting for something. I leaned up against the dresser staring at her back.

"Is this what you do at Natalia's house? Stare out the window and wait for bad shit to happen?"

She placed her hands on her hips and swiveled around to face me. The sweater she wore was cropped and exposed more of her stomach. "Nope, the witch makes us do helpful things while we are there because we can't just live there and be lazy, or however the fuck she explained it."

"That doesn't sound like a bad trade in exchange for staying at that mansion of a home."

Elise gave me an unimpressed look. "Sure, whatever you say. Her rules will be the least of everyone's worries if that rip in the sky gets any bigger."

"You know it's getting worse too, hmm?"

Elise pointed behind her towards the window. "Anyone with fucking eyeballs can see that it's getting worse. That ripple is a lot of dark magic in one place, Dani. That is so much more than Lilith darkness. That's Hell darkness and I can tell you that they aren't having a fucking party."

I leaned my head back, staring at the ceiling. "There isn't much I can do until I get things under control. Feeling myself being balanced is one thing, showing the act of balance by not creating a chaotic ball of hybrid magic is another. That kind of issue is why they didn't want half breeds in the first place."

"I love a good history lesson, Dani, but we are in the present. Present day says maybe being chaotic is worth it."

I laughed, shrugging. "Sure, let's go with that plan and I'll just burn down the entire realm of Heaven's Gate. Sounds like a great fucking time."

Elise clucked her tongue. "Isn't that basically what Lilith and Dimitri want anyway? You'd be doing them a huge favor, or I could do what I wanted to do in the first place and go by myself and take care of everything." She swiped her palms together as if claiming that was the best solution.

I chewed on my lip. "Yeah, Nick told me about your little hero act."

"Not a fucking hero…"

I charged up to her, sticking my finger in her chest. "Let me just say this one time, so that you understand. I will push the light out of the way and shove my shadows down your throat if you ever consider that plan of yours again. You are either in this with us or you aren't in it at all."

She grabbed my finger. "If I found you repulsive, I might break your pretty finger, but I actually tolerate you so you can keep this finger bone intact."

A smile slid across my face, but stopped midway when I noticed her apprehension. "What is it?"

"Let me ask you something, when you broke that wall, do you think your power just dispersed? Became a million tiny little fragments that no one would notice outside of that training room unless they were looking?"

I tapped my cheek with my fingernail while I considered what she said. "I would assume so, why?"

She backed up, so she could drop down onto Nick's bed. "Do not quote me on this, but what if it didn't? I mean like what if you creating that much of a frenzy turned into some kind of unwanted calling card? Just enough power to alert, but not enough to retain itself. It will eventually disperse, but not quick enough to go unnoticed."

"That's a lot to sit with in a matter of hours, Elise."

"Your kind of power isn't something you see every single fucking day. It causes a disruption. I'm pretty sure people in Heaven's Gate noticed it, but Ariel just told them it's fine, please go back to putting your blinders on and follow me."

I stared at the floor. "You think I put a direct spotlight on myself?"

"Ugh, I don't know. It's just something to consider. More for your boyfriend to fret over."

I waved my hands in between us making an X with them. "Absolutely not. I'm not going to have him jump to any conclusions based on a theory."

She lifted her hands up in surrender. "Fine, but if I'm right it's only a matter of time before they sniff out where the power came from and find out you've been alive and well this whole fucking time. Believe me when I tell you that Dimitri isn't the nicest when he's pissed off and that's saying *a lot* coming from me."

I chewed on my thumb nail. "All I have to do is control it. I actually think I'm getting the hang of it, sort of." I looked over my shoulder at the speckled black marks on the wall. "Only then can we go back *together*. Garrett can find his family, Beetee can see her moms, and we can end both Dimitri and Lilith, black sky ripples and all that. Find a way to build a better Purgatory or something."

"Hmm, I doubt Purgatory will be the envy of all the realms, but fine, for some reason I'm with you." She rolled her eyes. "You don't have months or weeks though Dani, from the look of that dark magic and the way I feel, you've got days."

"How you *feel?*"

"Must you forget that I was born in Hell."

I nodded. "Right, hence your abnormally large hellhound you refuse to tell me the origin of or admit that you miss."

She ran a hand down her face, scooting further back so that she could rest her back against the wall, with her legs out in front of her. "Shut up now. And honestly, I can't take you seriously without pants on. I keep getting reminded that nearly an hour ago you were getting railed by your perfect angelic cock."

I twirled one of my spiral curls with my finger as I turned around to search for a pair of shorts in the dresser.

"Dani."

"Mmhmm?"

Elise let out a frustrated sigh. "I said it in Purgatory, and I'll say it again. Is he strong enough for this?"

I pulled the shorts up my legs. "Who, Nick?"

The demon across from me placed her hands in her lap. "Yes, Dani. The angel that would like us all to believe he is doing just fine and managing perfectly. He may very well be getting his mental stuff together but what about his personal shit?"

"He went to Purgatory with personal shit before."

"He was still on good speaking terms with daddy Cassial. Those terms are nonexistent now."

I went over to sit on the bed with her, pushing myself back to match her posture. "I can't make him talk to him. I've tried. I can't treat it like I did his pain in Purgatory. I took that darkness from him as best I could. Right now, he's already removed his father from his life, and I have no idea if he'll let him back in."

Elise ran her tongue over her front teeth, letting out a humorless chuckle. "If pretty boy loves you as much as he disgustingly claims he does, he will. If it means being by your side when Dimitri and Lilith bring a shit storm upon us...I guarantee his handsome lovesick ass will do whatever it takes."

Two whole days of focusing and harnessing something I'd assumed would be unwilling to tether to me was proving harder to control. It was always much bigger than me in some way, the power too great. They were like fire to the open air, where one breeze would take it and cause a massive catastrophe if I didn't get it to back down— and that was without Nick's added help.

It was a power within myself, but somehow, I didn't think it understood that. I was opening myself up but maybe I wasn't being stern enough with how I went about releasing it. Natalia could only do so much each time and I swore Zane was praying to whatever Enchanters believed in that I wouldn't fuck up any more of their infrastructure.

The ripple was getting bigger and the pressure made me antsy. No one was outright yelling in my face to get my shit together, but every time Morgan came in with Nick, it was like she was silently willing me to admit defeat. I wouldn't be doing that anytime soon, if ever.

Reese, Elise and I walked into the training room with wide eyes the next morning we met up. "Holy fuck," I said, impressed with what Natalia had done to the wall of her training room. The interior walls had some sort of translucent moving film over them. I stretched my finger out to touch it, feeling a tiny bite against my skin.

"So, you want her power to just go flying all over the place now? Explain to me how you're queen again?" Elise questioned, sneering at the moving Enchanter magic around her.

"The forcefield takes her powers into it, anyone with half a brain could piece that together," Reese explained, giving her an expression that stated that what he said was common sense.

Elise squinted at him. "I'm sorry, are you her mouthpiece, I didn't think I was talking to you."

"Ellie, be nice. It's actually pretty cool, I watched her make it." Beetee skipped over to Natalia, hopping from one foot to the other.

"I think it's *very* cool, Natalia. Don't mind the grumpy bitch over here," I said, slapping Elise's arm.

Elise shoved me to the side. "Oh no, I'm just grumpy because every time I go into your boyfriend's room, I see fiery, charred things everywhere, which tells me that you are just getting laid all over the fucking place and some of us are in a living situation where they have to refrain from *'reckless behavior'*." Elise made air quotes around her last words, looking over at Natalia.

Reese snickered. "Well at least we know Nick is well satisfied meeting with Morgan." He presented his fist to me, and I connected my own against it, laughing. "Are we starting or are we waiting for another army of lethal Enchanters to come and attack us without notice?"

Zane shook his head, while Natalia patted him on his bicep. Her shoulders were dusted with gold glitter and the magic surrounding the room seemed to make the glitter shine brighter somehow.

"Are we waiting for Nicholas?" Garrett asked, his thick braids were separated down the middle and braided into two separate braids and rested on his shoulders.

"No, Nicholas will be joining us a bit later. Ariel has him attending to other matters." The irritation in the High Priestesses voice wasn't lost on me. I felt the same way she did, but something inside of me hoped that Morgan made a move so that Nick could tell her to fuck off. "And no, no army this time. I just want Dani to have her moment."

Beetee made a hurried motion so Elise would come stand by her and Reese sat his bow down so he could comfortably prop his back up against the wall.

"So, you want me to just have a fight with the wall?"

Natalia opened her mouth, but Garrett spoke instead, "I think she wants you to look in yourself, no distractions, no fights. When it's just you. You can tell your own power what you want it to do and how you want it to act. The problem with most hybrids from what I've understood is that they let it take them over. It's *your* power. *Yours.* You rule it, not the other way around."

I gave him a curious smile, then looked over at Natalia. She raised both her perfectly arched, dark eyebrows and nodded. "Couldn't have said it better myself."

I leaned up and kissed him on the cheek. "Your kids are lucky to have you as a dad."

He gave me a smile that almost had no happiness in it, it felt lonely. "Let's hope they still think that, that they don't think I abandoned them."

"I have a feeling *your* kids could never think that."

Garrett placed his hand at the top of my shoulder and squeezed, silently thanking me before stepping back.

I took a deep breath in and closed my eyes. It was as if everyone around me took a collective breath inward, waiting. I rubbed my hands together stupidly thinking that that might light some kind of spark in me, but it didn't. I felt like I was being put on display and if I didn't do something extraordinary then I was useless. My closeness with Lilith and my dagger made me special, but both of those things were no longer a part of my existence, so achieving this one thing was all I had. I didn't have time to fuck it up and fix my mistakes.

I couldn't have all these people wanting to help me and then find out I wasn't worth all the trouble. Nick would follow me until the day I begged him to not, but what if all that commitment came up empty handed. I didn't want to have faced death at the hands of the one person who only ever wanted the best for me to mean absolutely nothing.

What if I'd worked this hard to find out that I wasn't deserving of all this power I held?

Without having to look, I knew the caress of wispy darkness skimmed across my arms and up my neck. I knew the shadows danced mindlessly in between my fingertips. This would always be my go-to, my comfortable place, the power I clung to whenever I needed a hint of familiarity.

And that was okay.

It's your *power.* Yours. You rule it, not the other way around.

Lilith also had me believe my power, the dark shadows, was who I was. I had a kinship with it, but after all this time basking in the light that was Nick, I decided I wanted a kinship with that as well.

I wanted to be vulnerable with it and let it become a familiar sensation. I didn't want it to be a foreign spark that only came out when I really needed it. I wanted it to feel free to be present when it wanted; I *wanted* it to feel wanted.

The room started to feel warm and a small hum echoed against my ears. It was a hum of satisfaction and contentment. The warmth mimicked my darkness, and I opened my eyes watching them chase after each other along my hands. I put my palms together, taking in one big, deep breath. I pulled my hands apart, letting my fingertips touch for as long as they could. A ball of black, highlighted in gold light stared back at me. It hovered between my hands and continued to grow the more I inspected it.

Tiny pieces of light fell off and stung my cheeks, but it didn't hurt. My skin absorbed the small amount of pain like eventually one day, it wouldn't be painful at all. Little micro flames puffed off of the ball of power, but nothing like what I'd done the other day. I tried to keep my mind right, trusting myself and the balance I wanted to maintain.

I counted to three in my head, before I shot it out of my hands and towards the wall, willing it to go nowhere else but where I'd aimed.

The ball of hybrid magic flew over to the magically layered wall, bursting into a fit of nothing as the wall puckered and rumbled, consuming the large amount of power. The room shook with the aftereffects when Natalia spoke.

"Do it again."

I did the next time with more ease, one hand grasping the power and not two. It wasn't cockiness I felt, although I was allowed to feel every ounce of that, but it was a confidence I could completely call my own. Nick's light would always be able to make this bigger and more blinding, but I could do just fine on my own.

"Okay, okay, how about a moving target?" I turned around to see Reese notching his bow. He pulled back the string as he aimed the arrow slightly above my head. I noticed him take a breath in and then let the arrow go with his exhalation. The arrow flew and I eyed its precise spot when I sent shadow and light its way. The arrow didn't stand a chance when it was caught in the crosshairs.

Reese didn't let up. He sent arrow after arrow, in multiple directions and at various speeds. I was breathing heavier when he slowed down, bringing his arm down so his bow rested at his side. He nodded his appreciation. "I have never been prouder."

"Your arrows are literally nothing compared to what she's training for." Elise scoffed, turning her head towards Beetee. "Go ahead, do your thing."

Beetee ran her fingers across the shaved side of her head. "What thing?"

"Don't get shy about your snake sense now."

Beetee's mouth formed an O before rapidly shaking her head. "I'm not shifting in here."

"She is one thousand percent *not* shifting in here," Zane agreed with a much more authoritative tone.

Elise gave them both a bored expression before she faced me. Her tail unfurled from behind her back and she snapped it against the air. Her eyes flashed a shade of red before she snapped her tail in my direction. "We both know what the venom does, so let's try to avoid it, huh?" Her tail lashed out, almost slicing one of my arms. I jumped back, nearly falling backwards.

"Is this a good..." Reese started but snapped his mouth shut when Elise flung her tail a few inches from his face.

She shot her tail over towards one of my ankles, but I darted away from it. I turned my head to look at her when a cloud of reddish-black magic hit my face. I was pushed back, landing on my ass as I coughed.

"You'll have to use that handy peripheral vision you were graced with." Elise taunted, flinging her tail at me again, but I scurried backwards out of its grasp.

"Ellie, be nice." Beetee made a hissing noise over at her friend.

Elise paid her no mind. "Not in my nature." She created a ball of that same-colored magic in one hand, while simultaneously letting her tail linger and wait for the next time it was to strike.

I placed my hands on the floor, pushing myself up. I flexed my fingers and rolled my neck, as I readied myself. I pushed off the ball of my foot as I ran towards her. Her tail swooped low, but I jumped over it gathering all the combined power of light and dark power that I had as she let two balls of her own dark power out, the red coloring surrounding it sparking every few moments.

I went to reach my hand up and stop one ball of dark energy at me, when I saw that a few inches from touching it, my power reached out to take hold of it all by itself. My power sucked it up and I threw it over to the left. The magical wall Natalia had added encapsulated it and the interior of the room vibrated. I quickly did the same thing with the other ball of energy, throwing it to my right. Garrett swiftly moved Beetee off the side before she got struck by it.

I felt something like a scaly rope wrap around my wrist and found that Elise's tail was cinching itself around my arm. My body was twisted around, and I landed flat on my back, while my arm was still suspended in the air by her magical appendage. The venom pulsed itself along my skin, the feeling in my arm slowly growing numb.

My teeth clamped together with how the venom burned as it sedated my right arm. Her tail unraveled and started to slither its way over to my other hand, but I snatched it up, feeling my own power eject itself against her tail. I didn't feel the venom like I thought I would, but I saw lines of golden light shoot down towards the base of her tail followed by dark shadows spiraling.

Smoke flared and she yelped in surprise, throwing out multiple rounds of dark magic as she pulled her tail back. The appendage was wafting smoke flames as she brought it back closer to her body. I was starting to get the feeling in my other arm again as I threw out my magic at her attempt at a counterattack; each one flying into the wall and being absorbed.

Zane went to steady his High Priestess each time, but all she did was simply watch in utter amazement at what she was witnessing. When everything had settled, I felt sweat along my forehead and the back of my neck. I looked down at my hands, creating my own balanced ball of power between my palms and then letting it disappear.

I really didn't know if in a different setting I could control it again. I didn't know if the same victory I felt now would be the same for when I was faced with something much bigger than my friends.

I supposed the what ifs were a nonstarter at the moment. Fretting would get me nowhere.

Elise patted her tail, letting it move behind her and then disappear altogether.

"That's what you get for fucking with her," Reese scolded, wagging his finger at her.

"Bite me." Elise did a flicking motion with her fingers, sending a red flaming stream of darkness in his direction that connected with his stomach. He landed against the wall behind him with a grunt.

Beetee started to get in between them, while Natalia strolled over to me, taking my hands in hers. "You really are a sight to see."

"Let's just hope everyone else feels that way when it matters."

Natalia laughed, which like always, came out like the more charming music. "Right now matters just as much as any other time. Every piece of progress you've made, every single time you give the light and dark a place to call home, that matters. A round of applause and praise doesn't make your success any less of a success."

The door opened causing all of us to halt our conversations. I felt Nick before I saw him, bringing a smile to my face. That smile was immediately eliminated when Morgan walked in behind him. Her eyes darted around the room and whistled.

"Well, this is nice." She pressed her finger against the magic. "We wouldn't want any more destruction now, would we?" She blinked over to me with a smile that made my blood boil.

"Heaven's Gate could use some modifications, so maybe a little destruction is what it fucking needs." Elise tilted her head to the side, getting a narrowed glance in her direction from Morgan.

Nick pushed past her, taking the longest strides possible to reach me. "So how did everything go?"

"I think I can do this."

I wasn't going to wait for whatever was beyond that dark ripple to come to us, even if Elise said it was only a matter of days. I would get Garrett his family back, Elise could have her furry companion she claimed to not think much about, Beetee could protect her moms, Nick would have an entire story to tell his father once they were on speaking terms again and I would take out this darkness, whether that was attributed to Dimitri or Lilith. Or both. Purgatory had been a place where I'd been manipulated, and I wanted to take that back. There would be no thinking when I got there; I didn't get raised from the dead for any more thinking.

Ariel could think I was doing his bidding and fighting for him to make this realm better, but once it was all said and done, he could kiss my ass. The day that Ariel picked up a weapon or lifted his fucking finger to protect this realm would be the day he got my respect.

He placed his hand on my cheek, letting his thumb slide along my jaw. "I already *knew* that. I meant like any issues."

"Oh, no, well I almost burnt Elise's tail off but that's not a big deal."

"Oh, fuck off, it is a big deal," Elise countered.

Nick opened his mouth to speak again but Morgan cut him off. "Since you seem to be doing so well, Soul Seether, then I'll be sure to tell Ariel that you are more than prepared to do what you do best. He is eager to know that you are right on track, following directions."

"I'm sure he is." I slid my arms around Nick's body, resting my head on his chest as I stared at her.

She flipped her hair over her shoulder, the translucent shine of the magic from the walls bouncing off the lens of her glasses. She placed her hands on her hips. "Nick, why don't you let her continue being the most obedient hybrid she can be, hmm?" She motioned for him to back away from me and follow her.

Nick looked down at me and then over his shoulder at the waiting guardian angel. She had already spent the entire morning with him and yet, she still wasn't satisfied. I caught Reese out of the corner of my eye, aggressively rolling his eyes and I caught my laugh before it tumbled out.

"I think she has done well for today, we can always end early," Natalia offered. I felt the buzz of pride in my veins.

Morgan hummed, disregarding Natalia's words all together. "Until I personally see that she's good enough for today, then you won't be leaving early. Another hour should suffice."

"Watch your tone." Zane stepped up behind Natalia as the High Priestess, pressed her lips together in an unamused smile.

She lifted her hand towards Zane to stop him from having anything to say to Morgan. "Alright. Another hour."

"You are quite literally the worst." Reese yelled from across the room, shaking his head.

I pulled away from Nick, after pecking him quickly on the lips. I blinked over to Morgan, innocently. "Fine by me. I would stand back though; I wouldn't want to hurt you."

13
NICK

After some very vivid descriptions of her sparring fight with Elise and then a shower that consisted of me burying myself so deep inside of her that she nearly cried when she came, she told me all about how she wanted to proceed.

Her brown eyes had looked so determined when she'd said, "I want to go tomorrow."

"Tomorrow?" My eyebrows raised in question.

She nodded, scooting over in my bed to burrow her face into my chest. "Yes. Whatever that is," she'd pointed to my window where the sky was calm and uneventful, "I want to end it."

I squeezed her, trailing my finger along her arm. "You will. We will. Can you just take a minute to consider that maybe you need one more day of figuring your power out?"

"No." Her voice was unwavering.

I'd groaned and shifted to my side, waiting as she readjusted herself.

I'd placed my hand under my head and looked at her. "All I'm asking for is one more training session with Natalia. We will let everyone know what you want to do, and we will all follow you into whatever is waiting for us." I grabbed her hand and brought it to my lips, kissing her knuckles. "If you haven't noticed, I worry about you."

She'd brought her index finger to my lips, tracing them. "I worry about you too. You worry sufficiently more than me, so if waiting a day will put some pep in your step then fine. Only a fucking day though"

I leaned in to kiss her nose. "Good girl."

She wrinkled her nose and started to make her way back over to the comfort of my body. "I know you don't want to talk to him, but do you think you'll regret *not* talking to him when we go there? The outcome of this entire thing is so up in the air, I just…"

I knew her words trailing away meant she felt my body tense up, she felt my halted breathing. I would have been lying if I'd said that I hadn't even thought about the fact that I would actually leave without saying anything to him. The last time I left, I'd made him promise to tell me everything when he came back. He honored that promise. It wasn't his fault that the things that he told me… broke my heart.

I didn't know how to piece that back together. I didn't know how to involve him in the reconstruction.

"I really don't know."

She'd let out a sigh. "I think you will." She didn't look at me when she spoke again right before she went to sleep. "You lost someone that you didn't even know you could miss, and he should have told you about her, but I think you tend to forget that he lost someone too. You are so quick to absolve Jonah of all his faults but why can't you give that same grace to your father. They were best friends who have a shared history when it comes to your past, when it comes to your mother and anything else. You don't have to forgive him entirely but go scream at him, stomp around your house, something…. he's given you all his love and attention for twenty-four years, you owe him at least some of yours back."

Every second I spent with Morgan gave me a better understanding of why we weren't together anymore. Her incessant need to casually touch me or make flirtatious verbal hints were enough to make me want to shake her and scream that I wasn't interested anymore. I knew I didn't need to do any of that because she was well aware; Morgan just liked to play games and be, yet another person, to get under my skin. She looked at Dani like she was the superior of the two of them. In the context of The Skies, she probably was, but when it came to my attention and heart…

She was no match for how I felt about Dani.

Now that….that was a feeling I knew I would never find again with anyone else.

"Nick, are you listening?" Morgan waved her hand at my face. I shook my head, suddenly remembering where I was and why I was here.

I had gotten here with the knowledge that today was it. Everyone had been on board, Elise especially, with us leaving tonight. Dani had promised me one more day and she'd given me that, so I was ready to stay true to what I'd said.

"Yeah, sorry, what did you say?"

Morgan pointed to the far-left wall of the giant ballroom we were in. I knew this space was used for big parties or for when the new incoming class of angels finished their introductory training and got their specific positions. I'd seen this room transformed in so many ways, but Ariel's ceremony was not something I thought I'd ever see, let alone be helping with.

Lights were strung along the stone walls, unlit. I walked over, leaning down to place my hand at the bulb at the very bottom. My light dispersed from my hand into the bulb, moving from each one until it reached the top. I had been doing manual labor ever since I'd been coming here with her, and I was getting annoyed with how unnecessary this was.

"Once Ariel gets here, he'll want to show you how things will go so that you are knowledgeable on the day of."

I scratched the top of my head. "Why would that matter?"

She slapped my bicep, playfully. "Come on, Nick. You can't make sure the ceremony is secure if you don't know the rundown."

"Make sure the ceremony is secure? Morgan, I'm not doing that."

She let out a sharp laugh. "It's really cute how you think you have a choice."

"Actually, I do, and the answer is no. The entire purpose of me being here currently is stupid."

Morgan took both my biceps in her hands and peeked up at me through her lashes. It would be an innocent gesture to anyone else. "You are slowly working your way into Ariel's good graces; you'll need that for when he takes over. I assure you this stain on your reputation won't last forever. Ariel trusts me, so when I tell him how good you've been, well then, you'll be back to your perfect place in this realm."

I shrugged away from her, running a frustrated hand through my hair and walking away from her. I stopped short and quickly walked back over. "My perfect place in this realm? Do you honestly believe I actually want to have the kind of relationship I had with Jonah…with *Ariel*? I did all of this because as long as Dani was doing everything she was supposed to, he would leave her alone and keep up his end of the deal."

Morgan inhaled deeply, her calculating brown eyes narrowed. "She *is* doing all she needs to do and when she goes to take care of whatever the hell is happening, saving us all from everything her existence nearly caused then Ariel might, I don't know, give her a medal or something. Happy?"

My ears perked up at something she'd said. "You are aware, she isn't going back to Purgatory alone?"

"She can take her weird friends with her. Ariel made it clear that you and Reese are to stay here. He's trying to give you a second chance, Nick. I would advise that you take it."

I pinched the bridge of my nose, staring up at the ceiling. Decorated ivy hung from above, various flowers intertwined throughout it. "What are you not understanding? I don't want a second chance with that asshole. I also don't plan to stay here and pathetically follow him; I'm going with her."

"No, you aren't."

"Morgan, stop. I am and Ariel can whine about it all he wants, but it's already been planned. You said it's her mess, but it's my mess too."

Morgan scoffed, crossing her arms over her chest. Her freckled nose wrinkled. "You go and he could banish you, kick you out. It happened to your father. You aren't invincible, Nick."

I cocked my head back. "How do you know anything about my father?"

"Ariel likes to talk about a lot of things. When you get brought up, so does your dad. He sure as shit doesn't like that man, but he always makes a point to say that if you would just move your pride over just a smidge, look at the bigger picture, then well you could miss out on your father's mistakes…"

I pointed my finger at her, leaning down a small bit so I could meet her face to face. "My father did look at the bigger picture a long time ago and decided not to slaughter people that didn't deserve it. My father and my future aren't his fucking concern, nor is it yours. You want to help me, Morgan? Help this realm? Then stop thinking Ariel can do you any favors and start really looking at who you're working for." I backed up, needing to get the fuck out of here.

"You want to help the realms, Nicholas, well then, I suggest you stay on the side of individuals who have the power to legitimately change things."

"Ariel's version of change isn't something I'm interested in."

"It's in your best interest." She took her glasses off and started to clean them with the bottom of her shirt. She was so casual about all of this, like this was a conversation she assumed she'd be having. "You used to want to be the best, be at the highest tier. Don't you miss being envied and sought after by higher ups."

I rolled my eyes. "You have no idea what's in my best interest, believe me, you never have."

She placed her glasses back on, sticking her tongue between her teeth. "You seriously think *she's* in your best interest. She came as

Lilith's pawn, she manipulated you into following her to Purgatory, she's brought all this into our home and somehow you think…."

"She didn't manipulate me Morgan, I went all on my own." I closed my eyes, thinking over my next words carefully; I wanted them to matter, make an impact. "You're right, I did used to want all those things and I would have fought sword for sword just to keep it, but things change. *People change.* There are way too many people involved for me to just consider *myself* anymore and maybe that's where you and I differ."

"She's a demon, Nick. Oh, sorry a hybrid, not that it matters. You can't honestly tell me that you've just…"

"I'm in love with her!" My eyes widened at the need for her to fucking hear me.

Morgan's mouth closed quickly as she looked around at the different angels that glanced our way. I had seen them looking before but now they weren't even trying to act as if they weren't paying attention.

My chest could have exploded from the relief I felt. I had told Dani I loved her plenty of times, but saying that statement out loud, even if it had to be to my ex-girlfriend, made me feel a certain way. "Ariel doesn't matter. This fucking ceremony doesn't matter. There are plenty of other sentries that can stand guard and make sure he is still alive by the end of it. I am going with her tonight, Morgan. She isn't a stain or a problem, she's…she's *it* for me. I don't know when it happened but she's it for me. Whether it's Purgatory or Hell itself, I am going with her, because I'm *in* love with her."

"Nick." Morgan's face turned a shade of red, almost as if she was embarrassed that I wasn't professing my love for another person. I almost chuckled to myself thinking about that. I turned on my heels as I headed out of the ballroom.

If Dani thought she was ready for whatever lay ahead of us, then she deserved to get out of her head while she was still in Heaven's Gate.

14
DANI

I laughed at Reese's joke during our short break in between sessions when the door opened and I swung my head around to see my very frazzled angel charge through it. His eyes were a little wild, but his steps were determined, like he had thought about being in this location and *only* this location. The door slammed behind him as he looked around the room and found me. There was always this raging electrified energy whenever I became the focus of Nicholas Cassial's attention and it made me feel loved and comforted, it made me feel like I could do anything.

It also made me feel something else between my legs, but right now was not the time to consider that, at least not unless he wanted to.

"Where's your number one fan?" Elise asked.

Nick waved her off. "That doesn't matter." He rushed over to me, leaning down to kiss me with the aggression of someone who hasn't kissed in years.

"Uh…okay. I love the love, really, I do, but did something happen with Morgan?" Reese questioned, causing Nick to break away from me and focus his attention on everyone else.

"It did and while I'll be getting Ariel's wrath once we're back from Purgatory, I'm not really in the mood to care," Nick explained, laughing more to himself than to us.

"If we make it back…OW!" Elise mumbled, jumping a tiny bit when Beetee ran up and pinched her.

"I swear if you don't stop saying shit like that I will shift and swallow you whole." Beetee pinched her again, but then giggled.

Reese laughed along with her. "That's hilarious because you know, she's a snake and…they do that." He sighed, wiping his laughter induced tears.

Elise glared at him. "Yes, we get it. We aren't fucking idiots."

"Okay, okay, everyone simmer down. So, I'm just going to assume Ariel doesn't know you are here, without Morgan? And I'll also assume he doesn't know you all are leaving tonight?" Natalia stepped up next to me.

Nick pressed his fingers to his temple. "Yes…on all fronts."

"I think you're right, he won't be happy. Especially not with all the things you've told me about him," Garrett said, nodding his head towards me.

I rolled my eyes, refocusing my attention. "Are we leaving right now? I know we talked about tonight, but are you here to say *hey, change of plans, let's head out now*, because I am completely and totally for that plan."

Nick shook his head, twirling one of my curls around his finger. "Um, no. I don't love Elise's mindset and I don't want to alarm anyone with the idea of not coming back, but I think you more than deserve to do something fun."

"Using my powers and feeling amazing *is* fun, Nicholas." I tapped the tip of my finger against his nose.

"I mean something a little more mundane."

Elise made a gagging noise.

I looked over my shoulder at her, silently telling her to shut up.

"What is your version of mundane? Normalcy isn't our forte if you haven't noticed."

He rubbed the back of his neck, that nervous habit making an appearance. "I was thinking before we left that I could…take you out."

Beetee made a noise that was almost like a squeak. "Isn't taking someone out, like killing them?"

My eyebrows immediately turned down, my brain a little frazzled. I heard Garrett chuckle. "No, Beetee, I think he means a date."

"It's about fucking time," Reese said his voice muffled.

Nick let out a groan. "Yes, a date. I know we don't have time for a well-planned, fancy type of thing, but I just want you to have a little bit of fun before…"

"Okay," I said, pressing my finger to his lips. "Where are we going?"

I looked out one of the windows as Nick waited outside. The sun was going down, so there was this pinkish hue to the sky. I wanted to give him my full attention tonight, but I knew that this was just a small relief from all the work I'd done. This date would be something good that I would keep with me, whether it be a memory I'd have forever for the rest of my days, or it could be the last good thing I'd remember before the end came.

I fiddled with the thick straps of the dress Natalia let me borrow. Her various closets were filled with long flowing garments made of velvets, silks and other fabrics I couldn't even name. They have jewels that shined off of them and most were longer than I preferred. She had tapped her cheek, but then gave me a tiny smile before sending one of her Enchanters to fetch something more my style.

The dress was black with a small triangular slit at my right thigh. It wasn't super tight, but shaped my body enough to where you could still confidently make out every curve. She'd given me heels that weren't too high, but they accented the length of my legs. I pressed my fingers to the glass at the window as I watched Nick playfully shove Reese back as they spoke.

"Can we just pretend that you guys are going on a date when in reality you will find a dark corner to fondle each other in?" Elise said, as I walked by her to make my way outside.

"I mean if that's what they want to do then I say have the best date possible." Beetee gave us a thumbs up.

I giggled, locking eyes with the one person who could make me nervous. He let his eyes roam their way down my body and then bit his lower lip which quite literally made me feral. I made my way over to him, leaning my body as close to him as I could. "So where are you taking me, hm?"

He brought his hand up to cup the side of my neck, so that his thumb could graze my jaw. "You'll see."

I couldn't help feeling a tiny bit giddy as he dipped his fingers inside his shirt, pulling out his portal key. I placed my hand over his. "Is where we're going flying compatible?"

"Most places are flying compatible, but yes."

I rubbed my lips together. "Could we do that?" I tugged on his arm, feeling like I wasn't asking too much.

He dropped his key and in a matter of seconds, scooped me up and cradled me in his arms. He pushed out his wings, their mass causing a slight breeze to pass.

"I guess that's a yes." I hooked my arms around his neck and he pushed off of the ground. It wasn't long before the trees were nonexistent, and we were right in the heart of the sunset. I remembered being like this with him when we were less familiar with each other, when he was so much more apprehensive around me. I shamelessly flirted as if my life depended on it, but there was something about Nicholas Cassial that made me want to keep pushing his limits.

This time was different though. He was carrying me the same as before, but now his hands were more comfortable with their placement. He squeezed my body closer to his because he wanted to and because he could. He kissed me mid-flight for the hell of it and I didn't stop him. There wasn't a dark ripple in sight, but there was a tiny inkling that the next time it happened, it would be bigger and whatever was behind it angrier and more lethal with each pull against the threshold.

I pulled a piece of my hair away from my face as I shook off my thoughts, feeling Nick make a turn and then dip down every so often. We started to descend lower and lower, until I could see foliage and gravel. He swerved around trees and eventually found a solid landing spot near a building I didn't recognize. He sat me down, making sure I had my balance before making his wings disappear.

Nick held his hand out waiting for me to take it. Our fingers intertwined as he pulled around the building. Something about his place gave me déjà vu, but then it hit me.

"Are we at the North Village?"

"Mmhmm."

I chewed on my bottom lip. "Are we going to see your dad?"

His shoulders stiffened for a moment before he turned to look at me. "No, contrary to popular belief there are other things in the North Village besides my father."

The smell of apple and sugar reached my nostrils and my mouth instantly started to salivate. There were a few people walking around, giving him small nods of acknowledgement, but nothing more. The time of day told me that most were probably at home eating with their families and not out gallivanting like we were.

Nick opened the door of the shop with the delectable smells, pulling me towards the counter. A woman with tight blonde curls came out to greet us, but when her eyes found Nick, her smile grew ten times wider. She clapped her hands together and it was like her whole body vibrated with excitement. "Nicholas?!"

Nick gave her a genuine smile as she came around the counter to give him a hug. I backed up, watching their interaction.

The short joyful woman, reared back to look at him. "You never come by anymore. You broke my poor heart you know. Your father comes around telling me all about your adventures, or as much as he can tell me. Ah, he's so proud of you." She held his face, placing both her palms on his cheeks and something inside of me wanted his father to just burst in here. I wanted them to have a big cry fest where they both spoke at the same time, but then laughed and admitted that they still loved each other despite the secrecy and separation.

That wasn't going to happen. I knew that.

She let him go, placing a hand on her hip. "He doesn't come around much anymore. I've been meaning to stop by your house, but that girl, uh, Alex, she always seems to find herself here. Always gets a handful of things for the family. Are you headed there now?"

I muffled my laughter at the turn this had taken.

"Um, no. I'm actually here with…" He looked over at me and the woman followed his eyes. Her dark blue eyes widened as she took me in. It wasn't out of fear or nervousness. It was out of embarrassment.

"For the love of all that is ethereal, forgive me! I am just prattling on rudely." She stuck her hand out for me to shake. "I'm Josie."

"Dani. It's nice to meet you. This shop yours?"

She gave me a hearty laugh before she made her way back around the counter, grabbing two rectangular paper sleeves and stuffing cookies in them. "She's all mine. Nicholas has been coming here since he was a boy."

I raised my eyebrows at her. "Well, it smells amazing in here."

"Thank you dear." She handed Nick the sleeves and he started to reach into his pocket, most likely to pay. Josie waved her hands at him. "No, sir. You keep your money and tell your father I said hello."

Nick gave her a tight-lipped smile and nodded, thanking her. He handed me one of the sleeves as we walked out the door. I waved goodbye to her before I grabbed the cookie, breaking off a small piece and eating it. It melted on my tongue instantly and there were more flavors than I imagined.

"There has to be some kind of magic in here to make this taste this good."

Nick chuckled while eating his own and shrugged. "I've said the same thing, but she has yet to tell anyone her recipe."

"She's close with your dad?"

He stuffed another, larger, piece of the cookie in his mouth. He swallowed before answering me. "She treats everyone like family, so yeah I guess you could say that."

I kept eating until only small traces of crumbs were left, mulling over what I wanted to say next. "You are fully aware you could run into your dad here, correct?"

"Yes. I knew I wouldn't though."

"How would you know that?"

"My dad loves to make dinner and sit around at the table and eat food with his family, having conversations about their day. He wouldn't be out and about right now. Despite most things, my father is predictable when it comes to things like this."

I crumbled up my paper sleeve, throwing it in a nearby bin as we walked. I grabbed onto his arm, nuzzling closer to him. "Aha, well, you asked me on this date for my benefit, right?"

He kissed my forehead as we passed more shops and some kids playing. "Absolutely."

"Good because right now, I'm not asking you to speak to your father, I'm not asking you to tell me how you feel about him or the situation. All I want from you right now is for you to tell me about him, about you growing up, your time with Reese, and anything else that you can share. I'm told dates are about getting to know the other person, so spill it, Mr. Cassial."

Nick sighed, but it wasn't from annoyance, I knew that from the way he looked down at me with those brown eyes that told me he wanted to speak about the man that brought him up, but he didn't want it to be more than just conversation.

For the sake of my time with him, not to mention how in love with him I was, I could do that.

I found myself continuously looking at the sky. I kept thinking I saw something or at this very minute was when we needed to leave. Nick would follow my eyes and remind me that there was nothing there, but there were moments when I felt like that tiny ripples that I saw were for me, just to fuck with me. I kept telling myself that it would all be dealt with.

We had sat down at a small table near the end of the rows of buildings to talk. I let Nick talk about anything and everything. I'd fire my questions and he would ask what he wanted as well. There were things he already knew about me, but some things I surprised him with. He had ended up placing his hand on my knee, drawing tiny circles with his thumb.

He would occasionally move that hand higher up my thigh but then retreat back to my knee. I was no better with how I dragged my foot along his ankle and up his leg. It was nice to see him laughing when his father was brought up, rather than the tension filled moments that always seemed to happen.

"So, your father and Jonah both discovered that little path into the Divine Library?"

He nodded, leaning back in his chair. "Yeah, it was odd since he'd always huffed and puffed about Jonah ever since I started at The Skies. After he told me about the secret passage, I guess he was in a forthcoming mood to keep talking."

"And?" I pressed, intrigued.

"And he told me Jonah was always fond of the library. He liked going there at night and he'd drag my father with him. I don't know, I guess it became like a little secret meeting place. I don't particularly think Jonah's father was a fan of mine and Jonah himself was always busy with future executive things, that slowly I think they spent less time together but 'best friends will always find a way to meet up'. Those words are straight from my father."

"So, the library was Jonah's favorite place, huh?"

"Yeah, I guess so, the Divine Library is always quiet and it's a good place to think. I can see why he enjoyed it."

"Hmm, do you have a favorite place? I mean besides between my legs," I joked, getting an eye roll from him that made me giggle even more.

"You are so much more than just a very nice body, Dani, so..." His words trailed off while his eyes looked off to the side as if he was deep in thought.

I snapped my fingers at him. "Hello, Nick?"

"Wait, Jonah's favorite spot was the library."

I slowly nodded. "Yeah, you've said that."

"My father is probably one of the few people that knew him the best, so that has to be accurate, right?" He started to get up from the table.

"Sure. Nick, what's going on?"

"I'm not sure, but we have to go." He grabbed my hand, pulling me around a corner. He had his portal key out in seconds and started to create a circle.

"Go where? Context would be nice, you know."

Once the portal was done, he started to yank me inside the glowing circle. "The Divine Library."

I clearly wasn't processing what was happening fast enough, but I'd given up asking any other questions the minute the portal he had created led us into the closet that held the doorway to the secret passage into the Divine Library. Nick started talking as he maneuvered the bookcase out of the way, revealing the door.

Today was just filled with moments of déjà vu as we walked the same path, we had the first time we were down here. Everything from the smells to the darkness sent me back. Nick lit his own path, but his footsteps were faster and more determined. We were meant to leave soon and somehow this man decided to go rogue and tell no one his thought process. I couldn't say I was surprised.

The minute we got inside, away from the dank air of the tunnel, I took an easy breath inward. I hadn't been in the library for quite some time, but I'd almost forgotten how beautiful it was. The stained-glass windows collected the last of the sunset and it would be pitch dark soon. The tiny orbs of light started to glow as the inside of this building began to dim. Nick darted for the stairs while I followed behind him, my curiosity slowly morphing into annoyance. "Tell me why you couldn't just portal us in here?"

He took the stairs two at a time, placing his hands on his hips as he surveyed his surroundings. "The Divine Library is secured so that no one can just pop in with portals, regardless of their stature here. We would have gotten kicked back to the North Village. There are always loopholes, hence the secret passage."

I pushed my bottom lip out, nodding my head. I widened my arms and spun around. "And we are in here, why?"

Nick turned around. "The library was Jonah's favorite place."

"We've established this, yes."

"All this time, Ariel said they'd looked everywhere for it, but maybe they just didn't know where to look." Nick scratched his chin and then made his way over to the wall where the tapestries hung. The same wall where I'd found the book about Enchanters.

Something in my mind clicked. "We are here about Jonah's powers?"

He didn't answer me. He simply looked at the tapestries, examining them. He touched one of them, letting his fingers feel the golden tassels. He skipped the one of the Enchanter and angel, where I'd found the book and stood in front of the last one. It looked just like a simple picture of an angel etched into the fabric.

"Nick, you are making a big assumption on a conversation we had."

Nick pulled the tapestry away from the wall and started searching the wall. "I remember that they wanted to redecorate, make new tapestries, a bunch of things at one point, but Jonah had declined that request. He had made such a big deal out of keeping these here."

"Okay…Nick, when I found the book the last time it was behind the tapestry that made the most sense. This is just a picture of an angel; I don't get how that would lead you to…"

He pressed his hands to different stones, until one of them went further inward, as if he was pressing a button. When the stone slid back far enough another stone close to it popped out. "This tapestry was designed with the highest executive in mind."

I came up behind him, noticing that the stone was hollow on the inside. He reached inside to reveal a small book. There was nothing special about it. It was a leather-bound pocket-sized notebook with a plain leather strap that kept it bound. Nick swept his fingers over the front, tapping the bottom right corner. "Look."

I grabbed the book from his hands and found the impression of initials. "Are these Jonah's?"

Nick reclaimed the book from my hands and started to unravel the strap. "J. H. Z. Yeah, Jonah Henry Zuriel." We both waited with bated breath when he opened the book. I had this thought that magic would come zooming out, or words would appear, but neither of those things happened. Nothing at all happened. Nick stared at the blank pages, flipping through over and over again as if he thought something new would happen.

"I don't understand. I just...I have this feeling like this is it, this is where it is."

I leaned against one of the tables. "Maybe there is some special way to release it from the book. Jonah didn't seem like the type to just make it this easy. Or maybe it's cheeky and knows you aren't the one it's meant for so it's hiding." I poked his side, trying to be funny.

He let out an unamused laugh, closing the book and placing it in his back pocket. "As long as Ariel doesn't get his hands on it, then I guess we're good."

"We can hand this off to Natalia to keep while we're gone, maybe she can find a way to crack the code. She is the smart one."

"Yeah..." He seemed distracted and a bit disheartened.

I slid my hands from his stomach to his chest. "Fix your face, Nicholas, you should still be proud that you found it. Now you have something to rub in Ariel's face when we get back and you figure it all out. Dethrone him from his delusional place at the top."

He didn't look the least bit interested. I wanted to bring us back to the happy place we were in, especially since it wasn't like his detour was a failure. It just didn't end perfectly like he wanted; the answer required something more than just his good sleuthing skills. I huffed out a breath but chose to move my hands back down his stomach and closer to the button of his pants. "While we're in here, we could continue our date," I leaned up and kissed his neck. "You can't tell me you haven't considered what it would be like to do very inappropriate things in here."

His hand covered my own and removed them from the top of his pants. He backed up a few feet. "I haven't actually."

I walked back up to him, letting my fingers slip under his shirt. "Oh, come on, you can't tell me that it hasn't crossed your mind to bend a very pretty girl over one of these tables—"

"I think it's probably best that we just get back to the others." His voice was monotone and tired. I understood, I did, but I could still be upset all on my own.

I ruffled my curls, taking a few steps back. "*You* wanted to take me out. *You* wanted to give me a sense of happy freedom before I have to focus everything I have to lead all our friends into the literal unknown. *You* derailed our time to come here, which I will say was for a solid reason, but now since every little piece of the fucking puzzle isn't just falling into your hands, you're just done. No thought about me, the girl who is still trying to have a good time with you." I could have pulled my fucking hair out.

"Dani, it isn't like..."

I shook my head and smacked my lips. "Oh, no, it's alright. You're not interested. You want to leave and just head off to fight, then okay cool. Thank you for making my time before, I could potentially fuck up everything and cause even more chaos, a fantastic one." I pointed my thumb over my shoulder. "I'll just go be horny over there and finish our date by myself."

I turned around before he could say anything else, making my way over toward a row of bookshelves.

15
DANI

I was seething as I took note of all the books before me. Most of their spines were worn off but I'm sure the insides were legible enough if I gave a shit right now.

I felt a presence behind me, tall and familiar. I continued to stare at the bookshelf in front of me, not paying my increasing heart rate any mind. His hands came to my waist, as his body got closer to me until he was flush against my back. I held my breath as my hair was moved to the side exposing the side of my neck. His lips found my skin and traveled to my ear. "I'm sorry, baby."

His voice sent a shiver down my spine, and I felt myself leaning back into him. "It really isn't surprising that you turned this into part of a mission. Very you, Nicholas. Commendable, you wanting to help at all sides, but you are really frustrating." His hands explored my stomach, gliding down to my outer thighs and bunching up my dress slowly.

He continued to speak directly into my ear, his voice low and intoxicating. I was starting to feel a little drunk off of it. "I know, Dani. I know. I fucked up."

I let out a heavy sigh, attempting to collect myself. "It's okay, your heart was in the right place as per usual. You can make it up to me when this is all over, that way we both can be optimistic about everything."

I heard his deep chuckle before he whispered, "I would rather make it up to you now. I mean…" He ran his hand under my dress, letting his fingers slip into my panties, "I can't leave you all wet and needy now, can I?" His fingers massaged me between my legs, circling my clit and I nearly bit my tongue. I reached out towards one of the wooden shelves, hearing a small creak from the amount of pressure I was providing it.

"I could always say no and make you suffer," I snarked.

He removed his hand from my pussy and traveled up my dress to cup both my breasts with his palms. "You could. We both know that's not what you want. It's not what that pretty pussy is begging for."

He bent down, licking and nipping my ear. One of his hands moved further up my body towards the straps of my dress. Nick gently tugged one of them down, so that it sat limply at my arm. He fingered the top of my dress, pulling the material down and releasing my breast into the cool air around us. His fingers played with my nipple as he did the same thing to the other side, leaving me exposed on the top floor of the Divine Library.

"Are you so sure you've never—" I sucked in a breath when he started kissing my neck again. His lips brushed that perfect spot that always made my thighs push together, "done this before, had this little fantasy?"

He tweaked both my nipples with his fingers and shook his head against me. "No, but this isn't about me. This is all about you."

I felt my eyebrows turn in confusion. "What about me, hmm?"

"Tell me what you want, baby."

He pulled my dress straps further down my arms, allowing me to be free of their confinement. I reached back and grabbed his hair, eliciting a groan from him. "Tell me to make you come and I will. Tell me to make you scream and I'll fucking do it. Just be greedy and tell me what you want, right now."

"I want you to keep touching me," I ordered.

"Where?"

I looked down the length of my body, watching as his hands teased me. "Between my legs, use your fingers."

He did what I said and returned his hands to my pussy causing my thighs to tremble when his fingertips made contact. He circled my clit and applied just enough pressure to have me squirming.

"Fuck, Nick…" I wanted more, I wanted so much more.

"Is this enough for you, needy one?" He lightly grazed his fingers along my entrance but not putting them inside.

"No, *fuck*, no I want more."

He dipped his head down, kissing the side of my face while still playing with me. "Then use that bratty mouth and tell me."

I removed my hand from the shelf and tried to reach down towards his hand, guide him to where I wanted those skilled fingers. He was quicker than me and yanked my hand away, interlocking his fingers with my own and pulling me so close to him that I could feel his cock against my back.

"Not so fast…"

"Nick, please…" I whined.

He tsked, letting go of my hand and playing with my breasts again. "So flustered that you can't even tell the guy that loves you what you want him to do to you?" His smile against the skin of my face pissed me off in the hottest way.

"Put your fingers inside of me." I turned my head upward so I could see him, the frustration on my face so clear, but all he did was lift an eyebrow, never letting up on the rhythm of his fingers. "I want you put your fingers inside of me and fuck me with them until the only thing I can think about wanting is your cock."

His eyes closed for a moment, a restrained *fuck* leaving his lips.

"Is that detailed enough for you?"

He didn't answer me. He just quickly lifted the bottom of my dress up and moved my panties to the side. He pressed one finger inside of me, then without hesitation added another. He angled his body over me as he curled his fingers inside of where I was relieved to have them.

I whimpered at the rough movement of his fingers. His thumb skated over my clit, continuously making my eyes flutter open and closed. The sound of how wet I was filled my ears, and I bit my lip wanting more than just those two fingers.

As if he read my mind, Nick slipped another finger inside, stretching me but it was in no comparison to his cock. I reached back out for the shelves, steadying myself as I watched his forearm pulse with each flick of his wrist. His other hand played with my breasts, the stimulation overwhelming. "Don't stop, that feels so g-good."

"So needy the way your pussy is squeezing my fingers."

My thighs started to shake as his fingers kept slamming into me, touching that spot that had me dropping my mouth open. "Fuck, I want your cock."

His low groan at my ear had me coming on his hand, squeezing the shelves and attempting to jolt away from him even though all I wanted to do was be closer. He removed his fingers, his cock rigid against my back. My breathing was harsh and I ran a hand through my curls, nearly hearing my heart beating through my ears.

I felt his hand wrap around my throat gently, pulling me back against him. "Be specific, baby. Telling me to fuck you isn't enough. Use your words."

"I…fuck…"

His fingertips squeezed both sides of my throat and I brought my ass back, rubbing the front of his pants. We were so alone in this place and I had released this unhinged version of the man that I loved. All he wanted to do right now was please me and I knew he could. He was causing my senses to malfunction, but I wasn't so far gone that I couldn't articulate what I wanted. I slammed my hand against the wooden shelf, hearing the wood creak and rattle. Some of the books shook in place but then it was quiet again. I pulled away from him and spun around, standing on the tips of my toes, attempting to reach his face. He was thrown off guard a bit but rallied, raising both his eyebrows.

I grabbed his shirt, pulling him into me. My lips brushed his as I spoke each word with conviction so that he didn't misunderstand. "I want you to fuck me like I'm no one else's but yours. I want you to pound my pretty pussy so well that I scream in this perfect little angelic library of yours. I want you to make me come all over your cock so fucking hard that I'm shaking and unable to form sentences, that I'm only able to utter one word and that's your name." I grabbed his cock through his pants and licked at his lips. "Can you handle that, hmm? Or does the thought of fucking me senseless, hearing your name echo off the walls in a place full of so much history too much for you, baby?"

He took my face in his hand, grazing his thumb over my parted lips. He eventually stuck it in my mouth, and I clasped onto it, sucking and looking right into his hooded eyes. He pulled out his thumb, moving the wet digit to one of my nipples.

I shuddered at the contact, right as he leaned down, his voice wrapping around me like warmth I didn't know I could crave so much. "Oh, my needy one does know how to follow directions." He brought his lips to mine but then pulled away too quickly for my liking. I was about to demand more when he turned me around, pushing down between my shoulders so I was forced to reach one of the shelves near the bottom as I bent over.

The fabric of my dress tickled my skin, the material being maneuvered so that it was out of the way and exposed my ass to him. I felt his hands explore each cheek, small squeezes here and there that lit my skin on fire. He hooked a finger into my panties and moved them over again so he could see my pussy. I sensed a shift behind me, so I dipped my head down and tried to see what he was doing. He had knelt down so that he was eye level with my backside. My eyes instantly closed, a pleasurable hiss leaving my lips when I felt his tongue against me. He continued to lap at me with what seemed like every intention of making me come on his tongue. My teeth sunk down into my bottom lip so hard that I tasted blood when he used his hands to spread me open, his tongue licking from my clit up to my ass. My breath caught as he swirled his tongue around my tight hole, using his fingers to rub my clit. His tongue pressed into my ass as much as it could, pulling out and then going back in. I moaned out loud, pushing back against his mouth.

Nick got up from where he was settled between my legs, the sound of him undoing his pants making my ears perk up.

"What the fuck? Why did you stop?" I whined, wiggling my ass towards him.

His cock rubbed against my pussy, and he hummed. "Here I thought you wanted my cock." His palm landed hard against my ass making me squirm. "I thought you wanted me to fuck you."

I nodded towards the bookshelf, whimpering, "I do, *fuck*, I do."

"Say it."

I groaned out my response, "I want you to fuck me, *plea*—" My words were cut off when I felt him push inside of me with enough force to have me readjusting my stance. He grabbed my hips and started moving, pounding in and out. He kept a steady rhythm, never faltering as he pressed his fingers into my skin. His grunts bounced off the walls and caused a shiver through my whole body. I nearly wanted to cry from how good he felt and how I wanted him so much deeper than he already was.

He smacked my ass again, causing me to let out a moan. He pulled me harder against him, our skin smacking together violently. "Is this what you wanted?"

"Yes, Nick, yes, yes."

He grabbed my hair and yanked my head back, his cock moving inside of me at a different angle that made my legs buckle. "Does your needy little pussy feel better?" He spoke against my ear, his voice dominant and demanding. He wrapped his other arm around my body, holding me in place so I wouldn't fall forward. He let my hair go so he could wrap his hand around my throat.

I tried my best to give some sort of nod since I had seemed to lose all ways to speak. He wasn't tentative with his hips as our bodies collided over and over again. I fell apart when my orgasm ran through me. I felt his breath against me, his free hand traveling down to my clit. I squirmed just a bit, still coming down from my climax.

"So perfect." His fingers played with me and I could feel myself being turned on all over again, while his cock was still settled inside of me.

"N-Nick…" I hesitated, wanting more of his fingers or for him to start moving again.

"You still want that? For me to make you scream?" He kissed the side of my face and bent a little to trail his kisses to my neck.

I tried to steady my breathing. "Yes, make me scream."

Nick pulled out of me, turning me around and lifting me up into his arms before my legs could give out. His lips found mine as he carried me to one of the sturdy wooden tables, setting me down near the edge. I worked quickly when removing his shirt while he ran his deft fingers over my nipples. A small moan left my lips, but he took that moan and swallowed it whole as his mouth molded to mine.

"So dirty for such a well brought up angel." I teased, letting my hands travel down his skin. My fingers traced over his abs and wrapped around his cock. His shaft was still wet from me, twitching at my very touch. "Anyone can come in here and catch us. They could watch you taking what's yours…you aren't worried about that, right?" I tugged on his cock, and he pressed his lips together in a mild groan.

He grabbed my hand and yanked it away, gripping thighs, forcing me to fall back as he tugged me closer to the end of the table. The sound of him ripping my panties off filled the room and then I hissed out in pleasure as his cock slid over my clit. "As long as the only name you scream is mine, I don't care who sees us."

He pressed his cock into me, holding onto the outside of my thighs as he pulled me back, meeting him at every single thrust. Nick looked down and watched each motion, watched the quick way he slid out and back in.

I nearly bit my own tongue as I massaged my breasts, wanting to pull him in deeper. I looked down my body to see his stomach muscles contract as he pumped his hips. One of his hands released my thigh and he started playing with my clit again. He fluttered over it with his fingers and with the way his cock hit every perfect way imaginable, I knew this orgasm could probably kill me. He wanted to please me, whether it be sexually or emotionally; it was jarring knowing that this man would get on his knees for me yet have me dropping to my own when the moment called for it. "Fuck, I love you."

He let out a small laugh, leaning down as he spread my legs out wider. "I love you too." He pushed inside of me with short, quick thrusts that had me holding onto his biceps. "Now tell me you're mine."

I tried to kiss him, but he moved away, waiting. I let out an annoyed groan, which quickly turned into a satisfied one when he circled his hips. "I'm yours."

"Say it again."

"I'm yours. It's all yours, all of it."

Nick backed off and pulled out, disappearing as he bent down between my legs. I managed to lift myself up to my elbows right as he pressed his face into my pussy, devouring me with that skilled tongue he had. He pushed my thighs back so that his tongue could swipe over my ass and my pussy. I grasped the sides of the table at the sensation, nearly hearing it whine.

"You want me to make you come?" He asked between licks and kisses against the little bundle that had my thigh muscles clenching.

I nodded, my teeth pushing into my bottom lip.

Nick took my clit into his mouth, while his smallest finger delicately played with my ass but never tried to push inside. His eyes flicked up to me, as if saying my nonverbal answer wasn't good enough.

I whimpered, knowing he could make me come at any moment, but he was withholding. "I want you to make me come, *please*."

He let out a satisfied hum before licking at my clit again, circling it and giving it so much attention that my legs were already shaking. "And who owns this pretty pussy, Dani?"

My curls fell in my face as I panted, the room felt hot and I could have passed out from his incessant edging. "You."

He landed one more kiss to where I was wet and needy, standing up to his full height. "Good *fucking* girl." I practically yelped when he landed a quick but well-placed smack on my pussy, grabbing my thighs and pushing himself inside of me again.

The table rattled from how hard he went, how rough he was being and when he placed his hand under my head to lift me up, I widened my legs needing to chase that orgasm that was building and building. Our faces were inches apart and sweat decorated our skin. I kissed him but used my teeth to yank his bottom lip out. "Don't forget you're mine too, Nicholas Cassial."

He grabbed my hair as he pounded up into me, tilting my face back so he could lick up my neck and towards my ear. "Then come on my cock," he wrapped his arm around my body, his cock filling me continuously until stars started to shine behind my eyes. "Come for me, baby. Scream for me just like you want to."

I pressed my fingers into his bare shoulder, seeing small pieces of light come from my palm. He'd told me before, the burns I left didn't scare him or push him away. He'd said his skin would heal as would everything else. I loved him for saying that, even when my love tended to hurt him. I now knew how to control this light and what he did to me, what his own light added didn't need to hurt. The light dimmed and shuttered as if it was simply going back to sleep, dormant until I needed it.

It was all so much that I closed my eyes, letting out a scream that burned my lungs and his name followed behind it. He pumped his hips a few more times, shaking when his own orgasms released. I was trembling from the sheer satisfaction of the moment when the sound of a door opening stilled us both.

"I know it is late, but this is the best time to make note of the changes I need fulfilled. After the ceremony, the turnaround time will need to be quick. New windows, new tapestries, the works." Ariel.

A group of angels in teal suits followed behind him as he entered the library. They must all be executives, just clearly not at the caliber that Ariel was.

Nick mouthed the word *fuck* and closed his eyes, probably wishing to go back in time.

I couldn't help but cough out a laugh which Nick immediately shut down, clasping his hand over my mouth. I managed to get one of his fingers in between my teeth and bit down.

He hissed out and removed his hand.

"Maybe I wouldn't be laughing if you weren't still inside of me." I whispered, flicking my eyes down to where we were still joined.

He rolled his eyes and quietly pulled out, tiptoeing over to where his pants and shirt were still on the floor. He plucked my ripped panties from the ground and placed them in his pocket. Where we were was out of sight of anyone down below but the idea that they could look up and see us was a little thrilling. A lot thrilling actually.

"Maybe Ariel should have found us. We could have showed him what actual sex looks like." I muttered, realizing Nick could hear me when he shushed me from his spot near the railing.

I moved my dress back into place and without a mirror attempted to fix my hair. Nick looked over the railing, trying to see what was going on. He turned around, noticing me fiddling with my hair and whispered, "stop, you're beautiful. Your curls are perfect."

I could feel myself blushing. "I'm rightly disheveled"

"You're welcome."

I hopped off the table on shaky legs and bent down so I could rest my knees on the cold ground while being able to fulfill my curiosity. Nick followed suit and we both tried to listen as best we could.

"Those tapestries have been there for quite some time, Ariel. These changes do not need to be made in haste." A woman with gold hair said.

Ariel laughed as if her words meant nothing. "I didn't ask for opinions. I said what I needed, and I expect it to be done. I do have other matters to attend to. Much more pressing matters."

"Is everything alright?" One of the men in the back of the group said.

Ariel hummed. "Yes, just angels without discipline, that's all. Easily dealt with."

"Does this have anything to do with the ripple in the sky?"

The red-headed angel laughed as if nothing was wrong. "I can assure you that that issue will be taken care of. I have someone who is an expert in that matter fixing it."

"The Soul Seether, right?" The woman from before asked.

Ariel licked his lips, clearly through with his line of questioning. "Yes. Unlike my predecessor, who seemed to think she was trusted to do whatever she wanted; I know she will do as she's told. We have a very solid agreement. It seems as if she has much more control over her actions then some angels. Funny, how that works out."

Ariel motioned for them to follow him. "We will look at the exterior of the building and then we can move to the Ethereal Bastille. I have a feeling I'll be needing it quite soon." The others scurried after him. We ducked our heads down, moving away from the railing when a few of them looked up in our direction.

The moment the door shut, Nick patted his pants pocket to make sure he still had Jonah's book and we ran downstairs.

"According to Ariel, I am much more disciplined than you." I joked, punching his shoulder as we turned the corner down the hallway to his room. It was quiet enough at The Skies but with the way Ariel had spoken, I had assumed we would be ambushed by sentries by now.

I had told Nick I wanted to change and then we could go. I could have fought in this dress if I really had to, but it wasn't my first choice.

"You do follow directions nicely." He winked over at me.

"You're out of your funk I see."

He grabbed my hand when we were at his door, pushing my back against it. "Mmhmm. Like I've always said I want to be a team with you and I can't help my girlfriend fight *her* demons if I'm overthinking. Dimitri and Lilith were able to sniff out my bad spots before and I won't let that happen again. Satisfied?"

I kissed him, pulling back only when he wanted to keep going. "Very." I kept him close to me so he wouldn't immediately pull away. "Girlfriend?"

"Is that okay?"

I turned the knob to his bedroom, and we tumbled inside. "I've never been someone's girlfriend, but I'm more than okay with being yours." He leaned down and kissed me. I went over to the dresser, yanking out the first pieces of clothing I saw.

Nick snapped his fingers as if he remembered something and pointed towards his door. "I have to stop over at Reese's room to grab something for him before we go."

"Isn't that down the hall?"

"Yeah."

"Why are you acting like it's miles away? Go ahead, I'll be here, ready to go when you get back." I shooed him away as he opened the door, stepping into the hallway.

I grabbed the clothes and went into the bathroom. In the mirror, I looked back at myself and let the memories of how I got here replay in my mind. It was hard for me to think about Purgatory and consider that place somewhere to go back to and live happily. It would always hold a place in my soul, or whatever I had, but it didn't own me anymore.

I finished getting my other boot on when I heard a thump. I opened the bathroom door, ready to leave. "Well, that was quick…"

My words were cut short when I saw who was standing in the middle of the room. My breath caught in my throat at the intrusion. "What are you doing here?" It was all I could muster.

"Well hello to you too, sweetheart. Death really does look good on you." Dimitri smirked over at me as if he had every right to be here. His button-down shirt looked expertly tailored as if he had made sure he looked perfect for this reunion. One of his sleeves was rolled up tightly to conceal the place where his other hand should be. There were tiny scar lines on the side of his face where Nick had struck him with his light.

His eyes pierced into mine as if he was waiting for me to respond.

"No need to be rude. You could at least say that it's nice to see me."

I suddenly found my words. "How did you get here?"

Dimitri released a full smile in my direction. "That did take some time, this realm is quite tricky to get into, especially with those silly little wards these people drew up as a show of protection. Laughable, really. I was going to save the intrusion for a later date, but well, then you came back to life." He shrugged as if this all made sense. "You were always so attractive when you were mislabeled as just a demon, but now with what I know you can do, oh, you are just exquisite."

I narrowed my eyes at him, but then Elise's words hit me like a punch to the stomach.

What if you creating that much of a frenzy turned into some kind of unwanted calling card? Just enough power to alert, but not enough to retain itself. It will eventually disperse, but not quick enough to go unnoticed.

That's what he meant by 'came back to life.'

"The ripple was you."

"Lilith wanted to come see you, but well, you know all about her little confinement issue. A Son of Hell, now, with a little determination I can travel wherever I like, especially when it's for things that I want. And I wanted to be right here."

"For what?"

"To bring you home."

"No fucking way." I shot out my shadows towards his face, willing the light to stand down for now. I didn't want to cause some kind of mass explosion while there could be potential lives at risk. I darted for the door but felt a hand grab my wrist and throw me into the wall near the bathroom door.

I tried to shove him off of me, but he grabbed me by my shoulder and shoved me back again. His tattooed covered hand grabbed my neck and deep red shadows cinched around my wrists and every time I made an inch of movement it burned. It wasn't like a regular burn, no, this was burn with Hellfire. It was debilitating if you attempted to suffer through it. I'd seen Dimitri burn demons from the inside out by making the shadows into a ball, forcing them to eat it. I overlooked his sadistic nature because well, I rarely saw it. He did it behind closed doors, but there were moments, few and far between, when I was a witness to it.

Every single dark power I had disintegrated when it met Dimitri's. He had the power of Hell on his side. I wasn't prepped for this. I was prepared to use my newly balanced powers on a larger scale, not in the confines of my boyfriend's bedroom. "I really don't want to make a mess, so I suggest you stand down. If you make this difficult, I will do what I should have done in the first place and make you watch me rip your little pathetic angel limb from limb and then burn all the remains along with this entire realm, which really would ruin all my plans. Is that what you want?"

I fought against him, but he pulled me away from the wall, throwing back against it, my back aching from the pain. "Your powers weren't made for the use of angels, so why do you let them confine you? You have the power fit for a queen." He grabbed the restraints at my wrists and tugged. "Let's go. We have so much to discuss."

He moved his hand in an eloquent circle until a dark portal opened up. I yanked against his hold, the burning bite of his restraints eating into my skin. "I've been tortured by Lilith before; it doesn't scare me."

He pushed me in front of him, placing his lips at my ear. "Lilith isn't the one you should be worried about."

PART TWO

"however vast the darkness, we must supply our own light"

TW: severe panic attacks, physical assault, mental abuse

16
NICK

I huffed out an annoyed breath when I opened drawer after drawer to find a tiny carved wooden arrowhead that Reese had kept with him since his first time ever successfully using a bow. He'd asked me to snag it for him when we came back to the room before heading back to Oculus. I didn't quite understand it, his need to keep that tiny thing in his pocket like it truly gave him additional luck. He could survive without it, but I remembered him being the most nervous I'd ever seen him when we started really practicing for our assessments at The Skies.

It was a training bow and arrow, but nevertheless, he treated that weapon like his life depended on it. He'd used that bow to pass all the tests but retired it when he got a shiny new one that was sleeker and more elite. He'd kept the arrowhead though. He would say it was his first look at what he could do, even with the fragile wood and unreliable structure of the older bow. He kept it with him for nearly every single thing we did, even if I was the only person who ever knew about it.

I shook my head as I closed my fingers around the lucky charm, placing it in my pocket. A long dark ripple caught my eye at his window, but this one was *different*. This one felt more aggressive than the rest, it felt closer. That darkness felt like it was right in front of me, circling around Reese's room and there was nothing I could do about it. I had this odd feeling that I was being watched, but this time it wasn't from other sentries or Ariel himself. This gave me goose-bumps so intense that I found myself swiping my hands down my arms.

I ran a hand through my hair as I opened up Reese's door and walked back down the hall to my own room. "Are you all ready?" I asked, looking around to find an empty bedroom. I furrowed my brow, stepping into the bathroom and finding that free of Dani as well. I ran to my bedroom door, swinging it open, looking from side to side before slamming it closed.

She wouldn't have just left without me, especially since she didn't have any means of transportation to Oculus. She did have her wings, but her flying on top of all the chaos with Ariel wasn't the smartest move.

I was gone for five minutes tops...she couldn't have just disappeared.

I felt dumb looking under my bed as my heart started to speed up to the point that I felt like I couldn't breathe. I did a circle around my room as if she would appear somehow and proceeded to check my bathroom for what felt like the tenth time. "Where the hell are you?" I muttered to myself, the panic starting to set in.

I looked down, noticing something small and red, like the tiniest charred pieces I had ever seen. They were dusted around the floor near the bathroom door. I placed my fingers into the mess, feeling how warm the particles were. I didn't have to bring it too close to my nose to smell brimstone.

I didn't understand, where would she go? My chest felt tight when I rose from the ground, dipping my hands into my shirt for my key. She had to be somewhere safe, she just *had* too. There was a simple explanation, and I just needed someone to tell me that I was overthinking, that this was all some joke.

When I'd stepped through my portal, I realized that I'd managed to make it into Natalia's foyer. One of the Enchanters walking by yelped at my sudden presence, but I didn't pay her any mind. My eyes locked with the honey-colored ones of the High Priestess when she appeared from around a corner, hurrying down the stairs.

"Finally. We've been waiting for you both." She searched around me, confused. "Where's Dani?"

I opened my mouth, but no words came out. She didn't know where she was either. My throat felt tight and I rubbed my hand along my neck, hoping to ease some of the pain.

"Nick." Her voice was steady, but cautious. She subtly held her hands out, almost as if she thought I might fall. Her eyes flared with this look of understanding. "Nick, what happened?"

My voice came out small and hoarse. "I don't know. I—I don't know."

Her hands finally touched my arms, steadying me. "Zane!"

The large Enchanter, followed by Reese, Elise and everyone else hustled down the stairs, all of them flanking me from every side.

"Your Highness, what's wrong?"

Natalia pressed her lips together before sighing. "I'm unsure. Nick, where is she?"

"She? As in Dani?" Elise chimed in, mimicking Natalia as she looked around the room. "Where is she?"

I repeated my earlier answer. "I don't know."

Reese placed his hand on my shoulder. "Weren't you with her? How do you not know where she is?"

I took one breath in and then another. I tried to quiet all the things around me. Every person continuously asking me questions needed be silenced or I would fucking combust.

"You don't think she would go off by herself again, right?" Garrett asked no one in particular.

"No, she wouldn't. She made a big fucking deal about me not going alone, so I hardly think she would go and be a hypocrite about it," Elise explained. I peeked over at her the moment she decided to look over at me. "So what? You went on your silly little date and somewhere between then and now she just vanished? That hardly makes any sense."

"Ellie, maybe it's not that…" Beetee started but her voice was drowned out by my own thoughts.

I placed my hand on my chest, feeling like a weight was causing my breathing to become harder and harder. I was supposed to protect her and now I had no idea where she was. I didn't even know where to fucking start.

"Nick, hey, Nick." I heard Reese calling out to me, but his voice sounded muffled and far away.

No one was getting it. I didn't know what happened because I had left her for five *fucking* minutes.

She had been out of my sight and I left her.

I *left* her.

"I left her!" I screamed, placing my hands in my hair and pulling. "Five minutes! Five *fucking* minutes!" I ripped myself away from all their hands. The air was too dry, the temperature too hot. I felt like I was sweating as I started to pace.

Reese ran over to me, but I waved him away, hearing my breathing turn shallow, nearly to the point of wheezing. I groaned from the tense pain in my chest and I stopped walking when nothing seemed to stay in place. The room spun in one direction and then the other.

I couldn't help her because I left her and now, she was gone. This wasn't like Lilith's castle where pinpointing her location was simple. I couldn't think straight as I coughed, closing my eyes and backing up, hoping that my spine would hit a wall of some kind.

"Zane, go get Xander and some others from the infirmary," Natalia delegated. "Nick, take a deep breath, okay?"

I shook my head, finally feeling a solid backing so that I could lean my head back against it. "I—I can't."

"Hey, hey, yes you can." Reese gently grabbed my face and forced me to look at him. "One deep breath in, one deep breath out, okay? Do it, Nick."

My body vibrated as the pain became too much and I could feel tears starting to fill my eyes. My head was heavy as I nodded. Reese sucked in his own breath and let it out at the same time as me.

One big breath in, one big breath out.

"One more time, let's go." He placed his hand on my chest to steady me.

One big breath in, one big breath out.

I kept going as I slid my body down the wall, hitting the floor. I brought my knees up to my chest, continuing my breathing.

Reese cleared his throat. "You went to my room to get my lucky charm, didn't you?"

"Y—you asked m-me to," I answered, getting the words out as best I could.

"And when you came back, she was gone." Beetee wasn't asking a question, just summing up the situation.

"You didn't hear anything?" Garrett pressed, but his voice was soft when he spoke.

I shook my head slowly, as I waited for the vertigo to pass. I heard multiple footsteps round the corner.

Natalia spoke to the Enchanters she had ushered over. "He seems okay, just be careful with him."

Elise leaned down so that she was eye level with me. Her usual menacing glare had cracked just a bit as she watched me. She looked all around my body when something caught her eye. My heart didn't feel like it was going to rip out of my chest, so I followed where her eyes led her.

I recognized Xander when he came around to look at me, but Elise shooed him back before she yanked my hand away from where I had it placed on my leg. She flipped my hand upside down so my palm was facing her. "Nick, what's this?"

I swallowed down the thick lump that had developed in my throat. I narrowed my eyes towards the red dust on my fingertips. "It was on the floor in my room."

It only happened for a moment, but I could have sworn her eyes flashed a violent red before they settled back to their normal grey.

Beetee bent down next to her, also examining my hand. She immediately started chewing on her bottom lip, her chest flushing a slight red. "Ellie..."

"What is it?" Natalia asked, quickly looking at Zane before focusing back on the group.

Elise swiped her fingers along mine so that they were also coated in the remnants of the last place my girlfriend was. She rubbed her fingertips together, before she brought it to her nose. She inhaled deeply, a sigh leaving her lips. "This is Hellfire residue."

"Hellfire?" Reese and I both said at the same time.

Elise tilted her head to the side, the ends of her black bob swishing near her jaw. "Lilith doesn't have your girl. *He* does." The way her voice inflected told me everything I needed.

"He?" Zane said, raising a thick eyebrow.

My mouth went dry all of a sudden and words were hard to come by. "Dimi..." My vision started to get spotted, and I could hear the incessant pounding in my head getting louder. I tried to breathe deeply again, focusing on a spot across from me.

Dimitri.

Fucking Dimitri.

"Nick, hey, you okay?" Reese asked, but his voice faded.

"I need to—" I tried to get up from the floor but couldn't, the spots in my vision getting thicker. "I have to go get—"

I needed to save her. I needed to find her, but any thoughts I had were lost when my body felt limp, and everything went dark.

I thought I would have been brought into the dungeons of Lilith's castle when we exited Dimitri's portal. It's where she confined me when I was disobedient and back talked her enough to make her not want to see my face for a while. I was used to that kind of torment as sad as it sounded.

Dimitri had thrown me to two of his henchmen while he walked behind us. These walls were different. The smell and aura made me uneasy and slightly nauseous. The stones were crusted in dirt and cobwebs. Blood was splattered in nearly every crevice I could see, even along the bars that were cemented in the rectangular openings right in the center of the solid stone cell doors. Creatures barreled towards their small windows to the outside hallway.

Every movement of my wrists sent a heat wave through my veins, but I tried my best to fight through the pain. I took in the creatures I saw, realizing that they weren't the normal ones from Purgatory. I couldn't say that I was an expert on every species and entity that all the realms had to offer, but Purgatory wasn't super eclectic with its residents. There was something oddly familiar about this place, like I'd heard about it before in grave detail.

This place smelled like brimstone and Hellfire.

He had taken me to Hell.

I had been sitting on Dimitri's lap on a normal day while he worked in his office at Leviathan when he told me about these dungeons. His eyes lit up when he spoke about some of the pain he'd inflicted, thinking it would turn me on. The memory made my stomach flip in the worst way.

We stopped in front of a door that looked like all the rest, while Dimitri maneuvered in front of us, placing his hand against the stone while red and dark grey sparks illuminated from his hand. The door creaked open and before the room was even halfway exposed, I was pushed inside. I tripped over a piece of broken stone and fell to the ground with a thud. My wrists were still secured so I rolled over, blowing my hair out of my face. My cheek throbbed from how I'd landed, letting me know it would likely bruise.

The Son of Hell waved his hand towards the guards, providing them the okay to leave. Once they were gone, Dimitri ran his hand across his mouth, keeping his fingers at his chin as he looked me over. His green eyes were piercing and had me feeling a tiny bit unsettled. "I really would prefer you to make this easy."

I sat up, shifting around so I could finally get back on my feet. "This? What is *this*?"

"You just like to be so very difficult, which I'll be honest, it is always a pleasure to see you so feisty, but sweetheart I would suggest you dial back your attitude if we are going to be in each other's company," he said, ignoring my question.

"If it were up to me, I would never be in your company again," I spat out, looking right at him.

He chuckled, nodding aimlessly around the cell. "Well maybe you should be a bit more discreet with the way you use that newfound power of yours, hmm? I wouldn't have had to gallivant into that horrendous place just to retrieve you."

"It wasn't like I was summoning you."

He tilted his head from side to side. "Perhaps not, but alas here we stand. I would love for you to explain some things to me."

I lifted my chin, feeling his magic dig into wrists as I stood my ground. I didn't answer him, causing him to lift one corner of his mouth.

"How are you here?"

I narrowed my eyes, confused. He waved his hand, rephrasing. "I don't mean *here*. I mean here in general, alive and breathing. How are you standing in my very presence?"

I ran my tongue over my front teeth. "Just great luck I guess."

He placed his tattooed hand on his chest. "So modest. We both know that's not true. Your pretty body should be rotting in Purgatory by now, but no, you've found a way to resurrect yourself. You wouldn't have gotten the help of your little necromancer friend now, would you?"

"*No*, he has nothing to do with this. None of them do."

Dimitri hummed. "It would be very interesting if you were lying and something happened to that sweet little family of his."

"What did you do with them!?"

He raised his hand in his defense. "Nothing, yet. They are just fine. Locked away somewhere safe, don't you worry. I have my best demons looking in on them, just in case something goes wrong."

I opened my mouth to speak, but he wasn't finished. "Something tells me that you have an inkling to save them and perhaps we can work something out. You just have to show me that spectacular power."

"My hybrid powers?"

"Yes, yes that luminous explosion of light and dark. That masterpiece of havoc that you possess..."

I interrupted him, wanting to break through his magic and break his neck. "You want to destroy Heaven's Gate, turn it into a demonic free for all? Well, why don't you just fucking do it yourself!"

He lifted his eyebrows, pushing out his bottom lip in thought. "I could, honestly, I could. It isn't much fun to achieve that kind of success by myself.

Even so, my father and Lucifer are very adamant that I don't cause too much of a disturbance between our realms. Simply coming and destroying everything wouldn't look good in their eyes, but that doesn't mean it can't happen." He reached out and ran his hand across my cheek. I shuffled away, sneering at him. He clucked his tongue. "You are a sought after prize, pretty girl. Telling my father that I have the Soul Seether alive and well, while also telling him she was made to submit to her hybrid powers by the very angels she so stupidly trusted. Ah, it's going to be a wonderful story."

The smell of blood and burning flesh filled my nostrils again and I nearly gagged before I responded. "You haven't gloated to your father about this already?"

"No, it would be in poor judgment to tell him and Lucifer himself that you have achieved this great hybrid power without seeing it first-hand while I have you here. They will be thrilled to know that we will be able to take what those angels thought would be a weapon for them and use it to destroy them. My father can't say no to something like that. I can go in hellhounds blazing as long as you burn it all down around us. Lucifer himself wouldn't be able to say no to you being aligned with the Princes and Daughters of Hell."

He said everything like it was so matter-of-fact. Like it was all set in stone, as if I didn't have a say.

"You are out of your fucking mind if you think I'm going to go along with this pathetic plan. A pathetically ill thought out plan makes sense for a pathetic—" I felt the sting of his palm hitting my cheek, silencing the rest of my words. I stumbled back, instinctively wanting to raise my hand to my face, but the burning at my wrists had me keeping them in place.

I blinked a few times as my mouth dropped open. He hit me. I had been put in fighting arenas when Lilith needed some amusement and I'd been struck while causing my own fights when I was bored in Purgatory, but this had never happened. Surprisingly, I realized in that instant that Lilith had never slapped me before; that seemed too small and simple for her.

If I thought about all the torture she'd put me through, it didn't measure up, but the way my cheekbone throbbed...I didn't know anymore.

He took in a sharp breath as if he had just released some much needed tension he had been harboring. He pointed his finger at me, the tattoos there pulsing as if they too had some darkness to emit. "Lilith wanted to make you a pet for her bidding. I want to make you an equal, yet I can't do that unless I know that you've become worth all my efforts." He flicked his wrist, his deep red magic releasing itself from my wrists.

I tentatively relaxed my wrists, the painful burn gone as I swiveled them around to gain feeling. What the fuck was he doing? In such a small space, I could wind up hurting myself, but right now that didn't matter. I needed to conjure up everything I had—

"I forgot to make something clear." Dimitri placed his hand into his pocket, casually shrugging his shoulder. "You do anything to hurt me, plan to use those delicious powers to heroically save yourself, I would think about refraining."

My fingers twitched, aching from the shear strain I felt holding in what I knew I could release.

"You do something as stupid as that, well, your necromancer friend can be expecting his family's head's sent to him soon after. Contingency plans and all that. And with me gone, there will be no reason to hold back on erupting the entirety of Hell on that place you love so much." His voice settled into a whisper. "Just think, you saved yourself, just to watch all the people who thought better of you get mutilated."

Dimitri gave me a small smile that was filled with so much fake sympathy. "You can make it simple. You can show me that power and we can keep that castle they have intact so you can still hold onto some memories. I'll even let you keep that demon friend of yours alive so you won't be lonely, and perhaps I'll even let the necromancer keep his family, hmm? How does that sound..."

I rubbed my lips together, mulling over my options. I didn't trust him or anything he offered. I wanted to burn him alive and see his insides seeping out from every orifice in his body, but I couldn't be hasty. I wanted to defend myself and show him that he was nothing, but

Dimitri wasn't the type that made threats for fun. If he could pop into Heaven's Gate and whisk me away, there was nothing in my mind that assumed that he wouldn't make good on his words at this very moment.

"I can't."

Dimitri narrowed his eyes at me, skeptical. "What do you mean?"

I shook my head. "What you saw…what made you come and get me, that was a one time thing. It was spontaneous. I have no idea how I did it." The lies rolled off my tongue easily.

The Son of Hell hummed, considering me. "No idea?"

"This is harder to nail down than I thought, so maybe I'm not good enough to be your…" I almost choked on the word, "queen."

Dimitri sighed, his green eyes sparkling with a kind of newly found delight. "Oh, no, sweetheart. Those angels just didn't know what they were doing and that witchy queen they have, don't get me started…" He ran his hand through his hair, the pieces that were out of place, suddenly back to being perfect. "I will get it out of you by any means necessary. You did it once, no reason you can't do it again. I promise I'm an excellent motivator."

"But you won't…"

Dimitri stood in front of me, bending his knees a bit so his face was inches from mine. "Believe me while you are here, I can still fuck with your little friends while we wait. No big messes, but just enough to satisfy me. You think I still can't taste that pitiful angel's blood—"

I shoved him with both my hands, but all he did was laugh. I balled my hands into fists at my sides, feeling warmth in my palms that I desperately wanted to stop. "Just leave him out of this! Has Lilith somehow decided that you can be in charge now?" It was amazing to me how I wanted to be faced with the Queen of Darkness right now and not with an obsessive Son of Hell.

"She's *around*. It didn't sit right with me, what you said about me acting like Lilith was in charge of me, how it seemed like I was the one answering to her. It made me think and well, the woman has fucked up with you endlessly, but she made you what you are so I will still involve her. She just has no say, which is honestly how it always should have been. It is quite a shame when we put our trust in the wrong people." He raised his shoulders as if he was done for the day. "I think you'll like the solitude here. It will give you time to think. No distractions from useless boys that can offer you nothing. You should be grateful I'm offering you a chance to redeem yourself."

I nearly growled. "You are fucking insane if you believe I'll ever be grateful." I snuck a look down to where he was missing a limb. "I think you should be grateful I didn't remove your other hand. At least you have something to help please you during all your obviously lonely nights."

He snarled and quickly wrapped his hand around my throat, throwing me up against the nearby stone wall. He pressed his fingers against the sides of my neck, his palm crushing my windpipe. His eyes raged from their bright green to a bright red. Even with one hand, he was still strong and lifted me off the ground, scraping my back against the wall. He brought me forward just to slam me backwards again.

I gasped for air, clawing at his hands. I wanted to fight back, but his earlier threat echoed along my mind. Steam and red shadows pulsed from his hand and I bit my own tongue feeling the burning at my throat. My skin was on fire and my throat was screaming for oxygen. I felt his lips at my ear as he eased the flaming heat at my neck. "I adore you with everything I have, but if you think I won't make you regret all the things you've put me through then I suggest you think again."

He released me without another thought and I collided with the ground, my throat hurting from the desperate gasps for air. I reached up and touched my neck, my skin felt raw and burnt.

I tried to clear my throat but that hurt just as much, but I had to know something. My voice was hoarse when I spoke again. "What if I don't?"

"Hmm?" Dimitri was already opening the door, completely forgetting that he'd just strangled me.

"What if I achieve what you want, but I don't want to destroy things?"

Dimitri let out a low chuckle as he turned around, opening the door as he moved. "Dani, you try to kill me, everyone hurts. You refuse my offer, everyone hurts. In the end there is only you alone with your thoughts making what should be the easiest decision, but like I said, you take your time and I'll have my fun while we wait." He closed the door behind him as he left, but I heard his voice through the opening in the door. "You have caused far too much damage to that realm for anyone to want to come and help you, so consider that fact while you are pining for a way out."

I pressed my back to the wall, wincing as I swallowed. I pressed my fingertips to my cheek, closing my eyes. I held onto the only thing I had at the moment. He was wrong. I had people wanting to help me, wanting to find me.

I looked around and considered where I was. This wasn't a place where people were found. This was a place where demons were tortured until the outside world, the realm, forgot about them. I swallowed roughly again, shaking off the thought.

I had people wanting to find me. I couldn't forget that.

18
NICK

I opened my eyes, the instant harsh lightning causing me to close them again. I slowly opened them again, adjusting to the sudden change. My head was pounding and I was hyper aware of each breath I took and the pain in my chest with every exhale. I realized that I was staring at the ceiling of whatever room I was in, and my head was laying on a pillow that could only be described as featherlike. I flattened my hands at my sides feeling a mattress underneath me. I was in a bed, I knew that much, but it felt way too much like the kinds of beds you find at an infirmary. I moved my eyes from side to side, searching for something that could give me any indication of where I was.

"Oh, it's about fucking time." I heard Elise near one side of the room.

I heard a chair scoot back and then a head of blonde hair filled my view. "How you feeling?"

I reached up, running my hand over my face. "What do you mean? How am I feeling?"

"Yeah, you—you kind of passed out from a panic attack. Natalia and Xander brought you to this cool little healing spot so that you would be more…" Reese trailed off, pressing his lips together.

I closed my eyes tightly, not really understanding. I opened them again, staring into his concerned hazel eyes. "A panic attack? Why would I…"

Beetee tentatively stepped up to my side, so that she could place her fingers gently on my arm. "Yeah, about Dani and Dimitri…"

"Beetee, shush!" Reese shooed her away. The pink haired demon widened her eyes, a look of regret forming on her face.

It only took a few moments, but it was like my mind replayed the last time I'd seen Dani all over again. The date, the library, and when I'd left her to go to Reese's room for just a few minutes—

Fuck, fuck, fuck.

I shot up from the mattress, my head spinning instantly. I pushed through the mild nausea, nearly kicking Reese out of the way when I swung my legs over the side. They couldn't really expect me to sit here and not go out and find her. I couldn't sit here and have her think that I wasn't running around breathless trying to bring her back.

I got up from the bed, but both my arms were caught by Reese's hands. "Slow down, Nick. Just breathe."

"I can breathe just fucking fine." I shoved his hands off of me, shouldering him out of the way. Beetee fast-walked past me to open the door, closing it behind her.

Reese snaked his hand around my arm, pulling me back. "You won't be if you don't stop and take a minute to wake the hell up."

I ripped my arm away from him and turned on my heels so that we were face to face. "I really don't need to be coddled right now. What I *need* is to find my girlfriend." The label rolled off my tongue like it was always meant to be there and that fact alone hurt my heart even more.

"What you *need* to do is sit the fuck down, so we can talk to you." Elise stepped up to me, the look on her face cool and collected.

"I would think you of all people would want to head in there magic blazing. You care about Dani just as much as I do," I argued, leaning my head down so that she heard every word I said. I honestly didn't give a fuck if she kneed me in my balls right now. I wanted to get out of here.

Elise let out a soft laugh. "I would love to fuck some shit up, you are right. I am also someone who just saw you hyperventilate and pass out thirty minutes ago, so personally I don't think you are even remotely prepared to fight for your girl's honor

I rolled my eyes. "Fine, you don't have to come with me, I'll go by myself. So, move." I pushed her out of my way, wobbling a bit on my feet before heading towards the door.

"Nick, *fuck*, just stop," Reese pleaded, the frustrated tone in his voice hitting me for a moment, nearly making me turn around. I almost did, but then I felt a searing pain in my ankle. That pain traveled up to my calf, my knee and then to my thigh. I stumbled, hissing at the sudden burning, but then I couldn't feel my leg at all. I tried to take another step, but fell forward on my hands and knees, looking back over my shoulder.

"You could have been nicer about it, you fucking psycho." Reese stared daggers at Elise, who swung her tail behind her. The tip of the magical appendage dripped with the inky black venom that she used to temporarily paralyze.

Elise ignored him. "Now be nice or I'll make sure the other leg matches, alright?"

I tried to move my leg, but it wouldn't budge. I managed to flip myself over so I could sit on the floor. The door opened, revealing Xander and Beetee.

I looked up at Xander, whose teal eyes squinted down at me confused. The last time I'd really seen him was when he'd cleaned everyone up after our time in Purgatory. I knew Reese had gone to see him multiple times about his leg, stating that angelic nurses had nothing on the kind of medicine Xander made.

The Enchanter scratched his head. "Didn't I leave you on the bed last time I was here?"

I let out a huff but didn't answer him. Reese decided to do it for me. "He wants to go to Purgatory."

"Right now?" Xander asked, crossing his arms over his chest.

Elise and Reese both nodded. The fact that they seemed like a united front against me was scary enough despite everything else going on.

Xander hummed, squatting down and taking my face in his hands. "I mean, let me look you over first and then well, I can't advise you to go gallivanting off to be the hero we all already know you are, but I can't very well stop you either." He placed his hand on my chest, and I felt an odd vibration as a pulse of color came from his hand. "How do you feel?"

"Like I've told them, I'm fine. I feel fine."

"Muscle soreness, any pains in your body, exhaustion?"

I shook my head, severely annoyed.

"Your chest feels fine, and I don't believe you hit your head on anything when you passed out, so no need to worry about injuries there. How about shaking or trembling?"

"Nope." I nearly popped the 'p' when I spoke, so fucking tired of this.

"Uh, Nick." I looked over at Reese who pointed toward my hand that was closest to Xander. I lifted my hand, bringing it to my face and watched as it shook slightly, twitching. My fingers flexed in tiny spurts, and I closed them into a fist.

"Look, that's nothing. It's just stupid aftereffects." I eyed Xander, running my shaky hand through my hair. He looked at me with a sense of understanding, but at the same time it was his job to look after people. "I feel fine. It's one little fucking slip. I'm allowed to do that, like I don't understand the big deal. It's one little panic attack." I felt like I was fighting in a losing battle.

Xander sighed. "Like I said, I can't stop you from doing what you want to do. But just take this." He pulled out a tiny bottle with a cork at the top. "It's a lavender blend. It will soothe you internally. It's pretty nasty going down, but it should help."

I took it from him, yanking out the cork and downing the liquid. I scrunched up my face, wishing the bitter taste would quickly subside.

Xander looked over his shoulder and nodded, swapping places with Beetee. She gave me a small smile as she fanned her neon pink dress around her so she could sit on the floor. "I know you want to save her; believe me we all do." Her voice was almost like a whisper. "I know I haven't known you all that long, but I have a pretty good assumption that you wouldn't want to go into something without all the information. Something so tiny could mean everything when it comes to getting her back. We would never keep you from her, but you are just as much of a priority to us as she is to you." Her lilac-colored eyes were almost imploring me to side with her.

I didn't know if it was whatever Xander had given me or the way Beetee spoke with a friendly softness, but I nodded. She reached over and pinched my leg.

"Ow, fuck."

She giggled. "It looks like you got feeling back."

Reese walked over, offering me his outstretched hand. Once I was off the ground, he steered me back to the bed, nearly forcing me to sit down. Xander clapped his hands together, pointing his thumb towards the door. "Should I go get Natalia?"

Elise swung her head towards him. "No. You and the witch have done enough, thanks." She gave him a forced smile and half assed wave.

Xander raised an eyebrow, but simply chuckled. "Feisty one, aren't you." It wasn't a question, just an observation. He winked over at Reese while he walked backwards towards the door. "Watch your leg in Purgatory. I didn't spend all that time healing you for nothing."

When he was gone, I dug my hand in my pocket, pulling out Reese's lucky arrowhead. His hazel eyes narrowed when I presented it to him. "I almost forgot to give you this."

He plucked the charm from my fingers, flipping it over in his palm. My best friend let out a heavy sigh. "Doesn't seem too important anymore." He let out a short joyless laugh as if everything that that arrowhead stood for was some kind of joke now. "Really don't know how lucky this thing is."

"Listen, you asked me to go get it for you and I did. No one could have assumed that Dimitri would blow everything to shit."

Reese slipped the charm into his pocket and rubbed the bridge of his nose. "I know, I know. I just know that if you didn't then everything would probably be different right now. Or maybe everything would be fucking worse, I don't know. I guess the only thing I really want to say right now is I'm sorry."

I tilted my head to the side, nudging his bicep with my fist. "The only person who needs to be sorry right now is Dimitri." I pointed at his pocket that held the arrowhead. "That thing still might have some luck in it, don't doubt it now. We'll need it for finding her in Purgatory."

Elise clucked her tongue. "Right…about that."

We both glanced over at her as she slid her eyes over to Beetee who was nervously biting her lower lip. After a moment of silence, I spoke. "About what?"

"Purgatory. We aren't going there."

"Of course we are," Reese argued, waving his hand at her dismissively.

Elise pointed her finger at him. "Good luck with that because you won't fucking find her."

My eyes narrowed and her words stung. "Well that's super fucking shitty of you to say."

"What she means is that she's not there," Beetee explained, her eyes not really looking at me. She almost looked as if she was too nervous to say anything else.

"That doesn't make any sense." I shook my head in disbelief.

Elise rubbed her forehead, letting out a frustrated sigh. "Oh yes it does. I would love to tell you that Dimitri has taken her back to Lilith and she's held up in some prison in her castle. I would be stupidly over-joyed to proudly tell you that very notion, but I can't because it would be a fucking lie. And it would be a waste of my fucking time to have you believe everything is that simple."

I licked my lips, reaching up and rubbing my finger along one of my eyebrows. "Then where is she?" My voice was steady but concerned.

Elise pressed her tongue into her cheek, her gray eyes piercing into my brown ones. She looked as if she knew exactly what she was going to say but my reaction was the thing holding her back. It was almost like she cared just a bit about my wellbeing. "She's in Hell."

"I'm sure being with Dimitri *is* hell, yes." Reese said, sarcastically, rolling his eyes. The air left my lungs when I considered what she said, what it meant. I swallowed the lump down into my throat and I could feel the nausea starting to build up. I felt myself wanting to nearly dry heave.

"I mean *literal* Hell, Blondie." She shook her head at him, but focused back on me.

My mouth felt dry, but I was able to form words as difficult as it was. "How do you know that?"

Elise crossed her arms over her chest and shrugged. "I've known Dimitri for longer than I'd like to admit and he's fucking pissed. You made him look like a fucking idiot in his own club, Dani took his hand and you faked him out with her death. He thought he was getting something promised to him by Lilith and he's now an embarrassed entitled piece of shit. His father runs the prison down there and what better way to keep your ex-girlfriend in line then to bring her home and make her wish she had respected you all along."

"So what? He's keeping her stowed away, nice and pretty, for what?" Reese asked, leaning against the bed.

Elise looked over at Beetee again who met her gaze and furiously started biting her fingernails. They both had this look of hesitation. "I told Dani a few days ago that that little blast of hers might have caused an issue. Something with that much power is hard to miss no matter what realm you're in. Clearly I was right." She looked up at the ceiling, groaning. "Dimitri isn't like Lilith though, that bitch wanted Dani to do all the work, but Dimitri....he sees her as an equal, a partner in destruction. He knows she can produce that kind of power now, so unfortunately I can't tell you what that means to him. If I know Dani at all, she'll fight against that asshole."

I rubbed the back of my neck. "Dimitri in his own sick way cares about her I guess, so maybe he's just hiding her away and that's it." The look in Elise's eyes sent a shudder down my back. It was almost like she cringed at my optimism.

"Hell is the kind of place that doesn't want fuck ups and mishaps unless Lucifer himself calls for it, hence why Dimitri hasn't caused a scene and the reason why nothing has happened since she's been gone.

Nothing has happened *here*, Nick, that doesn't mean nothing is happening over there."

"The fuck does that mean?" I said, jumping off the bed and turning my body to face her.

I heard Beetee clear her throat, running a shaky hand over the shaved side of her head. "There is a lot of chatter about Dimitri not being the…nicest. Especially when it comes to that place. Creatures get menacingly tortured there…"

"And since his father is letting him have a little more control in everything, Dimitri is usually the one calling all the shots. He puts on a really nice fucking façade I'll tell you that. Demons at that club worship him. While I love the idea of blood and torturing for the hell of it, Dimitri is just fucking cruel." Elise scoffed, looking off to the side as if a small memory ran through her mind, but then she blinked back over to me.

"The simple fact that those words came out of your mouth says a fucking lot." Reese ran both his hands through his hair, the blonde locks becoming a messy mop on his head.

My heart was pounding in my chest and I almost felt like I could hear it. I took small breaths, trying to steady my composure. My blood boiled when I'd seen him touch her at Leviathan as if he had the right and now my blood was boiling over thinking about him hurting her. My hands were shaking, but not from any sort of aftereffects, but from literal rage that coursed through my veins. I always saw myself as the type of person who fought when I needed to, became violent when it was called for, but right now I wanted more than just the typical violence.

I wanted him to suffer the kind of torture that Elise probably couldn't even dream up.

I pushed past her more than ready to storm out that door and have her take us straight to the pits of Hell. I would spend an eternity down there if it meant I would find her. I turned on my heels back to my friends. "You know how to get there?"

Elise gave me a look like I was stupid. "Of course I do."

I grabbed my portal key from around my neck, snatched her hand and placed the magical item in her palm. "Then take us there."

Elise closed the portal key in her fist and scrunched her mouth to one side. "You forget there are other people involved here Nicholas, like Garrett. You want to clue him in on the plan?"

I opened my mouth to speak but she cut me off. "I know you are very set on this rescue mission and I am with you one thousand percent. I am more than ready to obliterate his other hand at this point. I am ready to remove him and Lilith from this equation all together, but going there might cause a lot of backlash for this place you call your home. It may not mean anything to me, but from where I'm standing it's not fucking fair to just portal out of this room and leave them to their own devices."

Reese whistled. "Damn, it sounds like you actually care."

I could see her jaw tense and the way she ground her teeth together. "I fucking don't. I just don't want to come back here and you send your-self into another spiraling mess because you weren't thinking. You don't have to be forthcoming with that shithead Ariel, but all of these people have risked their fucking lives for you and for some odd reason care about you. Dani is strong and can hang on, even when it comes to Dimitri, or did you fucking forget that despite what Lilith likes to claim, I'm the one that taught her how to survive."

I pressed my lips together letting her scold me like I was a child. Maybe she was right. I had let Garrett cry on my shoulder and promised him that he would get a chance to collect his family. Natalia had been this enchanting rock holding us together most times and I wanted to just leave without any sort of acknowledgement or parting words to them.

Elise's voice filtered into my thoughts as she fiddled with the portal key in her hand. "In case you didn't remember, you nearly buckled and lost yourself in Purgatory due to everything you wouldn't say. Dimitri got a taste of your blood down there, so as scary as it seems he will always have some tiny connection to those deep seeded parts of you."

Reese raised an eyebrow. "Nick's been handling all of that. We've all made sure he's been good and he has."

Elise hummed, her words coming out sarcastically. "Oh yeah, I totally see that." She casually sniffed the air. "You wanna know what I smell on you, Nicholas?"

I furrowed my brow.

"Resentment."

"Ellie…." Beetee started, but Elise put her hand up to silence her.

Elise grabbed my chin and lightly shook my head. "Resentment is a nasty thing to hold onto Nick. Believe me, I know, I do it every fucking day, but I'm aware of it. I speak it into existence so it isn't something to use against me. The reason why all the sadness and pity ganged up on you in Purgatory is because you couldn't admit to yourself that they were a *part* of you. Resentment works the same way and if you think that Purgatory was bad, Hell will eat you alive if you walk in with that hefty fucking baggage looming over you. I'm honestly surprised Dimitri hasn't dug his demonic nails into your little brain by now and fucked around in there."

I looked over her shoulder at Reese who was looking at me, but then his hazel eyes flashed with silent understanding. His mouth gaped open and he scrubbed a hand down his face.

"What the fuck are you talking about? I don't resent anyone."

Elise cocked her head to the side. "Oh really? No one at all?"

"Elise just back off," Reese warned, moving around her and standing next to me.

Elise waved her hands in front of us as if she was done with this conversation and our attitudes. "All any of you guys have done is coddle him. You will be no good to any of us, especially Dani if you don't talk to your *father*. I don't think you are afraid of the story or the knowledge you've learned. I think you're afraid of what it all means. For your future, for the past you can't remember. You think you had it all figured out and now it's all fucked up and you don't like that. You. Are. Afraid."

My blood ran cold and my shoulders stiffened. "I…I'm not…I don't…"

"You need to run into Hell with the idea that nothing is holding you back. When your father came to Oculus and explained things to us, it sounded like he told you a story that you ultimately gave no feedback on. You didn't yell at him, you didn't cry, you didn't do anything, you just stormed out and removed him from your life. You don't go into places like Hell with a small inkling that you might not make it out when you have unfinished business. If *you* die there, you don't have your pretty soul moved to Heaven; you'll go to Limbo because you have no idea what else to do and you won't get a chance to do it again." Her tone was filled with agitation.

"You can't make me do anything. You can't push me to do something I'm not ready for, that's not fair." I wanted my words to make a statement but all they did was bounce off her guarded exterior as if she knew that's exactly what I would say in retaliation.

"No I can't, but you can sure as hell believe that I'm not going with you and neither is Beetee."

Beetee let out a tiny gasp.

"So you just plan to leave Dani to fend for herself!"

"No, you fucking idiot. If you go there assuming you'll be fine, you won't save her either way. We will all be stuck taking care of you. I refuse to have a repeat of Purgatory and you honestly shouldn't want that. You want me to *trust* you? Have faith in you as your people like to say? Then do what I fucking say!"

"You want me to tell you that I wish my dad had told me the truth? You want me to tell you that I feel like I've been lied to by the one person that I trusted more than anything in the entire realm? You want me to say that sometimes I've considered never speaking to him again and then hated myself the minute it crossed my mind? There I said it!" I heard my voice start to shake and I didn't feel better saying it. I thought I would feel better.

Why didn't I feel better?

Elise put her hands over her face, letting out slow breaths. "Your honesty is riveting but this isn't like Purgatory where just speaking it into existence is all it takes. You felt all the things *yourself* while you were there, it was all internal. You had to forgive yourself." She pressed her index finger into my chest. "Everything you just said is all about someone else. It needs to be directed at *someone else*. That is the only way it will attempt to resolve itself. That is the only way you are making it in Hell."

I ran my hands roughly through my hair and turned around, catching Beetee's eye. She looked sympathetic but it also looked like she agreed with Elise.

"You should really give him more credit. You want people to just be ready on your timeline Elise and that's a bit fucked up," Reese insisted.

"He isn't going to ever be *ready*. You know your best friend better than any of us and he is going to put it off. Please, Blondie look me in my face and tell me I'm wrong."

I waited for Reese to say the things he always did, find some way around her statements, but all I did was hear him sigh. I fucking hated this. I hated knowing that in a way, I was being forced to do something, but on the other hand I understood why. I wanted to find Dani and bring her back to me, keep her safe. There was a tiny part of me that almost wanted her there when I decided to speak to my father, but then I would second guess and think that it would be better if I went alone. I would wish that I had never questioned him about anything and been left in the dark. I had even considered leaving things and just moving on, attempting to carry on a relationship without ever bringing my mother up ever again.

My head hurt from my thoughts and my skin felt overheated. Hands were on my arms and my body was being turnt so that I was facing Elise yet again. She didn't look any less irritated but something about the look in her eyes told me that she was forcing herself to soften just a tiny bit. "I am going to say this and you are going to never *ever* fucking ask me about it."

I waited patiently as she pressed her lips together, tucking a piece of her dark hair behind her ear. "I know what it's like to have a less than great parental figure and I am more than aware of what a major fuck up in that department looks like. I stare my resentment in the fucking face and it runs and hides from me. Let me be super clear when I say that your father is far better than great. I hardly believe in second chances, Nicholas, but in this case and for the sake of saving my…*friend*, I can make an exception." She scratched at her neck as if admitting that Dani was her friend would give her a rash.

I peeked over at Reese who looked just as surprised as me. He lifted one his shoulders in a shrug. "You know my parents aren't the greatest but I've owned that. Do I wish it was better? Yes. But I've come to terms with it. I think it's time you come to terms with this too. If we cry, we cry, right?"

I let out a choked laugh. Beetee crept up to my side. "As much as you think she's being a bully, which she kind of is…" The pink haired demon side-eyed Elise who rolled her eyes, "but she isn't wrong. Maybe you can go there and knock on the door, if you want to turn back then turn back. If he answers the door and you can't do it then, okay, you took that step. It's just time you took any type of step in general."

Elise dangled my portal key in front of me. "We all sat around and heard your father's hot little heart break over your past and your mother. You are allowed to be upset with the man, you are even allowed to hate him, but what you aren't allowed to do is hold him accountable for the actions of someone else. Your mother made the decision she did. He was honoring what she wanted because he *loved* her Nick. Take pride that you came from a fucking man who honors his word even at the expense of his son's trust."

Her words caused my breath to catch in my throat. My hands shook as I grabbed the key from her. The chain swung in my grasp as I tried to control my trembling fingers. My mind started replaying the last thing Dani had said about my father.

You don't have to forgive him entirely but go scream at him, stomp around your house, something…. he's given you all his love and attention for twenty-four years, you owe him at least some of yours back.

I was doing this because I was in love with her and even before she had exceeded in learning her powers, she was worried that I would falter and she wouldn't be able to help me. I gave a quick look around the room at people worried about the same thing. It wasn't that they thought that I couldn't do it, it was simply that they knew I *could* but I was the only one who needed convincing.

"Do you need us to go with you?" Reese asked.

I shook my head. "No, just umm, let everyone know to be ready when I get back. We'll meet outside of Natalia's, okay?"

He nodded, along with Beetee. Elise wiggled her fingers in a goodbye gesture.

I made my portal and held my breath the entire time.

I landed near the back door, outside my house. I let my eyes roam over the exterior wanting to take in everything I hadn't seen in what felt like forever. It had been only about a month, but this was probably the longest amount of time we'd gone without speaking. I rolled my shoulders, taking in a deep breath.

One deep breath in, one deep breath out.

I heard voices inside and I recognized them easily. It felt like a weight on my heart. I rubbed my hands together, feeling how sweaty they were. I could turn back now, but something in my gut told me not to. I was doing this for the sake of my own mental state and my life when going to Hell, but I was also doing this for—*me*. I was doing this for the relationship I legitimately wanted to mend, but I was afraid.

Elise was right. I was *afraid*.

I curled my hand into a fist and without thinking I knocked on the wooden door. I heard footsteps on the other side. I realized how fucking late it was and I started to feel like this was a mistake.

"Coming!" I heard Daya yell.

I counted backwards from ten in my head, but didn't even get a chance to get to one when she opened the door and I was met with her stunned face. Her shiny dark hair was pulled over one shoulder and her nose ring twinkled in the tiny lights my father displayed no matter what time of year it was. Her olive skin looked smooth and untouched with age, except for the crinkles around her eyes.

Her shocked expression morphed into something else. Her eyes started to water but the way she smiled looked as if she was trying to hold the moisture from leaving her bottom lids. She placed her hand on her chest and I had a feeling my own heart was beating faster than hers. Her mouth moved but no words came out.

"Daya, who is it?" I heard my father say and I started to chew on the inside of my cheek.

Daya simply looked at me, as if she was asking me for permission. If this was what I wanted.

"I want to talk to my dad." It sounded like I had whispered it, but I wasn't sure. I wasn't sure of anything at the moment.

My father's girlfriend cleared her throat, making sure her voice didn't sound like she was about to burst into tears. "Maurice, it's Nick."

She stepped aside to let me in, but not before opening her arms to embrace me in the biggest hug. Everything looked exactly the same and little by little, the ambiance of this place I called home started to settle against me. I heard footsteps that I knew well enough and I immediately looked down at the floor.

"What are you talking…" My father's words were cut off when he stepped out of the hallway and into the living room. I didn't know what it was, but I instantly felt myself wanting to cry. Something wrapped around me, almost like a familiar comfort, but nothing was touching me. My eyes were still towards the ground as my heart hammered against my chest.

One deep breath in, one deep breath out.

Inch by inch I let my eyes float upwards, until they were looking into a face that looked just like mine but older. They looked at familiar brown eyes, a mustache that was always trimmed, and a look of pure stunned joy at my presence. His lips pulled into a small smile.

Mine did the same before I opened my mouth. "Hi, Dad."

I knew it had likely only been a few hours, but it was something about this place that felt like it had already been an eternity. There was an odd type of muted sadness to my surroundings and it made me work even harder to not give into it. So much was riding on my ability to keep it together and withhold my powers. If this was an entirely different situation I would have eradicated Dimitri and everyone else helping him, but from his threats I now knew that my once hasty behavior came with consequences. Those consequences weren't just things I could shrug and mutter some noncommittal *I'm sorry* towards.

No, those consequences were bigger than myself. I bent my legs, bringing them to my chest as I rested my head on my knees. I thought back to Nick in Purgatory and how he fought so hard to keep his shit together even though everything inside of him was disintegrating. He saw the bigger picture and put himself last, which ultimately could have cost him his life. I tried to think about what he would say to me right now.

Would it be something similar to what I told him?

Would he think up something just for me, to get me through this?

Maybe I didn't need him to say anything at all…maybe I could just picture him coming in here with his heroic attitude.

I didn't particularly love the idea of *needing* Nick to save me. I didn't like the idea of *anyone* needing to save me. I could hold it together. Dimitri had to maintain his destructive boundaries unless he wanted the wrath of Lucifer on his ass. I had yet to meet the man, but he didn't seem like a fun time when he was angry. I thought about Nick's mind and the tiny threads of darkness I still felt there, the pieces that lingered.

He was hardly waking up in a sweaty mess anymore and he was doing better with his breathing techniques and just handling everything that I didn't really think to bring up something I'd noticed. The hollow piece of him, the place where his father should reside was thick with an essence I could only label as resentment. It felt sad and betrayed but not in a hateful sense, it was like it wanted to bust out of its place inside of him and come to terms with whatever was holding it back, but the opportunity never presented itself.

It wasn't necessarily a debilitating thing if it was handled properly, but since Nick had never even attempted to talk to his father, I would say it was *never* handled at all. I wondered if Dimitri could sense that. Was it that potent for him to latch onto and fuck with him all the way from Hell?

I should have said something….

I put my hand up to my face and focused. Tiny golden sparks flickered at my fingertips and skinny wisps of black curled around my knuckles as if they were greeting each other.

I heard footsteps outside the stone door, quickly ceasing any sort of power I had on display. I swiveled around on the floor so I could look at whoever was coming inside. My face scrunched up in distaste when Dimitri entered the room, but he wasn't alone.

I felt her presence before I saw her. Lilith glided in after him, tilting her head to the side when she noticed me on the floor. She looked almost like she was trying to figure out where she had gone wrong. Her long flowing dress bellowed around her feet, the silk texture more than likely collecting dust as she stood there.

"I thought you might like to see a friendly face." Dimitri gave me a smile as if his gesture was anything but annoying.

My eye twitched at the term *friendly* but I never looked away from her.

"He really does have you down here, doesn't he?" Her long platinum blonde hair flowed past her shoulders, moving as she shifted her stance. "I thought he was joking."

Dimitri glanced over at me and grimaced at my silent response. "It is rude to not say thank you when I'm bringing you visitors."

It was my turn to grimace. My shoulders tensed when Lilith started to walk up to me, squatting down when she was closer than I would have liked. "I thought you were dead. I thought that stupid boy of yours killed you and I dreamed about his agonizing suffering everyday since. I did wonder if he was wallowing in self pity thinking about what he'd done, but no, of course you are *still* here. My resilient girl." She reached out, her blood red fingernails grazing my neck. I hissed when they made contact with the raw skin from Dimitri's burn.

"Your disobedience has gotten you into so much trouble, hasn't it." It wasn't a question and even if it had been I wouldn't have been in the mood to offer up an answer.

"It was just a little warning. That's all." Dimitri cracked his neck. I flicked my eyes up to him to find him fiddling with the cuffs of his button-down shirt.

Lilith moved her hand to my cheek, the area still tender from where his palm had struck me. She pressed her fingertip into my cheekbone and her eyes sparkled at the way I winced. "I forgive you for hiding from us and thinking you could live some life you think you deserve."

I narrowed my eyes at her. "Fuck you."

Dimitri tutted. "You should be kinder to someone willing to offer you something we all know you want."

"I don't *want* anything from you," I said in a steady voice. My throat aching just a little with each word.

Lilith smiled at me. "Oh, I'm sure that's not true. Dimitri and I came to an understanding while you were playing hide and seek. And once we saw your beautiful display of power, well even though I was quite upset with you, I knew the perfect thing to get you to trust us again."

Dimitri came up behind her, placing his only hand on her shoulder. I noticed the Queen of Darkness stiffened a small bit. It was an odd gesture, one I'd never seen her display before. She exuded the same power she always had, but it was almost like I was seeing what Dimitri had been talking about. He'd taken into consideration my words about it looking as if Lilith called the shots, made the rules and outranked him.

The fact that he was gracious enough to include her in this at all was beyond my realm of understanding. Then I blinked, considering that he still needed her in some way. Maybe as a scapegoat, or maybe he actually thought I still had any desire at all to please her and bend over backwards for her attention. I nearly cringed at that thought.

There was something about the way he held her shoulder, like he was constantly reminding her of who was in charge and that her stance in this realm could be revoked with a snap of his fingers.

"I talked Lilith into bestowing a gift to you. You do remember how much I loved giving you gifts, sweetheart." He snapped his fingers and she opened her palm out in front of her.

Ribbons of darkness and clouds of gray smoke came from her hand. Something started to form, the smoke became bigger as the ribbons spun around it. I furrowed my eyebrows, irritated and annoyed at this.

"I don't fucking—" I started but Dimitri shushed me, placing a finger to his lips.

I was prepared to tell him where he could put his fucking finger when the smoke melted away and the ribbons unthreaded themselves from one another to reveal this 'gift'. My hands trembled at the item staring back at me. No, not just an item. A weapon.

My weapon.

My dagger.

I never took my eyes off the curved pointed end, the razor slits down the middle, the brown leather hilt that always felt so natural in my palm. I felt my fingers twitch wanting to feel the indentation of my name along my fingertips. It looked exactly the same, nothing was out of place and it was crazy how I still felt the connection toward it.

"What the hell is this?" I asked, my eyes unmoving.

"A little incentive, pretty girl." Dimitri knelt down so that he was right next to me. They were boxing me in and right now, I didn't care.

Lilith removed her hand, but the dagger floated in place. "I remember the twinkle of mischief in your eye when I gave you that dagger. Don't you remember how powerful you felt? Imagine what that will feel like along with those hybrid powers. You would be unstoppable." She flicked her fingers forward and the dagger swayed over to me. I kept my hands at my sides, but everything in me wanted to snatch it up and let every single ounce of power she'd given it mix with mine. "Imagine what you could do if something you used to enhance your darkness could handle all that light as well."

Dimitri lightly dusted my curls from my shoulder, running his fingers along my neck. "Do you really think those angels in that less than perfect realm would let you be who you are? Do you think they deserve to go on hiding behind all those fake smiles and deceit? We demons don't try to be something we're not. You'd be free to wield this weapon as you wish." He leaned into me as if he was inhaling my scent. "They would make you work for their respect but you would never get it. That is no way to live, especially for someone of your stature. The only thing I desire from you is a simple show of power and we can make *them* work to respect *you*."

I felt his breath on my neck and I tried to imagine the picture he painted. I wanted power and I wanted the dagger that gave me comfort. I liked the power of compulsion, but it wasn't my torture of choice. Most lesser demons who watched me loved when I used it and so I did but....the dagger wasn't all that I *was* though.

I didn't want to expand Hell, but I also didn't want Heaven's Gate to be run by a tyrannical dictator. I didn't want to be used and abused for what I could do by anyone, not Ariel and not by *fucking* Dimitri.

My hands stopped shaking. I felt the presence of both their bodies and I had to hold back my vomit when I became more aware of how close Dimitri was to my skin. I turned slightly toward him. "I appreciate your offer, but kindly go *fuck* yourself." I managed to keep my light at bay as I shot out shadows at the Son of Hell, causing him to go flying at the wall.

The dagger disappeared from my view as Lilith moved away from me, standing up straight. Dimitri growled as he shoved away from the wall, stomping over to me and striking my other cheek with the back of his hand. I instinctively went to grab hold of my hurt cheek, but he grabbed my hair, pulling so hard I felt a burning sensation in my scalp. He tilted my head back so I was forced to look at him. His face started to distort, melting away into the one he was born with.

His green eyes that turned up in the corners started to sink in, almost to nothing but black holes. Dimitri's skin started to decay into a gray color and sparks of red and black flames feathered off him. They singed my skin each time they made contact.

"You would do well to be reminded of what is at stake when you decide to be disrespectful." His voice was hollower now, less casual. It was almost like an echo and it vibrated through every part of my body. He pulled my head back harder and tears started to form, but I didn't let them fall.

I felt the tingles of warmth at my fingers wanting to come and protect me.

No, no. Fucking no.

I held on while the tension and pressure at my head increased.

"Dimitri, your father is waiting." Lilith, who looked unfazed by his transformation, caught his attention.

He tightened his hold on my hair, but then swung me backwards so that my head landed on the stone. I heard a crack and there were small stars behind my eyes. I blinked rapidly, clearing my vision as I grabbed the side of my head. I pulled my hand back, noticing that blood stained my fingers.

My vision was becoming less blurry, noticing that Dimitri was finger-combing his hair back into place. His tattoos were all back in the same spots and his green eyes pierced into mine. "Ah, yes. I forgot.

Planting important seeds for when everything comes to fruition." He winked at me as if nothing had just transpired between us.

Before he could keep my attention for long, I looked over at Lilith, rounding up shadows in my hand, thinking that if I couldn't hurt precious Dimitri then he wouldn't mind me causing some damage to the first person to fuck me over.

My shadows were halted when he spoke, "before I forget, let me remind you, sweetheart, that lives are at stake." He waved his hand in the middle of the room and a dark flat circle formed, almost like a portal. There was nothing but black until something began showing up. There were faces, three distinct faces.

It was Garrett's family.

Leah, Yuri and Jasmine. Their faces looked dirty and wherever they were appeared to be cold and damp. It was likely another area of this place, but just further below. Jasmine's face looked blotchy as if she'd been crying and Leah had Yuri tucked under arm, soothing him.

"You said you just had people keeping an eye on them," I accused, tearing my eyes away from them.

Dimitri sighed. "I do. I never said I didn't have them in a safe place for safe keeping. You never asked and I don't just offer up information without reason, sweetheart. I truly don't like hurting others who don't deserve it. This sweet little family could live in peace in the world I'd like you to help build. I don't have anything against Enchanters, by all means they are the true victims of those angelic beasts." He gazed over at the magical screen and shook his head as if he was visibly distraught. His green eyes narrowed when he looked at me again. "You try to move against me with your cute little shadows again and I'll slit one of their throats in front of their mother. Lucky for you I'll let you choose which one and if you decide you can't choose then I'll just kill them both."

He sauntered over to me, placing his hand underneath my chin, tilting my face up. I tried to pull away, but his grip just got tighter. "And if by some chance you get out of this after that, have fun explaining to your necromancer that you couldn't behave enough to save his children. You see Dani, like I said, you make the wrong move, everyone hurts.

You make no moves, people *still* hurt." He pushed my face away and turned around, preparing to leave.

Lilith watched me, a look of pity in her eyes. "And you thought I was bad. Stupid, stupid girl."

I reached toward the place where my head throbbed, pulling my hand back and seeing more blood coating my palm. "The only stupid thing I've done was think you ever gave a shit about me. You wanted to create something that obeyed you and did your bidding, yet all you've done is made me *hate* you."

She laughed. "Hate is a powerful feeling. I would lean into it, I'm sure all those angels who don't understand you do. The ones who see you as a threat, the ones that see you as a *monster*."

My hands curled into fists at that word. That wasn't what I was.

"A beautiful monster if I might add. Stubborn, but beautiful," Dimitri added before removing the visual of Garrett's family.

Lilith hummed, leveling her glare at me. She unfolded her hand towards me, streams of dark magic enveloped me. A whooshing sound filled my head and sounded loud in my ears. I tried to cover my ears, apply pressure to the sides of my head to make it stop. "Without me and my efforts, Dimitri would not have you. You would just be a pathetic girl dying by a tree in the woods if it wasn't for me. You would just be a fragile angel, nothing special. You let those soft creatures get into your head, so let me remind you that I will always be the evidence of how far you've come and sadly from the looks of it, you haven't come far at all." She looked around the dirty, stone covered cell. The dirt caking the corners and the blood dried up on the floor.

Dimitri cleared his throat, causing her to stop. I felt instantly exhausted and more of a throbbing sensation in my head.

I licked my lips, taking a deep breath. "I *used* to admire you. Now I feel sorry that you feel the need to follow behind a man whose ego is big enough to fill this entire prison." I spat back, watching as her lip curled.

Dimitri opened the door for her before she could say another word. "Rest up, pretty girl. If you can't be motivated by *things*, I'll just have to be a bit more forceful now, won't I? We will figure out a way to get that power out of you." He turned on his heels to begin walking out of the cell, but then he turned back, rubbing his chin. "I do wonder how that angel with the feeble tasting blood is doing. I should pay that mind of his a visit, nothing drastic."

My hand felt hot, like it wanted to create a giant ball of power like it had in Natalia's training room. I dug my nails in my palm so hard, I thought I might rip through my own flesh. "Just leave him…"

Dimitri wrinkled his nose and shushed me. "Unlike your previous advisor, I won't need to rip out your soul to get what I want, trust me. I need you fully intact. Now your spirit, well *that* I am willing to break."

20
NICK

There was this awkward silence that surrounded us and I almost feared swallowing down the lump in my throat, thinking it would be too loud. My father was dressed casually as if he and Daya were planning a night to just sit on the couch and talk about each other's days. My eyes left my father to dart around the room quickly, seeing that nothing had changed and for some odd reason that had me breathing easier.

I heard the floor creak as my father took a step towards me and I didn't know why, but I caught myself taking a small step backwards with a small shake of my head. I knew he wanted to hug me or even just take my arms within his grasp to look at me, but I didn't want that right now. My father stood his ground, giving me a shallow nod as if he understood.

"Mom, do you still have my…" Alex, Daya's daughter, asked trotting down the stairs. Her words ceased when I came into view. Her whiskey-colored eyes that were identical to her mother's grew wider as she did a small jump of excitement, darting in my direction. "Thank the realms! Oh my god!" Her arms flung around me and the momentum at which her body met mine caused me to stumble backwards.

I let out a soft chuckle, hugging her back. "I missed you too."

"Did you come here for the latest midnight snack in history?" She nodded over to the window that showcased how bleak and dark the sky was.

"Umm…no." My eyes drifted to my father whose face remained neutral even though I knew he was anxious to speak with me.

Alex scrunched her mouth up in thought. "Why the fuck else would you come here so late? I mean we haven't seen you for nearly a month, so all I'm saying is…"

"Alex, honey, why don't you and I go upstairs?" Daya grabbed her daughter's arm, casting an apologetic look over her shoulder at me.

Alex threw her mother a confused expression. "Upstairs, for what?"

Daya let out a long sigh, dragging her daughter behind her as they crossed the room. "Because I said so." She stopped to kiss my father on the cheek, likely saying encouraging words in his ear before walking past him.

Alex looked from my father to me and then back again, her mouth forming into an 'o'. She tugged her arm away from Daya and wagged her finger at her. "Why didn't you just say they were going to have a father/son moment? Stop making things so dramatic, Mom." Daya rolled her eyes, giving me a reassuring smile before she followed her daughter out of the room and up the stairs to the second floor.

"Would you like to sit down?" I jumped a little at the sound of my father's voice. It was steady, but there was a small sense of hesitation in his tone. It was like I was a wounded animal and he didn't want to startle me.

He waved his hand over at the couch and I nodded. My feet felt like they weighed a ton as I took the few steps over to the piece of furniture I was all too familiar with. I watched as my father took a seat on one end and I stood there, staring at the other. It took me a moment, but with a heavy breath I sat down, leaving a large gap between us. I leaned over, placing my hands on my knees and looked at him.

His body was turned so that I had his full attention and one of his arms was propped up along the back of the couch. He had this look of patience that I always admired and had tried to emulate my whole life, but he made it look effortless.

"It's good to see you."

I closed my eyes, not wanting those five words to affect me so much. It wasn't the words themselves because he'd said them to me before. He was *always* happy to see me. This time when he said them, there was something about them that had an air of sadness but still somewhat happy. He was happy that I was here, in his presence, but clearly the circumstances of my visit were never going to be a good thing. I cleared my throat before responding. "It's good to see you too, Dad."

When neither of us said anything else, I rubbed my palms over the front of my thighs. "How are Daya and Alex?"

"Good, actually. They're good."

I nodded, not really knowing what to say next. This felt so off and uncomfortable. I didn't know how to navigate this broken relationship with my father. I had every instinct to just up and leave but there was something that kept me planted on this couch. I caught him staring at me out of the corner of my eye.

He readjusted his legs, bending one and crossing it over the other. "Ask me whatever you want, Nicholas."

I ran a hand over my face, feeling some kind of pressure that no one else but myself was instigating. "I want..." My voice sounded smaller than I would have liked. "I want to go back to a time when I didn't know any of this." I looked down at the floor, focusing on the rug underneath the coffee table.

"You asked me for the truth and that's what I told you. I can't take that back."

I blinked over to him. "You waited *years* to tell me the truth. I practically had to back you into a corner for you to say anything."

He rubbed at his eyes, thinking over his words. "I knew you would never like the answer. The truth would never be something that invoked happy memories."

"Yes, I know. You made that abundantly clear, how you didn't want to interrupt my happy life with this kind of information," I said, my tone harsh. I ran a hand roughly through my hair. "Dad, does Daya know?"

His eyebrows pulled inward.

"About Mom, about all of it."

My father pressed his lips together, turning his head towards the hallway that led to the stairs. "She does."

I clucked my tongue, scoffing. "Of course, she does."

"Nicholas—"

"I get it okay. You needed someone to vent to who wasn't your son. *Your son*, who also happens to be the person you were lying to." I lifted my hands in frustration. "Oh, I'm sorry, I guess you were *omitting* things since you never seemed to give me a clear answer on anything at all. I didn't ask the right questions since I had no idea where to start and literally all I ever fucking did was just let you keep me in the dark because I don't know, maybe I thought it was better that way." I had never been so harsh with Maurice Cassial before, but I was just done with tip toeing around anything.

"You're right you never pushed with your questions. It was almost as if you inherently wanted to keep your life in order, no outliers in sight. You wanted to do things your way and so I let you…"

I shot up from the couch, looming over him. "I'm really not in the mood for excuses!"

"You were seven years old, Nicholas!" His brown eyes bore into mine when he matched my stance as he got up from the couch. "For one second please consider that I did not want to look my child in the face and tell him that his mother was…" His words cut off and he let out a low breath.

"You let me believe that she left," I accused, my voice shaky. "That's not fair. That's not fair to *me*! I didn't ask questions about her or damn near anything else because something would cast over your eyes anytime she got brought up. I wanted to make you happy, Dad. I didn't want to cause problems, because well, I thought anything having to do with her was simple. Fuck, it's *not* simple!"

My father took the few steps left to get to me and braced his hands on my biceps. "You're right, it isn't fair. I am *sorry*, Nicholas. I told Daya about a year or so ago because I felt like the time for telling you had passed. I thought she would help me try to bring it up somehow, but then I kept putting it off again. This is my fault, not hers."

I shrugged my shoulders to get his hands off me for a moment. My eyes stung from trying to hold back the tears I wanted to conceal. I looked up at the ceiling. "There was never going to be a perfect moment, Dad." I closed my eyes tightly; I felt the tears starting to slip through. "There was never going to be a perfect moment to tell your son that his mother didn't leave her family, she didn't abandon us. She didn't abandon *me*!"

My father took a step toward me, but I pointed my finger at him causing him to stop and I felt my cheeks getting damp from the slow-moving tears I'd tried to keep at bay. "You told me she…she died loving me, when I have spent my entire life thinking that she didn't care about me. I know you didn't mean to, but you had me resenting a woman who *loved* me. And you can tell me that story a million times, but I will…I w-will…" I stuttered on my words because they didn't sound right in my head, but I didn't know how else to put it.

"Tell me what you want to say, Nicholas." My father looked defeated, but ready for whatever else I had to say to him.

I took a deep breath, wiping my tears away with my fingertips. "I will never know what being loved by her even meant, what it felt like. You are the *only* person who knows what that's like. Even fucking Jonah knew what it was like to be around her and love her in his own way. And I get that she asked you to take away my memories and give me a happy life, but *fuck*, it hurts knowing that everyone had a say in something about *my* life. You, Mom, Moira, everyone but fucking me!"

I dug the heels of my hands into my eyes. "You get all these memories whether they are good or bad, while I have *nothing*, Dad! All I have is this power that I have no fucking idea how to handle. It served its purpose when I needed it, so do I just say thank you so much mom for providing me with the power to resurrect my dead girlfriend, but now it will have to go dormant in my mind again. Is this the only thing I'll have from Mom? A power that I'll have to keep hidden from angels like Ariel because for some reason she thought I was the most viable option for an outlawed magic skill.

"I went from resenting someone I don't remember ever knowing to resenting you and I don't know how to deal with that Dad. Fuck, *fuck*, I am so angry at you." I wanted my voice to be louder, but I heard it soften. My body vibrated with anger and hurt, but my voice sounded like it was the opposite. "And what's worse is that I'm angry at her. I'm angry at a dead woman for making you promise to lie to me. I am angry that you went along with it. I'm a-angry that J-Jonah knew about things and hid it from me. I-I'm a-angry that y-you let me r-resent her f-for fucking *years*."

He licked his lips, taking a step closer to me, tentatively reaching out to touch me again. When I didn't flinch away, he reached up and placed his palm on my cheek, letting his thumb remove some of the tears. A rush of déjà vu hit me, remembering his tender touch whenever I would come to him crying when I was younger, hiccuping from my incessant crying. Back then my problems were so small and trivial, yet he always spoke to me like they mattered. "You have deserved to know for a very, very long time. Your mother and I, we had this entire plan for how we wanted you to grow up and the kind of person we wanted you to be. I could see tiny pieces of what we envisioned as you got older and I was…I was selfish." His voice started to crack. "I wanted to keep you in this bubble where the only bad things that happened were just normal everyday problems, things you knew how to fight against. That's on me; that is something I will have to live with for the rest of my existence."

He cupped my face in both his hands, a small twinkle in his eye appearing. "That power she gave you is something big and over-whelming to have, but no Nicholas, that is not the only thing you have of hers. You have her nose, her smile, you both have this laugh that always told me when something was truly funny and," he placed his hand at my chest, "you have her heart. Despite your feelings towards her, please know that you loved her with every fiber of your being.

Every time I tried to tell you I only ever saw her looking back at me and breaking a promise to her was not something I wanted to do, whether she was alive or not."

I placed my hand over his, whispering, "I deserved to know."

He nodded solemnly. "You did."

"You told me I died, Dad. Mom saved me and you think that's something I wouldn't *want* to know. Moira took my memories. All of these people that were involved in my past and I can't ever ask them anything. I won't get to know any of them." I was talking more to myself than to him.

My father lowered himself onto the couch, putting his head in his hands. "I should have thought about the repercussions of the choices we were making, but Nicholas, I didn't know what to do. And I know, I know this sounds like an excuse, but I promise it isn't. I'm just trying to get you to understand that I wasn't a forty-year-old man with time to think clearly." He lifted his face to look at me and that's when I noticed that while my father looked like he always did—a mirrored version of myself—there were tells that he hadn't been sleeping, his eyes lacked their normal Maurice Cassial shine. Dani had mentioned once before that she could feel like something was missing when it came to me, when it came to my heart, since that day in the infirmary and maybe the same went for my father. There was a piece of him that was missing that was always meant for me and I'd removed myself from that spot for the time being.

He rubbed the back of his neck, giving me a hard look as if this was something he wanted me to understand. I remained standing, not quite ready to sit down. "I was not that much older than you with a son I had nearly lost and a wife I was about to have taken away from me. I didn't mind the power transfer part, but I want you to know that I wasn't fully supportive of Moira taking your memories. Your mother looked me in my eyes and begged me to do it before they took her away, there was no discussion, no pros and cons. The choices were I forget what she said and listen to you cry another night until you threw up over those sentries taking her away or I take you to Moira like she asked.

"And son, until you have children of your own, you will never understand what it's like to have your child screaming and pleading for someone who is never coming back. I did what I thought was best for you. Not for *me*. For *you*. I know you don't see it that way, but at the start of everything it was just me and you. You had no more bad dreams, no more crying until your throat was sore. Moira had offered to take some memories from me too, but I knew one day I would tell you everything so I kept them. I wanted to handle all the baggage for you, so you could go on and be the person standing in front of me. I pushed through the tears and my own nightmares so that everything your mother wanted for you could be achieved. You deserved the truth and answers Nicholas. You deserved to know what an incredible person your mother was and I have a million stories I could tell you if you'd like, but if your trust is something that is no longer on the table any longer then I will leave you be but know I'm always here. I'll always be your father, even if you hate me."

Elise's words came back to me, but I realized something about them was off.

Your mother made the decision she did. He was honoring what she wanted because he LOVED her Nick. Take pride that you came from a fucking man who honors his word even at the expense of his son's trust.

He did love my mother but despite doing what she asked because of his love for her, Maurice Cassial did what he did because he loved…*me*. We both had fractured hearts from the same series of events but in different ways. I felt my eyes start to fill with tears again, but these weren't the kind of tears that came from rage and hurt, these were from the overwhelming realization that I could understand where my father was coming from, but also be angry at the situation. There wasn't a wrong or right way to feel about it.

I moved some of the items on the coffee table to the side, sitting down on the wooden surface. I pressed my lips together as I watched him wipe his hand over his eyes. "Are you leaving anything out?"

My father tilted his head to the side, running the back of his hand under his nose.

"Anything about the past, my mother, Jonah, anybody or anything?"

He ran a finger across his mustache. "I don't know all that much about the man your mother was with before, the one who transferred his powers to her. Saving your life was the one and only time Scarlett had ever used those powers and we didn't really discuss it further than that."

I hummed, leaning back a bit. "What about…" I stopped myself before I could finish.

My father leaned in, placing a hand on my knee. The amount of comfort I felt from that one touch was profound. "No, what is it? From this point forward, I'm an open book. No more secrets."

I gave him a small smile, but then it faded. "What about what happened to her?"

"Your mother? You mean how she died?"

I nodded, slowly. Did I really want to know all of this? Something in my gut told me I did, but then again, maybe some things really were better just left unsaid.

My father swallowed and shook his head, more to himself then at me as if the thought was too much for him. "I don't know exactly what happened. No one ever really knew what happened to angels who disobeyed Jonah's father or what he did with them afterwards. Only the guards at the Ethereal Bastille could hear screams and there was always apparently massive amounts of clean up. Jonah is the one who made those rooms soundproof after a while." He bit his bottom lip, taking a deep breath. "The only thing I do know is that Isaac Zuriel apparently had a thing for angelic wings. I'd been told that he would have them ripped out, the open wounds burned closed so that healing would be obstructed." He tilted his head down, squeezing my knee. "I wasn't allowed anywhere near The Skies, but I tried. I had so many broken bones and bruises from trying to fight my way in. Jonah had no real pull when it came to his father, *especially* when it came to me. He tried to talk to him but it was too late."

I held down the bile that wanted to erupt from my throat thinking about that. I felt a phantom pain in my back from the very thought of having my own wings ripped out. I collected myself, removing the imagery from my mind. "And the person who outed Mom…did they ever tell the truth?"

My father opened and closed his mouth, mulling over his next words. "In a way."

I raised an eyebrow, not really interested in any more evasiveness.

"Do you really want to know this?" He furrowed his dark eyebrows, but a look of concern fell over his eyes.

I ignored his question. "Did Jonah have something to do with it?"

My father looked off to the side, like he was remembering something. He blinked away from the distant memory and looked back over at me. "No, but from the way I've talked about him and the strain you've witnessed on our relationship, I can see how you would think that."

I wanted to just be upfront and ask who it was, because the need to know was gnawing at me. Of course it was. I was realizing that some things were so far in the past that staying there might be best. If I had the information what would I do with it? I was quite the expert at spiraling and I was trying to work on that. "I guess I just want to know if this person was brought to justice?"

My fathers hand moved to my shoulder and something about the way he looked at me told me that he knew I would respond like that. "Yes, Nicholas. Maybe not in the most violent form, which is what I would have liked, but justice nonetheless."

My chest felt heavy, as I took a deep breath out. I hadn't realized I'd been holding my breath until the weight of it started to dissipate. I opened my mouth to say something else, but then a sharp ringing erupted in my ears. I shoved my palms against them, closing my eyes and clamping my teeth together. There was a whooshing sound and then the ringing again, they interchanged as if one wasn't enough.

"Nicholas!" I heard my father say, but it sounded so far away. He started to reach out to grab my hands, but once his skin touched mine it felt like my flesh was on fire. I hissed, leaping off the coffee table and backing away from him.

"Nicholas, what's going on!" He yelled, reaching for me again.

"No, stop! Stop!" I screamed, backing up against the wall near the fireplace. I rapidly opened and closed my eyes, seeing images behind my closed lids. The pictures changed each time, starting out distorted and fuzzy but eventually clearing up. The colors and imagery were more vibrant and distinct. The high-pitched sound rang in my ears again.

I saw a flash of Dimitri's face and his hand so tightly wound around Dani's neck. She was up against a wall, the look on her face told me she was holding in her own screams. The image painted itself red with blood and body, after body, littered my vision. I didn't recognize who I was seeing, but there was a pull in my chest that made me think it was my fault and I couldn't make myself think otherwise.

Every single piece of darkness I tried to keep at bay, all the time I'd spent working on myself felt useless as I tried to push the overwhelming feeling of dread away from me. My chest felt tight from my increased breathing pattern. My skin felt hot as if it were a million degrees in my house.

There were hands surrounding the sides of my face and they stung when they hit my skin. The haunting images repeated over and over again, but my father's face became more vivid and his voice echoed out, almost past the insane ringing I was forced to hear.

"Nicholas! Please look at me!" My father shouted.

I was being crowded now by Daya and Alex, but my father pushed them back, telling them to give me some room. My father pulled one of my hands away from my ear and placed it on my chest. He didn't let go when he said with pure conviction and honesty. "Look at me, Nicholas. Whatever this is, fight it."

I tried to think of all the good things I had, all the good things I *would* have. I thought about how I was still a good person despite everything. I thought about how much better I felt that I could have my father back in my life, as different as it would be now.

I thought about the darkness that threatened to ruin me, but in reality, I accepted it for what it was and lived with it, rather than hide from it. Rather than fear it.

I thought about how I loved a girl who made me want to explore the darkness just to know that there was light on the other side.

The ringing simmered until it was gone. The temperature around me cooled to an acceptable degree. My vision was slightly blurred from the tears I didn't know I'd let fall and I looked down, noticing that my father's hand was holding onto mine for dear life. I caught my breath, leaning my head back against the wall. My eyes caught the look of concern on Daya and Alex's faces. They remained a few feet away from me, likely not wanting to do anything to startle me or set me off.

"Hey, Nicholas. Hey, look at me." My father patted my chest and I glanced over at him. I was breathing heavily and words were hard for me to get out at the moment. "What was that, hmm?"

I licked my lips, pulling my hand away from my head. Tiny specks of blood came back on my palm. I swallowed a few times before I spoke. "Dimitri."

"The Son of Hell?" Alex chimed in, getting a stern look from her mother. I nodded over at her.

"What about him?" My father asked, running his knuckle along my ear to remove some of the blood.

"He has her, Dad."

His eyes widened at my words. "He took Dani? When?"

"Earlier tonight. She's not okay. I have to get to her. I can't let Purgatory or Hell get to me like it did before."

My father grabbed my chin and forced me to look at him. "Like it did before? I know you've had your dealings with this Dimitri fellow before, but what was this, Nicholas?"

I removed his hand from my chest and slowly walked over to the couch, collapsing on the cushions that were never truly comfortable to begin with, yet right now they felt like the best piece of furniture in the realms. "I didn't have the easiest time in Purgatory."

I flinched at the look my father gave me as if anything that hurt me, hurt him. "I'm not okay, Dad, but I'm working on it, I promise. I wasn't okay when I went there and it just got worse as time went on. Dimitri is *very* aware of that." I flashed him my arm and his eyes went straight to the faint scars there. The three lines left by Dimitri's extremely sharp demonic fingernails.

"I thought you'd just had a fight with him. I thought it was a battle scar and that was it. I didn't know you...I should have known that you..." Maurice Cassial looked truly the most defeated I'd ever seen him. It was his turn to sit on the coffee table, folding his hands together and placing them in front of him. Daya sat on the arm of the couch, while Alex leaned her body over the back.

"It is in the past, Dad." I explained to him about my time in Purgatory, not skipping the rough parts that I knew he hated hearing. I told him how I finally opened myself up to the help that was around me, despite my incessant harping that I was fine. "I haven't blamed myself for Jonah or anyone else in a good while, so progress, I guess. Dimitri is holding onto the little piece of darkness that's still left, but I'm working on it." I eyed my father, curiously. "How did you handle that so well?"

My father huffed out a small, short laugh, which was odd given the situation. "Nicholas, your mother used to have panic attacks as well. They weren't as hostile especially given your situation, but they could be pretty bad. She learned to manage them and also accept that they were something she had to work to get through when they happened," He ran his knuckles over my cheek. "Just like you."

I had the strongest instinct to hug him then and that's just what I did. I'd hugged my father so many times before, but this time felt different. I didn't have to like what he did to ultimately accept the past. I could wish for a different outcome but not let it fester away at me. He had lost someone the same as me and beyond whatever time had passed, that kind of pain still hurt. He needed me just as much as I needed him; I hadn't realized how much I'd wanted to hug my own father until right now.

When we let go he whispered *I love you* to me, which I whispered back, seeing a tiny glaze form over his eyes as he held back tears. Fuck I missed him.

"Are you going to be okay to even rescue her?" Alex inquired, taking in my mildly sweaty appearance and sudden breakdown that happened only minutes ago.

I let out a slight chuckle, shocking myself with the happy sound of it as I sat back down. "Yeah. I needed this." I snuck a look over at my dad, the twinkle that was missing from his eyes was back—where it belonged. "Now I just need to find her. I know where she is, just not *where* she is, if that makes any sense at all."

"You'll find her son."

"Always the optimist."

"When it comes to you, always," Daya added, her nose ring twinkling in the little lights around the living room.

My father tapped on my chest with his index finger. "Optimism, yes. It's also because you love her."

"*Fucking finally.*" I heard Alex muttered, tugging at a blue strand of her newly dyed hair, getting a slap on the shoulder by her mother.

I sighed, knowing my heart was a lost cause. "I do."

My father clasped both my hands in his. He looked as if he was in awe of me. "Somewhere between all the pain, blood and sacrifice, you fell in love."

Daya got up from the couch, leaning down to kiss me on my temple before doing the same for my father. "We'll be right here when you bring her home."

Home. That's exactly where I was and it's exactly where I wanted her to be.

"I know what that kind of love feels like. This love you have for her, the love that makes you fight without a single thought, the love that makes you worried and nervous, the love that lets you know that she is worth everything you've put yourself through— that is how you know you'll find her. That's how you know you'll win."

21
DANI

Every single time I made a movement with my head, it was like my scalp screamed for mercy. I'd managed to close my eyes, nodding off for a few moments until the image of Jasmine and Yuri flooded my mind. I would evade sleep happily if it meant not having to see that cross my mind again. The look on their young faces, filled with so much fear. Leah had tried to look strong for them and I knew she was anything but weak, yet being stuck in a Hell prison can make everything feel damn near impossible.

I felt like I was belittling myself with the way I had to make it out to be like I had no power at all, when all I wanted to do was rip Dimitri's head from his body and give it to Garrett as a prize for even considering touching a hair on his family's head.

Was I doing them a disservice by not doing anything at all? Making them rot in that disgusting place they were in.

Maybe Dimitri was bluffing and I was the one keeping them here longer. Perhaps if I just killed him and all his guards then I could set them free. I stood up from the ground and ran a dirt covered hand through my curls, getting my fingers caught on a tangle. I ripped through it in frustration, yelping at the pain in my scalp.

I scoffed, maybe I deserved this pain.

I gently moved my hair over my shoulder, letting my mind wander to things that lifted me up. I thought about how once I was out of here, tangles would be the least of my worries since I had my angel to carefully remove them for me. He had gotten so good at meticulously finger-combing my hair when I washed it. Time could tick by and Nick wouldn't even so much as let out a groan of annoyance when he had still another section of my hair to go.

The pain in my scalp wouldn't even be something to consider since Nicholas was insanely too good at giving scalp massages. I caught myself smiling, at the soothing feeling of someone delicately alleviating this pain in my head.

I rolled my neck and shoulders, my happy ideas halting when I heard the door opening. It didn't feel like Dimitri though outside of it. No, two of his bodyguards stalked into the room with their eyes trained right on me. I scanned my eyes over both of them. One was bulky and extremely tall; he reminded me a little of Zane but with shorter hair. The other was of average height, but his thighs and biceps bulged, even under his clothes.

"Can I help you?" I wasn't intimidated if that's what they were going for. All I felt was annoyance at their intrusion.

They casually looked over at each other, giving one short nod. The shorter one cocked his head towards me. "Grab her arms."

I reared my head back, blinking rapidly. "The fuck you will," I protested, backing up.

The taller one snickered. "You can make this real easy and just oblige us."

He took one long step over to me, reaching for my arm, but I swatted it away. "I'm not a fan of making your lives easier."

The short one rolled his eyes, lunging at me. I jumped back, nearly laughing when he almost fell flat on his face. The other one trapped my arm in his grasp, twisting it so that the bones there were on the verge of breaking. Before the shorter one could grab hold of my other arm, I collected shadows into my hand and reached over my shoulder. I shoved the dark magic into the larger one's face, thrusting backwards to get him off of me. He stumbled backwards, shaking his head and clawing at his face.

I pulled my hand back, shooting the shadows towards the shorter one. I spun around but had to lean back to escape the flying fist that was aimed at my face. The larger one huffed, moving a few steps to the side quickly when I shot out another stream of shadows. The other one pushed out his own dark magic, hoping to battle against mine.

The taller one saw that as an opportunity to gain the upper hand on me, but I'd let shadows rise from the stones, wrapping their ribbon like appearance around his legs, up his thighs and around his ribs. They cinched him in, letting me give all my attention to the one currently thinking he could win in this shadow fight with me.

I was about to propel a large amount of dark magic at him, something that would likely send both of them into unconsciousness when I felt something wrap around both my wrists. I instantly felt the burn. My eyes flicked to my wrists, ropes of black and dark red had a hold of me and the heat it created was fucking unbearable.

My power stopped flowing and everything the shorter guard had thrown at me hit me all at once. It looked so much like simple transparent wisps but they felt like stones. I tried to raise my hands and shield myself but the ropes at my wrists kept me in place. The larger guard broke through my shadow holds, beginning to barrel towards me, but he halted when he was so close he could have picked me up.

I started to turn around and add yet another person into this fight, but my head was yanked back by another rope that circled my throat. I didn't get a chance to catch my footing when I was pulled backwards, my back hitting a hard chest.

I knew that chest and I tried to force my hands up to my neck. I wanted to rip away Dimitri's hold on me, move my body as far away from his as possible. He still had a solid grip on my wrists, the burning a slow continuous feeling. It was a never ending heat cycle that thrummed through my veins and it was starting to make me sweat. I felt his hands move my hair away from my ear, so he could touch his lips to the shell. "Always the little fighter, aren't we?"

I looked straight ahead, refusing to even give him an ounce of my attention. I focused on the two men in front of me. They had gotten themselves together again and seemed to be waiting for his instructions.

Dimitri sighed in disappointment before directing his next words at them. "Grab her and hold her in place. One simple task, for fucks sake boys, do I need to do everything myself?"

"We had it, boss, I swear..." The taller one started, but suddenly there was a long cut along his neck, blood trickling out. I peeked over to my right as much as I could, seeing that Dimitri had extended one of his fingers at his guard. His fingernail had become long and pointed, the same way it had when we fought with him in his office at Leviathan.

He didn't have to take a step at all to cause harm and the tip of his fingernail was coated in blood. The guard's hand flew up to his neck, but before he could get any words out the blood started to bubble as if it was boiling. The color red caught in my peripheral vision and I knew Dimitri's eyes had turned. He wasn't angry enough to shift into original demon form, but he was pissed enough to make things count when he needed to.

"I am so sure you did."

We all watched as the blood started to rapidly pour out of his skin and sizzle as it hit the ground. Blood started to come from his mouth and his body shook with pain. His hands flew everywhere, not knowing where to go and how to help himself. His body fell to the ground, soaking up his blood.

Dimitri chuckled, grazing my ear again with his lips. "Oh, no, look what you caused. Don't worry, what I plan to do to you will be much less horrifying—on the outside."

The air turned cooler when he finally let me go. I didn't get a chance to enjoy it when his hand dug into my hair, tugging backwards, then forcing my head against the stone wall. Black dots decorated my vision and I blacked out.

My wrists stung with pain as I tried to stretch them out but to no avail. I pulled and tugged but nothing worked. I slowly blinked my eyes open to see the stone ground below me, but also that I was on my knees. I realized quickly with a few more tugs that my wrists were now placed around my back and secured. Pieces of my hair clung to my mouth and I blew tiny breaths out, trying to get them away from my face.

I tried to conjure up my own dark magic, but I felt nothing happening. I knew it was in there; I could even feel the light magic bottled up in myself, but nothing was willing to release itself from my fingertips. I couldn't feel anything wanting to come from my skin or any thrumming in my veins. I almost felt human and I ground my teeth together at the thought. I rallied when I brought my thoughts back to my captured wrists. Heaven's Gate had their golden magic dampening handcuffs, so what would stop Hell from having their own version of it.

I hadn't noticed the two guards standing on opposite sides of the room, staring at me as if they had nothing better to do. One of them was the shorter one from earlier, but there was a new one to my left. He had cropped blonde hair and dark brown eyes that looked black in the dim lighting of the cell. I glanced over at where the other guard had seized and died in front of me, his blood still staining the stones.

A throat cleared as the door opened and a smiling Dimitri sauntered in as if he was the biggest piece of shit in the realms. He wasn't alone though. Lilith walked in after him, her black silk dress flowing behind her. Her platinum blonde hair was swept up in a high bun and it almost looked as if she was about to attend some elegant dinner party rather than come and torment me with her presence again.

"Ah, you're awake. Excellent." Dimitri rubbed his hand down his fitted shirt, nodding at his guards.

They rushed over to me, grabbing my elbows and lifted me up. My knees ached and my legs felt wobbly from how I'd been placed on the ground. Dimitri stood in front of me, taking my hair in his hand and brushing the curls over my shoulder. His green eyes looked at my face as if he was considering something but then thought better of it.

"I admire your work with her Lilith, but I think you were quite foolish in how defiant you made her. I love a woman with her own mind, but hmm, I do believe it is a bit misguided." He looked over his shoulder at her, tilting his head towards me as if to tell her to come closer. She obeyed, standing next to him. He brought his gaze back to me. "I had a lovely meeting with your delicate little angel. I forgot how good his darkness tasted, although perhaps he isn't quite as delicate as before. He put up a fight and I probably have *you* to thank for making him so resilient. I could taste his need for you, his need to *find* you. It was actually kind of pathetically sad. Poor sad, simple Nicholas, loving a girl who was never his to begin with."

I tried to pull away from him, hating the way he said Nick's name. I hated the way he thought he was better and that somehow I was the missing puzzle piece in his deluded love story.

Dimitri raised his hand and placed his fingers at my shoulder. He twisted his hand so his knuckles slowly ran down my arm. "You don't want to work with me Dani, well then unfortunately, I will need to use a method I've tried to avoid with you. You really do bring out the worst in me." He looked over at Lilith. "Watch and learn."

I furrowed my brow, when Dimitri's long nails extended, pressing into the skin of my arm and slicing downward. Lilith took in a sharp breath, but it wasn't from shock, but as if she was impressed or awestruck. An excruciating pain ran along my arm and I closed my eyes, biting down on my tongue to keep the whimpering sounds I wanted to make at bay. I heaved out a breath, glancing at the damage he'd done. Blood ran down towards my elbow, dripping onto the stone.

Dimitri ran his fingertips along my open wound, smearing the blood there. I watched with my mouth half open as he brought his fingers to his lips, tasting my blood. He sighed as if he was so content with what he was doing.

"Such rage. Such overwhelming hatred for me, when all I'm trying to do is help you. We wanted the best for you and you went and decided that living with *them* was a better choice." He laughed. "We should be enraged with *you*, yet, I desire you too much to show you such malice."

Lilith reached out and touched my bleeding arm, pressing her fingers into the long cuts. I grunted, her nails digging into the broken skin.

"You can keep me here forever and I still won't want you. I will *never* want—" The back of his hand came down across my face, his knuckles connecting with my jaw and *fuck*, it hurt. I tasted blood on my lips, verifying that he had in fact, busted my lip open. I looked into the fiery red that were now his eyes and the way his face began to distort, but then he pulled himself back together.

Dimitri flexed his hand, chuckling. "I told you that I will break your spirit and I wasn't lying. I will see that power of yours, pretty girl. You will give me what I want." He nodded over to his guards who came up behind me, wrapping their hands around my wrists.

The Son of Hell ran his entire palm over my blood soaked arm, squeezing so that more of the dark red liquid oozed out. He pulled back, creating that reddish black magic in his hand, clouds of smoke coming from his palm. "I really do hate hurting you."

That was all he said before I felt the dampening magic at my wrists release but the guards still held my arms in place. Dimitri slapped his blood soaked hand over my eyes and it was like I was seeing multiple visions at the same time.

I tried to rip myself away from the guards holding my arms, tried to use my shadows now that they were free to run rampant, but it was like I was stunned into focusing on the things Dimitri was forcing me to see.

He had me seeing every single soul I'd tortured and I felt a shiver of pleasure roll down my spine from it. There were images of blood, so much blood. Blood I had spilled and the fact that I had desired more of it. He played off of my need for applause of lower demons and those that enjoyed my shows of torture. It was as if he was letting me know I could have all that again, that I could evoke pain and be praised for it.

My shadows molded and submitted to this idea, snaking around my arms with the need to do something like that, be something like that again.

I felt his hand press harder down on my face, his Hell shadows filtering into my eyes and it stung. I wanted to cry from how much it hurt and burned. It wasn't enough to fuck up my eyesight but I knew what was coming would be painful in a way I wasn't prepared for. Dimitri had tasted my blood and he would have found things he was knowledgeable of, but then he would have also tasted my desire for Nick, my love for him and everyone else I had let myself care about.

I flinched as he slammed image after image into my mind. The way he'd sliced down Nick's arm and the amount of agony he'd put him in. My angel's declining attitude at the fight outside the hostile and how he'd so much as put himself in the fetal position to make it stop. Dimitri sent feelings of despair and fear into my mind. He made me feel hurt and scared. I wanted to pull his hands away and make him stop.

He kept showing me Nick bleeding and then I would be the one over him as if I'd done it. Nick's screams and agony filled pains echoed continuously in my head.

Make it stop! Make it stop!

The warmth in my hands started to surge. I felt the familiar pull of my shadows rally around the warmth as if it wanted to protect. I willed the sparks to stop and I pushed myself to not explode. I couldn't give Dimitri what he wanted, I couldn't give up because the visuals were too much to bear.

I squeezed my fists together as he pushed images of him tearing Nick and everyone else to shreds. Blood flew everywhere and it was almost like I could taste it in my mouth. I wanted this to stop.

"Let me go! Stop it! Stop it, now!" I shoved the light down and it retaliated by nearly burning my insides with its rage to get out. For something that was supposed to be light magic, it had quite a temper. I used all the strength I had to force one of the guards away from me, while driving the other in the opposite direction. I grabbed Dimitri's hand, but it burned my palms the minute I made contact.

I wasn't scared of him. His power could shake me to my core at times, but I wasn't scared of him. I reached back up and hissed at the sizzling sound that came from our hands connecting. I tugged while screaming and pulling.

A growl of frustration came from his throat as he released me and I staggered back. The guards moved towards me but stopped a few feet from me as Dimitri grabbed my throat before I could get too far from him. My eyes burned and seeing him was a struggle but I could see that his eyes were tinged red again. "Silly, frustrating girl, you are."

He tossed me backwards and I fell, landing hard on the ground. I didn't get up immediately, I just placed my hands on the stones and let my breathing try to get back to an even level.

"You care far too much. Caring for them in the first place was your initial mistake, my love," Lilith said, the look of pity in her eyes was nauseating.

"How would you know a fucking thing about being cared for!" I screamed at her.

Dimitri rolled his eyes as if he was bored and annoyed at this entire interaction. He moved his hand to the side of him, the image of Leah and her children appearing. "You truly care about an entire realm of angels who would rather use you and fear you, than save these precious little faces right here, right now."

He made things sound so easy, but Dimitri was also a businessman, just like his father. I knew the things he said weren't always as simple as he made it seem. There was always some caveat that no one noticed. I stared at the image of Yuri and Jasmine; they were sleeping, their mother huddling around them to make sure they were safe.

I blinked and then blinked again, thinking my eyes were playing tricks on me when I saw a shadow in the back of the cell. It swished back and forth, almost like….

Like a tail.

Like a dog tail.

No, not a dog. A hellhound.

Before I could let myself be happy that they were being watched over, Dimitri took the image away and shook his head. He had shown me horrible things, things I would be haunted with when he left me alone in this cell for the next few hours.

Dimitri shrugged. "Or maybe you are waiting for your adorable group of friends to find you and then you can make everything right in the realms and pretend like you will have made any difference at all. If that is how you'd like it well then…I promise, I have my plans for them if that plan should come to fruition as well." He ushered Lilith along with him towards the door.

The guards followed after them and once they were on the other side, I pushed myself off the ground, running to the door. I grabbed hold of the bars at the only opening the stone door had. With all the confidence I could muster I said, "he will find me. Nick *will* find me."

Dimitri's shoulders stiffened before he turned around. His larger tattooed hand crowded my smaller one as he held it against the bars. "Oh, I sincerely hope he does find you. I'm planning on it." His mouth curved into a smirk and my stomach turned.

I felt my hands tingle as tiny light sparks trickled out. Not enough to do any damage, but enough to give Dimitri something to grasp onto. His eyes danced with delight as he watched the light drift away into the dust that percolated in the air. "Well, well, isn't that interesting. Next time, I advise you to be a bit more forthcoming with what I know you can do. It brings me so much pleasure to crush every little piece of hope you have, pretty girl. Though, my patience will run thin, even for you."

He let go of my hand and walked away, leaving me alone. Leaving me to my own thoughts. I pressed my forehead against the bars and felt my eyes burn from the tears that threatened to fall. Lilith had offered him so much before, while he only had to do so little. He hadn't gotten what he wanted, so he was ruthless enough to take matters into his own hands. Dimitri wasn't the kind of prince-like hell born demon that *preferred* to just sit back and he was proving that now. He was greedy, like Lilith, but he had all the power to back it up and no one to answer to —except for his father and Lucifer, but from the looks of it he was doing a pretty good job of maintaining his stature while mapping out an entire plan for a domination of realms. The Son of Hell, honestly, didn't even *need* me, but the fact that he *wanted* me to just gain power and hurt others…

I made sure the tears stayed where they were as I looked into the darkness of the hallway. There was a part of me that knew Nick would find me, but there was an even worse part of me that hoped that he wouldn't.

22
NICK

We stepped out of the portal, landing right in front of Natalia's large residence. After so much back and forth, my father had told Daya and Alex to stay put while he went back with me. I'd told him he didn't have to, but Maurice Cassial was stubborn. He was also a really good dad and my biggest supporter; I'd mentally hit myself realizing that there had been a time that I'd forgotten that. We still had some rebuilding of our relationship to do, but for now I felt like something had reset inside of myself. I would always feel a sadness and slight anger at the past. The future, though, that looked clear. There didn't seem to be anything muddling my mind and despite Dimitri's complete lack of personal mental space, I knew I could fight against it if I had to.

What lay ahead was finding my girl. If I knew Dani at all, she would hate to be in the position of the one in distress. I knew that it nearly hurt her to not have freed herself and come back to us—come back to *me*—already.

My father placed his hand on my shoulder, grinning over at me as if just being beside me made him the happiest man in any realm. Once the portal minimized and closed, Reese and Elise rushed down the front stairs and headed straight for us.

Elise looked my father up and down and then did the same thing to me. She casually sniffed the air, but I had a feeling what she was searching for. "Seems as if you took my advice to heart, pretty boy."

I raised an eyebrow at her. "Seems like I did."

Reese shoved her shoulder. "Leave the guy alone. You had one good idea and it looks like it worked out. What do you want? A fucking cookie."

Elise narrowed her gray eyes at him. "No thanks. I would like to go murder, rather brutally, a Son of Hell."

I looked over her shoulder to see Garrett and Beetee coming out the front door. "Is everyone ready?"

"Yup. Weapons are in the house as we speak. You coming on this little life-threatening adventure, Mr. Cassial?" Reese asked, rubbing his hands together.

My father chuckled. It was a genuine laugh, one that came from his belly. "No, but I'll be right here when you get back. And just in case you all decide to end up at my house again, Daya and Alex are waiting as well."

Reese clapped him on the shoulder but placed his hazel eyes on me. "Hey, Zane said he got this off the floor when you collapsed earlier." He reached into his back pocket, pulling out Jonah's leather-bound notebook Dani and I had found in the Divine Library.

"Collapsed?" My father eyed me carefully. I could see the various things going on in his head and the million and one questions he, yet again, wanted to ask.

"I'll tell you later. I promise." I snatched the book from Reese and turned so that I was facing my dad. I didn't know why I felt the need to tell him about this notebook as if it was a secret. Maybe because it was, but the only person that needed to not be aware of it was….

"We all thought you would be long gone by now, disobeying orders and such." Ariel.

We all swung our heads to where his voice echoed from. He emerged a few feet from us, sentries surrounding him.

"Ariel?" My father sounded confused, as if he had no idea why the executive would be here. I forgot I hadn't told him much about the sparring matches I'd gotten into with the red-headed angel.

Ariel gave him a little smile. "Ah, Maurice. I'm sure you are quite proud of your son. He is just like you. A spitting image in looks and idiotic choices."

I swiftly moved the notebook so that it was behind my back. My fingers clenched around the leather as if my life depended on it. I felt a small tug and quickly looked over my shoulder to see Reese giving me a small nod as if he was silently confirming that regardless of understanding anything about this notebook, it was important. I let my fingers release it into his hold, right as Ariel started walking over to us.

"I think his choices are quite solid in the grand scheme of things," my father said, trying to sound like the bigger man. When it came to personality and actual physical size, he was.

Ariel ran a hand down his lapels. "You *would* think that wouldn't you. You made a choice to disobey Jonah's father so long ago and letting your son inherit those bad habits, ugh, Maurice I would have hoped you learned. I would think you would want better for your own child."

"Cause what you offer is better? This coming from a guy who treats all his subordinates like shit." Elise rolled her eyes.

Ariel ignored her, though I could see his jaw working overtime from the way it tensed up.

I could hear commotion behind us, letting me know that the others were leaving the house. Natalia's voice surrounded us like some kind of lyrically royal blanket. "Ariel? I didn't know we had a meeting."

The executive kept his eyes on me. Just me. "We don't. I hate to intrude, truly. They were right where you'd said they'd be. See *this* is what a true leader, a true angel looks like." He waved his hand over to the side and I pressed my lips together when Morgan walked up, glancing over at him proudly.

She stood as if she was waiting for some kind of medal or maybe she just liked to bask in the glow of thinking she did the right thing, when in reality she had just fucked us over.

"We aren't going anywhere with you," I finally said, keeping my eyes on him with as much intensity as he was giving me.

Ariel smirked, but Morgan opened her mouth before he could. "Where's your adorable little girlfriend?" Her eyes searched around the area in faux concern. "I thought she was the entire reason you make so many bad decisions nowadays."

My hands curled into fists, but I felt my father place a hand on my back. He didn't rub circles or do any sort of movement to try to rectify my mood. He just settled his hand there, just simply being present. "She isn't here."

Ariel cocked his head to the side, intrigued. "And where did she go, Nicholas?"

Elise scoffed. "We don't have time for this."

The sentries started to surround us, but as they circled, the people who had my back started to surround me as well. Beetee and Garrett stood near my right, while Natalia and Zane were at my left. Reese and Elise flanked the immediate outside of me and my father. Ariel didn't scare me and neither did his guards. He was an inconvenience at best.

"She was taken," I answered. My voice was even and steady.

"By whom?"

"That part doesn't matter. What *matters* is getting her back."

Ariel nodded as if he understood this completely. "Ah, that ripple in the sky I presume. Maybe this is all some miracle then, the darkness has taken what it wants. Whether she went willingly or not. Now instead of living in fear of her, the people can fully hone their skills and increase our chances of fighting back."

"Fighting back...from Dani?" Beetee squeaked. Morgan shot her eyes over to her, giving her a less than friendly smile.

"From what I was told she has impressively found the balance of her hybrid abilities, but now she's been taken. You can't honestly expect me to believe that she isn't just dying to show her filthy demon buddies her new skills," Ariel said, incredulously. "I respect you immensely Natalia, but clearly your wards were not enough to keep a simple demon out after all the work you did. Or maybe you wanted her gone as well."

"Ariel, that is absolutely absurd…" Natalia started, but Elise interrupted, her neck tattoo thrumming. "It was a Son of Hell, you shriveled dick piece of shit. Even with High Priestess magic, wards are nothing when it comes to determined Hell spawns. So for the love of fucking Satan can you move so we can go retrieve her, before I decapitate you and feed your head to my hellhound."

The sentries made a move towards her, but Ariel stopped them. He clucked his tongue. "Retrieve her. Yes, of course that's what you mean to do. Always the hero." He pointed a finger at my father. "Idiotic choices like I said. *She* didn't want to fight in the war, so *you* didn't want to fight in the war." I noticed my father press his tongue into his cheek. Ariel was talking about my mother. I knew by the way the inflection in his voice and the way my father's shoulders tensed. The red-headed executive continued. "The Soul Seether travels to Hell, so Nicholas travels to Hell. Do you see the resemblance?"

"Let me get one thing clear, she doesn't make me do anything. I'm going because…" I was speaking through my clenched teeth, trying to maintain my composure.

"You love her. Yes, Nick, we got that." Morgan shook her head as if I was being ridiculous.

Ariel raised his hands, making it seem like whatever he was about to say had merit. "Let *me* get one thing clear, Mr. Cassial. Whether the Soul Seether is here or not, you are coming back to The Skies and continuing to do your duty."

"*No.* I'm not."

He didn't look surprised by my answer. "I'm not asking. She is already gone. You will not be following. Please come along." He moved as if he was assuming we would follow him.

"I said *no.* Dani would never put us in danger willingly. She isn't the bad guy. She isn't the monster you so clearly think she is." I walked past my father and right up to Ariel. He watched me approach, a glint in his eye as if he enjoyed me defying him just so he could say more hateful things. "I am going there and I'm bringing her back."

Ariel licked his lips and flashed me a cocky smile. "I think you are going to look back at his moment, Mr. Cassial, and consider that you could have made a better decision. That maybe what you wanted to believe isn't what's true. Maybe the girl warming your bed at night isn't the person you thought and that she is simply a demon with immense power. She and her power should either be harnessed by the side of good or disposed of, which is likely what I should have done in the first place." I flexed my fingers, feeling my molars grind together as I kept my mouth shut.

He kept going, placing a hand on my shoulder. "Or maybe the demons in Hell have just done everyone a favor and realized, like you said, that she won't help them either, so they've disposed of her for me. You could be going straight to Hell to find her dead body, but hmm, maybe I should let you go and see that for yourself. You can wallow in the mistakes you've made and learn that you are putting all your efforts into the wrong things. Nicholas, trust me, when I say she isn't worth it."

All I knew was that I was vibrating with anger right before my fist connected with Ariel's nose. He stumbled back, but I was already rearing back, slamming my knuckles against his nose again. His hands flew up to his face, shielding his bleeding nose. Morgan's eyes widened, rushing over to him. I shook my hand, feeling the urge to hit him again and again, until his awful words ceased to exist. I was ready to hit lower this time, maybe in his stomach, or maybe even lower where it would *really* hurt. Ariel pulled one of his hands away, pushing past Morgan. "You ungrateful little…" He reached for me, but my father pushed me out of the way.

"That's my *son*, Ariel. I would step away."

Ariel nearly growled at him, pointing at his guards and then at me. "Seize him, now!"

They came charging at us and without our weapons, it was magic and hand to hand combat at the moment. One came up behind me and I brought my elbow back, hitting him right in the jaw. I shot out my light right in the eyes of another one. Elise slung out her tail, making a sweeping motion through a handful of them.

Garrett shielded Beetee as best he could as he expelled his own colorful magic at the sentries that came their way. He looked as if he was trying to keep her in check. And the look on her face told me she was mere moments away from shifting if she were given the okay. A large snake would be a distraction, but it would cause more problems than solve them. Reese pushed out his wings and headed for the sky while other sentries did the same, sending their light magic up at him. He sent his own down as well, but we were all on the same level when it came to our magic expertise, so it was a fight amongst equals.

My father fought off a sentry that barreled towards us, gripping him by the waist and swinging him over his body so that he collapsed on the ground in a defeated heap. Zane secured Natalia, but the High Priestess huffed out an exasperated sigh, pushing her hands out and a jolt of yellow and pink magic moved over all of us.

We all paused—motionless.

I couldn't move my feet or my arms. Nothing hurt, but I was paralyzed. I could blink my eyes and move my mouth, but any motion in my joints and appendages were a lost cause. Natalia moved around the immovable sentries, stalking over to where me and my father were.

"Ariel this will not happen, not on my land, not in my home." Natalia stood with her back straight, her arched eyebrows rising. "You will *cease* this fighting." She looked at the executive, waiting for him to speak.

Ariel narrowed his eyes at her but conceded. "*Apologies*. Of course."

She looked skeptical as if she didn't believe him. "Very well."

She waved her hand eloquently; the feeling returned to my body almost instantly. She let Reese come back to the ground with a soft landing which by the look on his face, he greatly appreciated.

Ariel gave her a half smile as he stretched, his nose covered in blood and staining his suit. He brought his hand up and released a white-gold rope in my direction. It circled around me and in a matter of minutes I was being yanked over to him.

"Ariel! That's my son!" My father yelled, heading for me. Ariel wiggled his fingers and suddenly my father's wrists snapped together and gold electrifying circles encapsulated his wrists. He couldn't move them apart, no matter how hard he tried. It wasn't just him either, it was everyone. Everyone except for the Enchanters.

Elise violently tried to escape hers, but to no avail. "The fuck is this?!" The sentries came up behind each and every one of them, shoving them to their knees. Almost like they were bowing.

Ariel rubbed his knuckles under his nose delicately. "Executives have been able to conjure up magic dampening skills for quite some time. Your precious Jonah didn't want us using it anymore unless it was dire and had us reverting back to the manual ones. Same effect, just in my opinion, less *eventful*." I was finally all the way over to him as I strained against the roped restraints that circled my body. "I wanted you to come willingly Nicholas, but it looks as if we have come to a bit of déjà vu. I threatened to put you in the Ethereal Bastille once, didn't I?"

"Ariel, you will let him go or…" Natalia had the trees rustling around her house and the gravel under us shook. Her fingers sparked different shades of colors.

"Your Highness…." Zane started but was quickly cut off by Ariel's laughter.

The red-headed executive tutted. "He is *not* your charge, High Priestess. He may be your friend, on your land, but he is one of *mine*. He is not an Enchanter, so you have no right to stop me. I do with him what I please. I have left your people free of my magical dampeners because I understand the rules. If you would like to harm me for simply disciplining an angel that works *for* me, then so be it. I would hate for your people to have a tragic repeat of the past because their leader doesn't know when to stand down, hmm."

Garrett and Zane stomped over to where Natalia stood. Garrett opened his mouth before Zane had a chance. "You will *not* speak to her like that."

"I am simply speaking facts. And by the look on her face, she understands what I'm saying." Ariel looked her up and down.

Zane leaned down to be close to his face. "Do *not* threaten her. You are not the highest executive. She ranks higher than you from where I stand. She *always* will." He reached for me, but Ariel nodded over to Morgan to pull me away.

"Hmm, that may be, but the people see me as their leader, so for all intents and purposes that's what I am. And like a good leader, angels that go rogue do not need special treatment, they need discipline." The golden ropes evaporated, but the glowing cuffs surrounded my wrists and two sentries grabbed me by my elbows.

"You let him go, Ariel! Let him go!" My father pleaded and yelled, pushing off his knees and running for me, but a sentry got to him in record time and shoved him to the ground again.

Natalia looked lost, but Zane and Garrett stood by her side, yet they were giving me looks like they hadn't lost faith in what we were all planning to do no more than thirty minutes ago.

"We'll get you out, Nick!" Reese yelled, grunting as a sentry kicked him. As he sucked in a breath, he said, "we'll find her!"

Beetee looked as if she wanted to cry but they were almost like angry tears, her eyebrows pulling downward. Elise stared daggers at Ariel, likely plotting his death over and over in her imaginative head.

Morgan came around and created a portal with her own key, letting the sentries past her so we could go through. Ariel came up next to me, a smug look on his face. His broken nose was the only thing that made this moment worthwhile.

"Rogue angels rot in the Ethereal Bastille. They don't get to be the hero."

I backed up, holding in my body's protesting ache. My back hit the wall gently and I let out a heavy well-earned sigh before I swallowed. I blew out two quick breaths before I raised my right leg up and then my left, bending my knees. I eyed my right thigh, blood coating that entire part of my body. I reached down, tentatively touching the four open gashes in my skin. The blood was warm to my touch and I couldn't help but glance over at the already open wounds on my arm from Dimitri's first physically debilitating brand of torture.

The wounds on my thigh were deeper than my arm. He wanted to make this one hurt. As much as he claimed to *care* about me, that didn't mean that he would be seen giving me any sort of special treatment. I didn't want it anyway. I started to stretch my leg out and hissed at the pain. I leaned my head back, closing my eyes and mentally counting down until he came back in here and did it all over again.

I frustrated him with my resistance which in any sort of situation would have made me laugh at how red-faced he would get, but Dimitri was getting more hostile. He'd come in here with Lilith pathetically at his side and had his guards slam me up against the wall. The stone ground against my back as he'd, without hesitation, relinquished his claws and tore into the skin at my thigh.

I'd let out an unbridled scream that was silenced the minute he slammed his hand over my eyes. The visuals had been instant but they were darker and more brutal. Images of all my friends getting hurt, all the mutilation and harm was in clear view. I *felt* everything. Every single blade that went through their stomach, every punch to the face, every single fucking bone that broke and cracked rattled through my body.

I'd wanted to vomit from the never-ending pain. Dimitri could have been with me for three minutes but it felt like three hours. He'd let me go and before I'd let myself rally and focused on rational thinking; I'd let my hands get hot. I welcomed the little tingles from the light. I saw Dimitri's green eyes light up with amusement and I looked down at my hands, wobbling on my feet.

Fuck, fuck, fuck.

The shadows were just starting to emerge but hissed at me when I immediately told them to retreat. They obeyed as they always did, taking the light with them. I'd had this feeling that the light somehow knew it needed to avoid this situation all together, it knew what was at risk, but heroics were its calling and if I was in dire need to help people, it was right there whether it wanted to be or not.

My hands had returned to normal but Dimitri had gotten all he needed. It wasn't enough to boast to his father about, but it was enough for him to adjust his shirt collar with his only hand and smirk. He'd brought my chin up towards him, lightly burning me for my lack of immediate compliance. "Now, was that so hard?"

He'd stood back, waving his hand in the air and revealing a frightened Leah. One of the guards had her by the hair, pulling her head back and a silver blade was to her neck. Her children stood in the far corner crying over their mother.

"You told me that you…" I'd started to yell but he shushed me.

"Now, now, be quiet. This was just a precautionary measure. Simply for if you failed me. I told you that my patience was wearing thin and like the impressive girl you are, you have come through." I didn't speak so he'd continued. "I'll make sure to tell him to let her go, for *now*. Remember though, when you let that little hybrid beast of yours out, you aim at one of them, not at me. We all know what happens if you decide to be the most beautiful heroine in the realms." He pointed his finger towards his guards who swallowed so loudly it echoed throughout the room.

He'd snapped his fingers, removing the visual of Garrett's family. The guards let me go, my legs giving out on me from the lack of support and I hit the ground.

I opened my eyes, blinking away the memory. I scanned the ground, letting my eyes fall onto the pool of blood my thigh wound had created before I was left alone and had decided to move.

I looked back down at my leg, seeing a flash of platinum blonde hair. I tried to shake my head at the thought, but the same thing came back when I tried to look again.

Lilith had come over to me as Dimitri left, kneeling down beside me. She hadn't even tried to move her dress away from the blood that trickled around the hem.

She'd reached her hand out, stroking her knuckles against my bruised cheek. I'd attempted to pull away, but even the smallest movement had my muscles aching. "We both know you're holding back and I can't say I'm surprised. Stubborn stupid girl. This will all be worth it if you let it be. And then it will be a distant memory when things are how they *should* be."

I'd gritted my teeth. "I don't listen to you anymore. It's funny how there was a time I was mildly afraid of you." I'd peeked over at her as she'd eyed me. "Now, you are the least scary thing in the room."

She'd chuckled lightly, pressing her fingers into my wound, drawing out more blood. She pulled the skin apart further and tears threatened to spill at the corners of my eyes. "My ruthless, relentless Soul Seether would have shown her skills and risen up above all the rest, damn the consequences. Now you let the lives of others rule your decisions. You

owe them nothing. It is everyone else that owes us, can't you see that."
It had been more of a statement than a question. She'd casted a look
over her shoulder at Dimitri who looked as if he had been impatiently
waiting for her. Her eyes focused back on me. "You had your fun in
your false sense of happiness, now it's time to come home and *stay*
home. We can create a much bigger home, a more powerful one."

I'd narrowed my eyes at her, steeling myself. "Get away from me."

She'd dug her nails into my wound and I ran my fingertips into the
stone. Lilith ripped them out before getting up and smoothing out her
dress. "It truly does make me sad to see you like this. You've let love
cloud your judgment and I taught you so much better than that. Who
would have thought that along with all this glorious power, you are still
so weak."

I placed both my hands into my curls, feeling them shake against my
head as I forced myself to rid her voice from my memories. It wasn't
loud within my head, but it was constant along with Dimitri's hands on
my face, his claws slicing through my body were on a loop as my
muscles remembered tightening at the feeling of him breaking skin.

Lilith had always made it a point to tell me that we loved ourselves
and only let people in for short periods of time, only when we needed
them and then swiftly let them go. Maybe I should have known I was
different the minute I wanted Elise to be closer than an amicable
acquaintance, or maybe it was when I'd started to want to open up to the
angel I once thought was just a fun entity to tease.

Perhaps things would be so much easier if I didn't give a shit about
Garrett and his family or Natalia and her people. If I had just sustained
my emotions, my feelings, then this whole thing with Dimitri would be
smoother; it would possibly be fun seeing things crumble and rebuilt
with me at the forefront. I pressed the heels of my hands against my
head, hoping that the pain would rid myself of these unnecessary
thoughts.

I couldn't. I couldn't. I couldn't.

24

NICK

My fingertips rubbed at the place Morgan had yanked my portal key off my neck and the memory of her smug face seemed to flash every time I closed my eyes for even half a second. There was a wooden plank that protruded out of the wall that I'd been sitting on for the past hour and despite my ass hurting from the uncomfortable seat, I was more antsy than anything.

I had never been inside of an Ethereal Bastille cell, let alone been a prisoner in one. There was almost a muted blue tone to the room and there were no windows. I had been looked at by every angel we passed since Ariel had told the sentries to take me the long way, as if he wanted me to feel some sort of shame.

Ariel didn't even speak when they'd tossed me in here; he simply nodded and turned on his heels to leave. His words came flying back at me once he'd closed the door.

You could be going straight to Hell to find her dead body, but hmm, maybe I should let you go and see that for yourself.

"Fuck!" I yelled, pushing off of my seat and starting to pace. I had tried really damn hard to not consider that alternative the moment I realized she was gone. I mulled over the fact that Dimitri wouldn't have taken her just to rid himself of her. That wasn't the way he operated and with the way he was fucking obsessed with her, maybe I could breathe easier knowing she was alive and—

I ran a hand through my hair. I couldn't say alive and *well* because the second part was still undetermined.

Right now was when I wished my mother had left me with some sort of telepathic magic and not just resurrection as a parting gift. Not only did I want to talk to Dani in any way I could, but I wanted to tell Reese and Elise that they should just go on and find her without me. I hesitated in that thought, since maybe for my own selfish reasons I wanted to see Dimitri myself and ram my fist into his face.

My mind raced relentlessly causing my breath to become shallower and my chest to constrict. The air in here wasn't helping but I knew it was so much more than the less than quality air filtration in this place. I stood in the middle of the room and placed a hand on my chest, closing my eyes. I could feel myself wanting to go to that place, that dark place I accepted but chose not to visit by choice. My heartbeat raced underneath my hand and I took one long deep breath in.

She would be found and if not by me, it would be by people I trusted.

I let out one big deep breath.

I repeated this over and over until I felt the tension from my body start to release and I opened my eyes. My vision was a bit blurry from the amount of pressure I'd used to keep my eyes shut, but my heartbeat started to slow to its normal rhythm.

I heard the door open, a tiny line of dim light coming into the room as Morgan stepped in.

I gave her one short look, before turning away, not in the mood for whatever useless conversation she was planning to have with me.

"Oh, don't be like that."

My shoulders tensed at her cavalier tone.

I heard her cluck her tongue before she continued. "Fine, I guess you *are* going to be like that. You are getting so emotional over some demon who honestly shouldn't have been here in the first place."

I shook my head, rubbing my chest. I didn't turn back to look at her.

"Nick, maybe this all happened for a reason and it's for the best."

I spun around. "Is Ariel delusional in thinking that just because she's gone that we're all safe? Taking over Heaven's Gate has always been the plan, no matter who was in charge. He would fucking know that if he wasn't so dead set on targeting my girlfriend."

She blinked as if the term girlfriend took her by surprise. Morgan licked her lips, brushing a piece of her long brown hair over her ear. "That's no one's call to make but *his*. So, I guess, like he said, you'll sit here and rot until you can find that guy you used to be who always had a stick up his ass for the rules."

I raised my hands up and backed away, turning so I could go sit on the wooden bench. It was like talking to a wall with her.

"You should be happy he only came after you and not the rest of them. There is a silver lining in everything."

I placed my head in my hands. "I just want to find her Morgan. That's all I'm asking."

My ex-girlfriend shrugged, adjusting her glasses on her nose. "Well then you are asking a fucking lot." She turned to go, but I called her name, gaining her attention.

"I don't think I'll ever really understand why she threatens you so much, but I do know that when I get her back, she'll aid in making this place better because she's a good person. Despite what you think, she's a *good* person. That's more than I can say for you. There are a million angels like you that Ariel can boss around and answer to him without a care in the world, but there is no one like her. So yeah, I would probably be threatened by her too."

The air between us crackled as if she didn't know what to say. She smacked her lips together before she started to exit the room. "One flaw in your little speech. *If* you find her, not *when*."

The door closed with a loud bang and I knew I'd hit a nerve. I was pissed off, even more so because what she said wasn't a complete lie. I was optimistic that I would find her, but I also needed to be a realist and take into consideration that maybe Dimitri was smarter than he looked.

The wooden bench was long enough for me to lay back on it, stretching one of my legs out while bending the other. I placed one of my hands behind my head while the other casually rested at my stomach. I needed to think about all my options when there was a tug at my chest.

No, not at my chest. *In* my chest.

It didn't hurt and it wasn't trying to physically move me, but it was like an aching sensation to be somewhere else. I placed my hand on my chest, feeling it start to burn. Again, it didn't hurt. It felt like the light that I'd always expelled from my hands, the light that radiated even from my pores was harboring in my chest.

A prisoner's inherent powers were nullified in these rooms. Any sort of outward attack would cease the minute an imprisoned entity tried to use it, but just because I couldn't release it, didn't mean it wasn't present. It felt bigger than me though. There was a thump against my chest and I sat up, pressing my fingertips to my shirt. A much harder ache and more light magic. I recognized my own, it'd been growing with me since the day I was born, but now something had been added to it.

Something that felt far away, but close enough to meld itself with my own.

I knitted my eyebrows together but then relaxed them. I had no need to try to expel away whatever was invading my magic because I knew the intruder. I'd been burned by it.

Her light did like me after all. I understood as much as I could about how light magic worked, but even after so many years of studying and reading…some things were still an anomaly. I didn't have the mental capacity to dig any deeper, but in an odd way, I knew Dani was at least alive.

My father's words came back to me.

The love that lets you know that she is worth everything you've put yourself through— that is how you know you'll find her.

I had told Morgan that I was in love with Dani and that she was *it* for me. And even though it didn't *need* to be proven, I think it just was.

25
DANI

I slid my hands down to my neck, being delicate as I touched the raw skin there. I licked my lips, opening my hand flat in front of me, palm up. I felt my skin warm as my light flickered to life, making this dank, brimstone smelling room palpable.

I watched as the light danced across my palm, little pieces of it falling around my wrist and arm. My shadows couldn't heal my pain, but they came out and wrapped themselves around me in thin wisps, somehow trying to shield me from my problems. The wisps intertwined themselves with my light as well, almost as if it wanted to preserve the golden light I held.

My shadows didn't want my light to go out and neither did I. This room had no windows and it was made with a force so strong that no one would hear me scream if I felt so inclined, yet, I felt something pull at my light as if it was on the other side of these stone walls. Almost like something in another realm wanted to connect with it. My light never reared back from it, it just molded itself toward the pull. I didn't know what it meant but I wanted more of it.

My light felt protective of this pull. And I did too. That pull was familiar, like I'd felt it once upon a time in a secret pathway to a certain angelic library, or while in bed with probably the most handsome man I'd ever met. That pull was *familiar* because it felt a lot like Nick's light. I wasn't going to think too hard about it, but Nick's light and *love* felt a lot like the same thing.

Natalia's house was all chatter and nonsense the moment we all plowed inside. Elise, the little psycho that she was, was the loudest of them all. Well, she rivaled Maurice, that was for sure. I wasn't surprised by the visceral reaction everyone was having because *what the fuck* even just happened. The leather bound notebook I had taken back from Nick was burning a hole in my back pocket. I didn't know what it was, since I'd never bothered to open it. The moment he'd hid it from Ariel's sight told me that it was of importance.

What kind of importance and to whom, I wasn't sure.

I heard Beetee crying, but when I looked over to her, her face wasn't one of immense sadness. No, her body was shaking and her tears streamed down her golden brown skin in anger. I noticed her eyes shift over to a yellow color and then back to their normal lilac. They did it again and again, faster with each shift. She held her head in her hands and kept mumbling, *"I c-can't."*

"You can't what, sweetheart?" Garrett asked, reaching for her arms.

"She is trying really fucking hard not to be an enormous snake right now, so I suggest that if you enjoy the interior of this room, you take her out back," Elise crossed her arms over her chest.

"I'll take her," Zane offered, walking up to her, attempting to place a hand on her elbow.

Beetee shuffled away, her skin starting to flake away in tiny pieces and her eyes now permanently in their yellow color.

Zane huffed. "Yeah, not in this house, you aren't." He bent down and placed his arms behind her thighs, hoisting her over his shoulder. She was still shaking, small hisses releasing from her mouth.

As we watched him go, Maurice spoke, "Ariel has no right to put him there! I'm going to get him out."

"As much as I love your spirit, Mr. Cassial, Ariel isn't going to just hand him over because you tell him how much you care for your love struck son. If you go, it will only make things worse, since from how that looked, the guy can't fucking stand you," Elise pointed out.

"Can you have a fucking heart for like two minutes?" I asked, furrowing my brow.

She rolled her eyes. "It's the truth. How else would you like me to put it?"

Natalia cleared her throat. " Please, before you both start, none of this bickering will get us anywhere. Instead of using your minds to think up insults for each other, how about you start thinking of ways to get your friend back."

Elise opened her mouth in what looked like a protest towards the word *friend*, but Natalia gave her a pointed look. "You could have decided to find a way to Purgatory since the last time you threatened to go, yet here you stand." Elise narrowed her gray eyes at the High Priestess but remained quiet. "Whether you admit it or not, you are content being a part of this little family we've all created so stop resisting it and start working together."

I wanted to say something snarky but a rumble came from outside and I noticed a set of black scales lined in pink through the window.

"Is she going to be able to change back in the emotional state she's in?" Garrett asked, concerned.

Elise nodded. "Yeah, super heavy emotions tend to overtake her. She can control it for the most part, but sometimes, it's just too much." Her voice had lost its attitude as she worried her bottom lip.

I looked over their heads to see Maurice sitting on one of the steps of the grand staircase. I moved around everyone else and came over to him, plopping down next to him. "He's going to be fine, you know. Ariel isn't going to do anything to him."

"Ariel doesn't have to, Reese."

I narrowed my eyes at him, trying to understand.

He sighed. There was a tiny second of silence before he sighed again and turned his face to look at me. "You know he loves that girl, right?"

"Dani? Yeah, I'm pretty sure we all knew before he did."

Maurice ran a hand through his dark hair, the gray strands contrasting with the dark. "Then like I said Ariel doesn't have to do much of anything. We both know Nick has thought of nothing but getting her back and now that is out of his reach. There is a brick wall in his path, no way out to be seen." He sounded tired and sad. He sounded like a dad that cared so much that it physically hurt him to see his son in this predicament.

I couldn't say I was familiar with that ideal. The only thing my parents cared about was making sure I didn't fraternize with people they deemed unworthy and the man next to me was one of them. After Nick explained as much of his missing past as he could to me, I had somewhat of a better understanding that my parents were bigger assholes than I thought.

They had to have known about Nick's mom, but maybe allegiance to something they considered was the purest in the realms was more important to them. They were far too old for it to still be blinding them, so for now I had to just assume they were the most stubborn fucking angels in the realms.

I placed my hand on his knee. "We'll get him back, Mr. Cassial. I promise."

He placed his hand over mine, squeezing it. "You're a good friend, Reese. Probably the best my son will ever have."

I smiled, scrunching my mouth to the side as I thought something over. "At this point, we've already proven that we don't follow the rules. The time for talking is over. Ariel wants to steal him; we might as well just steal him back."

Maurice huffed out a small laugh. "A rescue mission?"

I opened my mouth to speak, but an irritating voice plagued my ear drums.

"Rescue mission?" Elise repeated, leaning against the railing of the stairs.

I clucked my tongue, whipping my head up to her. "Yup. And please spare me your insanely unhelpful words of wisdom that are likely something like 'you are far too stupid to rescue your friend' or 'he's Ariel's problem now, we might as well do it on our own.'" I pushed off the stairs so that I could look down at her from where I stood. "Frankly your moody bullshit is not on the menu for tonight so if that's how you plan to be, your ass can sit here and wait for me to get back because I'm sure as shit getting my best friend back."

I didn't realize my chest was heaving, until I sucked in a breath. She blinked up at me as if she was unimpressed at every single word I'd said. Her silence frightened me just a little and I could feel myself wanting to flinch as if she would surprise me with a punch to the face.

"Are you finished?" She asked, sounding bored.

"Yes…"

She gave me a tight lipped smile. "As surprising as it is to both of us, I was going to ask you what you had in mind, Blondie?"

Natalia let out a noise, almost like a choked cough. Maurice had raised both his eyebrows and Garrett tried to hide his smile, but it wasn't fucking working.

"Oh…" I tried to muster up all the confidence I'd had a second ago, "well, I…I didn't really have one. I thought we could brainstorm a plan."

She groaned, placing her hand at my face and pushing me back.

"Yeah, *okay*. I generously give you an opportunity to impress me and you fail. Not surprised but, oh well, I tried."

"And what do you want to do, just go in and slaughter everyone? No angel left alive?" I countered, chasing after her as she walked away from me.

She swung around, pushing me back. "Actually, that's a fucking awesome idea. Good job, Blondie. I am so happy we have the same idea. Everyone let's go!"

Maurice and Natalia both held up their hands, halting her idea.

"No, Elise. I understand that some blood may have to be shed, but you cannot just go in with violence being the intended solution," Natalia said, sounding exasperated.

Elise tilted her head to the side, her black hair swinging above her shoulders. "Tell me, witch, why the fuck not?"

"Because your hot-headed little temper might get us into more trouble than it's worth," I taunted, gaining a growl from her.

Garrett spoke next. "Then what do we do? The sooner we get Nicholas back, the sooner we can head to Purgatory and find Dani. The sooner I can have my family and Beetee, her moms."

Footsteps sounded as they rounded the staircase. "Are you all aware that there's a rather large snake outside?" Xander hooked his thumb over his shoulder.

We all nodded.

"That's Beetee. She had to uh, let off some steam," I answered, receiving a look that said *ah, okay makes complete sense.*

Xander's teal eyes surveyed each of us. "Am I missing something?"

"Nothing to concern yourself with, hot stuff, just go back to healing the weak and wounded." Elise waved him off. He wrinkled his nose at her, but didn't make a move to leave. Xander looked towards me for answers.

I rubbed the bridge of my nose. "Ariel took Nick to the Ethereal Bastille. We want to get him out, but the *how* is proving difficult."

He nodded in understanding. "So, you need to get past a bunch of guards?"

"Clearly." Elise made a face like it was the dumbest question she'd ever heard.

Xander ignored her, his ears perking up when his High Priestess's voice rang out. "Yes, what are you thinking?"

He smirked. "I might have something that could help you with that."

"You're sure this will work?" Natalia asked, skepticism lacing her tone.

Xander eyed her with a mischievous glint in his eyes. "Of course, I wouldn't steer you wrong."

"You've made this kind of thing before?" Elise said, turning her nose up at the glass ball he was filling with a green liquid. Smoke bellowed around the ladle he used.

The Enchanter poured the last bit of the solution into the glass sphere, swirling his hand around the top, closing the opening. "Yes and no. I've made it but not this large of an amount. I had to eyeball the ingredients, especially if you want the dosing to do the trick on your stubborn sentries."

Xander had taken us to the Apothecary, explaining that a sleeping spell would give us the easy in we needed to retrieve my best friend. He'd told us that he'd formulated many sleeping aids for Enchanters, some of them suffered from insomnia or just fucking terrible nightmares and a good nights sleep was much needed. He made sure to explain that we shouldn't linger too long just in case, but he was good at what he did, so we should trust him.

I didn't trust easily, but for some reason I trusted this Enchanter that had nursed my fucked-up leg back to some sort of health and made sure Nick had his bearings after his overwhelming panic attack.

He turned and handed the glass ball to me. I held it delicately in my palm, watching as the liquid sloshed back and forth.

"Don't drop it, Blondie. It will be nap time for all of us." Elise moved past me, rolling her eyes.

I bit my own tongue as I stomped after her. Xander and Natalia followed behind us as we walked out the front door. A back to normal Beetee and grumpy looking Zane met us outside.

"Sorry," Beetee mumbled under her breath, looking embarrassed.

I knitted my eyebrows. "For?"

She casually moved her hand in the direction of Natalia's home. "For what happened? I just…sometimes…."

I chuckled. "Ah well, I would expect nothing less from our favorite reptile queen. If you didn't care so much I would think you weren't the real you." I winked at her, which caused her to grant me one of her genuine smiles.

"Are you two fine going by yourselves?" The skepticism in Zane's voice was more than apparent. His dark eyes looked between me and the less than appealing demon next to me.

"Awe, your concern is adorable." Elise batted her eyelashes at the large Enchanter. "Makes me want to fucking vomit."

Natalia cleared her throat. "I've been thinking about that as well. As much as I'm concerned for Nicholas, I…" She raised one of her defined eyebrows, her array of jewelry shining in the moonlight.

I raised my hand up to stop her. "It's under control. The little one will be on her best behavior." I gave Elise a smug smile, which she responded by giving me a middle finger.

"Um…a question?" Beetee's voice rang out as if she thought she might be intruding on something.

We all looked at her expectantly.

She hooked her index fingers together, strands of her pink hair hiding her right eye. "How do you plan to make it into the Ethereal Bastille? You can't use magic to just portal into that place and no way Ariel or any sentry will let you through without a valid reason."

I snickered, giving the cute little shifter demon my attention. "Oh, don't you worry, reptile queen. I have an idea."

We walked across the lawn of The Skies, the sentries at the gate coming into view. Natalia had sent us through a portal that had us landing a few yards away, so that we wouldn't cause a commotion. Elise had incessantly asked me about the plan, but I'd just shrugged and told her that she would find out soon enough.

My body was vibrating with what was about to happen as I fingered the strap of my bow that was behind my back.

"Blondie, you really need to fucking tell me what's going on, or..." Her words were halted when I kicked behind her knees, causing her to fall forward, but I caught her by the arm right before she fell to the ground. "What the fuck!?"

I reached for her other arm, twisting her wrists between my hands and dragging her the rest of the way to the sentries. I pulled her back towards me, so that I could whisper, "settle down and let me do the talking."

She opened her mouth to protest, but the sentries cut her off. "What's all this about?"

Elise tried to break from my hold, but I yanked her back over to me so hard that I'm sure she got whiplash. "I'm sure Ariel would *love* another potential threat in the Ethereal Bastille."

"Blondie! You little..." She whined but I shushed her.

The sentries eyed each other and then looked back at me. The taller one spoke. "Isn't your friend already locked up in there?"

The other one, a female with corkscrew dark curls spoke next. "Yeah, we saw him get hauled away."

I shrugged. "Yeah, well I'm not trying to end up like that, so I'm thinking this could be a nice way of getting into his good graces."

The female tilted her head. "Okay, sure. We'll tell Ariel."

I hummed. "Well, *actually*, I want it to be a surprise. I want to tell him myself. Listen, with everything going on, he's probably really busy with his ceremony and all that so I don't want to be more of a problem then I've clearly already been. Let me just get her settled in her new home. I know the way, so you guys don't have to bother with leaving your post."

I squeezed Elise's wrists as she continued to stay quiet. Her breathing was even as if she was stewing in her anger over this situation. She was smart enough to understand what was happening, so I was silently thanking the realms that she had decided to shut the fuck up.

The taller sentry nodded and stepped to the side.

My heart thundered in my triumph. Before we started walking again, I leaned towards the female sentry. "Do you happen to have the magic dampening handcuffs on you?"

"*Handcuffs*...you fucking..." Elise started, pulling away from me.

I twisted her wrists harder, so she winced slightly, baring her teeth. "It would be much appreciated."

The female sentry smirked and reached into the satchel she had at her side, pulling out the golden handcuffs. When they clicked into place, I took Elise by the arm and strutted past the two guards.

Elise huffed. "I *fucking* hate you so much."

"We're in aren't we," I stated, heading down the hallway and making the trek to the Ethereal Bastille.

She scoffed, shaking her head. "I still hate you. You aren't as dumb as you look, but I still hate you."

I wanted to let out a booming laugh, but held it in, releasing a small chuckle instead. "Aw, tiny psycho, the feeling is mutual."

27
ELISE

I was going to *kill* him.

He was going to die when this was over and I would make it slow and so agonizing. I had so many options to run through in my head yet none of them seemed good enough. The handcuffs bit at my wrists each time I flexed them, but I was vibrating with so much annoyed anger that I couldn't help it.

I peered up at the blonde angel and noticed he looked pleased with himself. I could strangle him, watching the life leave his hazel eyes and I probably still wouldn't be satisfied with my choices.

He had caught me by surprise, which I was mentally beating myself up about because that hardly *ever* happened. I wasn't a total idiot, so I wasn't going to implode the plan before it had a chance to even evolve. I'd nearly bit my own tongue through his short exchange with the sentries and maintained my silence as we passed by various angels, making our way to the Ethereal Bastille.

Once Blondie had his friend back and Dimitri was dead to all of us, I would formulate my own plan to lure him away and kill him. I would do it, I swore to *fuck*, I would do it.

I could feel the difference in the air as we descended some stairs and began to walk down a darkened hallway. It felt less airy, like the light that this place seemed to think it exuded was snuffed out.

I kind of loved it here. The Ethereal Bastille was the first place in this entire realm that felt normal to me.

"You going to remove these anytime soon, Blondie?" I wiggled my wrists.

He arched an eyebrow at me as we walked. "Not yet, just shut up and wait."

I growled at him.

He snorted, pulling me along. "You keep making noises like that, I will have to flick you on the nose for bad behavior."

"You touch my nose and I bite your fucking finger off." I deadpanned.

I chuckled to myself as I noticed him flexing his fingers out, clearly thinking about what I said.

Two sentries were at the large door to the prison and I heard Reese suck in a breath. He cleared his throat as we settled in front of them. "I'm just bringing another one in for Ariel."

The sentries glanced down at me. One of them stepped closer, kneeling down to get closer to my face. "Demon?" He asked, eyeing Reese.

The blonde angel nodded. "Yup, thought it would be nice for Ariel to find two of his problems in a cell down here."

The sentry not invading my personal space spoke next, "Aren't *you* one of Ariel's problems?"

Reese rolled his shoulders. "Yeah, that was before, but like I told the sentries at the front gates, I'm not trying to end up here, so can I please take my prisoner to a cell?"

The sentry with his face in front of me, pressed his finger into my cheek. "She looks harmless."

I let a growl radiate from my throat and I opened my mouth, snapping my teeth together just shy of his finger. He reared back, pressing his hand against the door quickly. I heard it creak open, a gust of smoke blew out near my face.

The sentries let us go past them, but they followed us in, closing the door behind them.

Reese glanced over his shoulder. "Oh yeah, I don't need you to come with us. I got this."

The one who got in my face tilted his head at me. "Yeah…I think we need to make sure this one stays in line. Vicious thing, aren't you?"

The blonde angel snickered. "You are *not* wrong."

"Hmph. Keen observation. Get in my space again and I'll rip your face open with my teeth, crunch your bones into dust and drink every last drop of your blood until you are nothing more than useless flesh. So *yes*, I am very, very vicious."

Reese let out a nervous laugh, pulling me closer to him. His voice carried to my ear, whispering, "Cool it, you psycho."

I looked up, giving him the most charming smile I could muster. He rolled his eyes, ignoring the horrified expressions of his fellow angels. He turned around, tugging on my arm.

"Do it now, Blondie or I swear I'll shove my foot so far up your ass you'll be afraid to take a shit for the rest of your life."

He huffed, slowing his pace. Reese casually reached into his jacket, pulling out the glass ball of the sleeping liquid. I looked behind me, watching as the sentries kept their eyes on me, but also kept their distance.

Smart.

I saw Reese tighten his grip on the ball and then we stopped walking. The rest of the hallway and numerous doors to my left and right lay ahead of us, but we had halted.

"Sorry guys, but I have a best friend to spring," Reese announced before he slammed the glass sphere onto the ground, watching as it shattered into a million tiny little pieces.

The liquid inside instantly morphed into green smoke. It became bigger and thicker as it continued to grow. The smoke curled and ran along the stone floor, nearly encompassing the entire Ethereal Bastille in minutes.

I practically gagged when Reese placed his hand over my face, shielding my mouth and nose from the smoke. Natalia had spelled us so we wouldn't be affected by it, but Xander had told us to try and not breathe it in directly if we could help it.

We watched as the sentries tried to dart towards us, they tried to yell for help but their movements were slowed and their eyes got droopy. They stumbled on their feet and eventually collapsed to the ground with a thud. It was amusing watching them drop like insignificant entities. I heard more thuds and groans as more angels succumbed to Xander's spell.

The smoke started to clear and I needed to get Blondie's fucking hand away from me. I stuck my tongue out and licked his palm. He awarded me with a hiss and disgusted expression.

"Ew, ew, why?" He pulled his hand away, shaking it vigorously.

I motioned to my wrists. "Get me out of these things."

He narrowed his eyes. "What's the magic word?"

"*Now.*"

He rolled his eyes, using his own magic to release me from the handcuffs. Once they were off, I twisted my wrists. He started to speak, but on instinct I slapped him across the cheek.

He stumbled back, holding the side of his face. "What the fuck was that for?"

I cracked my neck and shrugged. "Let's go find your friend."

"Nick!" Reese yelled as we ran down different hallways, searching for the love struck angel. None of the doors had openings, so we had no way of knowing what was behind them. Reese had yanked my hand away the moment I tried to open one of the doors.

He'd made a point to harshly tell me that we didn't need a shit ton of prisoners running around. I had spat back that they wouldn't make it far if I had anything to do with it. He'd simply scoffed and continued to shout his best friend's name.

"Shit." Reese placed a hand over his face.

"What?"

He raised his hazel eyes to the ceiling, shaking his head. "Jonah made these rooms soundproof forever ago. The log of each cell's inhabitants is probably with Ariel somewhere."

I raised my hands above my head, exasperated. "Oh well, that's *fucking* great, Blondie! What does that mean for us now?!"

"Stop yelling at me or I swear I will slap those handcuffs on you and leave your ass down here!"

"I would love to see you..." My words were cut off by a voice that made us both whip our heads towards where it came from.

"Reese?!" It was Nick. He sounded both excited and slightly confused.

I rolled my eyes. "Soundproof, huh?"

The blonde angel ignored me, his eyes widening as he pushed past me, walking down the hall. His head swiveled as he spoke. "Nick? Keep talking!"

"Reese, what the hell?"

I followed after him, really listening to where Nick's voice was coming from. We continued to get Nick to keep talking when his voice got louder as we approached a door at the end of a long and dark hallway. It seemed as if Ariel had put him in the most distant part of this prison. If I was Ariel, I would have done the same thing. Isolation could do wonders to destroy someone's mental state.

"Nick!" Reese yelled one more time, making sure we were in the right spot.

"I'm in here!" Nick responded, his voice clear as day on the other side.

Reese pressed his hand to the door. "I thought Jonah soundproofed this entire building?"

Nick let out a humorless laugh. "I have a feeling Ariel undid it. The asshole probably enjoys hearing the screams of others."

"Lucky for us then, huh," I said, pulling the door open when it slid away from the threshold.

Nick stood on the other side, utterly surprised by seeing us both. He hadn't been in here long, but it already looked like his incessant over-thinking had torn some of the light from his eyes. Reese ran over to him, clasping him in one of the biggest hugs I'd ever seen.

I tapped my foot on the stone. "Are you fucking done? We have to go."

"You guys really did this as a team?" Nick asked, raising a dark eyebrow.

"I don't have time for your annoying ass questions, so please for the love of Satan can we get out of here."

Nick looked a bit defeated. "I can't. I don't have my key."

"What?!" Reese and I both said.

Nick shook his head, a grimace on his face. "The minute I got here, she—"

I felt a sharp heat hit my back that sent me flying against the wall. I rallied quickly, my eyebrows furrowing when my eyes met the only person at the moment that rivaled Nick's blonde friend for the top spot on my most hated list.

Morgan let her long silky dark hair swish over her shoulders as she aimed her light at Reese, who tried to counterattack, but she was just a tiny bit quicker. His back hit the wall alongside me, but I didn't have time to figure out a plan against her. I was already too pissed to form words.

"Nicholas, what have you done?" She asked, her voice playfully scolding. It was almost like she thought this whole thing was funny. It was shocking to think that Nick had seen anything in her because all I saw was an angel that needed their pretty ass kicked.

I unleashed my tail, whipping it around and curling it around her legs. She had started to walk over to Nick, but I had her calves trapped and scooped her up. Her glasses fell off her face as I held her upside down, flinging her body outside the door and into the hallway. Before she could collect her barings, I grabbed her by the neck, sliding her body up the wall. I slithered my tail across both her wrists, coiling itself so she couldn't move her hands. Inky black lines formed along her skin and she hissed in pain as my venom was leaking into her veins.

I brought my face close to hers. "You have his key?"

She pressed her lips together, refusing to speak. Nick and Reese watched from the threshold, not bothering to interrupt.

At least they weren't *complete* idiots.

"Okay, let's try this again. I *know* you have his key, so be a good girl and just fucking give it to me." My hand squeezed her throat a tiny bit and her body tensed as if she was scared. She should be. If I truly wanted to, I could snap her in half before either of the men behind me could blink.

She narrowed her eyes at me. My face was so close to hers that I could practically count all the freckles along her nose. I pushed my venom out harder and she cried out.

"P-pocket," she stuttered.

I gave her a full grin, before I reached my free hand into one of her pants pockets, producing Nick's tiger's eye key. I tossed it over to him, as he caught it easily.

"You'll regret this, Nicholas. You'll regret choosing her." Morgan's words were full of malice and something else that tasted a lot like jealousy. It was heady and delicious. She was the kind of woman that made me want to tie her to a chair and torture her for days on end, just to watch her cry. Ugh, but this so-called team I was begrudgingly a part of needed me to be fully present and alert.

"I think *you're* one of his biggest regrets, sweetheart." I brought her forward and then threw her back against the wall. Her head hit the stone and she slumped down the wall. I ruffled my bangs, casting a look over to the boys. "What? She isn't dead, be fucking grateful."

We stepped out of the portal and onto Oculus grounds, our little group waiting to greet us the minute the portal closed.

Maurice pushed past everyone to get to his son. The two men hugged and then the older Cassial patted his son's body as if he was searching for any wounds. Nick waved him off. "I'm fine, dad. I promise."

"Ariel has some nerve. Jonah and I might not have always seen eye to eye or been in the best place, but he would have never resorted to those measures." The anger radiating from his father's tone had me itching to see Ariel and Maurice in an all out fist fight.

Nick hummed. "Ariel is a giant bully and we'll deal with him, but now…"

Beetee borderline hurled herself into Nick's arms, embracing him in a hug. Maurice moved back, smiling over at the amount of love his son was receiving. Nick stumbled back, but hugged her with just as much appreciation. The pink-haired demon pulled back. "Are you okay?"

Nick nodded and then waved over to Reese and I. "Who thought it was a good idea for this to happen?"

I clucked my tongue. "Your best friend, surprisingly enough."

Nick raised both his eyebrows at his friend but Reese just shrugged, punching his shoulder.

Natalia and Xander laughed. The witch shook her head. "What matters is that you're here now and we can proceed as planned. I wouldn't waste any time though. I'm not daft enough to think that Ariel won't catch wind that you're gone soon enough."

Garrett sidled up to Nick, his long braids held together by a thick ribbon. "We're by your side, Nicholas." He placed a hand on Nick's shoulder.

Beetee bounced on her feet. "Always."

"You got yourself under control there, snake girl?" Xander asked, looking her up and down.

She rolled her eyes, but then her lilac eyes found my own. She gave me a look that told me she was fine. It was as if she inherently knew I was about to tell her she wasn't going because she had just busted into snake mode a little over an hour ago.

I looked up at the sky, realizing that it was almost close to dawn. The place above the trees was still dark, but I knew light was on the horizon.

I walked up to Reese and Nick, observing the moment Blondie reached into his back pocket. He pulled out a leather bound notebook, handing it to Nick. "That important?"

Nick took it in his hands and pushed away from the way we were crowding him. He walked over to Natalia, handing her the book. "Can you hold onto this for me?"

Natalia cocked her head to the side. "Me?"

The pretty boy angel nodded slowly.

The witch's bangles clanged together as she grabbed the book. "Sure, Nicholas. As you wish."

Nick wrinkled his nose skeptically. "You aren't going to ask me what it is?"

Natalia ran her fingertips over the letters on it. I couldn't make out what they were from where I stood. "Hmm, something tells me I don't have to." She gave him a small smile, the glitter that dusted her dark skin shimmering. "Be safe please. And bring her home."

Maurice grabbed his son and tucked him into his arms. "We will deal with Ariel when you get back." His father whispered something to him that had Nick squinting as if he was trying not to cry.

Reese nodded over Nick's shoulder when they stood in front of each other. Zane stalked over to us, handing Nick his sword. He gave him a short nod before taking his place at the side of his High Priestess.

Nick adjusted his sword at his back then grabbed his portal key. His brown eyes locked on my grey ones as he tossed the key over to me. A small knowing smile played at his lips, but there was something in his eyes that told me he would follow my lead. His priority was Dani, so long as I took him to Dani, he didn't care what I chose to do.

Reese waved towards the space in front of me. "Lead the way, little one."

I recognized Purgatory the minute we stepped out of the portal. No, I didn't just recognize Purgatory, it was The Hearth that caught my attention. Beetee's hostel.

Why the fuck were we here?

Beetee nearly squealed the moment she took in her large establishment. Everything about my time here flooded into my mind. The images that passed by were good, bad and downright traumatic, but they were things that would always stay with me. There was something about each of them that led me to where I was right now and I didn't regret them. Would I have done things a little differently? Probably, but that wasn't something to ponder on anymore.

The door to the hostel opened and Beetee's moms barreled out, running towards their daughter. They were all talking at once and it was like everything they'd left out about her life didn't matter right now. The pink-haired demon wiped under her eyes, removing some of the tears she let fall.

"I'm so happy you're alright." Beetee placed her hands at each of their cheeks.

The red head with the pixie cut, Louise, I think, smiled at her daughter. "We are just fine. We kept this place running while you were gone. We were a mess when you didn't come back, but you're a fighter my love. Always have been."

Reese asked the question on my mind. "I am very much loving this reunion right now, but there was a plan in place here, yes?" He looked over at Elise, who had my portal key dangling from her fingertips.

"Yes, Blondie. It's just a pit stop. Next stop Dani, *okay*?"

Garrett hummed. "Let me guess you plan to leave Beetee here with her moms, while we go find Dani?"

Elise turned her eyebrows inward in frustration.

Beetee whipped around, her pink hair flying over her shoulder. "Ellie!"

Elise rolled her eyes. "Listen, just hang out with your moms. We'll come back for you when we have pretty boy's girlfriend back. It's not up for discussion. It is happening and that's that. End of story."

I let out a short laugh, which surprised me since I was already on edge knowing that in some way Dani was so close. I leaned into Beetee, knocking my shoulder against her. "She cares, but don't let her know you know."

That made her giggle a little. Elise bared her teeth. "Do you really want to get on my bad side right now, Nicholas?"

"You have a good side?" Reese quipped, smirking at her.

Elise held out my portal key, making another circle that would ultimately lead us to Hell, or at least a prison in Hell. Beetee touched her wrist. "You *are* coming back for me. That's that." Her lilac eyes were wide and innocent. Something about her had me thinking that it wouldn't take much for her light to come to fruition. Beetee was so inherently good that it was hard for me to consider she could shift into a menacing snake until it was happening.

"I'll think about it." Elise winked at her, then focused her eyes on the rest of us. "Hustle people."

I nodded over to Garrett. "You don't want to go find your family? I promise we'll come back for everyone." I side-eyed Elise, but she just glared at me.

He looked up at the trees and the sky that looked like a sunset, but it was always like that. Always an orange-red color that never changed unless it was the dead of night. "They aren't here."

"And you know this how?" Reese asked.

A ghost of a smile haunted his lips. "Leah and I are bonded. It's special in marriages for Enchanters. It's not a requirement but we wanted to do it for ourselves. I can sense her, feel her aura and presence. I don't feel that here."

I nodded, not knowing what to say. It was kind of beautiful when I thought about it. It wasn't something they needed, but something they wanted. That kind of love floored me. I wondered if that was how my father felt about my mother. I let that thought morph into one that had me considering that my current love for Dani could become even bigger than it already was.

"We good?" Elise asked, bringing me back from my thoughts.

"Yeah." My father's whispered words to me earlier settled in my head.

We are so similar, yes, but you are also your mother's son. You have her heart.

"Good. Now let's go get your girl."

Purgatory was a breeze compared to this. Elise had tossed me my portal key when we exited the glowing circle and the instant heat hit me. Purgatory was humid but you got used to it, it became palpable over time. My mouth was starting to go dry the moment we stepped into Hell. Everything had a red or coral hue to it and it smelled earthy, almost like clay. It was nothing to be disgusted over, but everything about this place made me uncomfortable.

Reese patted his arms and legs. "Oh thank fuck, I thought I would burst into flames once we got here."

Garrett and I both looked at each other and then back at my best friend. Reese looked confused. "What?"

I narrowed my eyes. "Why would you think that?"

Reese pulled his blonde hair into a messy bun on top of his head. "Angels in Hell. You can't tell me that this place isn't just itching to swallow us whole. We are like delectable treats."

Elise scoffed. "First off, angels don't come to Hell. They strictly go to Purgatory. Even I know that, you idiot. Secondly, don't ever call yourself delectable again, it makes me want to vomit."

I pointed over to the grumpy demon. "Where to now?"

She looked around, surveying her surroundings. The way her shoulders tensed told me that she was familiar with this place, but it wasn't somewhere she necessarily wanted to be. That made two of us.

Her eyes peered over our heads as she scanned the building behind us. "We're at the back of the prison."

"You portaled us right here?" Reese asked, looking around anxiously.

"Would you have wanted me to portal us inside, right in Dimitri's lap?" She said, sarcastically.

I let my mind travel away from their arguing, feeling my skin itch. The back of my neck was licked with sweat, but it wasn't that it was significantly hot, but something about this place felt like it wanted you to be on edge. It felt like the trees themselves were watching you and my anxiety was on a much higher level then I would have liked.

The ground was made of a red clay that kicked up easily and dusted around my ankles. There were pieces of gravel scattered throughout and it looked as if this place was on the outskirts of something larger. The building we were next to was wide, but had the same height as the castle-like structure of The Skies. The trees around us had no real leaves left on them, but their trunks were huge, providing cover for each of us, should we need it.

Broken and dead leaves were scattered at my feet and my thoughts halted when I heard a crunch. I noticed that none of us had moved, so I trained my eyes on various places it could have come from.

"What was that?" Garrett asked, trying not to make any sudden movements.

I was about to reach for my sword at the same time as Reese was about to take hold of his bow, but Elise held her hand up. A smirk played at her lips as she looked into the distance as if she was….waiting for something.

"The fuck are you doing?" Reese whispered harshly, looking at me as if to say *she is clearly trying to kill us*.

The crunch got closer and it was more constant as if whatever it was —was running.

The running was soon drowned out by the distinct sound of panting. Elise bent her knees a little and in a matter of minutes, a small black beast broke through the brush and jumped into her arms.

No, *not* a beast.

A hellhound.

Axel.

The little black creature licked her face rapidly as she stood up straight. Elise turned around to look at all of us. "You should see your faces. Priceless."

Axel wiggled out of her hold and bounded over to Garrett. There was a slight whimpering noise coming from the hellhound. He nuzzled his little wet nose against the Enchanter's neck, while Garrett stroked his hand down Axel's furry back.

"You knew he was here?" I asked, staring wide eyed at the hellhound.

Elise shrugged. "Yes. Axel likes to explore between Hell and Purgatory. He always comes back to me, well me or Beetee. He is mostly a good boy."

Axel ripped himself from Garrett and nearly flew over to me. I caught him, allowing his tiny pink tongue to give me kisses. Even though his eyes were black pools of nothing, something like adoration could be found there if you looked hard enough. He missed us.

I wasn't fast enough to keep my hold on him when he leaped from my arms to an unsuspecting Reese. My best friend awkwardly caught the small dog, tripping over a tree stump and landing on his back. Axel sniffed him, letting out soft barks and panting against his face.

"Why do we keep meeting like this!" Reese groaned, but his voice had no anger in it. He scratched behind Axel's ears, causing the hellhound to lift one of his legs, kicking at the air as if the scratching felt good.

"*Mostly* a good boy." Elise repeated watching them with annoyance. "Axel come here." She snapped her fingers and in the most dopey obedient way, he padded over to his mom. Elise got on her knees and Axel faced her, sitting down and puffing his little chest out.

Elise tilted her head to the side, her black hair swaying along with her. "Is she here?"

"How would he know that?" I narrowed my eyes at our surroundings, wondering how this would help us.

She ignored me and continued to stare at her pet. Axel let his tongue droop out, but then he was gone. A puff of black smoke took his place, leaving nothing else behind. Elise sat back on her heels. Reese was wiping red clay off his pants as he sidled up to me, confused.

Garrett, like Elise, didn't look phased by what had just happened. Before I could ask any questions, the black smoke returned and so did Axel. Reese and I slowly walked over to them, careful not to make any sudden movements that could throw off whatever the fuck was going on.

Axel raised his head to stare at us, showing us his sharp canines as he happily panted. He sniffed the air, right before thin veils of smoke bellowed off of him. He slapped his tail against the ground as if he was pushing the smoke towards us.

"Elise what the hell is..." I started, but then something stopped me. The thin smoke floated right under my nostrils and I tentatively breathed it in and my breath caught.

It was cinnamon.

I nearly fell onto my knees with the way my heart started to constrict in my chest.

Axel started to whimper, pawing at Elise's knee and then he pointed his snout over to Garrett. He pawed harder at Elise and then turned back to Garrett again.

"Leah? The kids? They're okay?" Garrett bent down, placing his hand on top of Axel's head. I was too stunned at everything to even consider the fact that we were all talking to a hellhound as if he was going to start speaking to us.

Axel nuzzled his face against Garrett's palm and licked his skin. He did one solid hop and let his tongue connect with the Enchanter's cheek. I was going to assume that was a yes to Garrett's question.

"Can he.." I let my words trail off, not really knowing how to ask my question.

"Can he what, Nicholas?" Elise pressed.

I bit my bottom lip, readjusting my sword at my back. "Can he in some way let me know if she's okay?"

Elise raised an eyebrow at me over her shoulder, but turned back to Axel. "Is Dani okay?"

Axel's playful grin contorted quickly into a sneering growl. He snapped his teeth and his claws dug into the clay under his pads. Elise placed one of his hands under his chin, causing him to freeze and look at her. There was a small moment between them and then she huffed out a breath. "Shit."

"What? What's wrong?" I questioned.

Elise pushed up from the ground. "She's in there, yes. Dimitri has her in a Hell locked cell."

"Which would mean…" Reese pressed.

"Every cell in this prison is locked by Hell magic. Axel can move in and out of those cells in a shadowy form without issues. Dani's cell is locked by Hell magic as well, but it's also sealed with infernal fire." She held her hand up to Reese. "And no I don't have time to explain to you what that is."

He rolled his eyes, but let her finish. "It just means, no entity from Purgatory or Hell alike can enter, unless he's given permission. Axel can't shadow in there, like he can for wherever Leah is, but he can waft her scent to us."

"What in the demonic fuckery?" Reese muttered, pining his hazel eyes on the black dog.

Garrett stared up at the large building. "He can take us to her though? To all of them?"

Elise scoffed. "Of course he can."

Axel wiggled his way around us, heading straight for the wide, ominous building that lay ahead of us. A breeze went by but instead of pushing heat towards us, it felt like ice. The sweat that was at my neck froze in place at the sudden disturbance.

The heat came back with a vengeance when the cold air had moved on. Elise followed her hellhound with Garrett right on her heels. I wiped my hand across the back of my neck, looking around at the trees, trees that acted as if I was an intruder. In some type of fucked up way, I was. I felt my insides wanting to rage against me.

The darkness I'd managed to place at a simmering level since we got back from Purgatory, it boiled inside of me. I swallowed hard, resisting the urge to let it ruin this for me. I knew when to ignore it and when to acknowledge it enough so that it didn't think it had power over me.

I curled my hands into fists at my sides and took short breaths in, letting my mind adjust.

I wasn't going to let it win.

Half of my heart was locked away in that building and I wanted it back.

29

DANI

Lilith had gotten one of her loyal Enchanters to come stitch up my wound, only for Dimitri to come and tear it open again. There was never a moment to breathe. There was less time for my thoughts. Lilith would laugh along with him, at the way my resolve was crumbling.

Was it crumbling, though?

No, *no* it was sturdy and it could withstand all the torment.

I *could* withstand it.

I would nearly choke on the copious amounts of blood he would show me inside my mind. My shadows would shift and caress my body as I was put through his torture over and over again. The light peaked out this last time, more than normal. It didn't like this, it hated my pain. As much as the shadows were my shield, the light wanted to offer me some sort of barrier as well.

Dimitri's green eyes sparkled with delight at the way the light threaded through my fingers. He leaned down and went to touch my hand. The light at my fingertips sparked against him and he reared back, shaking his hand as if it stung. He didn't have an upset expression when he stood back up. His face looked almost as if he was delighted. "Marvelous."

I brought my hands to my chest as I turned away from them. My reopened wound stung, my face hurt and my neck felt raw and mistreated.

I wanted a way to get Garrett's family away from here so I could just eliminate this Dimitri problem all together. At this point, I didn't really care much about myself, but they didn't deserve this. My head hurt too much to be able to think straight. My body ached with every move I made and I missed when I didn't have so much to lose.

I wasn't weak, but I was *fucking* tired.

"Are you ready to surrender, pretty girl?" He sounded so close to me, but I knew he wasn't. He let his voice echo off the walls and right in my ear.

Lilith's laugh echoed along with it. "You are being far too kind, Dimitri. She is stubborn, rightfully so. Waiting for that precious little angel to come and save her, it's sweet really."

Dimitri huffed, but the sound of him conceding had my ears perking up. "Bring me one of the children."

Lilith hummed. "Why not just bring both."

Dimitri snickered and I looked over my shoulder. He spoke to one of his guards that stood outside the cell. "Excellent idea, bring me both."

My heart thundered in my chest and though my limbs were sore, everything inside of me barreled on without glance at my pain. I winced as I quickly spun around, my palm heating at the amount of upset and agitation I felt. Lilith had her back turned to me, but I felt the throat clawing scream that released from my mouth as I held out my hand, the calculated explosion of light shrouded in darkness releasing itself.

The magic hit her back, spreading itself along her skin and I heard a sizzle that popped, like music to my ears. Lilith was hurled against the wall and I huffed out a breath. My arm shook as if I was feeling the after effects of my decision. Lilith whipped her head around, her face full of fury and pain. She narrowed her eyes at me as she stalked towards me, but I shoved her back with my shadows, pinning her against the wall. I pushed her back with so much force, that the destroyed skin on her back scraped against the stone.

Dimitri doubled over in laughter, reaching his only hand out and I felt a phantom hold on my neck, my blood starting to boil. My shadows ceased and Lilith was let go. Before she stormed over to me, Dimitri held her back the same way he did me. "Now, now, what do we have here?"

He'd given Lilith a pointed look as if to say *stay put* while he held me in place, seated on the floor with no more than his heated magic surrounding my throat. He gave me a full grin as he stared down at me. "Was that so hard?"

He still looked at me but was speaking to the remaining guard at the door. "Keep the children where they're at."

Lilith huffed, but didn't make another move.

I felt like my blood was going to start leaking from my pores with how violently it raged inside of me. Dimitri didn't let up. "A little behind schedule, but you always do what you're told, don't you?" He smirked at me, then released me from his hold. "Next time you can aim all that power at something that matters." He turned around, placing his tattooed hand in his pocket, sauntering past Lilith as if he hadn't just insinuated that she was nothing.

He nodded his head towards the open door, silently telling her to follow him. "We must set up a meeting with Lucifer and my father. Our little monster has decided to finally be oh so forthcoming."

My blood settled and all the pain flooded back to my body. I held my hands out in front of me. They were almost blurry with how much they shook. I would kill Dimitri, I *fucking* would. And if I had to go down with him to do it, then maybe it would be worth it.

I thought I heard panting outside my door as I laid my body down on the bloodied stones.

Panting and the rapid thud of a tail.

30
NICK

Axel led us around the side of the building, causing Reese and I to have to duck under some low hanging branches. No one had said anything about how we planned to get in there, find Dani and get out, but it seemed like Elise and her hellhound had this under control.

Reese had other ideas. "You do know that we can't just pop in and out like Axel, right?"

"Yes, Blondie, I am well aware."

"Okay, so then—"

Elise turned around so fast that we both collided with her. "I am honestly really not in the *fucking* mood for your questions. Would you like to get into this Hell prison or not?"

We both were silent, but nodded.

"Perfect. *Stay here.*"

"Stay here...Elise..." I argued, but she cut me off.

"You show up with me and this whole thing will go to shit. Stay *the fuck* put." She nodded towards the door that was just a few feet away from us. "I'll meet you there and let you in. Any issues and I'm sure magic man here can figure out something. Or Axel will take care of it." She pointed towards Garrett and her pet.

"Elise why can't we just go with you..." Reese insisted.

She had already turned away and was heading towards where I assumed the front of the prison was.

"Unbelievable," Reese mumbled.

Axel was already pacing near the door, clearly anxious for his owner to come back, or he was just ready to get this entire thing started. I pressed my hand to the exterior and it was like dark radiation emanated from it. My head throbbed with the pulsing of everything I'd tamped down trying to bubble to the surface.

It was minutes before there was shuffling near the door and Axel lifted himself on his hind legs to scratch at the wood. Elise peeked out, motioning for us to come inside. The amount of damp air that flooded out from the open door nearly suffocated me.

Elise hadn't even closed the door all the way yet, before I noticed the smell of fresh blood and the small groans before silence. I walked further into the hallway we found ourselves in and noticed four or five men and women laying on the ground in a small sized cell. The entire door was solid stone but there was a rectangular opening near the top.

Reese pushed past me to look, then he huffed. "We could have helped you with that."

Elise waved her hands at us as if to show that she didn't give a flying fuck about how we felt. She looked at Garrett. "Cover their angelic scents, will you." It came out like a demand and not a question.

Axel led the way down the empty hallway. It felt lonely here and a lot like death. The smell of brimstone flooded my nostrils and I had to stop myself from having a coughing fit. I didn't like the idea of anyone being locked up here, let alone Dani and Garrett's family. Axel stopped at the end, peeking his head around the side.

As we followed him, I walked closely near Elise, whispering, "did they just let you in or something?"

"No idea what you're talking about."

"Why didn't you want us with you from the beginning?"

"As much as I love an all out brawl, Nicholas, I would rather the fights be when it counts. Fighting front gate guards is not high up on my list of priorities."

That still didn't completely answer my question, but I decided to let it go.

"Did you run into Dimitri?"

We halted, hearing voices, but then they faded. Axel sniffed near a closed door, right as we heard footsteps again. Without another thought, Garrett yanked the door open and we all shuffled inside. None of us moved as the footsteps went past the door, their sounds retreating.

"To answer your question," Elise pushed away from the wall and followed Axel as he descended the steps that were in front of us, "no, he isn't here. Apparently, he left a short while ago."

Axel stopped after two flights of stairs and turned to shadows, disappearing from our sight. We heard him on the other side of the door, pawing at it. Once the hellhound had all of us on the other side, he bounded down the dark hallway that was littered with cobwebs and smelled so much like fire that my lungs were burning. The sound of soft crying filled my ears and Reese turned to look at me, his blonde eyebrows raised.

Garrett made a beeline behind Axel as if that one sound had given him more speed and energy then he knew what to do with. The large Enchanter stopped in front of a door and his face turned into something like relief.

"Leah?"

I sidled up next to him, seeing his wife and two children huddled together near the corner. I saw shadows form near them and Axel appeared, running over to the kids and burying his face in their small bodies. Leah looked up from where she held her children and it looked as if she wanted to burst into tears.

"Daddy!" Jasmine yelled, while Yuri scrambled to get up and ran towards the door.

"Are you alright? Everyone okay?!" Garrett said hurriedly as if he couldn't get the words out fast enough.

They all quickly nodded and Elise placed her hand on the door, red sparks and black mists flowed from her palm and there was a resounding click. Garrett all but yanked the door open as he barreled into the cell and grabbed his family.

"Alright, we love the reunion but..." Elise started but then a loud, gravelly growl came from outside the cell. I took a few steps out and noticed Axel's black hair standing on end near his neck. His tail was stiff and his stance was something I could only classify as immovable. The growl wasn't one of a small animal, no, it was something bigger and much more destructive.

I looked up from the hellhound and noticed three guards coming through the door.

"Who the fuck are you?!" One of them yelled, heading straight for me. Axel's teeth grew larger, extending from his mouth as he clamped onto the guard's leg, causing the man to fumble and fall forward. The other two, a short man with cropped dark hair and a female with two braids down the side of her head ran towards us. Their hands were encapsulated by dark magic which they threw in our direction.

I grabbed my sword from behind my back and blocked one of the streams of magic. The female stopped in front of me, giving me a mischievous smile before holding out her hand and letting her blackened magic mold itself into a sword of her own.

Garrett hustled his family back into the cell, while he shot his foot out, kicking the male guard in the stomach. The man stumbled backwards right into Reese, who grabbed hold of him from behind, shoving one of his arrows into his neck. Blood spurted out when he removed it, the guard grabbing his injured neck and crashing to the floor.

I moved my sword from side to side, blocking each of the female guards' blows. She was pushing me back, so far back that my spine hit the wall. She slashed up high, causing me to raise my arm and block the blow, but she took that as an opening to raise her leg and kick my side.

I blew out a pained breath, but I kept my stance, using all my strength to shove her back. I stepped forward, cutting downward to hit her ankle, but she spun away, conjuring dark magic in her palm and throwing it at me. Elise's hand shot out, collecting the magic in her grasp. Her body shivered like she was absorbing it.

"You need to pick one, magic or weapons, you can't have both you bitch."

The female guard looked at Elise, but then she really looked as if something had dawned on her. "You must feel right at home, huh."

"I have no idea what you're talking about," Elise said, but her shoulders stiffened a small bit as if those words hit exactly how they were supposed to. She shook it off, but the female demon had her sword raised but it went clanging to the ground when one of Reese's arrows went through her chest.

Axel bounded towards his owner, his face covered in blood as I looked past the female guard, noticing the one Axel had fought had the most mangled face I had ever seen. The female guard held the arrow in her hands and slowly pulled it out, blood leaking from her wound. Elise wrapped her tail around the guard's waist, holding her up.

I held my sword out and placed it at her throat. I said my words slowly, just in case anything I said was misunderstood. "Where. Is. She?"

The female guard narrowed her eyes at me. It was hard to make out the color of her irises when it was already so dark down here. She coughed, blood coming from her mouth and I realized Elise was squeezing her middle. "So many creatures down here, you'll have to be *fucking* specific."

She was taunting me.

I pressed my blade towards her neck, the silver wanting to become one with her skin. "Just *fucking* tell me."

"Or what? I'm dead anyway. And so are all of you when he's done with her." Blood trickled down her lips and onto her chest.

"So forthcoming aren't you. Axel can help us more than she can, but we'll just need one thing." Elise unraveled her tail from the guard's stomach and without even blinking, slashed the appendage across the female's wrist. A sound of intense pain left her lips as she slumped to the ground. Elise caught the guard's newly severed hand in her grasp. "Thank you for your service."

Reese made a gagging sound as he hustled over to us, Garrett and his family behind them. "What is that for?"

"Like I said, Blondie, only demons that have permission can open Dani's cell. I might have the dark magic to maneuver the lock but I don't have the physical permission." She dangled the hand in front of us. "Now I do."

"We will have to find her fast and hope no one comes down here before we've gotten her out," Garrett explained, nodding over to me. I looked down at Axel who was already staring up at me, like he wanted this just as much as I did.

"Get me as close to her as you can." The hellhound wagged his tail and darted out the door.

Months ago, if you would have asked me if I could see myself following a hellhound through a Hell bound prison, in search of my hybrid girlfriend, I would have said you were out of your mind. I pressed my back against the stone hearing the groans from cells around us. Axel had stopped and sniffed the air, licking at his blood stained teeth. His ears swung left and right as he looked down the hallway and trudged onward.

He led us down a narrow hall that seemed to diverge into two paths like most of them did, but this time we heard voices. Elise pressed her finger to her lips, placing her hand up as if to say *stay here.*

Garrett and Leah held each of their children, surprisingly having refused our offer to send them straight to Beetee and her moms. Their reasoning was that the portal from inside the prison could cause too much commotion, so they would stand by us or at least hide when they needed to.

Elise walked around the corner and started talking. I couldn't make out what she was saying, but then I heard a grunt and gurgled noises of choking. The dark haired demon brought her head around the corner and motioned for us to follow her. The narrow hall we walked out of, morphed into one that had a dead end on both sides.

"Axel…" I said, pining my gaze at the hellhound. He simply looked up and down the hallway as if to say *this is the place*.

"Start from that end and we'll start over here," Garrett delegated, bringing his family along as he walked down the hall.

My mind was racing with the amount of self doubt I felt. I didn't want this to all be for nothing. It wouldn't be. Axel wouldn't lead us astray and I wouldn't leave here without her. Reese was on one side and I was on the other, looking into the small rectangular openings at the tops of the doors.

Some of the prisoners were shrouded in their own darkness, not bothering to give us their attention while others stared right at me as if they were trying to dive into my very soul. Reese jumped back when one of them sprang over to the door, wrapping its hands around the bars. Every single time I looked into one of the cells and it wasn't her, I felt defeated and I was mentally counting down the time we had here before shit blew up in our faces.

I blinked down at Axel when I heard him whimpering. His claws were scratching at one of the stone doors. Each time he pressed against it, a wisp of dark red mist came from the bottom. I looked down at him, but he swiveled his head from me to the door. Then he barked at me. One stiff bark.

I ran over to the door, wrapping my hands around the bars at the small opening and peering inside.

I saw an empty room and splotches of dried blood littered throughout the space and then I saw…

I couldn't breathe.

I couldn't move.

My fingers flexed hard around the bars when I saw…*her*.

She was laying on the ground, her back to me. Those mess of curls I'd run my hands through more times than I could count were splayed out behind her. I noticed the large gashes on her exposed thigh and there was something about the way her shoulders were slumped that had my chest heaving.

I wanted to scream her name but something in my throat caught. It was like I was too pent up to speak. The already too hot prison suddenly felt like it was a million degrees. She was right there. She was right *fucking* there.

And I couldn't get to her. There was something in the way.

I felt like I could throw up from my array of emotions, I felt like I could fucking cry. I smelled that cinnamon scent of hers, but it was wrapped in that thick brimstone smell.

She was right there. Right *fucking* there.

My heart thundered, wanting to claw itself out of my chest. I blinked rapidly, the bars I was holding coming back into my view. They were in my way. This whole *fucking* door was in my way.

I didn't know when it happened, but I tightened my hold on the bars and started to shake them. I tried with all my strength to remove them from their place in the stone. I heaved out breath after breath as I pulled against them. I punched at the stone, pressed my fingers to the cold feel of the rocks. I couldn't focus on anything but this— but her.

"Open the door," I said more to myself than to anyone else. Axel was clawing at the stone with me as I tried to pry my fingers into the place where it met the threshold. "Open the door."

Reese turned away from his place a few doors down and tentatively walked towards me. "Nick."

I wrapped my hands around the bars again, nearly straining myself to find a way in. I heard someone call for the others, but they sounded so far away. My brain was overloaded with one thought and one thought only.

"Open the door! Open the door! Open the door!" I slammed my fist against the stone, thinking I had the kind of power to tear it down. I was losing my voice with how much I was straining it.

I saw her body move a bit, her shoulders shifting as she turned over. She pushed her curls out of her face and she winced as if she was in pain. Our eyes locked and I could feel my entire world collapse at the fact that she was too far away or I wasn't fucking close enough. It didn't *fucking* matter.

I nearly heard the metal bend on the bars as I tugged. "Open the door! Open the door!"

Someone gripped my shoulders and pulled me back. Elise was in my view now. "Okay, Nick. Okay."

She placed the guards severed hand against the door, pulsing out her own reddish magic. The area around the door dimly glowed a deep red, but then a click sounded. The stone pushed away from the threshold and whoever was holding me back didn't stand a chance of keeping me in place.

I ran into the room, sliding onto my knees the moment I was in front of her. Her mouth moved slightly, but she didn't say anything. It was at that moment that I realized she hadn't even been gone for long, not even a full two days and she looked like she'd been in here for months. I placed both my hands at her cheeks, noticing that my hands were shaking. My thumbs started to caress her cheek but she flinched.

I took a second to blink, finally taking her in completely. My thumb hovered over the large bruise at her cheekbone. She had the beginnings of a black eye and her bottom lip was cut. Her arm had large, long cuts and I surveyed the still bleeding open wound on her thigh, but then my eyes caught onto something else.

My hands traveled from her face down to her neck. Her brown skin was red and raw, like it had been burnt. She hissed as my fingers delicately traced the outline of a handprint. I clenched my jaw, wanting to remain calm for her but inside….inside I was fucking *seething*.

"Nick.." She started, her voice a little hoarse.

I brought my hands back up to her face, making sure to be gentle. "I'm here, baby. I'm right here."

She gave me a short nod, but leaned her face into my hands. She reached her hand out and placed it at the side of my face, bringing me closer to her. My lips touched hers softly and that's all I needed to know this was real.

The kiss was short and I would give her so many more when she was safe and away from his place. "I'm taking you home."

I started to get up, wrapping her arm over my shoulder so I could pull her along. We were out of the cell and I reached inside my shirt to pull out my portal key. My movements were stunted by clapping.

It wasn't a joyous clap, but one that told me whoever was on the other end of it was amused by this entire thing.

Footsteps sounded around the corner and the sight of a tattoo clad demon with only one hand had my fists curling at my sides.

"You really shouldn't take things that don't belong to you."

31
NICK

Dimitri reached his hand out for Dani, but I reared back, letting Garrett take hold of her. I pulled my sword out from behind my back and pointed it toward him. "She isn't yours."

The Son of Hell laughed. "Oh and she's yours? This isn't a game of who she likes better, it's simply a game of what's best for her. And that's being the most powerful being she can be. While on a throne."

Elise snorted, causing Dimitri to sneer at her.

"Back off and let her go," I demanded, holding the hilt of my sword so tightly that my knuckles were white.

Dimitri let out another laugh and snapped his fingers. The sound of multiple footsteps echoed and black smoke filtered in around our feet. The air became thicker and my vision was blurrier. I could see things, but most of it was distorted and misshapen. Something took a hold of my wrist, cranking it in one direction, making me hiss out in pain before I felt a blow to my stomach.

"Get the fuck off me, you little shit!" Elise yelled. I could make out the whip of her tail through my cloudy vision. A body collided with mine as we both fell to the ground. Reese shook his head, his blonde hair fanning out around him. I rubbed at my eyes, needing my vision to be clearer.

"Let me go!" Dani shouted. I watched as she kicked her legs out, scrambling away from whoever was trying to grab her. For a small moment, when my vision was palpable, I saw the way her fingertips sparked as if her light was brimming at the surface.

I pushed off the ground, heading to her, but my feet were pulled from under me and my face hit the stone floor first sending a painful vibration through my skull. My face was towards the entrance of Dani's cell and I saw Jasmine and Yuri hiding inside, peeking their heads out ever so slightly. I noticed a small floppy ear near their feet, telling me that Axel was with them.

I groaned, pushing off the ground and flipping over. I felt around for my sword, knowing it was nearby. Once I had it, I pushed every last bit of my light into it, watching it glow within my hold. The guard lunged at me from above, but I held my sword out, watching them fall onto the pointed silver tip. I lifted my legs and shoved them off of me, ripping my sword from their body.

Light cascaded around us and my eyes burned a little less. The blur that shifted my eyesight was gone. I shot my eyes over to Garrett whose hands were covered in bright yellow magic, magic that melted away the fog that loomed. A guard came at Garrett from behind, but Leah lifted her elbow, hitting him in the face. Garrett pressed his magic to another's face, using their body as a weapon to knock another one down.

Even with her less than healed thigh wound, Dani fought alongside Elise. Her shadows were easier to handle especially with the way she winced. Reese reached for one of his arrows and pierced it into one guard's leg, ripping it out and plunging the same arrow into their stomach, shoving them away from him.

Elise shot out her dark magic, connecting it to every target she saw, but a wave of dark energy swept her and Dani off their feet. A set of larger guards stalked over to them, their shadowy weapons at the ready. I held my sword out, slashing at them one by one. Elise shot her foot out hitting one of them in the knee. Her hit landed so hard, I heard the crunch of bone.

One of them hovered over Dani and she let her shadows come from her hand, sending them sailing backwards, causing me to shift sideways so I was out of the way. Before they could push off the wall, I turned my sword slicing diagonally across their chest, making my cut deep and deadly.

I heard a tiny groan from behind me. I turned to see the blood that slowly leaked from Dani's open wound, was bubbling. It was like it was being heated.

"You think I care about any of these demons you're slaughtering, Nicholas." Dimitri's voice rang out.

There was a ringing in my head. I staggered backwards, the hallway we were in fading in and out, while visions of blood and Dani's screams became more apparent.

Breathe, just *fucking* breathe.

My sword was strained in my grip. I closed my eyes, nearly tripping over a dead body.

I would never be fully rid of this panic, of this dark thing that still gripped me from the inside out. And I had to remember that I was… okay with that.

Dimitri kept feeding into that part of me, but something else crept in right beside him. Something wriggled its way through the cracks in my mind. It was still dark, but it was a darkness that wasn't my own, but it was a darkness I knew was safe.

I peeked over at Dani who gripped the wall as she pushed through the pain in her thigh. An arrow sailed by my head while Leah and Garrett were fighting back to back, but all I felt was the simple darkness of a girl I loved.

My light called to hers, so why would I ever think her darkness wouldn't do the same to mine.

The pain Dimitri tried to put me through felt so minuscule and unnecessary. I held onto my sword as I ran straight for the Son of Hell himself. I rammed into him pressing my side against his, digging my elbow into his side as we both collided with the wall. He shoved me off of him, his usually well manicured hair was now messy and unkempt.

I pulled my sword back to strike him but he grabbed the silver blade before I could pierce his skin. He held on so tight that it cut into his fingers, blood dripping down towards the handle. "She already took one of your hands. Don't make me take the other one," I threatened, ripping my sword from his grip.

I felt hands on my shoulders, trying to haul me back, but Elise wrapped her tail around their ankles, pulling. I wiggled out of their hold, before they descended to the ground, letting Elise finish them off.

Something yanked on my neck and it burned. I was lifted up and hurled towards the wall. Dimitri slammed his body against mine, while the tension at my neck held me in place. He extended one of his nails and sliced down my neck. His face was contorting into that thing I had seen for a short period of time when Dani and I fought in his office. The perfectly normal face he had was melting into nothing by gray matter and bone. His eyes sunk in and black whorls of nothing were starting to take the place of his bright green eyes.

"At least you got to see her before she destroys everything. She will create something so beautiful, but it saddens me to know you won't be here to enjoy it." His voice was so dark and unholy deep that it made my stomach drop.

He didn't *scare* me though. Dani could have given in to what he wanted, but she didn't. Could Heaven's Gate be better? Sure, but not like this. If Dani wanted to create a better realm, she could very well do it. He didn't need to be a part of any of it.

I gathered light in my hand, mustering all my strength as I brought my palm up and slammed it against his face. I wanted to blind him, shove the light down his throat and watch him choke on it. He coughed, still keeping me in place, but he stepped back enough for me to kick upwards, connecting my foot with his stomach.

He let out a guttural sound, holding his middle. I punched him with my free hand, watching as he clawed at his face to remove the remnants of the light I'd bestowed on him. I used the pommel of my sword to hit the side of his head. Flipping my sword around, I stabbed him in the shoulder, pulling out my sword so I could stab him in the stomach as well, before he could hit the ground. I extracted my blade from his body, getting on my knees and turning him over.

I clenched my hand into a fist and started to hit him. My knuckles collided with his jaw over and over again. I wrapped my hands around his neck, bringing his face up and slamming it into the stone floor. He continued to flood my mind with vicious thoughts and I pushed them away, even when my blood was on fire. My arm was getting tired but I needed him to hurt and get out of my head.

I kept going even when he stopped fighting back. Even when it seemed like he had stopped breathing.

"Nick! Nick! Nick, stop!" I heard my name and felt a hand tugging on my shoulder, stopping me.

I blinked up at Reese whose blonde eyebrows were furrowed. I looked from him to a limp Dimitri. His face was bloodied and almost unrecognizable. I tentatively touched my neck, feeling the blood from where he'd cut me. My hand suddenly throbbed from where I'd landed on the stones so many times.

"Nick," Dani called in a soft voice that still had every bit of confidence as the day I met her. She was hurt and needed more medical attention than this place could ever offer, but her voice still had me wanting to stand beside her in any battle, any war.

"He better be fucking dead." Elise wiped her face, removing any large remnants of blood.

"Nicholas, we have to go before more arrive," Garret pressed, gathering his family. Axel let out a huff, jumping into Elise's arms.

Reese let Dani hang onto his shoulder as I moved away from Dimitri's unmoving body and shakily got out my portal key. "Beetee, then home," he reminded me.

I nodded, giving Dimitri's body one long look before we headed out.

My legs gave out the minute we stumbled out of the portal. Dani rolled out of my arms and onto the grass. She blew out some of her curls that fell onto her face. A numerous amount of collective groans and grunts sounded around me. I made sure everyone was accounted for: Reese, Elise, Garrett, Leah, their children. Beetee, her moms and with a small bark, I knew Axel had come along as well.

My mind was still frazzled from the entire ordeal, pieces of Dimitri's mental torment still hanging on in my mind. I'd had to focus harder than normal to get us out of there.

We wanted to be out of Hell and back to somewhere safe. I had *planned* for Oculus.

A voice I recognized as not Natalia's caused my spine to go straight.

"Nicholas?" Daya called and nearly everyone turned their heads toward her.

I was looking at my dad's girlfriend, which meant I was looking at my house.

"I told you, you should have let me use your key," Elise grumbled, picking herself up.

Daya's eyes widened as she took in our large group. Alex pushed past her mother, a curious smile at her lips. "We really don't have enough room for this many people."

Daya shushed her daughter. "Nicholas, what's going on?" Her whiskey colored eyes found their way over to Dani, who was slowly pulling herself up from the grass. "You found her."

We heard rustling in the trees, causing everyone to stop.

"He sure did." A light shone near a collection of trees and Ariel stepped out, his voice giving my head the same throbbing sensation that Dimitri did.

"Oh for fucks sake, not this fucking guy," Elise whined, placing her hands on top of her head.

Sentries came from around the trees and wings fluttered as they shot down from the sky. Morgan sidled up next to the red headed angel, a bruise along her neck. I saw the way her eyes locked onto Dani. Next to me, Dani let out a low growl towards Morgan. More sentries surrounded us, but none of the people with me made a move to cower in fear.

"You honestly think I wasn't waiting for you to make an appearance again. The prodigal hero. I've been staking out your known locations since the moment I found out you broke out of your cell." Ariel gave me a disapproving look, almos as if he pitied me.

"Now isn't the time Ariel," I said, knowing that this conversation, this discussion would have to happen, but right now wasn't ideal.

"Break the rules, deal with the consequences. If you don't like it then you should have remained in your cell rather than do as you please." He pointed at Dani. "You have caused so many around you a great deal of pain. Are you proud of yourself, demon?"

"*Don't* talk to her like that." I took a few steps towards him, but the sentries that surrounded him stopped my movements.

"Collect them all. You should be happy I don't just sentence you all to death," Ariel said nonchalantly. His nose still looked swollen from where I'd punched him.

Another light flooded around us, closer to my house. It was another portal.

Natalia, my father and Zane stepped out.

My father ran over to me, pulling me in for a hug, before delicately taking Dani in his arms as well. He looked over at Ariel, his tone harsh. "This is my *home*, Ariel. Have some goddamn compassion for once in your existence."

"How did you find us?" I asked Natalia, who gave me a knowing look.

"Nicholas, I did once tell you that I can see your portal light, did I not?" The glitter at her cheeks sparkled.

Morgan scoffed. "Compassion for what? Disobedience? You brought back more problems, including a mutt." She nodded towards Axel who growled deeply, snapping his teeth at her.

Ariel looked around him, his green eyes wide with annoyance. "What did I say! Seize them! Or will I have to do it myself!"

Reese was readying his bow while I pulled Dani closer to me, but then a rumbling against the ground had us all stopping.

"What the hell is that!?" Ariel asked, looking around him.

Elise started laughing, as her grey eyes fell to her pet. Axel's fur was starting to shed and his floppy ears were decreasing in size becoming more pointed and short. Black eyes turned to bright red orbs and his nails grew longer as his body got bigger and bigger.

Alex cleared her throat. "Umm mom, aren't you afraid of snakes?"

I brought my head away from Axel and looked to my other side, seeing the Beetee had shifted completely as well. Her black scales gleaming with their pink lining and her hot pink tongue peeking out. Her yellow eyes peered down at Ariel as if he could be her next meal.

Daya had her mouth open, but no words came out. My father patted me on the shoulder and went over to her, his mustache twitching as if he wanted to laugh at her frozen expression.

"You can take us Ariel, sure. *If* you can get through a hellhound and a reptile queen?" Reese challenged, bringing his bow down. He went over to Axel, patting the side of the large hellhound

Smoke bellowed out of the creature's nose as he leaned towards the ground, ready to pounce.

Ariel regained his composure, swallowing hard. "This is not *over*, Mr. Cassial. These monstrosities are not allowed at The Skies." His eyes flicked from Beetee to Axel. "Enchanters stay in Oculus and so do your demonic friends. Including this one." He waved his hand over at Dani, but I held her closer.

"She stays with me and that's it."

"You are not in a position to make demands," Ariel said through his teeth, but the rest of his sentence faltered when Beetee let out a loud hiss, moving her large reptilian body towards him.

"Fine. *Fine*! She can stay with you, in your room as before. The privilege of roaming is gone now, Soul Seether. Dying in whatever prison they had you in would have been better than the lonely life you'll lead here." Ariel rubbed his hands down the lapels of his suit jacket and huffed. "I have a ceremony to postpone due to your selfish insolence. One that you will attend happily I might add, Mr. Cassial. I will work you so hard that whatever life you thought bringing her back to will be an afterthought."

He turned his back to us and was gone. The sentries made themselves scarce and within minutes Axel had returned to his small form, falling into Reese's arms and licking his face.

"That's a good boy," My best friend praised, rubbing the small dog's belly.

"Beetee, please change back before you give the woman a heart attack," Elise commanded, rolling her eyes as she snickered over at Daya.

Garrett put his hands up. "Wait, she needs clothes first."

Alex chimed in. "I have some, come on."

Dani limped over to Beetee, sliding her hand over her scales. I came over to her, placing a hand on her arm. She flinched at my touch almost as if she hadn't known it was me. Dani took a small step back, replacing my hand with her own, covering up what she could of the gashes Dimitri left along her arm.

"Are you okay?" I asked, knowing it was a question that probably didn't have a clear answer.

"I will be." She tucked one of her curls behind her ear, lifting on her toes so she could kiss my cheek.

She was the same person I was in love with but there was something missing. She fingered the wound on her arm again, looking down almost like she was lost in thought.

"Hey, I love you."

Dani lifted one corner of her mouth. "I love you too."

Elise took Dani by the arm and led her towards my house. I watched her walk away, furrowing my brow. I believed that Dani could do anything. She could fight anything or anyone and win. She didn't need me, but for some reason she wanted me in her life. That's where I would remain, until she told me to go away, but even then I probably wouldn't.

Something told me that Dimitri somehow still lingered between us. If the way she hugged her arm was any indication, I *knew* he still did.

PART THREE

"Claim the light. Claim the dark. Claim it all."

—

Beautiful Creatures

TW: discussion on past abuse

32
DANI

The shower water felt good, really fucking good. The heat had my bones relaxing and somehow comforted me. I tilted my head up, letting the water rush over my face and down my curls. I smoothed my hands down my hair, squeezing excess water out. I looked down seeing dirt and crusted blood circle around my feet before it made its way to the drain.

Natalia had taken everyone back to Oculus and then returned to Mr. Cassial's house with Xander, who inspected my wounds. He delicately touched over the places I was hurt and I couldn't help but flinch away from him. I'd had battle scars before, bled profusely and made it out the other side, but this was *different*. The Enchanter didn't let that deter him from doing his job.

He'd asked me how I felt. I'd tried to make a joke, something like *how do you think I feel* but all that got me was a raised eyebrow as if he wanted me to be serious. I told him I was okay for the most part; I was in pain, but I would manage. He planned to make me some items to heal the wounds quicker and even smooth out the scaring. He'd lightly placed his fingers at my neck and I felt my body wanting to shift away from him.

His lips pressed into a hard line, but he had let out a sigh and given Nick a nod over my shoulder. The Enchanter placed a tender hand on my knee. "I'm happy you're safe, love."

I knew there were creatures that had been in that place much longer than me, so I should be happy that I got out when I did. Time wise, I was only there for a day or two, but the way my body ached and this weird feeling I couldn't pinpoint, had me feeling like I'd been in there for months.

I had told Nick when it came to his own mental issues to take it one step at a time. I could do the same for myself. Especially when there was someone like Nicholas Cassial doting on me. He was probably right outside the door, waiting for me to come out, so he could tuck me into his bed.

He hadn't tried to talk to me about what happened in that cell when we made our way back to The Skies. He didn't try to push. The endless looks from multiple angels in suspicion or amazement was enough to keep my eyes forward before we were secure in the confines of his room.

Torture was something I was used to, so I *should* be able to take it as much as I've given it. Why did I feel like there was something holding me back? Why did I feel like I hadn't done a good enough job?

I placed both my hands on the shower wall, feeling my thigh pulse with the pain from Dimitri's long claw marks. The things that he'd shown me, the visuals that riled me up…they haunted me at the time, but I'd bared witness to so much worse that I knew it wasn't his mental debilitation that was gnawing at me.

I slammed my fist against the wall in frustration. Why couldn't I just be fucking happy to be out of there and alive? I was with the person I loved, the person I trusted with my entire heart, the person that…

Before I let that last thought out, I wrapped it tightly in the shadows of mind and held it hostage. That thought wasn't *fair*.

Lilith's words came back to me.

Waiting for that precious little angel to come and save her, it's sweet really.

I turned around pressing my back to the shower wall and sliding down so my ass hit the floor. I brought my knees up, resting my chin on them. The circumstances I'd found myself in required assistance, I knew that. I couldn't shake the feeling that all this did was make me feel weak, while giving the heroic side of his personality an ego boost. It made me yearn for what Dimitri had offered me: free to use power with no consequences, a fucking throne when it was all over and entities that thrived off fearing and adoring me. That yearning quickly started to make my stomach turn.

I knew it wasn't fair because I knew who Nick *was* and all he cared about was *me*.

But right now, how I felt about *myself* was all that fucking mattered.

TWO WEEKS LATER

I gave tight smiles to the sentries as we left for the day and to say I was tired was a fucking understatement. Ariel had decided that I'd had enough adventure, so mundane tasks for hours on end would be how I spent my time. One of those excruciating things being moving everything he'd set up for his induction ceremony from inside the grand hall to outside in the courtyard.

I'd widened my eyes, barely holding back the words I'd wanted to spew at him for seriously planning to go through with this whole ordeal. Surprisingly, when Ariel wasn't looking, I wasn't being shunned by my peers. They didn't quite understand my affection for the pretty hybrid stowed away in my room, but they chose not to question me about it.

Their constant inquiries about Hell ceased the moment Morgan would show up and inspect how things were going. I hated playing nice like this, especially towards those that didn't deserve it.

I headed down the hallway of The Skies, hearing chatter about all the changes Ariel was planning to make to this place. Each idea was more absurd than the next and I stopped listening to the gossip after a while. I opened my door and found Dani perched on my desk, running her hand down the leather-bound notebook Natalia had handed back to me before we left my house.

She looked up at me, her brown eyes soft and welcoming. Her curls were slung over one of her shoulders and she looked comfortable in one of my shirts. I leaned back against my closed door and stared at her. It was partly in what I now liked to call obsessively-loving adoration, but it was also in contemplation. The bruises on her face had healed and the swelling around her eye was less intense.

Dani sighed, holding the book up. "You plan to do something with this soon?"

I bit my bottom lip. "Maybe. Natalia said that she could feel some sort of magic in it, but it wasn't her place to mess with high executive magic, even in death. Or maybe she said especially in death. It was one of the two."

She nodded, slowly, placing the book down next to her. "I suggest keeping it with you, since you know, Ariel might have a means to raid your room randomly."

I let out a small laugh, rubbing my neck and feeling a knot.

Dani noticed the way I winced when I tried to release the tension. "I told you to stop sleeping on the floor."

"We've been over this." I walked over to the bathroom, picking up one of the glass jars that Xander had given us. It had a silvery gel in it that Dani had been using on her wounds. He wasn't lying about how fast they would heal up, but the scars were still sensitive.

I unscrewed the top and heard her huff out a breath. I scrunched up my face. "He said twice a day, Dani."

I sat in my desk chair and grabbed her leg. I pushed the shirt up, exposing her thigh and the three decently large gash wounds. My heart constricted each and every time they were in my eyesight. I placed the jar on my desk and dipped my fingers inside, feeling the cool texture of the gel. It sparkled slightly, but I knew that would go away the minute it was rubbed into her skin.

I gently started smearing it on her scars and I noticed her thigh tense up. It wasn't the kind of tensing that told me it hurt, but the kind that had me thinking that Dimitri's torture wasn't too far from her mind. I eased the gel into her skin, seeing the way she tried to look casual, but her mouth would twitch as if she was holding something back. In a flash, she pulled away from me.

"Okay, I think that's enough." She put one of her curls behind her ear, grabbing the jar and scooting over. She started to spread some of the gel over the scars at her arm.

The burn at her neck had subsided tremendously, but there were moments when she would turn a certain way and it was like I could see a shadow of where his hand had been. I wiped my hands down my pants, watching her carefully. "And this is why I sleep on the floor."

"Excuse me?"

"I didn't mean it like that, I'm sorry. I'm just...I'm *trying*, Dani. I want you to feel comfortable and the first night we slept in my bed since you've been back, you nearly jumped from under the covers cause my leg grazed your thigh."

"You ever think maybe it just hurt or something." She wasn't even looking at me. She put the cap back on the jar, tapping her fingernails on the lid.

"Sure, maybe. Did it?" I got up from the chair and stepped between her legs. She didn't answer me, so I continued to speak. "I want to be selfish, okay. I want to be in bed with you, holding you and crushing you against my body so tight you can't disappear again. I want to kiss every single inch of you until what happened is something you can't even waste time remembering, but I know you work on your time and that's okay. I'm the last person who should ever force you to be okay when you aren't." I delicately reached my hand up, brushing my knuckles against her cheek. I heard her breath catch the minute my skin connected with hers, but she let out a long exhale when I didn't move and just let her relax.

She reached for my hand, bringing it away from her face so she could kiss my knuckles. "Nick, what happened with Dimitri…"

I shook my head. "This isn't me asking you to tell me what happened while you were locked away…"

She kissed my knuckles again, one by one. "I know."

I took a deep breath in. "So, what were you saying?"

She looked confused. "What was I saying when?"

"Before. You were about to say something involving Dimitri and then I cut you off."

Her mouth formed into an O and she stuck her tongue out to lick at her bottom lip. She looked as if she was thinking, like she'd had something else on her mind but now she was reevaluating. "Uh, what happened with Dimitri was awful but don't pity me or the scars he left me with. I still have my light and my dark powers; I can still fight the same. A million creatures end up there and don't ever get out so everyone should just save their pity for them." She clucked her tongue, leaning back on her hands.

I tilted my head to the side, trying to piece her words apart. "I don't pity you, Dani. I know you would fucking hate that. Do I wish the guy was alive and here right now so I could beat his face in all over again, well yeah. As for your scars, if you honestly think something like that makes me want you any less, then you don't know me at all." I let my voice get low, whispering, "existing with all the scars, remember."

Her lips twitched into a small smile, but it was a smile that wasn't planning on staying for long. I pointed to the floor. "I'll sleep on the floor until you give me an okay. Not chastising me for sleeping there but telling me that having me back in bed with you is what you *want*." I walked back up to her, placing both my hands on either side of her legs. "The moment you do, the minute you say okay and lean into my every touch, then I'll make you understand that I will *never* stop wanting you."

Dani placed one of her hands over mine, worrying her bottom lip as if she was fighting against herself with whatever else she wanted to say. "Nick, it's not…"

I waited for her next words, but a knock at my door caused us both to jump.

"Yeah?" I called, listening for a response.

"You called me here to babysit," Reese answered, saying babysit like there could have been a better word for him to use, but he didn't.

Dani cocked her head to the side, raising one of her eyebrows. "Babysit?"

I ran a hand down my face, turning to head to my door. I opened it, seeing him leaning against the threshold. I gave him a pointed look.

"What?" he asked, completely unaware.

"Nothing, absolutely nothing." I spun around to look at Dani who was already holding Jonah's notebook. "I'm heading to Natalia's and then my dad's. Ariels had me running around so much, I haven't had a chance to really sit down with them. I would take you with me…"

Reese clucked his tongue. "Lockdown, hence the babysitting. Nicholas here, didn't want any of Ariel's little bitches to bother you."

Dani laughed and it was a nice sound to hear despite everything else. "I can handle Ariel's little bitches, including the head bitch himself, okay." She shoved the notebook at me.

"Is that Jonah's initials?" Reese asked, craning his neck to get a better look. "Wait, that's the book with the Jonah high executive magic stuff or whatever?" He said it so simply like this notebook couldn't just rip away everything Ariel was trying to steal. I had told Reese pieces here and there, wanting to keep him the loop as much as I could. He was more interested in the part where Ariel got kicked off his self-made pedestal and less on how it happened.

"Something like that, yes. Maybe exactly like that." I patted him on the shoulder and walked around him. I leaned down and gave Dani a quick kiss. I wanted more than that, I wanted a deeper kiss that she was dizzy from, but I could wait. "I'll be back."

I didn't like leaving her, but I also didn't want to coddle her. That was our problem last time she was confined to my room.

Reese saluted me and jumped up on my bed, scooting back so he could prop his back up against the wall. Before I walked out, I thought about what that meant leaving those two alone together. I was about to turn around and go to Oculus another time, but then I heard, "Are you wearing pants under that shirt?"

Dani's laugh vibrated through my core. "Yes, you idiot, well—shorts."

"Oh thank fuck, I did not want to have to keep my eyes closed the entire time."

I chuckled to myself, thinking that maybe he was exactly the right person for this job.

34
DANI

I slid off the desk, climbing onto the bed and tucking in my legs so I could sit on my knees. Reese whistled as he looked around the room, his hazel eyes landing on me.

"How is cohabitation?"

I bit the inside of my cheek. "Um, it's fine. Different than before since Ariel keeps Nick out all fucking day."

Reese nodded as if that made sense. "You could always make a break for it, you know. Have a little explorative adventure." He gave me a mischievous grin that I couldn't help laughing at. Laughing felt good.

"Don't tempt me. I've thought about it, believe me." I looked at his shirt, the sea foam green color offsetting his lightly tanned skin nicely. He shifted up so that he was more comfortable against the wall and pieces of—*something*—flew off his shirt.

I leaned over so I could get a closer look.

"What are you doing?" he asked, cautiously.

I reached my hand out and plucked something dark and thin off his shirt. "Is this dog hair?"

The blonde angel looked down, as if he was just now noticing he was covered in remnants of a certain hellhound. Reese ran his hands down his shirt, pulling at the material to try to rid himself of the evidence.

"It's okay to admit you happen to like the little fur ball."

"*He* likes *me*, okay. I *tolerate* him." He shrugged, settling back on the bed. "And I just so happen to love the fact that his affection for me pisses off his mother."

I giggled, but then my mind went to Elise and the others. "How is everyone?"

"Good, Garrett, Leah and their offspring got settled in some house Natalia offered them, Beetee is stressing out since she has the whole Daya thing to deal with, especially with her moms here now but apparently Xander likes to whisk her away to help at the apothecary and Elise is well…*herself,* if that tells you anything."

"And Maurice, Daya, the rest of them?"

Reese ran a hand through his blonde locks. "Everyone is okay, Dani. I wonder if it would surprise you to know that all of them have asked about *you*. They're concerned. None of us were locked away in a prison cell by our deranged ex who for some reason can't understand that no means no." He raised his index finger. "Wait, I'm wrong. Your boyfriend was locked away in a prison cell, but that was by a different deranged individual."

My heart had gleamed with pride when Nick had gotten to the part of his storytelling where he'd punched Ariel in the face. I really wished I had been there to see it because trying to imagine it just wasn't good enough.

"I can't say I'm surprised Ariel threw him in there."

Reese snorted. "Nick would happily go to angelic jail for you. That's a no brainer, Dani. It was pure punishment for him being away from you."

I blinked away from him, focusing on the soft comforter underneath me. Nick had no other thoughts but finding me and bringing me back.

He was never going to settle for less than that.

I fingered the scars at my thigh, feeling how much the raised skin had decreased since I'd started using the gel Xander made. I peeked up to see Reese watching me with a raised eyebrow.

"What?" I asked, moving my hand away from my thigh and threading my fingers together, placing them in my lap.

He shook his head. "You look better. I mean Nick has told me that you were better. You heal up nicely—physically, I mean."

I wrinkled my nose. "What does that mean? Physically."

"All the wounds look good, that's all." He pushed away from the wall, pressing his index finger to my forehead. "I don't know exactly what's going on in there, so I felt I needed to specify."

I bit my bottom lip, pushing his hand away. "I'm fine *generally*."

He let out a small laugh. "Hm, you sound a little like your boyfriend there."

I rolled my eyes and turned my body so I could scoot up the bed, resting my back against the wall. My head was at his shoulder, but he didn't look down at me once I was settled. The sound of our mutual breathing was kind of soothing to me.

I lifted my hand, letting shadow and light intertwine in my palm. It felt so easy now, giving my all to the two things I'd thought would never become a united force. The power got a little bigger and began to grow higher, but I snuffed it out by closing my hand. His eyes were wide and alert when I looked up at him. "See? Totally fine."

He furrowed his blonde brows. "Somehow the use of your hybrid powers equals you being okay in the old noggin." Reese looked off to the side as if he was contemplating this.

"Is that a question?"

"Uh…well…mmm, no." He rubbed his thumb and his index finger along his chin. He shrugged at my stunned expression. "So, I was talking to Alex about how her mom is afraid of snakes. How Beetee plans to even talk about that part, let alone the fact that she is Daya's long lost family member is lost on me….."

I reared my head back at the sudden change in conversation. I blinked rapidly, shaking my head. His voice trailed off as he watched me.

"What, what's wrong?"

I ruffled one of my hands through my hair. "You aren't going to question more about this?"

He scrunched his face up to the side. "About what? Dimitri? Your time in Hell?"

I blew out a breath. "Any of those things."

He narrowed his eyes, thinking. "Do you want to talk about it?"

It was such a casual question. He was giving me the option to be as open or quiet as I wanted. The way he said it didn't give me the impression that he didn't care, but that he cared *enough* to let me make my own decisions. Nick had gotten better about giving me space during my recovery while still hovering just the slightest bit. I knew the bruises and scarring made him angry to think about, but he hadn't pressed to know more.

I didn't think about it constantly and I knew Nick wasn't the enemy, so every time I flinched away from him, I wanted to berate myself. I could handle the cut lip and the black eye. I could deal with the bruised cheek and even the raw, reddened skin of my throat. What was continuously racking my brain was the claw mark from Dimitri's nails. Those left an impression, not only on my flesh but also on my mind.

He had dug them in so deep that I felt the muscles tighten thinking about how my skin broke, about how my blood drenched the area around me as it flooded out of the wound. I had been so close to giving in at the end and all these stupid scars, all of that fucking pain I'd endured would have been for…nothing?

I would have fought against him for…. what?

I could have laughed at myself. For what? *Power*. That was it.

Every touch from the angel I loved along those long claw marks made me wince and it made me feel small. I had pushed Dimitri away and I'd said no, but every single time I'd stood my ground, he showed me all the reasons why resisting was making a mistake.

He showed me the pain of others that I had grown to care about which made my stomach feel like it was in knots because I shouldn't *care* that much. I shouldn't care enough to let others be able to cause my pain. That made me *weak*…didn't it?

Fuck, fuck, fuck.

I saw a hand waving in my face and Reese's face came into view, concern in his eyes. "Are you okay? Where did you go just now?"

"I…" I started, noticing that I was delicately touching the scarred wound on my arm. I pulled my fingers away and firmly placed them on the bed. "What were you saying?"

He let out a half-hearted laugh. "I asked if you wanted to talk about it?"

"Oh right." I pressed my lips together, thinking it over. "I don't know."

Reese nodded thoughtfully, as if he was considering my words. "Hm…okay. Would you like to tell me what you *do* know?"

I tilted my head to the side, moving my eyes away from him and pressing my back to the wall again. "You really aren't going to just unload a million and one questions at me, huh?"

Reese huffed. "Listen, maybe I *should* have done that shit with Nick. Asked him a bunch of questions and made him tell me what's wrong, *maybe* I could have changed his outcome. That's in the past now. You might be surprised to know that most of the time I do pay attention Dani and *surprisingly*, you aren't Nick." He gave me a look of faux shock. "It is highly unlikely that continuously asking you what's wrong would get me very far, so all I can really do is either try to keep your mind off of what's bothering you or allow you to tell me whatever you want to say, if it helps."

Again, his words came out casual. They rolled off his tongue without an ounce of hesitation. If I didn't think it would have freaked both of us out, I probably would have hugged him. I stuck my tongue into my cheek when I really looked at Reese. He'd gone to Hell with his best friend to come and find me. He wasn't complaining to me about it, nor was he boasting about their accomplishment in retrieving me. He was just sitting here…wanting to make me laugh because well—that's who Reese *was*.

I sighed, debating how I wanted to go about this. "I'm going to tell you something and it probably won't make any fucking sense, but just let me say it and then we can go back to you making a joke about Daya's distaste for reptiles."

Reese lifted his lips in a tiny smile at my joke. "Alright, hit me with whatever you got, halfling." He made himself more comfortable, giving me his full attention. His hazel eyes looked more patient than they ever had. There was a small part of me that thought he might take what I said and run to Nick about it. They were the best of friends and Reese had every right to choose Nick over anyone else.

The larger part of me knew that he wouldn't. Unless I was in some type of imminent danger, this conversation would stay between us, almost like this weird friendship we had been slowly building was using this moment to define itself and continue to build on our previous foundation from our moment in Purgatory.

I fiddled with the bottom of Nick's old shirt, the hem hitting right at mid thigh. "Have you ever felt like you were upset with someone for doing the right thing, but you know you shouldn't because well, what they did wasn't a bad thing, it wasn't wrong, but somehow you still feel really fucking upset?"

Reese didn't answer immediately, as if he was waiting to see if I had more to say.

"You can respond, you know."

He blew out a breath. "Oh well I don't know, the last time I interrupted a girl while she was spewing out her feelings I got yelled at, so I was just being polite." He narrowed his eyes playfully, but then they returned back to their casually serious look. "I guess, maybe I've felt that way. That seems like a very specific to *you* situation."

"Oh, you think?" I said, sarcastically.

He lightly shoved my shoulder. "Go on."

"This person, in their head and their heart, had no other option but to do what they did. Which again was a good thing, it was a.... heroic thing."

"But you don't think it was heroic?" Reese questioned, his eyebrows veering upward.

I shook my head. "Oh, no, it was. That's the thing."

"The heroism is the problem?" He scratched his head.

I pressed my face into my hands, clearly not explaining this right. It never sounded perfect in my head, so why the *hell* would it sound fine out loud. I said my next words into my palms, muffling my voice. "No, no it's not. Well, maybe it is. *Fuck*! I don't know." I lifted my face out of my hands and moved my curls to one of my shoulders. "It sucks not being able to help yourself, having to hide your strength for the sake of others and then someone swoops in and does all the things you couldn't."

I lifted my eyes to the ceiling. "And it sucks because they are a good person, the *best* person. They did what was right and you wanted them to find you, but you are left feeling like you aren't strong enough to stand on your own somehow, like you'll always be waiting for someone to..." I swallowed, letting out a deep breath. "Waiting for someone to save you."

Reese's eyes were pointed down as if he was in deep thought. I knew I had said too much, too soon. I knew this was a stupid fucking idea. I cleared my throat, wrapping one of my curls with my finger. "Just forget I said anything at all, okay?"

Reese chuckled softly; his eyes kinder than I'd ever seen them. "Dani, can I speak hypothetically?"

I raised one of my eyebrows. "Sure..."

He spoke with his hands as he weaved his words together. "Let's just say there is a guy who has been hardwired to be a leader, always making a plan and fighting for those around him. And yes, we all understand how fucking annoying that kind of guy can be because he overanalyzes nearly every situation." He rolled his eyes before looking at me again. "Hypothetically speaking of course."

I nodded, slightly intrigued.

"Now, let's fast forward and this guy just happens to fall in love with a girl who can clearly take care of herself, but being the guy that he is, well...." He trailed off, scratching at his jaw. He raised his finger up to me before I could speak. "This girl probably didn't want to feel like an afterthought to everyone, but she might feel like people will view her like she'll always need someone—*specifically*—this guy to help her.

Again, hypothetically speaking, if I was her, I might feel a little like I'm weak from being made out as if I'm begging for assistance." He peeked over at me the minute he heard my breath hitch.

My shoulders slumped when he caught my eye and I didn't know what to say to him. The blonde angel tilted his head to the side almost like he was waiting for me to respond, or maybe he was fine with us just sitting in silence.

"Which you aren't by the way," he added, "begging for assistance I mean."

I let out a small smile. "I thought we were speaking hypothetically."

He rubbed his entire hand over his face. "Oh right. Shit."

I shoved his shoulder. "Thanks though."

Reese leveled me with a hard look that had my shoulders tensing. "Hypotheticals aside, you aren't weak. I'm not asking you to explain anything about well, *anything,* but you aren't weak no matter what anyone has told you or what you've been made to feel." His eyes wandered towards the wound at my thigh. "Someone swooping down and removing you from a bad situation doesn't change that."

I scooted off the bed with a laugh, somehow feeling lighter and I wasn't sure why. My next steps were halted when he continued. "You know just because you're strong and can handle your *own* shit, doesn't mean you should. You'd be surprised by how much strength another person can give you. Especially when that person already knows how tough you are and they love you for it."

I swiveled on my heels, placing my hands on my hips. "When did you get so profound, huh?"

He shook his head, scooting to the edge of the bed, so that his feet hit the ground. "Eh, I am highly underestimated." He lifted his shoulders in a shrug. "*But,* I might have heard variations of those things from Maurice growing up."

"Sounds like good old Maurice."

Reese pushed off the bed and nodded, rubbing his chin. "You still scare the hell out of me, if that's any consolation."

"It means a lot actually." I bit at my bottom lip. "Dimitri, he just… he held a lot over my head and I just…" I held my hand at my stomach, feeling the nausea wanting to build. The overwhelming thoughts of what had happened occasionally had me feeling sick, but nothing I'd bothered anyone about. I'd taken soothing breaths whenever it came about and it subsided. I swallowed before speaking again. "I couldn't do anything and I wanted to do more, I wanted to do it all."

Reese ran his head through his hair. "It sounds like your decisions played a role in keeping others alive, which personally I think sounds like you did a whole hell of a lot." He took a deep breath in and sighed. "Coming from someone who probably does too much all the time, likely at the wrong time, *maybe* you should look at it like doing nothing was the strongest move you could have made." He wiggled his eyebrows and I pressed my lips together, letting his words settle but also wanting to laugh for some odd reason.

There were things I still needed to discuss with Nick, things I knew Reese couldn't talk me down about. It was nice though, having someone who loved Nick just as much as I did, but who could also move that love aside to see my views—or at least try to.

The conversation was heavy, but it didn't feel like it when he spoke to me.

Reese tucked his fingers into one of his jean pockets, plucking something out and holding it tight in his fist. "Before we jump into the Beetee-is-a-reptile-so-how-is-Daya-going-to-handle-that-without-passing-out talk, I want to say I'm sorry."

"You're sorry?" I was stunned he was saying that to me, but also confused on where this was coming from.

"Yeah, I…" He looked down at the ground as if he was trying to get his words right. The way his body language morphed from something casual and languid to nervous and slightly uncomfortable was a little shocking.

I crossed my arms over my chest, waiting. My eyes kept glancing towards whatever he had bundled in his fist.

"Dimitri wouldn't have had an opening to get you or Nick would have at least been there as a buffer if I didn't ask him to go to my room for me."

I blinked at him, my mind rummaging around in my memories to understand what he was talking about. Then it hit me. Nick had told me he had to go to Reese's room to grab something for him and that he'd be back. Dimitri had come and whisked me away to one of the worst experiences of my existence.

I hadn't ever added Reese into the equation. The only person I was deeply pissed at was Dimitri. I would have said I was equally enraged at Lilith, but she didn't deserve any of my emotions. "Reese, it's okay. It's not like you knew."

He nodded, solemnly. "Yeah, well, I may or may not have been beating myself up about it, but that's besides the point." He opened his hand and in the middle of his palm sat an arrowhead that looked old, but like it had been taken care of at least. "This is what he went to get."

I leaned in a bit to inspect it. "An arrowhead?"

He used his other hand to pick it up and held it out to me. "It's a long story that isn't important at the moment, but the only actual important part is that it's lucky for me or well, I don't falter quite so much when I have it. Yes, I know it's stupid because it's a random object but we all have our things, okay. Maybe, it isn't so lucky because of what happened, but I'd like to believe that it still has all the luck in the realms." He grabbed my hand, moving my wrist around so I could display my open palm to him.

I felt the arrowhead drop and I had no idea why but it felt like something so small weighed so much. "Wait, you want me to have it?"

He furrowed his brows, shaking his head. "Oh, fuck no. That is mine and mine alone, but I think maybe I could spread the luck a little."

I stuck my tongue in my cheek to stop myself from smiling as I closed my palm around the lucky charm. "That's surprisingly nice of you."

"Pretty sure I said in Purgatory that we were going to start a friendship and you just so happen to make my best friend the happiest he's ever been." He tucked his hands into his pockets. "Also, before there is any confusion, you don't need luck but having just a tiny bit, even if it's in your own head, can make a shit ton of difference. I am actually really fucking good at what I do Dani, I know I'm that good, but sometimes you just need that extra push."

"I think Axel is making you a softie." I poked his stomach.

He waved me off. "I'm hard where it counts, ask any of my previous girlfriends."

I wrinkled my nose up and started to joke back with him when a voice caught my attention from beyond the door. My ears perked up at the feminine voice that made my spine stiffen.

"What's wrong?" Reese sounded like he was suddenly on high alert.

I shushed him, turning towards the door and placing the arrowhead gently on top of the dresser. I pulled the door open a crack so I could attempt to listen better, slightly hoping my ears were playing tricks on me.

Her voice filtered into the room, almost as if she was standing right in front of the open door.

"He has to learn his lesson, that's why Ariel is working him so hard. It does kind of suck seeing him this upset, but I mean Nicholas Cassial is the type to deal with the consequences," Morgan said, a nonchalant tone in her voice. "He does look really good doing all that hard labor though. The more he understands that she's the culprit of all his bad luck, the faster he'll be back in my bed and we'll be back to being the perfect couple we were always meant to be."

I heard her and another person giggle as if that statement was the funniest and most truthful thing to ever come out of someone's mouth. My eyes narrowed and I felt my body start to shake with this kind of overwhelming anger. It was her attitude about everything that made my blood boil. It was her lack of respect.

I was *very* good at making people give me a little respect. It was time I made that clear.

"Uh, Dani…" I heard Reese say as I swung the door open, feeling the cool stones underneath my feet as I headed towards her voice. "Dani, where are you going?"

Morgan wasn't that far down the hall, having stopped midway as she chatted with other angelic females. I heard hushed tones and whispers as I approached. One of the females pointed to me and Morgan turned around, her brown eyes widening when she finally took me in.

She quickly gave me a once over, but before she could say anything,

I had my hand around her throat. Gasps surrounded me as I shoved her body against the wall. Before I'd grabbed her, I'd noticed the bruising around her neck, remembering Nick telling me that Elise had been less than gentle with her when they broke him out of the Ethereal Bastille.

She clawed at my hand, letting out little grunts of frustration. I held on tighter pushing the others back with the shadows I conjured.

"Let me go!" She shouted, her words coming out a little strangled.

"Ah and why is that? Why shouldn't I just snap your little neck? It would release you from these delusions that you and Nick are meant to be. It's sad really, when you just can't get the hint that you aren't wanted."

Her eyes burned into mine and then I saw sparks come from my palm and light flash within my shadows. I felt her swallow under my palm. "You should have stayed down there, exactly where you belong. He would have gotten *over* you."

I narrowed my eyes leaning towards her and my shadows followed. I held my light back, not wanting to burn her skin, mark her body…*yet*. I let out a dark laugh that caused goosebumps to rise along her skin. "There is no getting *over* me. He went to Purgatory for *me*. He went to Hell for *me* and somehow you think you have a *fucking* chance of being better than *me*." I put my lips at her ear, feeling her try to kick at me but my shadows locked her in place. My whispered words caressed her ear. "You kept him from me by helping put him in the Ethereal Bastille and don't try to deny it because it's what pathetic little bitches like you do. I will tell you this once and only once, you keep your worthless little claws out of my relationship and what's *mine*."

I pulled back, bringing her face close to mine. "If you don't, well… I'll slice your pretty skin off and then if you survive that, I'll burn you alive. I'll let my shadows drag you to Hell and see how much you *fucking* like it." I pressed my fingers into her neck, smelling her flesh starting to burn slightly from my light, as I whirled around and threw her against the opposite wall. My shadows dispersed, bringing everything I'd blocked out back into my view.

Other angels gave me a wide berth but they looked on with shocked expressions, but no one made a move to help her or run away. I smelled sweat and fear among her friends, but all I felt when I looked at the guardian angel hunched over, cowering in much needed submission was success.

I saw Reese from beyond Morgan's group of friends, his hazel eyes perplexed at the scene I'd just displayed. It only took me one step before the angels that were in my way dispersed, giving me a path to walk through.

Reese whipped his head back and forth, from me to the now, very chatty angelic individuals. "Dani, as Nick's best and loyal friend, what the fuck? He wanted you to keep a low profile, not scare the everliving fuck out of his ex-girlfriend." I stopped walking when we got to Nick's door, facing him. His expression melted into a less frantic Reese and mischief played at the corners of his eyes. "*But,* as *your* friend, that was the best fucking thing I have ever seen in all of my existence."

I chuckled, rolling my eyes.

When it came to my dignity, my power and Nick, anything or anyone that tried to undermine those things didn't make me a little unhappy.

No. It made me lethal.

35

NICK

I stepped through Natalia's front door, instantly greeted by the High Priestess. Her hair flowed down her shoulders in a multitude of twists, thin strands of glitter string woven throughout. She gave me a smile that had me releasing some of the tension I'd been harboring from my shoulders.

I reached behind me, digging into my back pocket for the notebook. She tilted her head to the side as she looked down at it. Her smile began to disappear and her face started to carry a more apologetic expression.

"Nicholas, I already thought I told you…"

I stopped her. "I know what you said, but could you at least try?"

She pressed her lips together. "I understand you trusting me with this and I do believe this holds Jonah's magic, but even as powerful as I am, I cannot and will not intrude on this matter."

I let out a heavy sigh, realizing this conversation was never going to end in my favor. I held onto the notebook a little tighter, wishing that something in these blank pages would tell me anything at all.

Natalia placed her hand on my shoulder, not paying any mind to the busy Enchanters around her. "I know you want to stop Ariel by figuring this out, but you can't let this fill up your entire mind."

I nodded. "I know, I know. Believe me, I have other things to focus my energy on. It's just…this holds Jonah's power. This flimsy, slightly worn notebook, holds all the power that Ariel is trying to just claim without any right to it. It's just not fair to be so close, but feel like you have nothing to show for it."

Natalia took my arm and pulled me towards the left, out near the balcony. "If you want to consider the bright side, we both know that whenever that power would like to reveal itself from its place in the book it will never go to Ariel. All my years of knowing Jonah and I can confidently say that as regal as he was, he was also clever and smart. He would never let magic of that caliber land in the hands of someone like that."

"You're right," I agreed, wrapping one of my hands around the railing as I looked out at the front yard. "What he wanted, his power and everything else doesn't really matter if it's locked away and we have no idea how to coax it to come out."

"I am a strong believer in things revealing themselves when the time is right." She nudged my shoulder. "It makes the moments when you had any doubt laughable."

I tapped the notebook against the railing, flipping it open and fumbling through the empty pages. "Why would he do it like this though?"

Natalia raised her delicate eyebrows at me.

"Why would he entrap his powers in this notebook? Why not just have it go straight into the person he entrusted?" I furrowed my brows, my head hurting from all the times I'd gone over this.

The High Priestess turned, leaning her back against the railing. "Things are so much easier when you have an heir to bequeath something like extraordinary powers to. Jonah didn't have that so his decision was much more personal, less about magical nepotism. Perhaps…" She rubbed her lips together as if she was considering what she wanted to say, "perhaps his successor isn't an executive at all."

I pressed my tongue into my cheek, mulling this over. Natalia pushed away from the railing and moved to stand in front of me. "Even if Ariel gets through with this awful ceremony, he can always be removed by the real successor. Timing is everything to things such as this."

A throat cleared near the door. We both looked over at Zane who stood with his hands clasped in front of him. "Xander has been looking for you."

Natalia gave him a small nod before turning back to me. "If it helps, I'm still trying to figure out how to retrieve your memories. I know you didn't ask me to and maybe, you don't even want that, but I've felt awful about it. If there is something I *will* meddle in, it's my mother's magic."

"You rebel," I joked. "Dani made a point earlier before I came here. This might not be the best time to be harboring things in my room, so…" I held the notebook out to her.

She took it, running her fingers along the leather. "I'll keep it safe for as long as I can." She started to turn away, but I said her name, causing her to turn back towards me.

"I am curious. The whole memories thing. I don't really know if I'm completely ready to see everything I don't remember, but I'm curious enough for you to keep trying. I would like to think our mothers were close enough to where Moira would leave something open. Like you said a while back, magic has loopholes."

Zane, who had been standing silently in the doorway, held his hand out when Natalia gave him the notebook. She mumbled something about taking it straight to her room, which he nodded and hurried away.

"I have to get to Xander, but please stay as long as you need." She gave me a genuine smile.

"Thanks, but I'm seeing my father." I hadn't told my dad that I was coming to see him, but if we planned on any sort of normalcy, then I had never really planned my visits before so why start now?

"Good. And you? You're good?" She leaned against the door frame.

I shrugged. "More or less." I rubbed the back of my neck, giving her a lopsided smile.

"And what about her?" She asked this as if she had an inkling that I likely always had Dani on my mind. She was *not* wrong.

My smile faltered. "She's…okay. You've met Dani, you know how she is."

Natalia smiled fondly. "I do. She survived when she was meant to crumble and that is honorable. I do hope she knows that."

There was a glint in her honey-colored eyes that had me wondering if that last part was something she wanted me to hold onto. Natalia gave me a quick wave of her hand before she departed, leaving me to my own thoughts. I had decided that I could just fly off the balcony and head to my house when a voice caused me to halt.

"Nick," Beetee shuffled out to the balcony, her arms wrapped around herself.

I raised my eyebrows. "Hey, are you okay?"

She nodded, pieces of her pink hair flapping in the breeze. "I had a talk with my moms while you guys were off getting Dani. We talked about Daya and pretty much everything under the sun."

I had been completely engrossed in getting Dani situated and trying not to hover over her, that I had pushed the Beetee/Daya issue to the back of my mind. "How did that go?"

"Better than expected. They are the most understanding women I know. They're my parents, Nick, I just…"

I rushed over to her as she started to sniffle. "Woah, hey, you said they took things well. That's a big step, you don't need to rush anything. I just so happen to be excellent at prolonging things because I'm not ready."

She coughed out a tiny laugh. A few tears left her eyes as she sniffed. "They told me that…that they think it would be good for me to talk to her. They said she deserves to know who I am but that it's my decision how I proceed after that. If I don't want any sort of relationship, then I don't have to and if I do, then they fully support me."

"That's really good, Beetee."

She looked up at me with sadness swimming around in her lilac eyes. "Nick, I *want* to talk to her. Regardless of how my moms feel, I just don't want to have a great time getting to know Daya and Alex, but then I start to drift away from my moms because Daya is my *family*, by blood."

I placed my hands on both of her arms and squeezed. She rubbed underneath her nose, her face a little blotchy from her on and off crying. "Daya *is* your family, but so are your moms. They raised you, they taught you things and let you be this oddly bubbly snake shifting hybrid that cares so much about other people, that you created a hostel to keep creatures safe. You can have them both." I shook her just a little to get her attention. "You also have all of us, you know. You won't be replacing the family you've always known; you'll be adding to it."

She cried a little harder, wrapping her arms around me. I looked over her shoulder to see her moms at the door, waiting. They looked hesitant as if they wanted to make sure it was okay to proceed towards their daughter. I pulled back, watching as she smiled at me.

Beetee glanced over her shoulder, noticing her moms. "How long have you guys been there?"

The one with white hair, Willa, shrugged. "Not long."

Her other mom, Louise, walked over to her daughter. "We just wanted to make sure you were alright, that's all."

Beetee looked at all of us and nodded. "I'm okay." She focused on me. "Where are you headed?"

I looked in the direction of the North Village. "Uh, my house."

Beetee stuck her tongue out, licking at her bottom lip. "Can I go with you?"

I opened my mouth to speak, but it was like the words were caught in my throat. Beetee continued. "Can we all go with you? I don't want to intrude on your time with your dad, but I don't think I'll ever have the nerve to go over there."

Willa shook her head. "Honey, we don't have to go with—"

"No, if Daya is going to know me, then she is going to have to know you as well."

I scanned the three women, discovering that nothing more was going to be said and the decision was made. I huffed out a laugh. "Well, then I guess I'm not flying."

My father opened up the door, ready to embrace me in a hug, when he stopped. His eyes glanced over my shoulder at Beetee and her moms behind me. His eyebrows furrowed in confusion when he looked back at me.

I clucked my tongue. "It's a long story, but it's an interesting one."

My father moved to the side without another word, ushering us in. Daya and Alex sat on the couch, empty plates littered with crumbs on the coffee table in front of them. There was a soft grumble that came from my stomach. I could admit that I had wanted to come here to talk to my father *and* because I was hungry.

"Nicholas, it is so good to see you." Daya smiled at me and then looked over at Beetee. "And you brought friends?"

I pointed at her from over my shoulder. "Uh, yeah, you all remember Beetee and her moms, Louise and Willa."

The two women awkwardly waved, while Beetee plastered a friendly smile on her face.

Alex snorted. "Oh yeah, no one can forget the giant fucking snake in our backyard."

Beetee's lilac eyes bulged, her face turning red as if she was embarrassed. "Oh my…I'm sorry, Ariel was just…and I…."

My father came over, placing his hand at her elbow. She stopped stuttering and pressed her lips together, giving him an apologetic expression. "Sweetheart, it's alright. You got Ariel to flee with his tail between his legs. I'm kind of impressed."

"I second that. That was probably the second best moment of my entire life. It comes in right behind getting to play with a hellhound for a few hours," Alex chimed in, propping her hand under her chin as she rested her arm on the back of the couch.

Daya bit her bottom lip, peeking over at Beetee. "I'm not the biggest fan of snakes, but as Maurice said, you are an impressive sight."

I had a feeling that all Beetee got from this interaction was that Daya didn't like snakes, therefore, Daya didn't like *her*. It was irrational thinking, but Beetee was the type of creature that was all emotion.

She shuffled over to me, her moms close behind her. Her voice was low, like a whisper.

"Nick, I don't think I can do this," she said at the same time my father announced, "you all don't need to stand, we have enough chairs and food if you're hungry."

I looked from my father to the pink-haired demon who looked like she wanted to bolt out of my house at any moment.

Daya got off the couch and sidled up next to me. "Are you alright, honey? I'm sorry if what I said offended you in any way."

Beetee shook her head, turning her head to give her moms a swift nod as if confirming something silently between the three of them. She took in a deep breath, letting it settle in her chest before she blew it out. "There is something you need to know...or well, that we need to talk about."

Daya tilted her head to the side. "You need to speak to me about something?" Her voice was light and filled with understanding, even though she was about to be hit with something that would alter her life.

Willa cleared her throat. "Actually, Louise and I are the ones who really need to speak with you, first and foremost."

I could see my father from across the room, his eyes narrowed. I *knew* he wanted to pull me outside for answers but for now, he would just listen. Alex did the same, but her body was currently bent over the back of the couch, intrigue written all over her facial features.

"What exactly is going on?" Daya asked, worry laced in her voice.

Louise spoke next, "I've never been the type to try to make things sound pretty, so I'll just say it. When we were looking for a way out from under Lilith's reign, she asked us to do one last task. She wanted us to go find a baby and remove it from existence. We couldn't go through with it, so we raised it. We raised that beautiful baby girl away from Lilith and never looked back." She brushed Beetee's pink hair away from her shoulder, so that she could stroke her cheek.

"I don't understand what that has to do with me. It's a beautiful story and I commend you on not doing something so horrendous, but…" Daya started, but her whiskey-colored eyes moved to Beetee. She started to look as if she was rearranging all the puzzle pieces she had just been given, continuously placing them in different spots until something made sense. "Did you say Lilith wanted you to take a baby?"

Beetee's moms nodded. Beetee herself remained quiet.

"And you brought it to Purgatory to raise it….raise *her*?" Daya moved so that she was now right in front of Beetee. The pink-haired demon looked down at the ground, fiddling with the ends of her dress.

"Lilith told us the hybrid child would ruin her. Our Beetee would never do such things. If she wanted to showcase the immense power she had then we would let her, but she didn't. Thank Satan for it, because raising a snake shifter is difficult enough," Louise said, squeezing her daughters hand.

"Hybrid…" Daya's words halted when I heard her voice crack. Her eyes were glassy as she tucked her fingers under Beetee's chin, lifting her face upwards. Daya pressed her lips together as she examined Beetee's features. My father's girlfriend tore her eyes away from Beetee to look at me, silently asking if it was true. She was asking if the suspicions her mind was conjuring up were authentic.

I simply nodded.

She still gently held onto Beetee's chin, moving her hand to place her palm on her cheek. "You act just like her, you know. My cousin, your mother…she had this way of acting a little shy and she didn't like to step on toes, but when she loved, oh did she do it with her whole heart."

"That sounds just like our Beetee," Willa said, placing her hand over her chest.

My father slowly made his way over to us, assessing the situation. "So what you're saying is you're the baby that the whole massacre in Oculus was over? You've been alive this whole time?"

"She didn't know. We kept her in the dark for her own safety," Louise said, defensively.

My father raised his hands as if he meant no harm. "I get it. Believe me, I fully understand protecting your child by any means necessary." He didn't look at me even though I knew he wanted to.

"We would have come to talk to you sooner, but there was just a lot going on and we all wanted this to be her decision," I added, not really knowing the trajectory that this moment was heading towards.

Daya nodded as if she was absorbing every tiny piece of this conversation. She placed her hands at her face, discreetly wiping away her tears. "Layla would have done the same thing, if she had been in your position. I am eternally grateful for what you did."

"Layla?" Beetee questioned, her voice small, like she was testing out the name on her lips.

Daya tucked a piece of her dark hair behind her ear. "Oh. That's your mothers name, Layla. She and your father loved each other very much and boy, did they love you."

Beetee's eyes were shiny and her lip quivered as if she was holding herself together with the tiniest thread. "I wanted to say something while I was staying at Natalia's, but I couldn't. I should have said something after we all came back from the Dani mission." She shook her head, gathering her thoughts. "I just don't know what to say or where to go from here. I don't want to intrude on the family you already have..."

"Oh, honey no. Absolutely not. Distance and time will never make you any less a part of my family. It seems as though you have been raised by some wonderful women and I wouldn't want to force myself on you when it seems you've had a pretty good life." Daya smiled over at Louise and Willa, who granted her their own smiles back.

Alex hummed from her place on the couch. "So, what you're saying is that I'm related to a snake shifter?"

Daya ran her finger over her eyes, removing the last bit of tears. She gave her daughter a stern look. "Alex."

Her daughter giggled. "I know this is a heartfelt moment and I would love to know every single detail of this entire thing, but come on, we all need to admit that makes me ten times cooler in the eyes of *liter-*

ally everyone." Her eyes widened with amusement. She removed the humorous tone from her voice after a minute and gave Beetee a soft smile. "If you are nervous about the snake thing, my mom has always hoped that you were alive, so I think she will learn to get over her fear. When it comes to family, the woman would do practically anything."

"Yes, yes she would." My father leaned in to kiss Daya on the cheek.

Daya started to open her mouth to say something, but Beetee's incoming hug stopped her. I could see from the way her arm muscles tightened that she was putting all the strength she had into that embrace. Daya hugged her back with just as much fierceness. Neither of them said anything, but words didn't seem quite as important right now. Willa and Louise looked on, like they were happy that they were no longer harboring this secret from their daughter; they were happy she could be whole. Beetee could have the family that raised her and the family that shared her blood.

Both women pulled away, the air in the room feeling lighter. Daya held Beetee's face between her palms. "How about we all sit down and I tell you all about your mom and dad. And then you can tell me everything I need to know about you."

"She is quite the entrepreneur," Willa chimed in, wagging her finger.

"Mom…" Beetee whined, blushing. She turned around while Daya laughed and motioned towards the couch.

"Nice tattoo," Alex complimented, eyeing Beetee's back.

Daya pointed at her daughter. "Don't even think about it."

Alex stuck her tongue out, winking at Beetee. "We'll talk."

While they got settled on the couch, my father sidled up next to me. "You look like you thought that might take a turn for the worst."

I let out a small laugh. "Eh, I guess. I had every right to be worried that she might just decide to shift right in the middle of the living room."

My father held his stomach as he laughed. "Daya's snake fear would either get worse or be instantly cured if that happened." He ruffled my hair, wrapping his arm around my shoulders and pulling me close to him. "Should we go listen in on their conversation?"

"Um, I actually wanted to talk to you."

"About?"

"Dani."

My father nodded, looking over towards the chattering woman in his living room. He ran his index finger over his mustache before he nodded his head towards the backyard. I followed him out, rubbing my palms over the front of my pants.

"How are you guys doing over there, under Ariel's thumb?"

I rubbed the back of my neck. "Alright, surprisingly, Ariel isn't the issue. Well, he isn't the main issue. I can *handle* Ariel. He is a dick, but he is slightly predictable in how he operates. Dani is different...." I looked up at the sky, putting my hands on my hips. "And I love that about her. I love that she is this unpredictable creature that keeps me on my toes, but I can't help but wish that this situation was easier to read. I wish that it was, well....much more—"

"Predictable?" My father finished, crossing his arms over his chest.

"Yeah, I guess."

My father sighed. "You want to give her the world. You would damn near carry it all on your shoulders while she walked ahead of you if you could." He chuckled. "I felt the same way about your mother and there was a sort of pride in that kind of love, but Nick, there is also pride in understanding that women like Dani, they don't want you to just hand them the world or show off your muscles and hold it on your shoulders. They *know* you can do all that."

"I think Dimitri shattered her confidence."

"And I think that hurts worse than any physical scar he could ever leave her with."

"How do I fix it?"

My father walked over to me, placing his hand on my shoulder and bringing me forward. He tilted his head down so his forehead could touch mine. "You have decided to fall in love with a woman who can fight for herself which means when she's been pushed down, you help her get back up, but not by instantly taking her in your arms and carrying her. You help her by reminding her of who she is and the kind of power she has. Then and only then can you give her the option to be carried." He squeezed my shoulder before pulling away.

"She's not weak." I was talking to myself, but my father heard me.

"She isn't. *I* know that and *you* know that. But are you so sure that *she* knows that?"

Words I'd said to her pre-Dimitri's invasion sprang into my mind.

I'm not going anywhere, Dani. If Lilith or fucking Dimitri find out about you and come here, I'm right here. I want you to be ready, but I also want you to know I'm here even if you falter.

She was faltering, but she was strong enough to remember who she was. And I would be there to make sure she never forgot again.

36
DANI

I laughed at something Reese had said, while I fiddled with the arrowhead between my fingers. He leaned his back against Nick's dresser, speaking with his hands as if that made the story that much more enjoyable for the listener.

The door creaked open and Nick gave us a smile as he entered. The look on his face told me he had something on his mind, but there was also this look of relief. It was like he was happy that what he walked in on was two entities chatting like old friends and not like two enemies.

Reese gave me a small knowing smile before he patted Nick on the shoulder. He was headed for the door when he turned back, resting his hand on the doorknob. "Oh yeah, if you happen to hear anything in the next day or two, don't worry about it. Dani might have left the room for a few minutes and threatened your ex-girlfriend, but as you can see…" Reese waved his hand around the room, "all good here."

Nick's eyes widened in shock. "I'm sorry, what?" He looked over at me.

I shrugged nonchalantly.

He focused back on Reese. "Is Morgan at least okay?" The tone in his voice almost sounded like he was trying not to laugh and keep things serious.

Reese made a disgruntled noise. "Psh, I don't like her, so I don't care." He rolled his eyes, turning to me and winking. The door closed behind him as he stepped out.

Nick let out a loud sigh, shaking his head. His shoulders started to shake from the way he was laughing.

"If it's any consolation, the worse that happened was she might have pissed her pants. I didn't break any of her bones, or make her bleed profusely. I'd say I've been a very good girl, so she should be thanking me if I'm honest." I flipped the arrowhead in my palm, peeking up at my boyfriend.

Nick let out one more chuckle before sitting down next to me. "You are predictably unpredictable, you know that?"

I wiggled my eyebrows at him, leaning in to kiss the scar under his eye. "I think she'll move on from you with ease now. If not, well, death will be my only option for her." I lifted one of my hands and lightly patted his cheek.

"Hmm." Nick scanned my face with unbridled adoration. It brought me back to when everything had started, the kind of man he used to be. He had been all rules and no loopholes. The mission was key and side quests weren't something he gave a second thought towards. This Nick didn't flinch at my spoken thoughts of violence and I loved him for it.

His eyes flicked down to my palm. "What's that?"

I held the arrowhead between my fingers. "A borrowed gift from a friend." The words came out so easily and I had no intention of taking them back. Reese was stuck with me now.

Nick placed his hand gently on my knee. I flinched just a little and I knew he would remove his hand if I asked, but I took a breath and let him caress my skin with his thumb. "I stopped by Oculus again on my way back here. Garrett and Leah wanted me to thank you."

"They already did that when we got back."

"Yeah, I know, but they wanted to tell you again. I don't think they'll ever stop being eternally grateful."

I placed my hand on top of his. "It's really not necessary." I let out a strained laugh. "It was a piece of a cake over there."

His eyebrows furrowed. "Okay....well, Leah wanted you to know that the kids are calling you their hero…"

"Can we not do that please?" I said quickly, pushing off of the bed. My heart was beating so hard that my chest hurt. "I am happy they're okay and safe, but Axel is also the one who stayed in that cell with them and calmed them down. They can call *Axel* their hero. I'm someone who just sat there and…" I started to pace, holding the arrowhead tight in my grip.

"Woah, Dani, no one is saying you just sat there…"

"I *did*, though. Every option was blocked by a consequence," I muttered, letting out a heavy sigh before walking to the door. I needed to get out of here, anywhere that didn't have me almost spewing my entire thought process to Nick.

I pulled the door open a tiny bit, before it was slammed closed and Nick stood in front of me, blocking my way. "Please, stop."

"Move."

"No."

"Nick."

"*No.*"

I let out a groan, turning slightly and walking over to his dresser. I placed the arrowhead on top, looking at it. I gripped the edge of the wood, hearing it whine under my hold. I kept my eyes on the lucky charm as I spoke. "You don't get it. And it's okay that you don't because you grew up with the ideals of saving people and helping those around you. Those kinds of things made you happy and stronger."

He leaned against his door, listening.

I licked my lips. "Destruction and mocking those that ended up in my presence, those that had to endure suffering at my hands…that gave me strength, it made me happy. And then I started to…" I swallowed the lump in my throat. "I started to care about other things, other people. I wanted what I wanted, but I also felt the need to give a flying fuck about everyone else. That way of thinking didn't burn me like I thought it might, so I let myself lean into it. I could have both, the violent, lethal side and the side that cared and..." I glanced over at him, finding that he was staring at me, "fell in love."

I shook my head. "Then I was locked up by Dimitri. My intentions were to get out, fight him but then he took that away. He dangled a family in my face and had me holding my power back. Lilith and Dimitri, they both taunted and toyed with me, any emotion I had was contorted and what I wanted, what I had to do just kept changing or getting further away from me." I looked down at the ground, feeling my chest tighten. "I could sit there and suppress my power, letting him cause me so much pain in hopes of giving myself and everyone else more time, or I could give in and let him drag me towards destroying everything. He'd said he would let Garrett's family go, but what about everyone else I cared about."

"Dani..."

"Heroism looks so nice from the outside, you know? The act of saving someone looks so simple as if the choices are easily defined. No one tells you that sacrificing your own strength can be an option if it means others get to see another day." I ran my tongue over my front teeth. "I thought about how easy things would have been if I hadn't opened my heart to you, the light, or anyone else. I thought about how I would have adored Dimitri's plan forever ago; I would have thrived off of it, but no, I *care* far too much for that now."

I saw Nick run a hand down his face, keeping his hand over his mouth. I knew he was so eager to speak, but he kept quiet.

"Sitting there in a dormant state, pretending that I had no idea how to use my powers put Leah and them in danger, so little by little I had to bide my time and show Dimitri and Lilith *something*." I clenched my teeth together, nearly seething out my next words. "Hour after hour, it was *torment*, Nick."

I reached up and touched my neck gently. "I can *handle* torture, but it was like he was dangling who I was, who I am and what I could be in front of me, masking it together in this hopeful bloody mess that had me screaming with pride and crying in pain. I kept trying to figure out how I could save myself, but nothing seemed plausible. If I made a move to use my power to kill him then that would make matters worse…I just…"

He reached his hand out to touch my arm, but I moved away. I turned to look at him, my chest rising and falling as I heaved out breath after breath. "Eventually I let him see it all. I didn't mean to, or maybe I did. I don't know, but when it happened, it felt good. I didn't want to keep who I was hidden, but then what did that mean? Now I'd fucked everyone!" I heard my voice get louder, but I just didn't care. "Leah and her kids didn't have any more time to just *wait* for me to figure my shit out; I was going to be forced to become one half of a powerful duo I had no interest in being a part of and my only option now, the *only* thing I had left was…" My voice cracked before I could finish my sentence. I stepped over to the center of the room, turning my back to him. I crossed my arms over my chest, realizing I was shaking.

"Was what, Dani?" Nick whispered. I felt him coming up behind me, but he didn't touch me.

I pressed my eyes closed, dropping my head and feeling my hair fall around my face. "You."

I slowly turned around, wrapping my arms tighter around myself. He tilted his head to the side, but his eyes looked concerned and confused. "Me?"

"The *only* thing I had left was waiting for you."

He searched my face as if he was trying to understand what I was saying.

"In the end all I could do was sit on my ass and wait to be saved by the completely endearing, heroically well-brought up angel that I'm so fucking in love with that I damn near hate myself for even…. I didn't…" I placed my hands over my face, feeling so many emotions boil inside of me. I removed my hands, running them through my hair and ripping my fingers through a tangle. "There was a time that I didn't *want* you to save me. Maybe it was for your own good or maybe it was me wanting you to stay put so I wouldn't be forced to feel like such a fucking damsel in distress."

I pointed my finger at him. "I. Am. Not. And I never will be."

"I know you aren't," Nick answered, nodding.

I looked up at him, the smell of worry and love wafting off of him. It was heady and I wanted to bury my face in his arms, but—not yet.

"I wanted to hurt him. I wanted to use everything I'd learned about myself and stop him, make him pay. Enduring all that agony was worth it if I could just show him and Lilith that fucking with me was a mistake. I *wanted* a lot of things, but what I *got* was you and everyone else doing what I'd wanted to do!"

Nick let out a deep sigh, rubbing his finger at the place between his eyebrows. "We all care about you, Dani. We were never going to leave you in that place with him. *I* was never going to leave you."

"I know that. That's what makes this so fucking hard. I wanted you to find me, but then again, I didn't. There was a time before you, Nick, when I didn't need anyone and even during the toughest trials...I could save *myself*." I turned away from him, hoping I could head to the bathroom and lock myself in there.

He caught my wrist, causing me to stumble a bit before I righted myself. I swung my head around to face him. Before he could speak, I heard myself shouting again. "I couldn't even be my own hero, Nick!" I felt tears wanting to leave my eyes.

Nick pulled me closer to him, his expression something I could only describe as determined. "I *know* you can fend for yourself, Dani. I *understand* that you can fight and take on the worst kind of villain without me, but despite all those things I *know* about you, there is not an evil in the realms that will stop me from getting to you. I will *always* find you."

I bit my bottom lip. "I know you will. It's who you are." I inclined my head towards his. "*You* swooped in there, *you* killed Dimitri. I just... I vowed that *I* would kill him, *I* would make him hurt. Even if you were the one to open that door and save me, maybe I could at least do something that would make me feel less expendable and weak."

He let go of my wrist, placing his hands on my waist. "I will *not* apologize for beating the shit out of Dimitri. *Fuck*, Dani, I watched you die and I never want either of us in that position ever again. You keep saying I'm yours, well in case you need a reminder, you're mine. I am fucking ecstatic that I get to say my girlfriend is extremely strong, she's powerful and scary, she's beautiful and can probably make your death look like an art form. The fact that you think you are less than what everyone in the realms knows you to be makes me want to bring Dimitri back, just so you can show him all you've got. I'll stand beside you or behind you, whichever you'd prefer, but you are *done* standing alone."

I didn't know what to do with my hands so I tentatively placed them on his biceps. I hadn't realized how unsteady I felt until his skin was within my grasp. "Nick, they made me feel like you coming made me weak. I don't *want* to be weak; I can't. That's not who I am!"

He squeezed my waist, his brown eyes piercing into mine. "You are *not* weak. I will keep telling you that for the rest of our lives if I have to. Big shows of power are great, Dani. Perfect spectacles to gloat about later." He took one of his hands and brought it to the side of my face. I didn't flinch this time. I leaned into his touch quicker than I expected. "You are so used to fighting first and thinking later, which for a good while was how you survived and I commend you for it. You had to steel yourself and think about other people. You had to consider the risk of what a hasty decision would do. You continuously suffered Dimitri's... abuse" I noticed his jaw tick as he continued to speak, "and you made it out the other side. You really want to stand here and tell me that that makes you weak? You want to tell me that it doesn't make you some kind of hero?" He placed his forehead against mine.

"I don't know what I am," I murmured.

"Oh, baby, you are something to be afraid of. You are something to admire." He kissed my forehead, letting his lips linger there. "Once upon a time you told me to remember who I was, remember that I was a hero."

"I did."

"Despite everything I'd been through, everything I was putting myself through, I was still a *hero*. I'm telling you the same thing. Remember who *you* are, Dani."

"And who is that?"

"The *strongest* person I know."

I reared my head back so I could look at him. His eyes were genuine and I didn't have to think twice when I lifted up on my toes, kissing him. His lips were soft and inviting. I opened my mouth a tiny bit, hoping that he would mirror my movements which after a second, he did.

He gave me a tiny peck before we separated, but he kept a hold on my hands, his fingers intertwining with my own. My cheeks felt wet from the tears I'd let fly free.

"I know you have to believe in yourself when it comes to these things, Dani. I know just me saying all of this, as true as it is, won't be enough, but…"

"I just haven't felt like myself lately, that's all. I…hmm…" I wrinkled my nose, not really knowing how to say what I wanted.

Nick gave me a look filled with intrigue.

"When I manhandled Morgan, it felt….good. Like all I wanted to do was hit something to, I don't know, jolt the healing process."

Nick pressed his lips together. "Mhmm. Sounds logical."

I had let Morgan live so that said a lot about my progress.

"I'm gonna work on it, okay? I've had to be my own strength for a long time now. I've never let other people offer up their own whenever I faltered."

His fingers tightened and flexed around mine. "Existing together. You and me."

"You and me," I repeated, leaning in to kiss him again, but something stopped me. My palms felt hot, but not the normal heat that I was used to. This heat burned like it had doubled in temperature, but it didn't hurt. I looked down at my hands, noticing the light that filtered out from between our palms.

"Uh, Dani…" Nick started, pulling our hands up so that they were parallel to our bodies.

I slowly pulled one of my hands away from his, watching as the light that came between them was bright and nearly blinding. I grabbed his hand again, admitting silently to myself that what I'd seen was startling.

"What's happening?" I asked, more to myself than to him.

"I felt this while I was in the Ethereal Bastille," he admitted.

I looked between us, at the glow that illuminated between our palms. The tug I'd felt hours before Nick and everyone else had busted into Dimitri's prison. The familiar light that nearly matched my own.

"Me too," I said, feeling a tingle in my hands. It was like a caress that I never wanted to end. It felt comfortable and had a simplicity that I didn't know I could want. My chest tightened when I looked into his eyes, the white golden light from our hands casting a glow along his face.

I would find my way back to the powerful hybrid I knew myself to be, but I also knew that faltering was okay, since I had more than enough people to lean on. Nick had the biceps to hold me up, I was definitely sure of that.

Without a moment to waste I ripped my hands from his, placing them on either side of his neck as I kissed him. He let out a small hiss that had me pulling back. I blinked over to where my hands were, seeing that I had started to burn him.

An apology was on my lips, but he shushed me. "It's okay. You can burn me whenever you like."

"I want you back in bed. I don't want you sleeping on the floor. You want to be by my side, Mr. Cassial?" I asked, tilting my head to the side.

He nodded. "Like I said, by your side or behind you. I'm there."

"Then I want you back in bed with me." I made a move to walk forward, causing him to go backwards towards his bed. "I want *your* touch. I want *your* hands on me, being gentle and making me feel safe. I want *your* kiss making me forget and easing my pain." My voice got small as I spoke my next words, not really knowing how else to convey my feelings. "You're my home."

His mouth was on mine before I could say anything else.

"I love you," he said in between his kisses. He turned us around, so that the back of my calves hit the side of his bed. I sat down, scooting backwards and bending my knees slightly. The shirt I'd borrowed from him riding up my thighs.

He looked patient as he delicately placed his hand at my knee, gliding it down my leg. His fingers stopped once they touched the beginning of the long pink scars at my thigh. My muscles started to tighten at the feeling of his fingertips, but I swallowed, nodding at him. He kept going, tracing the scars with a feather-like touch.

He bent down, placing his face near my thigh and my muscles relaxed slowly as I felt him kiss the raised lines. I held in something I could only call a whimper because this had nothing to do with sex and everything to do with love.

He kissed every inch of my scar, making sure not to go too fast and then lifted himself up to kiss my lips again. "Okay?" He was checking in on me, making sure I was good with how things were going.

I felt myself starting to cry again as I nodded. "I love you too." It was wild how love and strength were so intertwined.

He kissed me again, before carefully maneuvering my body so that my head rested on his pillows. "I know you have some issues with me charging in and helping you, but right now, *please* let me make you feel good."

37
NICK

Dani didn't say anything. She just looked up at me with a few tears streaming down her cheeks and I reached up, swiping them away with my thumb. I saw her chest rise and fall as she let out steady breaths. It was times like this that confirmed I, of course, thought she was beautiful when she was confident and unyielding, but I also thought she carried the same beauty when she was unsure and vulnerable.

I hovered over her, preparing myself to go as slowly as I could. I would spend hours here with her if that's what she wanted, if that's what she needed from me. She reached for my shirt, making a motion to try and tug me down. I obliged, feeling her breath against my skin when I was inches from her face.

I caressed her cheek, watching as she leaned into my touch. I kissed her other cheek, trailing those kisses to her jaw. "It's just you and me."

I kissed her neck, remembering what it was like seeing that reddened handprint encompassing her throat. My shoulders tensed at the memory and then I blinked, bringing myself back and taking a look at her neck again. The handprint was gone now and she was okay. She was here. She was with me, safe.

If this were a different time, I would have let my kisses travel between her breasts and down her stomach, probably tickling her in between. This time I took a detour. My lips went to the fabric of the shirt at her shoulder. I dipped my head down to kiss just where the shirt sleeve ended and her skin began.

She turned her head to look at me, not stopping me, but something in her eyes told me that she wanted to witness everything I did. I moved my lips down her arm, pressing a light kiss to the scars she had there as well. These ones were deep but they weren't as bad as the ones on her thigh. Xander had said that the ones on her arm might fade with time, but her thigh scar could be a permanent fixture on her skin.

I peppered kiss after kiss to the raised skin, moving the rest of the way down so that I could place a kiss to the inside of her wrist. I peeked over at her. "Still okay?"

She graced me with a tiny smile. "Yes."

My hands were a little shaky when I brought them to the hem of her shirt. I had started to kiss her, letting her decide when she wanted to unleash her tongue. She let out a small moan, bringing her hips up to try and meet my own. I dragged the shirt up her body, exposing her stomach and tiny shorts she had on underneath. I pushed the shirt up some more so that it sat above her breasts.

My fingers ran over her miles of brown skin, her stomach hollowing when I splayed my fingers out across her skin. I would never fucking get over it.

Fuck, she was beautiful.

I kissed down her ribs and her stomach. I let my tongue out to lick at her skin. I thought I was hearing things, but I could have sworn her heartbeat was loud enough for it to travel to my ears. I kissed the inside of each of her thighs, mimicking what I did before and kissing the scars at her outer thigh. I would do it over and over again if that's what she wanted.

After each kiss, the pads of my fingertips would take its place. Her muscles weren't as tense and each touch of my fingers didn't feel like it was unwanted. I knew I wasn't the cure for her pain but if this eased just a fraction of hurt, then…it was worth it.

I had asked myself a while ago if I wanted her enough to fight for us. The answer was so clear now; it probably always was.

I tucked my fingers into the waistband of her shorts, feeling the elastic. She looked from me to where my fingers now were and then back at me, giving me a small nod of approval. I pulled them and her panties down her legs, tossing them to the floor.

I pushed her legs open wider, planting tiny kisses up her inner thighs. I ran my fingers over where she was already wet. She sucked in a breath and I chuckled a little. I spread her open, her arousal heady and inviting. I wanted to put my mouth on her. I wanted to take that perfect clit between my lips and make her come so beautifully that she would have nothing but happy thoughts.

But first…

I locked my eyes with hers catching her off guard. She looked a little stunned that I didn't just dive right between her thighs already. I softened my expression. "You don't like something or you're uncomfortable, tell me to stop."

"Nick…"

"If you are ever uncomfortable, you tell me to stop," I repeated, sternly.

She pressed her lips together, but adoration flooded her eyes. Out of the corner of my eye, I noticed black wisps coming from her fingers. They coiled around each other as they made their way to me, towards my face. Her shadows landed against my cheek and they felt… comforting.

They swept over my skin as if they enjoyed my company. Her voice sent my eyes flying back to where she was still lying back on my pillows. "Okay, I'll tell you to stop."

"Good girl."

I didn't waste another minute before my tongue was circling her clit. She cried out, instantly fisting my sheets. I didn't devour her like I wanted. No, I savored her. I let my tongue create lazy circles and lapped at her entrance like we had all of eternity to be here.

I stuck my tongue inside of her pussy, using my fingers to massage her clit, rubbing it gently. She moved her pelvis up and forward, trying to get closer to my face. I flicked my eyes up her body and saw that her eyes were closed. I liked when she watched me, but I also liked knowing that something made her feel so good that she couldn't help but lose herself to it.

I slid one of my fingers inside of her, curling it towards that spot that made her legs shake. I kept up my languid movements with my tongue, my cock hardening with every tiny whimper and moan she let out.

"Nick, *fuck*. Nick." Her voice was strained and breathy.

She lifted her hand to run it over her breasts as she came. I removed my finger from her, kissing her pussy and leading a trail of kisses up her body.

I nuzzled my face between her breasts, preparing myself to roll over and lie down next to her. Sensing my next movements, she stopped me. "What are you doing?"

I raised an eyebrow. "I was hoping to take a nap with my girlfriend."

She looked between our bodies. "But…"

I shook my head. "This isn't about me, Dani. I told you I wanted to make you feel good and I'm pretty sure I've done that." I shrugged. "Unless you'd like me to do it again."

She pushed up on her elbows, her face closer to mine. "You told me if I asked you to stop, you would. I haven't asked you to stop anything."

I smirked at her. The sassy demon I fell in love with making an appearance. I started to descend back towards that perfect place between her legs, but she pulled me back up.

"No, if this is about me, then as good as you are with your tongue, I don't want just that. I want you inside of me." She huffed out a breath. "Please."

"No need for pleasantries, needy one. You can demand things from me all you want." I kissed her before she could respond, moving over her so that she was forced to lie back down again.

My mouth was glued to hers as I undid my pants, pushing them down and kicking them and my underwear off. I reached behind me, pulling my shirt over my head. I placed my hands on either side of her head, feeling the heat of her near my pelvis.

"I love you," she said against my lips as she kissed me, bumping her nose against my own.

"I had a feeling." I ran my nose along her jaw as I grabbed my cock and slid it between her legs, coating myself in her arousal. "Remember what I said Dani…"

"I'll tell you to stop, Nick. Now can you *please*, shut up."

I could have laughed, but the moment I pressed inside of her was instantly too much. The way she felt around my cock was like pure magic. She gripped my biceps, burrowing her face into my chest as I thrusted forward.

I could have fucked her hard, made her come with ease, but that wasn't what this was about. I thought back to when she'd had her nightmare in Purgatory, how she had needed me to just let her take her own pleasure and find a way to be okay by doing something she knew made her happy.

She'd said I was her home.

And I never wanted her to leave.

I moved inside of her slowly, feeling the way my cock went all the way in and back out. Her pussy tightened with each thrust of my hips. I hit her deep, eliciting deep moans from her throat.

"Yes, right there." Her words were muffled into my chest.

"Hey, hey look at me. Look at me, baby," I coaxed, getting her to lift her head up so I could press my forehead to hers. Her eyes pierced into mine.

She moved her hands to my shoulders, starting to move the lower half of her body with mine. Each time my cock hit her in the right place it had my eyes wanting to roll back but I needed to focus on her. Her mouth dropped open with each drag of my cock.

I circled my hips, causing her to bite her bottom lip. I picked up my pace just a fraction, but I continued to let her feel all of me before pulling out and doing it all over again.

"Fuck, fuck, yes," she moaned and I felt heat on my shoulder. The burn was intense this time, like maybe it wouldn't fade like all the other burns she'd left me with.

The heat was gone when she snatched her hand away from my shoulder, attempting to hide it from me. Her hand glowed as she closed her palm. She was panting and her voice was shaky when she spoke, "I- I'm sorry."

I pushed into her continuously, fighting back the urge to shake my head and scream at her that it didn't fucking bother me. Her eyes were glassy and I could still feel the remnants from her burning light on my skin.

I quickly moved my hand up her arm and intertwined our fingers, slamming her hand down next to her head. Her light seeped out from between our fingers, but I pushed out mine as well, giving it something to mingle with. The heat thrummed but it was nice, soothing.

"*Don't*. Don't be sorry," I spoke against her lips, speaking each word clearly. "I've. Got. You."

Dani didn't cry very often, but the sharp cry that tore out of her chest nearly broke my heart. She closed her eyes, trying to pull herself together, but to no avail. Her breaths were shallow as I kept moving inside of her, legs sliding higher up my body so that I could go deeper. Her lips pressed together, whimpers leaving her throat.

I held her hand tight. "I've got you, baby."

Tears fell down the side of her face, disappearing into her curls. She nodded, tilting her head up for me to kiss her. Our mouths collided and I wanted to shield her from the entire world, but I knew her well enough to know that wasn't possible. I could have chastised myself for ever wanting to change her or thinking she would have been better living the way I did. I had wanted her to be mediocre at best when she was some-thing just above extraordinary.

I couldn't be as slow as I wanted anymore, my pace increasing. My pelvis hit her clit again and again. Her breathing was rapid now and I kept her hand safely within my own.

"Come for me. Let go for me, Dani," I whispered against her lips.

She dug her nails into my shoulder while her other hand flexed around my fingers, her light pushing out harder. I felt the slither of a shadow wrap around our bodies as if she was trying to keep us as close as possible. She cried out and I followed quickly behind her as I thrusted against her a few more times before finally coming. Her arm went limp and her body shuddered.

She released my shoulder to start clearing the tears from her eyes.

"Stop."

She ceased her movements, confused.

"I did mention how beautiful you are when you come, right?"

She giggled, sniffing as a small tear escaped from her lower lid. Her shadows retreated when I pushed up, bringing the hand still trapped in mine with me. I kissed her knuckles, eventually letting it go. She placed her hand at my side, wincing a tiny bit when I pulled out of her.

I rustled up the covers, watching as she removed her shirt before she snuggled underneath my sheets. I slid in next to her, laying on my back and she placed her head on my chest as I wrapped my arm around her shoulder. Her curls tickled my chest, but I wasn't about to move her anytime soon.

She traced circles on my stomach, sighing. "I know it wasn't a lot of time, but I missed you."

"I missed you too. Anytime you're away from me is too long."

She hummed, burying her head further into my chest.

"I'm sorry I didn't let you kill Dimitri."

She kissed my chest. "Me too."

"How about you tell me everything you planned to do to him? Every bloody, gruesome moment."

Dani looked up at me and blinked. "Really?"

"Mhmm."

She narrowed her eyes at me. I saw shadows swirl in her irises but there was a glimmer of light along with it. "Can I tell you every torturous thing I plan to do to Morgan and Ariel as well?"

I pressed my tongue into my cheek, fighting back a smile. "Go for it."

We had fallen asleep for about an hour or so, but my need for the bathroom jostled the bed enough to wake him up. Nick hadn't blinked an eye when I'd gone into depth about all the vile things I'd conjured up for the numerous people we both equally disliked. Months ago, if I had spoken like this, I would have been awarded with a lecture. Right now, it felt like some kind of high being able to speak so effortlessly and strongly about the things I wanted and could do if given the chance.

Just because I couldn't do those things when I wanted to didn't mean I was any less capable. Dimitri was a piece of entitled worthless shit for making me even consider I was anything less than who I actually was. I also knew from watching Nick and pushing him through his issues, that people don't always rebound so easily, so I would have setbacks.

I did tell him once: *Let yourself fall apart while you still have people surrounding you who care.*

Nick drew circles along my back, sending a happy tingle down my spine. He had been telling me all about Beetee finally speaking to Daya. He told me about his severe panic attack which caused him to have to calm me down after he'd finished speaking about it. He'd let me in on his conversation with his father and the amount of kisses he'd received from that admission had him batting me away. I had told him how Lilith had offered me my dagger, or at least a new version of it that was tempting. *Fuck* had that been a tempting offer. Nick had laughed, claiming that it was unsurprising that Lilith had seemingly been demoted to one of Dimitri's minions.

"Is it awful to say that I miss my dagger? I mean even if you were to say it is, I would still admit that I miss it."

Nick let out a small laugh. "For one, no it's not awful. It was a part of you and it probably always will be, even if it doesn't technically exist anymore."

"She presented it to me and I don't know, I knew it wasn't the same but that dagger was nothing without me and I guess I just missed something to tether myself to. Things feel different when all the power has someplace to go besides just inside yourself."

Nick hummed, considering my words. "With all the power you have, I can see how that makes sense."

We talked and laughed about so much until a small silence settled over us.

"Is Natalia looking into your memories?"

My raven-haired angel sighed. "Oh yeah, sorry, I thought I'd said it earlier. She is. I told her to take her time. If she can't find anything, I can say we all tried."

"She'll find something. She always does."

He hugged me closer. "It's in a few days."

His words caught me off guard. "What is?"

"The ceremony. Ariel's fucked up attempt to rule over all of us."

I let out a low whistle. "I can't believe that's still happening. What was the point of searching for where Jonah's powers might be, just to figure it out and still have literally nothing to show for it."

Nick pinched my side. "That trip to the library wasn't *all* bad."

I pinched him back. "I must *really* be rubbing off on you if you are making sex jokes, while your entire realm is in turmoil with an egoistic leader at the helm."

He readjusted himself in bed, making sure to keep me close to him. "Ariel has me running all over the place. He surprisingly let me off the hook for my Animus Seeking duties just so I could be around if he needed me. You should see the fucking spectacle that he's created on the lawn since he decided that an inside ceremony just wasn't grand enough." I didn't have to look up at him to know he had rolled his eyes.

"Does Ariel expect me to just stay in here forever, until I fucking wither away from epic boredom? Like does he think that I'm going to stand by him if shit hits the fan again? I can give you that answer right now. Absolutely *fucking* not."

"Dani, I don't know. The man has only spoken to me in monosyllables and gotten others to communicate to me on his behalf. The only time we've spoken for longer than a minute was when he sarcastically congratulated me on neutralizing a threat and doing something right, while in the same breath making sure to point out that I had to make so many mistakes to do it." He kissed my hair, burying his face in my curls. "I'll figure something out, I promise." He remained like that, taking in a deep breath as if he was inhaling my scent.

"I miss everyone and oddly or maybe not so oddly enough...I miss Elise."

Nick ran a hand through his hair. His bare chest rumbling with laughter. "Bored of me already."

I pushed away from his chest, propping myself up on my elbow so I could look down at him. My curls shifted over, cascading down my shoulder. "Don't be jealous. I've spent time with *your* best friend and not enough with my own. You men are great and all, especially your dad, but..."

"It's not the same. I get it. And I'll tell you right now, they miss you too." He shifted so that he was using his elbows to prop himself up.

"Ariel banned Elise, Beetee and nearly everyone else to Oculus and I don't know what exactly you did to Morgan, but I'm pretty sure she's run her mouth to Ariel—"

"Hmm, I don't know about that. I think if she cried to Ariel about what I did, we would have definitely heard about it by now." I snickered, remembering the way her eyes had bulged while I tightened my grip on her neck.

"Fair point. Still though, moving you out of The Skies would be a risk and trying to bring them here would be another one."

I bit my lower lip, closing my eyes and then peeking over at him by just opening one. "What about your portal key? Did Ariel confiscate it when we came back?"

He eyed me suspiciously. "Surprisingly no. He probably thinks we'll be good little angels now that we've been to Hell and back."

I walked my fingers over his chest and up to his lips, tapping my index finger against them. "Then he doesn't know me very well, now does he?"

"Dani…"

I moved quickly, maneuvering myself so I was straddling his waist. I leaned down to speak against his mouth. "Men like Ariel will never trust you. No matter how hard you work or how much you plead. You've proven you're a threat to his authority and he will make you work until the day you die thinking you will ever have a chance of getting him off your back. In his mind you've done a million and one things wrong." I gave him a peck on the lips. "Why not add another to the list?"

I pushed open the door of Natalia's home, feeling an overwhelming sense of contentment. This place felt safe. It was nothing like the feel of being in Nick's arms, but it was a close second. Nick stood close behind me, his sword strapped to his back like the showoff that he was.

Noise came from around the corner where the kitchen sat. A pair of black combat boots caught my eye and a familiar nonchalant snort made my ears perk up.

"About time you sprung out of that place." Elise tilted her head to the side, her black hair following her movements.

The last time I had seen Elise was at Nick's house. We had said a few words, but it wasn't enough. Everyone had been so frazzled about what happened and Nick had been so adamant on my healing that we'd left without so much as a goodbye.

Everything in me knew she would hate it, but my feet were already moving. I didn't hesitate when I threw my arms around her, pulling her into a hug, I felt her arms stiffen and her spine go ramrod straight. The air was sucked out of the room and the silence that surrounded us was awkward to say the least.

I didn't really care.

Her arms didn't move to hug me back, but she did place her hands on my forearms, pushing me back. She furrowed her dark brows. "You could have just said you missed me. I would have preferred it." Her lips quirked up into a small smirk.

"You should be happy someone *wants* to show you that much affection," Reese said, coming down the stairs. He looked over to me. "I'm guessing you got everything worked out?"

Once he was at the bottom of the stairs, I realized he was holding a sleeping Axel in his arms. I looked from the napping hellhound to him. Reese rolled his eyes as if saying *don't say a fucking word.*

"Yeah, basically. It helped that I had a little luck on my side, huh?" I reached into my back pocket, pulling out his arrowhead. Reese smiled at me. "I'm sure you'll be wanting it back."

He shook his head, slightly jostling Axel. "Keep it. Well, keep it for *now.*"

"Oh, Blondie, giving gifts so people will like you? That's so sad," Elise taunted.

Reese narrowed his eyes. "You're just mad because I'm stealing all your people to the side of team Reese. Even your fucking dog likes me more than you."

"Ha, right." Elise whistled, her eyes flashing a red so quickly that you wouldn't have noticed if you weren't paying attention. "Axel, come here."

Axel yawned and shuffled out of Reese's hold, causing the blonde angel to bend down a bit so he could scamper over to his mother. Elise leaned down so he could jump into her embrace, licking at her face. The dog nestled into her arms comfortably. She smirked over at Reese, who crossed his arms over his chest.

"I'm just going to safely assume Ariel has no idea you're here?" Reese asked.

"Not exactly," Nick answered, shrugging.

"Rebellious little angel. Who would have thought having a demon girlfriend would make you such a renegade." Elise placed Axel down right as he let out a little bark, as if agreeing with her.

Nick looked over to me, his mouth gaping open. "Well, I…"

Elise laughed. "Oh, no, pretty boy. That's a compliment. I only give out very few, so I would consider yourself lucky."

I nodded, letting him know she was right. My smile towards him faltered a bit when I caught her grey eyes falling towards the scars at my arm and my exposed thigh. I had changed my clothes before we left, but I wasn't ashamed of what had happened to me. I wasn't going to hide the evidence that my time with Dimitri had really occurred.

Her eyes locked onto mine and her expression wasn't one of pity or empathy. "Dimitri is a real piece of work."

"Yeah, that's one way to phrase it."

"You wear those scars proudly. Their reasoning for being on your skin sucks fucking dick, but we move on. You take your moments to deal, but then you get back up and you continue to be just as powerful as he wanted you to be, but—" she narrowed her eyes at me. "You don't do it for him or his agenda, you do it in spite of him. You do it for you."

I pressed my lips together, a crying laugh threatening to erupt. "What is with everyone being so profound lately? Like seriously, what the fuck?"

"I think they've spent way too much time with the High Priestess." We all jumped when Zane's voice echoed around us. He appeared at the top of the stairs, shaking his head. "I would really love it if any of you would find some way to announce your presence rather than loitering in her majesty's foyer as if you hold residence here."

"Some of us do, oh large one." Elise tipped her head up to speak to him.

Zane sneered at her. "The High Priestess allows you to seek shelter here, this is not…"

A throat cleared and Natalia came up beside him. "Oh calm down. You know you have a soft spot for the snake shifter and do not even try to deny it."

The large Enchanter kept his face neutral, not giving into Natalia's teasing. The sound of children laughing had me blinking in confusion. Axel wagged his tail and ran around us, bounding up the stairs. Another sound, a familiar male laugh, had me rearing my head back.

"Is that my father?" Nick asked, as if he read my mind.

Natalia nodded. "Yes. They've all been here for quite some time."

"They?" Nick and I both said in unison. Natalia winked at us and turned to walk down the hall, Zane following at her heels.

We all trailed behind them, letting Natalia lead us into a sitting room that was covered in gold wallpaper. A large chandelier hung from the ceiling and a large circular window brought light into the room that bounced against the golden walls beautifully.

A collective silence filtered through the room when I took in every person that looked back at me. Garrett and Leah sat closely on one of the couches, while their children played with Axel at their feet. Beetee and her moms stood near the windowsill, huddled closely with Daya and Alex. Maurice Cassial came into my view when he walked over to us. He looked from his son to me and smiled. He patted Nick's shoulder like there was some silent conversation between them.

I felt a warm hand against mine and fingers threading through my own. Mr. Cassial looked down at where we held hands and he chuckled, more to himself than to anyone else.

"You're all here?" I asked, my voice smaller than I wanted.

"Where else would we be?" Leah answered, giving me an encouraging smile.

"You can't scare us away," Beetee chimed in.

Maurice smiled. "Whatever happens we're with you. When all Hell breaks loose, we're with you."

"Plus, I personally am always going to fight on the side with two hybrids, especially when one is a snake shifter." Alex gave me a thumbs up, getting a sigh from her mother, before she walked over and sat on the couch.

Elise pushed past us to sit on the arm of one of the couches. "Ah, let's not forget that Dani wields some shadowy fireball of light that could melt all our flesh off." She blinked innocently at Nick. "You would know about that wouldn't you, since she nearly melts yours off every time you make her com…"

"Oh my god, please shut up!" Nick shouted, but not before Daya let out a choked cough at the same time Reese held his stomach trying not to keel over in roaring laughter.

Nick shot him an unamused look. Reese held up his hands. "I'm sorry. The grumpy psycho and I don't get along much, but that was funny."

I squeezed Nick's hand and leaned up to kiss him on the cheek. "He likes my burns."

Alex made a gagging sound before kicking her feet up and resting them on the coffee table.

Nick let out a slow breath, regaining his composure. "Are you all here about Ariel?"

"Well, Ariel and anything else that needs to happen with the Dimitri situation." Maurice leaned over the back of the couch, resting his elbows against the top.

I tentatively touched the scars on my arm. That was going to be a nervous habit, I could tell. "Well, Dimitri…"

"We know he got dealt with, but Lilith was there, right?" One of Beetee's moms, Louise, asked.

"Yeah."

"Is she going to be a problem?" Daya inquired, her whiskey eyes staring at me patiently.

I thought this over. I wasn't really sure how to answer the question since Dimitri had been the real issue. Lilith was an afterthought since she had been pushed down several pegs when Dimitri had decided he would be calling the shots. "I wouldn't think so. Dimitri was the one they all wanted to look up to, not her. It would be pretty hard for her to get the same sort of loyalty she had previously after Dimitri became her handler."

"No one to do her bidding, means no play time for the queen of darkness," Elise added.

"I suggest we stay vigilant but not let the idea of her threaten our lives," Garrett said, but he spoke while he gazed at his children. "Besides, with the way your leader is handling things, if she did come and propose a fight, I don't know how this realm would fare."

"So, are you suggesting we all fight Ariel head on?" I asked.

"If you do, it will be sooner than you think," Reese said, pressing his tongue into his cheek.

"What do you mean?" Nick stepped closer to his best friend.

"Earlier today, I got an invitation to his ceremony. The date was for tomorrow." Natalia gave us a sympathetic look.

I looked over at Nick. "I thought you said it was in a few days?"

Nick ran a hand through his hair roughly. "That's the last I heard. Like I said, the man hasn't really spoken to me much."

"Better to keep you out of the loop." Maurice ran a finger over his mustache, letting out a humorless laugh.

"So are we ambushing this thing or..." Reese offered, glancing around the room.

"Get a grip, Blondie. You're starting to sound like me." Elise blew him a kiss before jumping off the arm of the couch. Her grey eyes scanned me and before I knew it, she was grabbing my arm and yanking me out of the room, shouting, "I'll bring her right back!"

She looked behind her to make sure no one followed us out before she spoke in a low voice, "are you completely sure Dimitri is no longer a problem?"

I blinked at her, immediately thrown off guard. "You saw him, Elise."

She gave me an incredulous look. "I know what I saw. I'm not asking you what I *fucking* saw. I'm asking you what you know and how you feel. I'm asking what you fucking think."

I reached up and ran the pads of my fingertips over my scars. "Nick killed him. That's what happened."

Elise pinched the bridge of her nose as if she was annoyed. "The entire reason I'm asking you and *not* your boyfriend is because he would tell me exactly that. He got to throw down and beat the shit out of Dimitri, which great, good for fucking him, but just because the entitled piece of shit is unmoving doesn't mean he's dead. He looked it and I'd be really fucking surprised if he wasn't, but..."

"But what?"

"Ugh, pretty boy should have cut off his *fucking* head, that's what."

"Elise...*ah*!" I felt a sting in my arm. I thought I might have accidentally scratched myself, but my hand wasn't anywhere near my scars anymore. We both looked at the raised skin on my bicep and noticed that nothing was red, the scar tissue wasn't pulsing, it all looked so normal. I placed my palm against my arm and felt heat there as if it was simmering on the inside.

"Dani, what is going on?" Elise questioned.

"Nothing, it's probably just remnants of what he did. Case closed."

"You are fucking delusional if you think—" I gripped her arm, harder than I intended but I didn't let up.

"It's fucking nothing, so for the love of Satan can you just shut up."

She opened her mouth to argue with me, but the door opened. Zane stepped out, walking past us in a rush.

Elise shrugged away from me. "I really don't like playing the good guy Dani, but I shouldn't be the one to tell you to be honest here."

"I *am*. We both know that Nick and everyone else would dive straight back into Hell, so no, Dimitri is dead. This is *over*."

I heard stomping behind me, looking back and seeing Zane walking by. I looked down seeing that he was holding the leather-bound notebook that belonged to Jonah. I brushed past Elise to follow him back inside the room.

"Dani, we aren't done," Elise argued, but I shushed her, watching Zane walk over to Natalia and hand the book to her.

Nick looked me over when I stood next to him, silently asking me if I was alright. I gave him a small smile focusing back on Natalia.

"Nicholas, I've been doing some thinking about this book and I've replayed what I know about Jonah over and over again in my head." The High Priestess ran her fingertips gently down the front of the notebook.

Maurice came up next to this son, bumping shoulders with him as if he was curious about where this conversation would go.

Nick raised an eyebrow. "Did you figure out a way to release the magic? I know you had said you didn't want to mess with what this book held…"

Natalia shook her head. "My decision still stands true. I will not involve my magic with something that I am fully aware is set in its own ways. There is some magic that likes to be seen when it's ready." She peeked over at me but then focused back on Nick.

"Nicholas, what is this all about?" Maurice asked his son.

Without looking at his father, Nick answered, "Jonah's magic."

"You know where it is?" Daya asked, placing a hand over her chest.

"If the magic wants to be ready any time soon, that would be fucking fantastic." Reese rolled his eyes, leaning against the back of the couch.

Natalia rubbed her lips together. She patted her palm against the book. "Sometimes it just needs to be in the hands of the right person. I didn't need my magic to see something so glaringly obvious." She looked at Nick. "If Ariel wasn't so eager I would do this more delicately, but it seems that isn't an option."

My angelic boyfriend's eyes widened when the High Priestess turned slightly and handed the book to his father.

39
DIMITRI

"If you value your lives, you will make sure he remains alive and in one piece!" My father yelled from somewhere in the dimly lit room. The Enchanters that Lucifer had coaxed to come to Hell, thinking that being with him was better than being with Lilith, worked diligently around me.

The pain I felt wasn't excruciating but it was rather annoying at best. My sight had started to get blurry and my mind began to fade before the guards in the Hell prison had found me. I heard chatter among the Enchanters as they spoke to my father with stuttered words. His booming presence had them worried. They should be, to be fair.

My father snarled when they'd said my face would need some time to recover from the swelling. They said they could do what they could, but they weren't miracle workers. I heard a slap and a body falling to the ground when the words, "we aren't the High Priestess" came from one of their mouths.

Idiots. All of them.

I flinched as I sat up in bed. My father commanded them out of my room and I nearly laughed watching them fumble around. The Enchanters toppled over one another just to try to be first out of the room and into the hallway. My father let out a deep sigh, running a hand down his tired face.

He was handsome enough, his blonde hair closely cut. He looked at me with eyes that mirrored my own, green and turned up at the corners. He had scruff that settled at his jawline, which he scratched as he slowly walked over to my bedside.

"What the hell happened?"

"I can handle it." It hurt to move my mouth, but I pushed through.

He growled at me. "I didn't ask you if you could handle it. I asked you what the *hell* happened?"

"She got away, but like I said, I can handle it. Just let me handle my own business, father." I lifted my hand to my face, feeling the puffiness.

My father's eyes narrowed. "*She?*"

"That is what I said, isn't it?" I snapped.

He opened his mouth, but then closed it. A rumbling groan left his throat. "That girl. Lilith's little project."

I remained quiet. I wasn't a fucking child and didn't need a lecture of any kind. I needed to get the hell out of here, readying myself for my next move.

"You let yourself get attached to one of *her* problems and look where it's gotten you. The last thing we all knew about her was that she was dead! I told you not to go into dealings with that conniving bitch and you did! I wanted to give you more responsibility, so I gave you Leviathan. Holding down that property was all you had to do, but no you wanted more." He spat the words out like venom, but it didn't sting.

"I am my father's son." I smirked at him. One of my eyes seemed to be more swollen than the other, so my vision was limited. I didn't need both eyes to know that his facial expression was all but lethal.

I was suddenly seething with pain when he grabbed my face and turned me to look at him, head on. "What do you mean she got away?"

"You are a smart man. I am sure you can figure it out."

"She was in the Hell prison," he was talking to himself, mulling over the thoughts in his head. "Oh, no, you *kept* her in the Hell prison."

"You catch on quickly, don't you father?"

"You thought she was dead Dimitri!"

I snorted. "Well clearly she is not! I had to bring her here. I needed her here, *we* needed her here!"

My father's eyes widened. "You created a dark rift to bring her here. You stupid boy! Risks can be a wonderful thing, but you don't just make decisions based on some girl you fucked around with. You are not just any other demon! You cannot be this fucking reckless!" He slammed his hands down on the bed, huffing out a breath.

I chuckled. "I knew she wasn't dead, father. Is no one paying attention here? That pretty girl is a hybrid and a powerful one at that."

My father lifted his head up slowly to gaze at me. "Excuse me?"

"The whole story is quite long and obnoxiously boring, but the short version is Lilith had no idea how to get what she wanted. The angels were able to entice her to do both, she expresses both of her own volition."

"And you tell me this *now*?"

"I hate disappointment just as much as you do, father. I wanted to make sure she was good enough before a riot started. I am smarter than you may think. I know Lucifer doesn't like things rattling Hell unless he deems it worthy, so before a commotion was started, I wanted to make sure I had everything in place before bringing her to everyone." I practically bit my own tongue thinking about that fucking angel and his heroics. He had cost me so much and he would fucking pay for it, as would everyone else she deemed to care about. "She cares *too* much. She can be the final weapon we need to take Heaven's Gate by storm. She could either be a part of the masterful chaos or she could be yet another reason it manifests anyway. It was a perfect fucking plan."

"Until it wasn't," my father added, scoffing. "You let them take her back and now they are just waiting. You've made deeper enemies of the angels. Brilliant son."

I pointed my finger at him. "Ah, but they think I'm dead. They might be waiting, but the thought of my death will ease them into a settling kind of contentment. I was completely ready to throw my energy into Leviathan until Dani displayed her power and it was a thrilling surprise."

My father looked me up and down, eventually turning his back to me. "What are you even considering, Dimitri?"

"No more games, no more big plans. We come to them, death at the ready."

"She was brought up by Lilith, you really think that girl will come so easily." It was a rhetorical question meant to undermine me.

"Surrender will be her only option. If everyone is dead, she will have no one to save now will she?"

My father looked over his shoulder at me, a small smile full of mischief on his lips. "A hybrid, you say?"

I let out a sigh. "I could watch her burn the world, father. It would be mesmerizing."

He nodded, running his index finger over his eyebrow. "Angel blood is my favorite kind as you know and as much as I would love to approve of this endeavor…"

The air in the room became stale and changed from humid to ice cold in a matter of minutes. The temperature rapidly changed back and forth while the doorknob turned, swinging open. Lilith stepped inside, an impartial expression on her face.

A tall figure loomed behind her, moving around her thin frame to place himself at the center of the room.

My father cleared his throat, bowing his head. "Lucifer."

The King of Hell inclined his head towards my father. His hair was black, cut short on the sides with more on top that occasionally fell into his face. He had a trimmed beard that sat neatly around his cut jawline. His eyes were the color of charcoal and could burn into your soul whenever he pleased.

He smiled, but that smile could be so deceiving. That was the same smile he wore when he was sentencing deaths. Lucifer nodded towards me. "I do hope you are alright, Dimitri."

"I'm well, thank you."

"I heard there was quite a commotion in the prison. Was that of your doing?" He asked this casually, but I knew my answer mattered if I was getting out of his unscathed.

"I brought something into the prison, yes. The commotion was not of my doing."

He nodded thoughtfully. "And whose was it, hmm?"

I looked over to Lilith, but I heard Lucifer chuckle. His laugh was dark and almost brooding. "Don't look to her, my boy. She works for me, not you. She would not have her station if not for me and your father would not be where he is if I hadn't wanted it that way, so please let us not pretend like I don't know the entire story." He glanced at Lilith before giving me his attention again. "I am asking you what happened. Be careful about your answer, I assure you."

I liked to test my father on any occasion I got, but Lucifer was a different story. I told him what happened, every detail I could conjure up. He stood there and listened as if he wouldn't want to be anywhere else. He took in my words, almost as if he was committing them to memory and sizing them up next to whatever Lilith told him.

When I was done, he placed his hands in his pants pockets and closed his eyes. He tsked. "I thought you told me that girl wouldn't be a problem." It wasn't a question, but a statement. He looked down at Lilith, tilting his head to the side.

"She wasn't. I thought she was dead, I was planning on leaving it be."

"Yet, here we stand. A hurt Son of Hell and a hybrid nowhere to be found."

Lilith pointed a finger at herself. "That is *not* my fault!" Her voice grew louder.

My father nearly snickered when Lucifer got closer to her face, his eyes flashing a reddish color. "You *had* to go to the human realm and pluck her right from her death. You *had* to train her and give her that dagger. You *had* to recruit that idiotic angel and that Enchanter. You *had* me convinced that you could tear her soul out and keep her in line, but of course you could not. I gave you a second chance after you caused that mind numbing catastrophe in Oculus all those years ago and *this…* *this* is how you repay me!"

"Lucifer, I…" Lilith started, but he put a hand up, stopping her.

"You were something great once, but you let this idea of yours, this Soul Seether run amuck." He placed a hand on her neck, circling behind her. "I kept you around for so many reasons. Some of those reasons will forever remain between you and me, but it doesn't seem like Dimitri's plan has room for you."

"No, sir…"

My shoulders jumped a tiny bit when the King of Hell brought his other hand near the top of her head, twisting her neck so quickly a resounding snap echoed.

My father came over to him, stepping over Lilith's limp body. "Would you like me to find someone to clean her up?"

Lucifer flexed his fingers, waving them over her body. Her arms and legs began to disintegrate into black smoke; the rest of her followed suit quickly after. Lucifer smiled at my father. "No need. Thank you for asking though."

I swung my legs off the bed, getting to my feet. "I am sorry I didn't come to you with my idea and plan sooner, sir."

Lucifer walked over to me, placing his hand lightly on my shoulder. "You wanted to do it when the time was right, be sure you had something solid. I can admire you knowing an asset when you see one. You believe she is worth giving you my approval for?"

"I believe she can be more than Lilith ever was."

Lucifer grinned. "You will get no pushback from me, but like with Lilith, you will get no assistance from me either. Other than what I provide you, I am just an observer of your plan. I will not jump in to save you."

"I would never expect that, sir."

"Good."

A knock at the door sounded and a woman peeked her head in. "Sir, that thing you were asking about….it needs you attention." She looked nervous as if she didn't know if speaking about whatever she was eluding towards was permitted.

Lucifer gave her a curt nod. "Of course, if you will excuse me gentleman. Dimitri, heal up. You have much to do."

Once the door closed, my father placed his hands on his hips. He curled his lip when he looked at the empty place Lilith's body had been. "I never liked her. Always thought she was better for some odd reason."

I rolled my eyes. "I need to get some rest, father. You being here isn't going to help me get better faster, so please leave."

My father let out a loud huff before turning towards the door. "Do not embarrass me by thinking some girl is worth losing your place in Lucifer's good graces. I am not above disowning you, I swear to Satan."

"Don't worry, father. That girl will help change the realms."

40
NICK

My father looked down at the book, perplexed. He didn't make a move to hold it nor did he make an effort to speak. I took a glance around the room and it seemed as if every single person had also lost the ability to form words. Natalia stood her ground, patiently, like she knew this moment was one that would take some time to completely understand.

"Are you saying that…" I started, but my father finally spoke, cutting me off.

"Why do you have Jonah's notebook?"

Dani pointed to the book "You've seen it before?"

My father opened his mouth and then closed it again. He let out a breath before responding. "Well, yes. He would write in the pages with this disappearing ink he'd gotten from an Enchanter we were friends with. He housed all his ideas for the future in it, everything his father would have never accepted. He…" My father shook his head.

"He kept it in the Divine Library for safe keeping." I finished for him. He looked over at me and his eyes held curiosity at my statement.

I shrugged. "I've been looking for Jonah's magic. Ariel can't do this, Dad. I've been rattling my brain trying to figure out where he would keep it. I figured it out, but when we found it, the pages were blank."

"Explains that I guess," Elise said, walking over to us.

My father looked at each of us. "Are you trying to tell me that you think Jonah's magic is meant to go to…" He stopped talking, his words falling away.

"Yes, Mr. Cassial. That is exactly what I believe. It is your choice to accept it. You take the book, you read what's exposed to you and the power is yours."

"Why wouldn't he take it? Ariel or Maurice, it's really not a hard decision." Alex furrowed her brows.

Beetee looked at her thoughtfully. "That's a lot of magic for one person who didn't even know it was available to them until right now."

"Dad." My father was looking at nothing in particular, dazed and blinked when I called his name. "This could be all wrong, there is really no pressure."

"Maybe a tiny bit," Elise whispered, huffing when Dani shushed her.

My father chuckled softly, more to himself than to any of us. "No, it's not. It's not wrong." He sighed, looking at the book. "Jonah was my best friend. He confided in me about anything and everything. He always joked about how I knew every move he was going to make before he made it, but he got me with this one."

"Maurice, if you need to think about things…" Daya began, but my father ran a hand over his face and shook his head.

"No, the time for thinking is long past. The Jonah that decided this knew who I was—who I am." He cleared his throat, looking over Natalia's shoulder to give Zane a short nod. The large Enchanter mirrored it back to him, a small semblance of a smile playing at his lips.

My father reached forward to take the book and small sparks played at his fingertips, moving from him to the book's leather exterior.

"Woah, there isn't about to be some giant explosion while we're all in here, right?" Reese asked, making a valid point.

Before anyone could answer there was a humming sound that vibrated throughout the room as my father took the book into his hands. Golden magic lined the outside of the notebook, tracing along my father's fingers, over his knuckles and down towards his wrists.

His chest rose and fell, the light seeming to not bother him. The magic looked like it was working its way through his veins, the trail moving up his arms and over his shoulders. He opened the book, white-gold light flooding from the pages, causing me to squint.

The light simmered to a dim hue as words appeared slowly near the first page in a delicate cursive that I couldn't read from here. The only thing I could make out was that it was addressed to my father. His thick eyebrows pulled inward as he read it over. He then flipped through the book, wanting to read more, but pages moved on their own. The words that were previously hidden to us started to reveal themselves. The book ripped away from his hold, the pages flying faster and the dim light brightened, starting to tear apart into tiny particles of soft light.

The golden fleck began to decorate my father's body like falling snow. His body absorbed the magic, piece by piece. Dani took my hand, squeezing it as she looked on.

The book finally closed and flew over to my father, slamming into his chest. He placed his hands over it, hugging it to his body before he fell onto his knees.

Garrett and Zane got to him faster than Reese and I, but my father kept his eyes closed and just took deep breaths in and out.

Daya and Alex hovered over him, concern etched on their faces.

"Maurice, honey." Daya tentatively placed her hand on his shoulder.

His eyes opened and for a moment, they held golden magic within his irises before returning back to their normal dark brown. He held the book close, letting Garret and Zane help him up.

When he finally stood up straight there was a different aura about him. Maurice Cassial always held a presence of authority when he was around, but this was different. This kind of power was thick and...it suited him.

Natalia walked around everyone and stood in front of him. "How do you feel, Maurice?"

My father held the book out in front of him, tracing his fingers over Jonah's initials. "Like I'm a teenager again with responsibility I'm not completely sure I can handle. He had to know that."

I placed my hand over his. "I think he did. You are everything this place needs, Dad." I leaned my head in, whispering, "you deserve it."

Axel stood on his hind legs, running his claws against my father's leg. My father bent down and swiped his hand over the hellhound's head, petting him. Axel inclined his head as if he enjoyed this treatment.

"So are you as powerful as Miss. Natalia?" Garrett's son, Yuri, asked. His face was scrunched up in skepticism.

"Yuri!" Leah ruffled her son's hair.

Natalia chuckled, winking at my father. "Something like that."

"Do you think Ariel knows?" Reese asked, running his hand across his chin.

Dani hummed. "I think any angel probably feels like something is off. Just like Enchanters did when Natalia's mother passed. I don't think he'll directly relate any of it to Maurice."

I nodded. "She's right."

"Well, we can go right the fuck now. Daddy Cassial can blast him to pieces and we can move along because everything is totally *fine* on all other fronts." Elise's grey eyes danced over to Dani, who shook her head at me and shrugged as if she had no idea what she was talking about.

I bit my lower lip, thinking. "Ariel wants to prove to everyone that he's the one that deserves it. That's what this whole ceremony is for. He wants to make a spectacle, so can we." I looked over at my father.

Natalia cleared her throat. "Um, Nicholas, you might want to ask your father if outing himself as Heaven's Gates' next ruler so outlandishly is what he wants."

I winced, feeling a tad bit embarrassed. "Fuck, right. Sorry. We can do things however you want, Dad."

He placed a hand on my cheek. I could feel all that power that Jonah held radiating from his palm. It was a little unnerving, but I also felt an overwhelming sense of pride. "That man threw my son into the Ethereal Bastille, belittled my family and thinks that sullying the name of a fellow executive is a way to success. I am a sensible man, but I won't tolerate people who want to hold their people's respect yet they have no idea what the word even means."

"So that's a yes?" I asked, with a smile pulling at the corner of my lips.

"No, Nicholas. That's a *hell* yes."

41
JONAH

Dear Maurice,

    I know what you are going to say and luckily, I'm not there to hear it. My father would stomp around and rage if he were still alive and knew what I'd decided to do. I think I would have been a different person had I not known you. I might have ended up just like my father. Bitter and so afraid that your power would be diminished in some way. You took the verbal beatings from that man with a sharp smile and I applaud you for your efforts, but I saw through it.

    You had loving parents that celebrated your wins and soothed you during your losses. I envied that about you. I never quite understood why you chose to be within sparring distance of Isaac Zuriel. I never got it through my head why you would be in every meeting you could when I was summoned to meet with him or why you insisted that you wait outside for me if you were not allowed in.

You were my relief from the thin line I constantly walked on with that man. Even when I wanted to run away and never hear the word executive again, you stopped me. We could have portaled somewhere and been nomads, never having to be held down by obligation again.

You were my friend. As tarnished as that word might be between us.

I don't think I ever truly admitted to you how smart you actually were. You let me go on and on about my ideas for the future and you listened, adding in your own as well. When my father had you cast out and with everything that happened to Scarlett, I didn't know if I would have been worthy of the job you pushed me to do.

The last time we spoke, you told me to take care of your son. The son that has the same look of aspiration and confidence as you once did. A look you still have. He deserves to know a realm of peace and prosperity. The kind of place I wanted to create, the kind of place you always knew could be achieved. The kind of place to fly free and fall in love.

I am sorry that my father's cruelty stole your happiness and I am equally sorry for not finding the courage to help you restore even the smallest piece of your heart. He is your son, Maurice but when I see him fight, when I hear him speak, I am reminded of her.

He has a tenacity I haven't seen in a long time and I think he can make a real difference.

I know you didn't want the kind of power my father held and you thought that only I could do these things, implement these changes we'd envisioned. Maurice, these ideas, these notions are ours.

There is so much to do and I am working with the Enchanters to slowly try to find some peace amongst all our kinds. If I'm not here to do it, then I do not trust anyone else to see our plans out. You have a heart that's big enough to house this realm and the people deserve you at the helm. You deserve to be heard. If my father would have listened to your pleas not to fight, maybe things would be different.

Accept the power, Maurice. You were always stubborn, but you understood the necessity of when things truly mattered.

Accept the power. Please.

Your friend,
Jonah

We settled back into Nick's room, my anxious angel heading towards his door. He opened it slightly, peeking out to see if anything seemed odd or out of place. He headed into the bathroom and I followed him.

I leaned against the door frame with my arms crossed, watching him turn the faucet on and splash water onto his face.

"Your dad is the supreme ruler now," I pointed out.

He choked out a laugh. "It seems that way. I would really love to say I'm surprised but I'm not."

Maurice deserved this immense power he'd been given. He'd stayed back with Natalia and everyone else after we'd discussed a plan for tomorrow. Ariel was about to be in for a surprise when more than just his invitees showed up.

"Hmm, are you ready for whatever tomorrow brings?" I asked, biting my bottom lip.

He turned to me, his hands holding onto the edge of the sink. "I've only been absolutely sure about a handful of things and *this* is one of them."

"Oh and what are these other things, hmm?" I inquired, playfully.

He walked over to me, placing his hand on the wall and leaning down towards my face. "You."

"Oh really? I'm pretty sure you were very fucking skeptical about me."

He rubbed his nose against mine. "Technicalities, needy one."

I leaned up and took his lower lip between my teeth, biting down softly. He hissed when I released it. "Well, technically, you stink. Take a shower."

I winked at him before reaching for the door and closing it behind me. I jumped onto his bed, crossing my legs over each other, so my knees pointed out. I took this moment to consider Elise's words. I had every fucking intention of presuming Dimitri was dead. He had looked really fucking dead.

Fuck, fuck, fuck.

I placed my palm on my thigh scars and heat simmered underneath. Maybe I was scaring myself. We were so close to something good. A sharp burn hit my thigh and I flinched.

I was letting Elise's delusions get to me. I was worried for nothing.

I was spiraling just like my fucking boyfriend.

"Hey, are you coming?" Nick's voice pulled me out of my mental marathon. His shirt was off and it was hard not to look away from him.

"What?"

"You, me equals shower."

I gave one look to my thigh, but then narrowed my eyes at him. "Are you going to wash my hair?"

He laughed an easy laugh, like he was calmer. The calmest I'd ever seen him. "I was planning on it, yes. Amongst other things."

I pulled off my shirt and brushed past him to the bathroom. "Other things?"

He closed the door behind him when he followed me inside. I turned around, realizing quickly how close he was when my chest hit his. He tucked his fingers into the waistband of my shorts and pulled me to him. "Mhmm, like when I'm done, I plan to put your legs on my shoulders and bury my face in your pussy until you are screaming my name."

"Who knew Ariel's downfall would make you so feisty."

"How about no more talking."

I could hear myself giggling, but there was also this nagging feeling that something was amiss. Ariel was the last problem.

Ariel *was* the last problem. I could tell myself that until I believed it.

I had to hand it to Ariel as I looked up at the clear blue sky. He picked a pretty good afternoon to have his sham of a ceremony. I could see the tiny progress he was making on his update of the Divine Library. It was a ridiculous venture, but he was the kind of guy who made changes that were visually impactful. Nothing really improved from the things he wanted, the ideas he wanted to implement.

If any angels felt anything significant after my father took the power, they weren't saying anything about it. Maybe it was better that way. I rolled up the sleeves of my button down as the sun beat down on us. My sword felt heavier at my back; it was like something was weighing on me but I couldn't figure out what. Angels hustled around in preparation. I had begrudgingly helped this morning, but since Ariel was busy perfecting himself for what would happen in about thirty minutes, I was able to make myself scarce the rest of the time. At least I thought I had.

"You clean up nicely. You always did." Morgan sidled up next to me, her pink dress swishing around her knees.

"What do you want?"

She scoffed, pushing her glasses further up her nose. "I'm trying to be nice. You could do the same. I'm actually surprised you aren't."

"What do you mean?"

Morgan grabbed her dark hair and pulled it over her shoulder. "After your girlfriend's stunt, I should have gone straight to Ariel, but I didn't. You should be thanking me."

I huffed out a laugh. "She scared the shit out of you. That's why you didn't go to Ariel; don't twist it into you playing nice."

She looked like she wanted to throw a tantrum and stomp her feet. "When Ariel takes over, *she* is going to have to play nice."

"She doesn't *have* to do anything," I argued, peering down at her.

She started to argue back, but Natalia appeared at my side. Her dark hair was in multiple twists with gold threads interwoven throughout each one. Her lilac dress shimmered in the sunlight, contrasting nicely with her dark skin and the glitter that decorated her cheeks. "I am not interrupting, am I?"

Morgan plastered a smile onto her face. "Of course not, Ariel will be so happy you could make it."

Natalia gave her a half-hearted smile back. "I'm sure. Can I have a moment with him, please?"

Morgan nodded, giving me one last glance before turning away to yell at one of the other angels. Natalia put herself in front of me, raising one of her well manicured eyebrows. "I will tell you that your father is anxious."

"I would be surprised if he wasn't."

"He is eager to help you though, so I think the two emotions are canceling each other out."

I pulled at my shirt collar, looking around.

She swatted my hand away. "You are doing the right thing, we all are. Have faith in your choices. Ariel has made it seem like everything you've done is a mistake, but I like to look at it like everything you've done has led you to all these people that want to help you, it's led you to *her*." Her honey eyes looked at me knowingly, then she nodded towards something over my shoulder.

I swung my head around seeing Reese and Dani walking down the aisle of marble benches. Reese matched me in a button down, but he'd left more buttons undone than normal for a formal event. His bow strap settled across his chest and he nodded towards me, letting a half-smile play at his lips. Dani ran up to me, hooking her arm through mine. She wore a dark purple dress with thick straps that didn't hug her curves too tightly, giving her enough room to move around or run if needed.

I looked down at what was around her neck. Reese's arrowhead sat delicately at her chest, held in place with a tiny chain. "That's new."

She fingered it gently, looking over at Reese and then back at me. "Natalia did it. Made it so no harm came to the arrowhead and the chain can be removed when I give it back...eventually." She wrinkled her nose in the cutest way.

I kissed the top of her head, letting that cinnamon scent of hers waft towards my nostrils.

"The big guy is keeping his eyes wide and vigilant." Reese pointed towards Zane, who stood silently further back near the front of The Skies.

"She can't be here." I heard Morgan before I saw her. She nearly flew over to us, her finger pointed at Dani, accusatory.

"Well that's a real bummer since she's already fucking here." Reese rolled his eyes.

"Oh don't start..." Morgan began but she was stopped by Ariel clearing his throat behind her.

Angels were starting to take their seats on the benches and the final touches were being finished.

Ariel sneered at me and then rested his green eyes on Dani. "Always the disturbance, aren't you? No bother though. This is a joyous day, so why shouldn't you be here to witness it." He gave her a quick smile and gestured towards the benches. "Take your seats and High Priestess, I have saved you a place near the front. You and I will be working closely after today."

"We are waiting on a few more guests," I said, standing my ground.

"Guests? Mr. Cassial, you are not permitted to invite guests."

Natalia laughed, the sound of it musical. "Ariel, these are not *his* guests. These are mine. You wouldn't forbid the guests of the High Priestess, now would you?" She gave him an innocent expression.

Ariel looked around, noticing that some of the angels, including his fellow executives were watching our scene curiously. "No, I would never. As long as they are punctual."

Natalia nodded, laughing softly. "Oh they are. Right on time." She waved her hand to the side and a circle started to form to the far left. The edges were a blue mixed with a white hue, the center caving in a bit. We all stared at the portal as the light flickered.

Elise and Beetee stepped out first, followed by Garrett, Leah and my father. Axel jumped out right before the portal closed, sitting nicely next to his mother.

Ariel squinted, vibrating with anger. "I suppose if you want to bring your fellow Enchanters I cannot stop you, but I will not have unwanted demons and that disgraceful man on this lawn!"

I stepped up to him, using my hands to push him back a little. "I have no problems breaking your nose again. You do *not* talk about my father that way."

Ariel snickered. "Guards! Take him and his father away. Gather up the other trash while you're at it." He motioned towards where Elise and Beetee stood.

"Excuse me! I swear to fuck, I will rip your fucking dick off..." Elise shouted, practically running up to him, but Garrett grabbed her, holding her still.

Beetee's eyes shifted and Axel pressed his paws into the ground, running his claws across the grass. The guards moved closer to all of us, but my father cleared his throat.

"I think we'll stay, Ariel." His voice was calm and unmoving, his tone made my spine straighten.

Ariel let out a sharp laugh. "You have no authority here, Maurice."

"What the hell is going on?" Morgan demanded.

"I think he has *all* the authority," Dani said, ignoring her and placing both her hands on her hips, sizing Ariel up.

My father stepped up so he could be right in front of Ariel. He placed his hand on his shoulder, the tension in his forearm causing his muscles to pulse. "Stand down, Ariel."

The red headed angel's eyes that held a menacing stare began to morph into one of understanding. The settling nature of my father's newly found magic erupted over the entire space. The guards that stood behind Ariel backed away from him and looked at my father as if they were waiting for an instruction.

Ariel's mouth gaped open. He knew what had happened, he could feel it pulsing into his body with the way my father held onto him. That didn't mean he had to accept it, though. "It can't...you don't deserve it!"

"Neither do you. Jonah never thought highly of you, even all those years ago." My father seemed to press down on his shoulder harder.

"Guards! Seize them, *now*!" Ariel shouted, clearly causing more of a spectacle than he anticipated.

Mission accomplished on our end.

"They don't work for you now. You are back to what you've always been..." Dani started.

"Useless and disappointing," Elise finished for her.

My father let go of his shoulder, watching as Ariel crumbled to the ground as if the weight of my father's power was too much for him to handle. "Take him away," my father said to no one in particular, but guards surrounded Ariel and yanked him up.

They carried him halfway down the lawn when the ground started to shake. Quick vibrations at my feet had me looking down, watching the small pieces of dirt and rocks shake. Then a violent growl ripped through and a few angels were knocked off their feet, some of the marble benches cracking in half.

"What the fuck is happening?" Reese shouted.

I opened my mouth to speak, but then the sky shifted in color. The blue became muted, distorting into something darker. The trees whipped from a wind that came from nowhere.

"Your majesty..." Zane started, suddenly by Natalia's side and attempting to pull her away from whatever was happening. She batted his hands away, looking from me to Dani.

Elise was looking up at the sky, her face morphing into something I could only pinpoint as realization. "Why does no one fucking listen to me!"

"What are you yelling…" I started to say, but a dark circle appeared near us. It reminded me of the ripple in the sky but more fleshed out. This tear in the realms was more confident. The ground shook harder and the dark circle pulsed over and over.

Two hellhounds jumped out, but these looked different than the ones we fought in Purgatory. They were around Axel's size when he was angry but they had horns that protruded from the tops of their head, spikes trailed down their backs and their teeth were huge and oozing some sort of black liquid that sizzled when it hit the ground.

Axel growled more intensely, not backing down from them. I blinked and one minute he was the cute little black dog that napped in Reese's arms, the next he was matching the size of these new hellhounds, stalking towards them but still keeping his distance.

A manically casual laugh filled my ears and the figure who owned that laugh stepped out of the portal. I had to be seeing a fucking ghost.

I heard a deep hiss come from my right and that told me everything I needed to know about Beetee's state of mind.

"Nicholas…" My father started, but he was cut short when a scream pierced through the chaos.

I looked down to find Dani pressing a hand to her scarred thigh as she let out another scream of pain.

44

DANI

My thigh was throbbing and my arm didn't feel any better but at least *that* I could attempt to ignore. It felt like my thigh was going to explode from all the pressure it was harboring. I looked down at my skin and the wound was visibly pulsing as if at any minute, blood would start to gush from it. The area around the scars was red and raging. I pressed my lips together trying not to release any more screams, practically biting my tongue.

The ground shook and black mist collected around me and everyone's feet. Dimitri's laugh thrummed in my ears, but it was like the volume was turned up. I released the hold on my thigh and pressed my hand to my ear, hoping to block out the noise. It was no use, the fucker was in my head. The minute he'd cut me, the minute he'd had my blood on his nails, slipping down his hand…he had a way in.

Dimitri couldn't make me submit, but *fuck* could he make me hurt. He didn't have the power like Lilith did to make me do his bidding by a simple command. Even through all this sudden pain, I didn't feel the urge to make it stop simply because it would make my life easier.

"Dani!" I heard Beetee yell as she ran over, kneeling beside me. She looked across my body to Nick, who was also hunched over me. He placed his hand gently behind my head, scanning my body. He went to touch my pulsing wound, but he hissed, shaking his hand as if simply touching my scars caused him pain.

He opened his mouth to speak, but Dimitri cut him off. He clucked his tongue, running his hand along the side of one of the hellhounds. "You move against me, everyone hurts. I believe I explained this to you quite thoroughly, pretty girl."

I heard Axel growl as the hellhounds chomped at the air.

"Nicholas, what is the meaning of this!?" Ariel demanded, his green eyes wide as he took in the darkened sky, the massive hellhounds and the pretentious Son of Hell that wanted to act like he wasn't making a scene. Ariel shoved away from the guards, rushing past us. Nick grabbed my arm helping me up as we watched Ariel trudge towards where all the chaos was.

"Ariel, if you listen to me at least once in your entire life, please do so now! Move away!" Maurice urged, walking behind Ariel but still keeping a small distance. He grabbed at Ariel's arm, but the executive yanked away from him. He spun around, getting into Maurice's face.

"This is how people lead Maurice! I will not let what your son and that stupid girl brought here destroy this place!" Ariel moved to face Dimitri, hesitating a bit when the hellhounds eyed him. They dug their claws against the ground, creating deep lines that brought up the dirt underneath. Ariel made sure his voice was loud and clear. "You have no place here! You will not win today…"

"Ariel I really don't think…" Nick started, but Ariel looked over his shoulder, sneering at my angelic boyfriend.

"Do not speak to me as if…" Ariel spat, starting to reprimand Nick when his voice caught. A flash of reddish light hit his body and then… through his body. I heard Nick's breath hitch as his mouth gaped open. Ariel looked down, sputtering when he saw the large hole that was created in his chest. Morgan let out a sharp cry as Ariel fell to his knees, the light leaving his eyes as blood leaked from his mouth. Tiny flame sparks moved around the inside and you could see clear through his body, right at Dimitri who had a small smirk on his lips.

Screams and cries filled the open space as many of the angels that had been here for a simple ceremony had no place to go, no place to run.

"You should have really listened to the boy, hmm." The Son of Hell's tattooed hand was engulfed in a circle of red and black flames. He casually moved the power he had between his fingers as if he had all the time in the world to taunt us.

A large, very bright, stream of light flew at Dimitri, knocking him off his feet. When the light had retreated, I blinked, realizing that that level of power came from Maurice. His hands were in front of him as he stood in front of Ariel's dead body. "You will leave!"

Dimitri huffed, getting up and readjusting the suit jacket he wore. He let out a low laugh before thrusting his hand forward, aiming his dark power at Maurice. The red magic flew fast, molding itself to a sharp point.

Maurice readied himself to fight back, but a sharp blade came in front of him. The magic pinging off the silver, flying into the air. A sizzling sound surrounded us, but all I could focus on was the intense breathing coming from Nick.

He held his sword tight as he protected his father. Dimitri laughed again, pure amusement playing in his eyes. "Ah, showing off are we? A solid attempt, but misguided. That heart of yours will be quite a delicacy to the hellhounds."

The portal shuddered and moved behind him, but then shadows wafted out of it. Some of them were large and some were around my height. The darkness scattered over the benches and around our feet. The shadows lifted and grew, forming people and weapons for them to fight with. Dimitri's guards hustled out of the portal, flanking him on all sides.

"It's a shame you had to ask for Lucifer's help in all this. Too helpless to do it yourself?" Elise taunted, growling right back at the hellhound's that threatened her and Axel. Garrett and Leah stood next to her, hands already filling with their magic.

"Lucifer!?" Reese questioned, his voice rising just a fraction.

Dimitri cocked his head towards Elise, raising his eyebrows. She never let her grey eyes leave him. "We both know you don't hold the power to establish this much!"

"Perhaps not, but he did give me the okay to destroy all of you and we wouldn't want to let him down, now would we?" He blinked innocently at her.

I eyed the shadow demons and their holds on their weapons. I scanned the hellhounds and their vibrating need to strike. Morgan shook next to me, her fear easily identifiable.

She jumped, startled when I spoke to her. "You have a choice. You can run inside The Skies and wait until this is all over, no matter the outcome or you can fight with us. You want to prove something to yourself and actually show that you deserve that applause that you somehow think you're owed? Then I suggest you choose the latter."

"Kill them all, but leave that one..." Dimitri nodded over to me. "To me."

The descent upon us was quick. Reese got his bow out, notching an arrow and began releasing them in perfect succession. They struck a few of Dimitri's guards causing them to collapse around him.

Beetee shifted quickly, her black scales lined in pink shimmering even though the sky was darkened. Her large body slithered through the grass while her tail whipped around, knocking down shadow demons as she moved. She reared back, opening her mouth and hissing before collecting some of the guards that tried to fight her in her mouth.

I gave Morgan one last look before I forgot about the mild pain in my leg and charged towards Dimitri. He threw his deep red tendrils that held sharp points at me, but I dodged them. A flaming ball of red fire was sent my way, I crouched to the ground, feeling the heat right over my head. Dimitri continued to aim for me, but I managed to entrap one of his reddish black flames into my own shadows, harboring it in my hand and throwing it back at him.

It hit his shoulder, causing him to stagger back. He righted himself but I threw another one and he was pushed back again. I could have sworn steam bellowed from his ears as he threw his hand out and I felt a cinch at my wrists and throat. I was flipped over and thrown onto my back as he dragged me along the grass. He burned my wrists, the pain causing my fingers to tense up and the heat at my throat was enough to make breathing hard.

I looked over to see Nick and his father fighting back to back. Maurice had so much power now, it was mesmerizing to see. His hands glowed with an overwhelming amount of light that he nearly caused the guards to combust into microscopic light particles. Maurice took one by the neck, his eyes bulging out and light streaming out of them as he twirled him around. He stopped, letting his son finish them off.

A guard came up behind Nick, raising his sword to slash at his back, but an arrow came sailing down, hitting him directly in the back of his skull. Reese flapped his wings, readying his next arrow and letting it fly at a demon that was running for Leah and Garrett.

The two Enchanters rallied behind Beetee, catching all the demons that she had missed. A guard hit Garrett's side, causing him to keel over, but Leah moved around him. Blue sparks came from her fingers as she pressed her fingertips into the guards eyes, causing her to let out a scream. Garrett ran past his wife, creating dark blue magic that formed over his fist and punched a guard in the stomach, sending him flying towards the trees.

Natalia and Zane kept demons from running into the The Skies and attempted to keep angels from harm's way, but the damage was already being done. Not as much as Dimitri likely hoped, but there were angels littering the ground. Blood soaked the grass and wails of pain were filling the open space. Natalia let out streams of her magic towards demons that headed for the sky, trying to move past and overtake the castle-like structure.

Zane held his arm out, ramming his forearm into the throat of a demon that tried to pass him, while also grabbing another by the throat. Natalia forced tree branches to extend and entrap unsuspecting guards, holding them so tight against the tree trunks that she would close their airways and break their ribs.

Dimitri raised me up by his magic, forcing me to look at him. "I have missed you dearly." His eyes changed from their normal green to the black whorls of emptiness. He flung me towards the forest. My body moved fast and the wind felt harsh against my skin. I let out a loud groan as my back hit a tree trunk, the bark ripping at my scalp as my head collided as well. The trees around me trembled with the impact I'd made. I fell to the ground, landing on my shoulder and hearing something that sounded a lot like dislocation.

Dimitri moved faster than I anticipated and I had barely gotten up when he hovered over me. "You come with me and you won't have to worry about Lilith. Lucifer made sure she wasn't a problem for either of us anymore." He winked at me and I sneered at him barely flinching at the idea that Lucifer had killed Lilith. I had wanted to end her but Dimitri would be my prize in the end. She wasn't worth my efforts. "Simply being here for this short period of time has made you lackluster. I plan to change that." He reached down to stroke my head, but I grabbed his wrist and slid closer to the ground, kicking upwards towards his stomach.

I let my shadows grow in my hand and I released ribbons of them over to his hunched over body, wrapping him up. I let light litter my palm next and threw it over to him, sending him sailing towards a mass of bushes. The light traveled along the shadows causing more of an explosion than I had anticipated.

He didn't come back up immediately, but my head swung around when I heard a whimper. I saw Axel holding one of the hellhounds by the throat, swinging it around like a chew toy. Elise had somehow gotten onto the other hellhound's back and was plunging her tail into its body, causing the creature to stumble around, stepping on multiple shadow demons. Nick and Reese were both flying now, fighting like it was an art form with the way they weaved around each other and knew when to block and let the other have the final strike.

A shadow demon charged at Leah from behind, but to my surprise Morgan stunned it with her own light magic, giving Garrett the chance to kill it. Maurice was surrounded by another set of demons, but he blasted sparks of lights from his hand, letting it travel through each and every demon until they all were connected by his power and then he released a massive light explosion. There was a pop that sounded when each of the demons exploded, one by one.

The wind picked up and the startling heat that hit my neck was something I'd only felt when I was in Hell. The smell of brimstone was heady and the bush that Dimitri had been thrown in rustled.

"You think you can fight as you always have and *win*, pretty girl?" Dimitri's voice was harsh, as if he was losing that usual calmness he always showcased. The ground shook again and this time it nearly knocked me off my feet. I heard a crack and right between my feet a jagged line formed in the grass. All of my friends, the people I'd come to care so much for, continued to fight, but were aware of the shift.

The crack grew bigger and lengthened, moving past me. I noticed more cracks around me and smoke puffed out of the openings.

My shadows hissed at the thick black wafts of smoke seeping from the cracks. This was different from the mist Dimitri had created before. The sky grew darker and a deep red shone over us all. I went to back away, but a hand clamped around my throat. Fingers gripped me so tightly that a single gasp for air felt like a difficult task.

Dimitri's face was gone now and only the skull, decorated with gray matter and black eyes like a dull void, was in its place. The tattooed hand that had a hold on my throat vibrated and pulsed. His voice was deep and hollow when he spoke, "you will *not* have it all. You will *not* beat me, Soul Seether. You can have what I *tell* you you can have." He threw me onto the ground and I heard my shoulder pop back in place. The cracks only got bigger and bigger.

I couldn't bother trying to regain my breathing, so I tried to gather as much of the hybrid power I could in my hands, but something wrapped itself around my legs and wrists. The thick black smoke from the cracks in the ground had shot out and seized my ankles, holding them together tight; my wrists were the same, pulled in towards my chest.

My energy felt like it was leaving me, depleting. This wasn't Dimitri's magic. The Son of Hell didn't have this sort of power. The person he *worked* for did though.

"You really can't do anything yourself, can you?" I wheezed out, exhaustion hitting me like it never had before.

It was hard to see any kind of expression from him when he was in this form, but I knew he understood that I'd realized this power wasn't his. His laugh seemed to rumble through my very core. "To be fair, getting a little help isn't unheard of. We want the same thing, him and I."

I could hear my shadows crying as if they were suffocating. My light simmered and tried to shove through, hitting my chest from the inside over and over. My fingertips felt the heat from my light, but it wasn't enough.

"What the fuck?" Elise yelled, the thick black rope yanking her off of the hellhound and pinning her to the ground. Leah and Garrett tried to expel as much of their magic as they could but the darkness was too strong and it spun around them, pulling them in different directions before pinning them to the ground as well. The hellhound Elise had been on top of rammed into Axel, before it slumped to the ground, causing Axel to skid across the ground and be engulfed in the dark magic as well.

Beetee's tail got caught with one of the ropes, ceasing her movements. She hissed out, her yellow eyes locking onto me. Those eyes widened when a shadowy demon came up and struck with their blade. Not once, but twice. She whipped her head to the side, snatching him up into her mouth, clamping down and then throwing him to the other side. She slowly began to shift back into her normal self, pink hair and lilac eyes. The heat was turning thick, but she was naked and shivering.

She held her side, covering the bloody stab wounds that pierced her skin.

I pulled at Dimitri's restraints. The more I pulled, the tighter they got.

Nick and Reese continued to fight in the air, but the thick ribbons of dark magic shot up in the air, wrapping themselves around Nick's wings and yanking him down. Reese flew down to try to release him, but his own wings got caught up in the black ropes as well. Nick slammed into the pile of rubble from a broken bench, his sword landing a few feet away from him.

Maurice was on his knees, two restraints at his wrists as he held his arms out. Another black rope wrapped around his head, covering his mouth and restricting words of any kind. He didn't look afraid, though. He looked like he was still full of so much pride even if the odds of this ending well were slim.

I saw no signs of Morgan, leaving me to assume this had been too much for her. Hiding was always an option. Submitting was always an option.

No, no, no. *Fuck*, that was never an option.

"He let me have control of these beauties of his." Dimitri cocked his head to the side and motioned his hands towards the dark magic holding me hostage. "I will show you how *little* your resistance mattered." He snapped his fingers and a loud agonizing groan sounded.

It didn't sound like Nick. It didn't sound like Nick at all.

Leah let out a blood curdling scream as she watched the restraints hold her husband up and pull in tighter. Even from my small distance, I could see his cheeks hollow and his face grow more ashen as if his life force was being taken from him.

"Dimitri, stop!" I screamed as I watched Leah try to pull away from the thick shadows. Maurice yanked on his as well, along with anyone else I could see. Elise tugged and tugged but to no avail. Beetee, who was the closest to me, had small tears in her eyes as she winced at her wounds.

Garrett groaned louder, bones cracking and blood expelling from his ears. "I love you," he said to his wife in a strained voice. My fingers sparked a little brighter but it still wasn't enough. I *needed* it to be enough.

Dimitri snapped his fingers again and the ropes pulled so tight that Garrett's body crumpled in on itself as they let him go. He swiftly descended to the ground, landing near Maurice whose chest was heaving in and out. I saw tiny sparks of light in his fingertips as well as if he was pushing through.

Leah started to scream violently, but a black shadow clamped over her mouth. Dimitri laughed. "Who's next, hmm? Don't worry, I'm saving your heroic angel for last." I felt a burning sensation in my thigh. My blood was boiling and he didn't even need to be touching me to create visions in my head. I was starting to sweat and every time I blinked, the pictures I was forced to see just got worse and worse. "Perhaps we should just get rid of all the Enchanters first? I did tell you that you could keep your friend, didn't I?" He pointed at Elise, who was still pulling at her restraints, even using her teeth to try and get out. "I am nothing but good to you, even though you want to be ungrateful."

I felt tears brimming and my body was waning. My strength was straddling a line and every breath I took felt harder than the last. My light pressed hard against my chest and I wanted to tell it that I didn't know what it wanted. I didn't know…

I peeked up at Dimitri who was bringing Natalia over, letting her fall to her knees. The glitter that had decorated her dark skin was messy and her once vibrant demeanor was lost under the dark magic. Her honey eyes stared at me as if she still had all the confidence in the world, despite the circumstances. She wasn't dumb enough to think this situation was ideal, but she didn't think less of me…of any of us.

Her eyes moved to my thigh and then to the light that sparked at my fingertips. She looked back and forth from my hand to my throbbing wound. My deep planted scars were the only connection Dimitri had to me. It was shrouded in darkness and something needed to root it out. I needed enough light to eliminate it.

I used all the strength I had to push Dimitri's vile visions aside and searched my head and my heart for the memory I wanted. I thought back to when I'd let myself be balanced with my light and dark magic. I'd let Nick help me; I had been open to the added assistance. I needed to push through the debilitating force of Dimitri's restraints and so would Nick, if this was going to work.

Always here for me when I need you.

For you? Absolutely.

My light was strong enough to push at my chest and beg to be released. His light was strong enough to find me in a Hell prison. I *had* to hope it was enough.

45
NICK

I looked over at Garrett's dead body and I could feel my breathing getting rougher from the harsh breaths I was letting out. Leah was still screaming behind the black ribbon over her mouth and I couldn't blame her. I could barely make out the way Beetee's shoulders moved, telling me she was barely alive.

This felt like losing and I hated to lose. I especially hated to lose to someone who was unworthy of being victorious. My eyes had followed Natalia as Dimitri brought her over to where he had Dani. Zane was yelling at him to bring her back, but it was no use. I wanted to help her; I wanted to help everyone. I caught sight of all the bodies that littered the grounds. Some of them were angels I knew and some were ones I hadn't met yet, but it made me want to vomit all the same.

Thoughts about the last time this many angels were dead and scattered at my feet flooded through me and my head started spinning. It was already hot, but I felt myself starting to sweat profusely. The restraints kept my chest from rising like normal, so the restriction on my breathing wasn't helping. I should have seen this coming. I should have made *sure* he was dead. I was stupid to believe otherwise; this was clearly all my fault and I would never get to tell Garrett how sorry I was. My eyes burned from keeping my tears at bay.

"Deep breath in, deep breath out, Nick." Reese had his wrists tied together, his bow inches away from his feet. He gave me a look that told me to do what he said.

I nodded, taking in as much air as I could and then letting it out. My chest hurt, but I did it again.

My chest felt hot, but this wasn't from Dimitri's power. I *knew* this heat. I looked down at the way my chest had a slight glow to it. It wasn't bright and overwhelming but it didn't need to be. It soothed me in a way, but it also had this yearning to it. I let out slow breaths, letting my body mold to the welcomed invasion of light. I looked over at my father, who was staring right back at me.

I had my strength, sure, but I liked to think I owed so much of it to this man. He couldn't douse me with words of wisdom or sharp wit at the moment, but his eyes told me so much. I had to hope mine did the same. My father had so much power now and he had to use nearly all of it in the first fight since acquiring it. I was sure he was tired and drowning in the need to re-energize, but if I knew my father at all—that wouldn't stop him. I was able to raise my hand just a tiny bit, letting him see the light that formed at my fingers. His eyes roamed from my fingers to my chest, seeing the light that glowed there. He moved his head towards where Dani was and his eyes widened in what I hoped was understanding.

I kept pushing my own light, trying to mend together all the pieces of it I could feel. I gave my father a small smile, my voice a bit rough. "You are stronger than any of this, Dad. Jonah wouldn't have given the power to you if he didn't think so." I hissed when one of the shadow demons kicked me in my side.

I coughed, rolling over but keeping up the persistence of my light as I heaved out a breath.

My father pulled at his restraints, but this time I noticed he was *really* pulling. His face was strained and reddened by the amount of energy I knew he didn't have but he pushed through. Light ignited around his body, dimming and becoming bright over and over again. It was being shut down and amped up causing my father to have to push more, exert more power.

The guards that watched us were on edge but seemed to think nothing would happen. They likely assumed we were trying to fight against a losing game. The black ropes that held my father in place began to burn and melt. The one at his mouth glowed and started to shrivel up.

I squinted when the light became too bright to look at head on, closing my eyes for a minute. I heard a grunt and something that reminded me of a squeal before I opened my eyes again. My father was standing proud, his chest broad and the aura he presented was felt.

He opened up his hand, letting light protrude from it and towards me.

One day your light will be just as big as that all on your own, but sometimes

it's okay to get a little help.

My light would be just as big as my father's, but I wouldn't be the one using it.

I felt my restraints pull away, dissolving up around me. My light felt stronger and ready for anything. My father started to say something but stopped short, punching a guard clear through the chest with his power. My father was much different than Jonah when it came to his power. Jonah was never one for physical altercations so he used the power for more emotional situations, he let others feel his authority over them. My father would like me to believe he enjoyed talking things through, but a good rumble was something he appreciated and the power he now had molded to that.

I grabbed my sword and paused when I got to Reese. I heard my father yell in my direction, "I have them, now go!"

Reese gave me a solid nod before I seamlessly fought through demons that barreled towards me. I swiveled out of their holds, while also piercing through the chest of one guard. I shoved my sword's pommel into the head of another. I let my light amp up my blade before I plunged it into the shadow demons, letting them fall to the ground without a second glance. I got up to a tree, seeing Beetee and watching her breathe shallow breaths.

The snake shifter caught my eye and her eyebrows furrowed. Blood soaked the area around us and the wind rustled the leaves on the trees. The smell of brimstone nearly clogging my lungs.

I didn't know much about what Dani planned to do but I didn't think twice when I let light expel from my hand straight to her body. It was eager to get to her as if it wanted nothing more than to mingle with hers.

Another light caught my eye and I blinked looking to my left. My breath caught when I saw the pink haired demon extend as much of her hand as she could out to Dani. Her head rested on her arm as she let light flood from her fingers, as if it had been there all along and just waiting for a reason to be released.

The jolt I felt burned, but it was a good burn. It was the kind that made you hesitant at first, like you weren't expecting it. Then it becomes something that you can handle, something you can settle with and learn to enjoy. Nick's light flooded in and I watched as Dimitri reared his head back, continuing to press his nails into the back of Natalia's neck. It was quick the way my light no longer cried out in pain, but seemed to jump for joy over having its companion back. That joy doubled over when a new light forced its way in as well. This one was foreign to me. It wasn't uncomfortable, but when my light didn't shy away I didn't think to question it. My light embraced this new one while my shadows tried to fight back against Dimitri's own darkness.

My thigh was starting to bleed slowly and I took a deep breath in, letting my mind go numb enough to let both lights stand their ground with my own. I heard Natalia moan in pain as Dimitri dug his nails in deeper.

"You are so cute when you try, pretty girl, but all you can do is *try*." Dimitri gripped Natalia's neck harder and flung her backwards.

I pointed my fingers at my thigh, seeing the light grow bigger than before. It *had* to work. I had to rely on the light to help me, without my shadows. I had to hope that being vulnerable to it wasn't wrong and I wasn't completely fucked. "All *you* can do is wish you *never* touched me."

I let the light fly from my fingers and onto my own skin. It hit my wound, seeping in and I let out a scream at the way it burned. Dimitri pulled back, moving his head from side to side.

"What are you doing!?" he yelled, reaching for me, but then slinking backwards as his shoulders tensed. It looked like whatever I was doing was hurting him from the inside.

I pushed more light into my scars, seering my skin. Shadows flew out of my now open wounds, they snapped at me and shrilled at the way they were pushed out. Dimitri pressed his hand to his skull; he tried to morph back into his old self but the two parts of him kept shifting. I was disrupting his mind.

I bit my own tongue at the way my skin sizzled. The restraints loosened inch by inch and when I was close enough I gave it my all. I pressed my palm firmly to my thigh and Dimitri lunged for me.

"You stupid girl!" he roared, being thrown to his knees by his own destructive mind. His restraints slipped away from me, so I got up hurriedly, feeling the pain in my thigh almost immediately when I put pressure on it. Dimitri looked behind me as he continued to wince. "I will make sure you are *never* as happy as you could have been!"

He threw his hand out, black and red magic shaped like a web shot out. I glanced over my shoulder to see it slam right into Nick, sending him backwards. Natalia rubbed the back of her neck as she ran past me to aid him.

The feeling of so much light mixed with my freed shadows felt *good*. It felt like so much power that I didn't know what to do with. Dimitri tried to get up to his feet, but I stopped him, raising my knee swiftly and connecting it under his chin. He went flying backwards with a grunt. I didn't notice how dirty and ripped my dress was when I ran up to him, placing my foot at his chest. I let my own shadows grow from the ground and wrap around his wrists and throat. They shined with light as the other half of my power threatened to burn him like nothing he'd ever felt.

"I think you've always underestimated me," I said, moving my hand towards the shadow demons and guards, letting shadows of my own form into fighters just like them. They grabbed them and began tearing through their chests, slaughtering them. The sky crackled with lightning but the only storm that was brewing was the one inside of myself.

I straddled Dimitri, letting my eyes go black and light simmer at my fingertips. "You think I'm so *weak* now?" I grazed my hand up his chest and felt the way his heart thumped.

Light struck down from the sky and singed a tree. Another hit the ground, burning through a patch of grass. Shadows whirled around the tree branches and the winds felt rough, pieces of the broken benches being thrown around.

"Am I everything you ever *imagined*, Dimitri?" I let a maniacal smile form on my face and I let my mix of powers form in my hand before I slammed my fist into his arm, right at his shoulder. His face was back to his normal look, giving me the chance to see how his lips pressed together as if he was holding in a scream. I pulled my arm back to see his arm severed from his body. "Have you had *enough*?" I asked, not waiting for an answer. I pressed my hand to his throat and squeezed so hard, I swore I heard something crack and it made my chest swell with pride.

Light started to come down harder, almost like a rain shower. The shadow demons that I had created started to morph and contort into things from nightmares.

"Dani!" I heard Elise. "Dani, stop whatever it is you're doing!" I hissed at her complaints, seeing that my shadows were charging at her. They were charging at *all* of them.

They could handle themselves. I had something to do at the moment and he deserved all my attention. That was what he always wanted, wasn't it?

Zane's booming voice sounded around me. "Maurice, use your power!" The large Enchanter hustled over to Beetee, tenderly turning her body over.

It was like I could feel Maurice hesitate before he considered blasting his high executive magic at me. The magic came my way, but I quickly constructed a shield over myself. It was housed in my own magic of light and dark. The way the two worked together and fashioned themselves as one was astonishing. There was rumbling on the other side and I felt like something was banging against it.

Axel kept ramming himself into my shield over and over, clawing at the darkened dome I was settled in. He opened his mouth to let fire erupt over my shield, but to no avail. My shadow demons came to subdue him but he wouldn't relent. I saw Enchanter magic try to push through, a cascade of colorful sparks trying to penetrate.

I focused back on Dimitri, pressing my fingers into his chest. He winced but let out a half-hearted chuckle. "Even without me, you are going to destroy everything. You are a beautiful monster."

I reared my head back, while I let my fingers burn into his chest, digging inside. He opened his mouth to scream but my shadows snaked around and flew down his throat, choking him. I missed the ease of removing souls like I used to, but this would do. Blood spurted from his chest as I dug deeper.

I leaned in, whispering, "I want to know if you have a heart after all."

The inside of his chest felt warm as I searched around. The beating organ felt foreign in my hands, since I had always assumed Dimitri was damn near hollow on the inside. I pulled it out, letting my shadows flow deeper into his throat and watched as his eyes rolled back into his head. I let light move out of my other hand into the open space in his chest, burning him.

I held his heart out in front of me and his words wrapped around me like a vice.

You are a beautiful monster

I blinked, pushing away from his body.

I remembered back to what Daya had said when this whole thing had all started.

The energy in the hybrids was always fighting with itself, never knowing which one was more in charge, so when it was time for their powers to release, it could be a massacre.

I wasn't fighting with myself, I *knew* what I was. I understood my balance of power. Light showers hit my shield and I heard the grunts and huffs of fighting on the outside.

I shook my head, holding Dimitri's heart tight in my grip. Nick's voice fought its way to the forefront of my mind.

You aren't the villain in this story, remember that.

My own thoughts fought against it.

I couldn't even be my own hero, Nick!

I don't want to be weak; I can't. That's not who I am!

I held my chest, dropping Dimitri's heart. Nick's voice forced its way in one more time.

Oh, baby, you are something to be afraid of. You are something to admire.

I shuddered feeling all the power I'd let loose reel itself back in. The shield I'd conjured disappeared and I saw what losing myself to so much power had done. I motioned towards my raging shadow demons and they dissolved as if they were never there in the first place. I could be something to be afraid of but I didn't have to ruin the realm around me to do it.

Revenge was sweet, but not at the expense of those that tried to make my revenge possible in some way shape or form.

I felt hands on my arms, shaking me. "Do you understand that you literally tried to kill all of us, huh!?" Elise shouted.

"I didn't..." I shook my head, gathering my thoughts. "I didn't mean to."

I felt the burn in my leg and looked down seeing the amount of burnt flesh looking back at me.

"She needs help now!" I heard Zane yell, letting Reese huddle close to Beetee, whose eyes were flickering from open to closed.

Piercing wailing was coming from Leah and, oh god….Garrett. Maurice knelt down next to her, rubbing her back as she was hunched over where I assumed her husband's body was. Maurice's head flew upward when Natalia called for him.

Axel's large body that was covered in cut marks and dirt, crowded around Natalia. I narrowed my eyes at where she was, feeling a pull in that direction for some odd reason. The pain in my leg grew heavier when I saw what had her so concerned. Elise followed me, grabbing my arm when I fell onto my knees next to Nick's body.

His chest rose and fell, letting me know he was alive, but something was *off*.

Nick's body would jolt every now and then and his skin was hot.

"I can't wake him up," Natalia admitted. "I've tried most of the things I know, but without Xander or really any certified healer, I don't know what else to try."

Maurice laid his hands on his son, pushing his light into him. Nick calmed from his jolting fit, but his eyes didn't open. I scanned his body, trying to think.

"Before…everything, Dimitri threw something at him, it looked like a web or a…"

Elise let out a short breath as if she was realizing something. "An alarum net."

"A what?" I pressed.

"They don't always work depending on the prey and they are strictly a Hell born weapon. He throws the alarum net at Nick, it absorbs into his being, trapping him and his mind. He's eternally stuck in this net of distress and harm of his own mind. It's a pretty last minute move, but it's smart, especially with everything he knows about him."

Maurice cleared his throat. "Eternally?"

We all jumped at Leah's cries and Natalia nodded. "I'll send Zane to fetch the healers. We will need them. I'm sorry, I have to…" She looked over her shoulder at where one of her fellow Enchanters needed her. Nick may be unconscious but he was at least alive. That was something I could attempt to hold onto.

I grabbed Nick's hand. "He'll wake up."

Nick jolted again as if his mind was fighting against him, torturing him.

Axel let out whimpers as he started to shrink in size. He padded over to Nick and licked his cheek, nuzzling his nose against him. I looked over at Elise who gave me a hesitant look as if she didn't want to say what she was really thinking.

I moved in closer to him, pushing his hair back from his face. "You don't go down like this. *We* don't go down like this," I whispered into his hand.

A portal flashed causing us to all move our heads in that direction. Morgan stepped out and I wanted to combust, but then behind her came Xander and a few other Enchanters I remembered from my time in the The Skies infirmary after our time in Purgatory.

Xander looked around, a grim expression on his face. "Oh." He glanced over at Morgan, who was biting her bottom lip. "This is not what I thought we were walking into."

She gave a small shrug, placing her hand over her heart when she saw Nick. "I didn't either, but can you help or not?"

The healing Enchanter took in a sharp breath and nodded. He turned towards his fellow Enchanters. "A few of you head towards Zane, some of you stay here with Maurice and see what he needs and the rest of you follow me to the High Priestess. We are moving everyone inside and to the infirmary." The Enchanters followed his lead without question or doubt.

Morgan fiddled with her fingers as she took in her surroundings again. She settled her dark eyes on me, adjusting her glasses. "I may not know how to fight as well as you, but I know how to get help."

I hummed, not giving her my attention anymore, but focusing on Nick. "Thank you." She sniffed, seeming to take my gratitude as a reason to come closer. I put my hand up, letting my shadows push her back. "You come near him though and I'll ruin you."

47

DANI

The Enchanters worked diligently, never missing a beat as they rotated to every angel that needed assistance. They had checked on each of us, giving us the okay when they saw fit that we could walk around on our own. Natalia had done her normal once over, scanning her magic over us to check for things that you wouldn't see on the outside and having Xander go behind her and double check. A large bandage decorated my thigh and the knowledge that the wound would heal in time settled on my mind.

I assumed that went for all wounds and not just physical ones.

I walked down the hall of the infirmary, stopping to look in on Beetee, who had lost consciousness multiple times before they got her stable enough to feel comfortable leaving her alone. Well...*alone* was subjective. Elise eyed me from the corner of the room, pushing out of the chair she sat in and walking over to me.

"How is she?" I asked, crossing my arms over my chest as I leaned around the door frame.

"She's fine. She won't be shifting any time soon, but she'll survive. I had to calm her moms down, which was my second least favorite part of the day." I had been informed that Beetee had been my second light source. I didn't know how I would ever thank her, but I would spend every minute of time I had figuring out a way. Beetee wasn't like me. She didn't need rigorous training to find her light and nourish it. She quite possibly *was* the light and used it in a different way other than for fighting. For Beetee, it was a demeanor and not a weapon.

I sighed. "I'm sorry. I really didn't mean to…"

She held her hand up to stop me. "Yeah, I know. I would have been surprised if you didn't explode with your unhinged hybrid powers at least once. Never again though or I'll kill you myself."

I let out a small chuckle. "Right."

We heard crying coming from one of the rooms down the hall. I looked down at the floor and shook my head. Elise clucked her tongue. "She's been like that for hours."

Xander ended up having to give Leah a soothing tonic just to get her to stop convulsing into tears. She fought the healers that tried to take her husband away and she'd always tried to run out of the infirmary to find him. Natalia had attempted to talk to her, but she wouldn't listen. She'd respectfully asked the High Priestess to leave her room.

"How would you feel if your husband died right in front of you?" I asked, raising my eyebrows.

Elise shrugged. "I don't know. From what daddy Cassial says, Daya and Alex are watching her kids."

Fuck, her kids. I had fought so hard to control myself and keep the powers in check so that Garrett could reunite with his family. I wanted to do something good and for it to work out. I held myself back to keep a family together, just for Dimitri to tear it all apart with a literal snap of his fingers.

I could still feel the weight of his heart in my hand and I wished I had crushed it, burnt it to pieces and stuffed the ashes down his throat. My heart beat loudly and I fisted the fresh shirt I wore, giving my hands something to do. Before I knew it, I was walking down the hall towards Leah's room.

"Dani, if she didn't want to see the witch, what makes you think she'll want to see you?" Elise called after me but I ignored her.

I took a deep breath before I peeked into the room. Leah was huddled on the bed, her legs bent so that she could rest her chin on her knees. I took a tentative step inside, lightly knocking on the open door. She looked over at me, the area under her eyes was swollen from crying and red splotches decorated her face. "Please get out."

I pressed my tongue into my cheek. I should have left and done exactly what she wanted. I really was terrible at following orders. I stepped further into the room and she huffed out a sigh.

"Dani, *please*, leave." Her voice was small and the words that came out didn't hold much ill-intent.

"I'm sorry," I said, knowing that wasn't enough and it never would be.

She squinted at me. "You're sorry?"

I nodded, deciding that where I was standing was as close as I would get for now. Leah placed her hand over her mouth, shaking her head. "Dimitri should be sorry, not you."

"You shouldn't be dealing with this. You should be doing what you always planned together, whatever that may be. The two of you should be hugging your kids." She let out a choked sob for a moment, causing me to stop speaking. She wiped her hands under her eyes, collecting herself. I continued, "you can't punish Dimitri for what he's done, but you can punish me in his place. I let you down and you deserve some kind of justice for all your pain."

Leah swallowed, placing her hands on her cheeks as she stared at me. "Punishing you would be useless since you've done nothing wrong. I want to make someone hurt for Garrett, yes. I loved my husband and having him taken from me is the worst thing I have ever, *ever* felt. A part of me is missing, Dani. We were bonded in a way that makes my very soul weep." She held her hand to her chest, tears streaming down her cheeks. "He would want me to fight when the time is right. He would want me to save my energy for our children and be there for them because they are going to hurt, just as much if not more than me. I just need time to wrap my head around the fact that I am without the other half of my heart."

My heart thumped against my chest at her words. I felt my eyes burning from my own tears. "I want justice for you."

She nodded solemnly, moving her hair behind her ears. "I do too, sweetheart. Garrett, Yuri, Jasmine, they deserved it." Her eyes locked onto mine as if she wanted my full attention. "You gave my husband his family back by keeping Dimitri's men at bay in Hell. You let me hold my husband for far longer than I thought I might get a chance to." She scooted off the bed and leaned back against it. "He was one of the last resurrecting Enchanters and now there is just your Nicholas. We were hoping Yuri or Jasmine would start to show some signs of it soon, to keep their father's line alive."

"I'm sure Nick can learn right alongside them if they do," I said, hopefulness in my tone.

"I overheard that he hasn't woken up."

I rocked back and forth on my feet. "Rumors are true."

Suddenly, she was right in front of me, taking my hands in hers. She looked deep into my eyes. "You want to do something for me? You *never* give up on him. You stay by his side and wake him up however you can. Garrett was rooting for you two, as odd as your pairing may be. If you ever for a second think about faltering, think about how Garrett would have loved to see the things that you two would achieve. The moment you think Nicholas is a lost cause, you are hurting everyone who ever believed in you both. Sometimes healing medicine and wishful thinking isn't enough. Sometimes all they need is you and you alone to bring them back."

I swallowed the very big lump in my throat wanting to verbally commit to a *yes* but I simply nodded. She grabbed my shoulders and pulled me into a hug. I nuzzled my face into her neck. "Garrett was so lucky to be loved by you."

She cried harder, her words coming out choked. "Oh, I was so lucky to be loved by *him*."

I pulled back, planning to leave her in peace, but she stopped me.

"In a few minutes can you tell them to bring my children here. I don't know how I'll make it through it, but I can't leave them in the dark forever."

I gave her one solid nod. "Yeah, I can do that. If you want some additional strength, I'm here."

Nick let out steady breaths as he remained asleep. If you took out the random shaking and jolts he did, he looked serene in his comatose state. Reese had his feet kicked up on one of the tables as he leaned back in his chair, sleeping and Mr. Cassial was in the other chair, staring down at the floor.

Maurice looked up at me, giving me a wilted smile. "How are you feeling?"

I moved my head from side to side. "I've been better, but okay."

He hummed, looking over at his son. "No changes. His skin is still on fire and his eyes are roaming away underneath his lids. I wish I knew what was happening in that head of his."

"Nothing good, but he'll pull through. He always does." I sounded optimistic and I hoped he believed me.

He squeezed my hand. "Yes he does."

I licked my lips, giving Nick my full attention when I said, "can I have a minute with him?"

Maurice chuckled softly. "Of course you can." He walked over to Reese, jostling his shoulder. The blonde angel jumped, kicking the table.

"What, what's happening?" Reese looked around the room. "Did he wake up?!"

Maurice sighed. "No. We are going to give them a moment alone." He nodded his head towards the door.

I held onto the side of Nick's bed as I watched them leave. Reese spun around before he exited. "I've tried everything I could. You are probably the only person that can wake him up. Do what you can... please."

I cocked my head to the side, watching as he gave me a tight lipped smile before walking out of the room. I let out a heavy sigh, not really knowing where to begin. I ran my knuckles over his cheek, feeling the heat wafting off of him. "I don't think I need to ask you what's going on in that head of yours."

I leaned forward, grabbing his hand and placing it to my lips. "You worked so hard to keep those thoughts in check and now he's placed you with them without a way out." I didn't know if he could hear me, but I just didn't care.

I placed his hand at my cheek. "Was this what it was like when I was dying in your arms? Was there a sharp pain in your chest? That's what I feel right now and I don't like it, Nick. I can't stand it. So I *really* need you to wake up."

I kissed his knuckles, over and over again. "I told you I would fight your demons if I could and right now, I *really* fucking want to, baby. They are all clouded in your head, but I can't get to them. Fuck, Nick, you spent all that time making sure Dimitri didn't take me away from you, so do *not* let him take you away from *me*."

I dropped his hand and moved further up his body, placing my hand along his jaw. I leaned down and kissed his forehead. He jolted a bit and I could see his face contort for a short moment in pain. "I don't know how to fix this, Nick. You're my fixer. You're the one with well thought out ideas. You're the hero. You're the one who tells me when something is probably not a good idea, but I do it anyway and you tag along because you love me so fucking much. God, why do you love me so *fucking* much."

I didn't know why I was talking so much. Maybe if I spoke enough he would wake up just to shut me up. If I had to go to Hell to figure out how to fix this I would. Nick would never approve, but that was a risk I was willing to take. Too much had happened for me to go the easy route when it came to getting him back.

I placed my hand at his cheek, pressing my palm against it. I kissed his other cheek, my tears making his skin wet. "Leah said that when Garrett died it was like half of her heart was gone. You are right here and I feel like half of my heart is fumbling. I know what it's like to be lost in the dark, Nick, and I wouldn't put that kind of emptiness on my worst enemy."

I didn't have necromancer powers like Nick, but he wasn't even dead. I didn't have the kind of magic that could remove the net and kill all the demons in his mind. I wasn't this heroic figure he thought I was —if I was, I would be able to *fix* him. Despite everything, all the self loathing in that Hell prison, all the torture from Lilith and everyone else —I had never felt weaker than I did right in this moment.

I moved my head down so that I could rest my cheek at his chest. His heartbeat thrummed against my ear and it was nice. "You promised me you would stand beside me or behind me. Whichever I prefer. You can't do that if you're like this, so just wake up. We can't exist together if you don't wake up."

I sighed, sniffing against his chest. I would go to Hell. That was it. My mind was made up and I was going to fight for him, for my own happiness. I *deserved* to be happy and not have to destroy an entire realm to achieve it.

I pulled away from him, starting to make my way out of the room and alert the others of my plan when Leah's words halted me.

Sometimes healing medicine and wishful thinking isn't enough. Sometimes all they need is you and you alone to bring them back.

That was what I was doing. Me, myself and I were going to bring him back. I took another step and then stopped again. Maybe, that's not what she meant. I brought my hands out, palms up and stared at them. I slowly turned around and made my way back over to him. I leaned over, placing my hand to his chest and ran my nose over his.

"I love you Nicholas Cassial. Please come home to me," I whispered against his lip before I kissed him. The kiss was soft and I just held my lips against his. I pushed my light out against his chest, trying to dig it in as deep as I could. I tried to keep my shadows at bay, assuming that they weren't needed but I felt them caress his body and move in alongside the light.

I told Nick I would fight the demons in his mind, if I could.

I had to *try*.

48
NICK

I was sweating buckets and I could barely feel my arms with how they were tied up. I hung from a ceiling I couldn't even see, continuously poked and prodded at by shadow demons that changed into my worst nightmares. One minute it was Jonah punching into my stomach and the next it was Ariel whipping my back. Anytime I closed my eyes it was a fucking mess.

I saw blood everywhere and then it would be right in front of me, pooling at my feet as if it was my own. I saw Dimitri and the way he taunted and cackled in my face, somehow making me believe he won. The figures before me morphed into Dani or my father spewing out words of hate and discouragement in my face. I tried to block it out but this wasn't like the times where I could breath and make it all go away.

This was my reality and I wasn't waking up. I blinked and it got worse. I took a breath and my lungs constricted. The darkness in my mind was having a field day and all the progress I had made was pointless in a place like this. It was a prison of my own doing, even if I hadn't forced myself to be here.

I felt a knife stab into my side, but I knew it would heal like it did every few minutes. I was tired. So fucking tired.

The demons hissed, glancing at each other and then at something behind me. I couldn't move my head over my shoulder enough to see much of what it was, but it was bright. This had to be another trick. A ploy to say *oh you've gotten out*, but actually I'm still here, living in the dark.

I let my head hang down, not wanting to be met with utter disappointment. The light didn't move or shudder. There was a shift in the space around me. The demons started convulsing and transforming into one form to torture me and then to another. The images I was forced to see started to distort and become nothing at all.

The demons started screeching as shadows flew past them, slicing at their bodies and picking them up just to drop them on the ground. It was hard to keep my eyes open, but I watched, eyeing the shadows and waiting for when they would come for me next. The shadows swayed, whipping around towards me. Instead of cutting my skin or causing me pain, they stroked my skin.

The tension in my body melted and I wanted to lean into the shadows, but they moved behind me flowing into the light that was behind me.

I heard a voice that felt so much like a piece of my heart as the light got closer and shrouded me in its glow.

I love you Nicholas Cassial. Please come home to me.

My whole body was shaking from the amount of energy I was pushing out, but I needed this to work. It *had* to work. I pressed my hand against him, hoping that I wasn't hurting him. I broke our kiss and my power reeled itself back into me causing my body to be thrown back and I reached for the chair to steady myself.

I don't know what I tried to do, but if it was a waiting game, that's what I would do. I would wait for a long time when it came to this man. I settled into the chair, seeing my light and shadows dim over his body and then disappear altogether. My curls fell in my face as I looked at him, feeling myself start to cry just because I hated this. I hated everything about this.

I placed my head in my hands, considering my options. The *only* option I had was to permanently live in the infirmary until Nick woke up. I could make this chair comfortable enough, maybe pull a Reese and kick my feet up every now and again. I would make sure Morgan never showed her face in this room or she would see the end of my….

"Dani." His voice was groggy and a bit confused.

I peered up from my hands to see Nick leaning up on his elbows , looking at me. His eyes were squinted as if he had just woken up from a very good nap. His hair was messy in that boyish way I loved and his lips formed into a lopsided grin that I knew only came out when he didn't know what kind of expression to use, but he was sure it wasn't a sad moment.

I bounded up from the chair and launched myself at his bed. I wrapped my arms around him, feeling his hands at my back as he squeezed me. His body was at a normal temperature and he held me like I wasn't a stranger to him. The idea that he could wake up with some kind of amnesia haunted my thoughts constantly, but I knew that was a long shot. I ran my hands over his body checking for any wounds that could have popped up. I didn't know how this kind of dark magic worked but I wasn't about to get blindsided by something. I pulled back, placing my hands at the sides of his face. "I don't…"

He raised his eyebrows. "Did you…"

"I didn't know what else to do." I considered the things I *did* know about hybrid powers and how they had always been known for their ill-intent. I wasn't sure if anyone had tried to preserve them for things like this.

"Hey, hey, you saved me," he said this like he was trying to make a point. Even out of a coma he hadn't changed.

I pressed my forehead to his. "I would burn the world for you. You like saving me so much, I thought maybe it's high time I save you, hmm?"

He leaned in to kiss me. "You've always been my hero. Don't you know that?" I kissed him back harder, practically jumping onto the bed myself.

"Dani, I know you wanted your alone time…woah!" Reese yelled, holding onto the door frame. "You're awake!"

Nick yanked his mouth from mine and nodded over to his best friend. "Looks that way."

"Holy shit! You're awake!" Reese ducked his head out the door. "Maurice, he's awake!"

I heard the sound of footsteps as Maurice came into the room. I moved back to give him some space to hold his son. He took his face in his hands, moving his head from side to side, inspecting. "Nicholas, my boy, how are you feeling? Do you remember anything? How did this happen?" He looked from me to Nick, patiently waiting for an explanation.

"Oh pretty boy is awake?" Elise poked her head into the room. "I was wondering what all the commotion was."

"Yes he is. You can leave now. He doesn't need any of your negative energy." Reese rolled his eyes.

"Right and you are such a fucking delight to be around," Elise stated, scoffing.

"Alright, stop it you two. Any other time, but not now," Maurice scolded, pointing at both of them. They both mumbled a version of *I'm sorry.*

Nick pressed his fingers to the side of his head, rubbing. "I'm feeling okay, for what it's worth. I remember up until the point of getting hit by whatever Dimitri threw at me and nearly everything I was forced to endure while locked away in my head." He threw a look over to his dad. "No, I don't want to talk about that. And well, how it happened…" He snuck a glance at me, which caused everyone to look at me.

I ruffled my hair. "Why don't we get Natalia in here to give him a once over and I'll explain it to you."

50
NICK

Reese and Elise had surprisingly been in agreement that Ariel didn't deserve or need a funeral, but my father had insisted. He didn't like the guy all that much, but as the highest executive, he had to show his respects regardless of his personal feelings. Xander gave me a thorough once over—again—before I left the infirmary, letting me know I should come to them if I felt off at any time. Natalia had made sure Dani got a thorough check up as well, giving her a clean bill of health. The High Priestess gave both of us a small look of apprehension. She huddled with Xander and a few other healers as they released us, speaking in hushed tones as if there was more going on but she had simply smiled at us with a simple wave.

I chose to believe the weirdness was due to the fact that the amount of times she's had to check in on us was too many to count. She would likely have to continue doing it if remaining friends with us was on her agenda.

When Ariel's ceremony had finished causing me to lock eyes with a somber Morgan, I had a sense that she wanted to talk to me. I had nothing to say to her, but despite everything that happened she did bring the Enchanters to The Skies, so maybe she did have a heart somewhere in there. She started to make her way over, but when Dani came up to my side, pressing her body into me, Morgan paused.

She sucked in a deep breath and nodded at me before turning away. I laughed softly.

"What's so funny?"

I looked down at my girlfriend. "Nothing, just ready for things to get back to some kind of normalcy."

"You know that's pretty impossible."

"Normal is for the weak and grossly predictable," Elise said, sidling up next to me. Beetee walked over, wincing just a little, but not as much as she had been for the past two weeks.

My father placed his hand on her shoulder, causing her to jump a little. "Please take a seat. The last time you tried to move too fast, you opened up your wound."

Beetee huffed. "You are worse than my moms."

"Your moms love you very much, so you *let* them worry as much as they want." Daya slipped her arm in through my father's, swatting Beetee's arm lightly. She looked up at my dad. "Leah wanted to say she was sorry she couldn't be here. They are going to spend some time with Garrett today."

The conversation lulled as it normally did when we spoke about this. Oculus had a special place where they buried their own. Leah and her kids spent a lot of time there, which was understandable. I'd gone to speak with her, letting her cry into my shoulder and shedding my own tears as I spoke about how much Garrett loved them and how he nearly fought me just to get back to them. Yuri and Jasmine missed their dad, but they were resilient kids and they each had a ton of strength that carried their mother when she felt like she couldn't do it anymore.

My father and Daya let Leah know that they were always open to talk. They had both lost someone dear to them in manners in which they weren't expecting. They understood more than any of us ever could.

Reese let out a loud laugh, making his way over to us. "Why didn't you tell me this one was so hilarious?" He pointed at Alex who shrugged as if it was obvious.

"And what was so funny?" Dani asked, cocking her head to the side.

"Oh she was making a bunch of Ariel jokes."

I scoffed. "Wow, at the guy's funeral ceremony, seriously?"

Alex stuck her tongue out at me. "I cope with jokes, leave me alone."

A few angels came by my father wanting his attention and he leaned over to kiss the side of my head and did the same with Dani. "Excuse me would you?"

"He's so popular," Reese pointed out.

"Pretty boy should pay attention, he's next in line." Elise patted my shoulder as she walked past me. I closed my eyes, trying to forget this fact completely. The last thing I wanted was a high executive title looming.

"Hey, look at me." Dani brought my face down so my eyes were on her. "Your father will reign for a very long time. I'm not sharing you with any angelic followers. I have you all to myself." She pecked my lips and turned around running right into the High Priestess.

I looked around spotting Zane not too far away. Reese bent his elbows, holding his arms out for both Alex and Beetee to take. Natalia chuckled softly as we watched him escort them inside The Skies.

"Your father seems to be taking to his new duties well, despite the circumstances," Natalia said, running her hands down her dress.

"He was meant for this even though I don't think he'll ever admit it," I said, running a hand through my hair.

Natalia chewed on her bottom lip. "Nicholas, I have something I need to discuss with you."

I couldn't hide the skepticism in my voice. "What is it?"

The High Priestess fiddled with the earring in her ear. "You told me that if I could find out how to retrieve your memories then I should."

"Okay..."

"My mother seemed to believe you deserved them at some point in your life because I found them. If you want to know then please come by Oculus, but I would understand if you aren't interested. Time and life have gone by for you, you've grown up without them and it might alter you in some way by placing them back inside your mind. The choice is yours, always." Natalia pressed her hand to my cheek, his skin warm and comforting. She gave Dani a small smile before she retreated towards another group of people.

I opened my mouth but Dani cut me off. "You want to know what I think?"

"Even if I said no, you would tell me anyway."

She smirked up at me. "Personally, I think you should. You've been in this up and down emotional war about your mother for a while, so maybe getting the memories you have of her back could create something really beautiful for you."

"I don't know if it can patch up the giant sized parental hole that she left behind."

Dani pressed her lips together. "No, but it might help repair it just a little bit. Just enough for you to know that repair is possible at all."

Natalia ushered us inside the apothecary, leading us into an empty room. Dani held my hand the entire time and even when our palms got sweaty and separation of our hands was all but necessary, she didn't let go.

"Are you completely sure this is what you want?" Natalia asked for probably the tenth time since we'd gotten here.

I sighed. "Yes. I'm overly sure at this point." I walked over to the chair in the middle of the room and sat down.

Dani and I watched as Natalia went over to a bookshelf and pulled out a small square box with rose colored hinges. She placed the box on the table behind her and lifted the lid. When she walked around the chair, facing us again, in her hand was a sphere with white gold smoke floating around inside. The smoke was thick and I felt the need to reach out and touch it.

"What's that?" Dani asked, her eyes wide as she stared at the sphere.

Natalia held it firm between her palms. "It's a retention sphere. They are hardly used anymore, if I'm being honest, they were likely not used all that much back in my mothers time."

"My memories are in there?" I pointed to what she held in her hands.

"Yes, Nicholas. Most of the time the removal of memories was quite permanent. They pulled them from the mind and simply threw them away. My mother clearly didn't do that with yours."

Dani hummed suspiciously. "How are you so sure that's his memories?"

"As I've said these spheres are hardly used, but this happens to be the only one and— because of this." Natalia reached into the front pocket of her dress, pulling out a small note. "It was underneath the sphere.

I took it from her, unfolding the paper and reading the contents:

If you find this please forgive me and know she loved you very much, I never wanted you to forget that.

"It's written in my mother's hand and I don't know about you but I would bet all my magic she is speaking about you." She gave me a pointed look.

I folded the note back up, placing it in my pocket. "Okay, what now?"

"Nicholas, this isn't going to feel good. I have to be forthcoming about that. Extracting memories hurts but putting them back is a much more delicate process. You'll feel a lot of things all at once. The memories won't be in the right places at first and you'll feel like you want to push them out, but fight against that." She placed her hand on my shoulder. "The memories will find their place. You have to give them time. They are foreign to you, but you are not as foreign to them."

I looked over to Dani, who collected my hand in hers again. She kissed the inside of my wrist. "I got you."

Natalia stood on the other side of me and moved her hand around the sphere. The smoke started to recede from inside and circle around Natalia's hand. "Just relax Nicholas."

I settled back in the chair, watching as the smoke started to move towards me, collecting around my head. It tickled behind my ears and I blinked a few times as it got in my eyes. The smoke started to fall away as it absorbed itself into my head. I felt like nothing, but then I heard a ringing.

"Does anyone else hear that?" I asked, the sound getting louder and I shook my head, trying to get it to stop. Dani looked to Natalia, opening and closing her mouth. The ringing stopped and then nothing. I let out a breath. "That was odd, but I don't feel..."

The sudden feeling of bricks being cemented into place hit my head. It was like every memory was slamming in one by one, landing wherever they could. I jolted backwards, clamping my teeth together. The memories shifted, grating over my mind. Little pieces of things I hardly remembered began to take shape.

The memories continued to jump around and slam around in the interior of my mind, but I squeezed Dani's hand needing some kind of anchor to the here and now.

The pain halted, skidding to a stop. The memories moved more delicately now as if they knew exactly where they needed to be and why. I felt my body slump back as if I was dozing off, but then the memories started to play and my mind opened up as if it was the first time I was experiencing these things.

I saw my mother and the way she crouched down as I ran over to her. Her face bright with so much pride.

I felt the fear from when I'd woken up from a nightmare and my mother rushed in to soothe me.

I saw the way she snuggled with my father on the couch right before I jumped in between them.

I remembered the way she caressed my face and told me how lucky she was that I picked her to be my mother. She would tell me how I would grow up so strong like my father, but at the end of the day I would always be her little boy.

I saw the looks on peoples faces when my mother would take me everywhere with her, making sure she always spent enough time with me.

I felt the overwhelming joy from both my parents when my wings finally made their appearance.

My chest tightened when I saw the hill I'd tumbled down and things went black. There was a sense that I had lost time somewhere, but I saw myself blink and my parent's crying faces came into view. I felt like all my pieces were back together.

There was a sense of dread all of sudden and the memories were darker. My mother cried as she held me, but I didn't know why.

She would leave and be gone for long periods of time, but eventually she took me with her. I remembered looking at a lady who I'd met a few times and she'd pressed her hand to my mother's forehead and then to mine. It stung but I hadn't felt any different.

I remembered when we got home, I had asked her what she did. My mother had knelt down in front of me and said: *nothing for you to worry about. I hope you will never need to use it and if you do, it's on something that truly matters to you.*

I had decided to forget about it and then the memories got worse and I felt an overwhelming dread in my stomach.

I remembered men coming into our house and demanding she come with them. My voice had grown hoarse from screaming for her as they tried to drag her out. My father had shouted but he had to hold me back from running to get her.

She'd held my father's face in her hands and told him something that I couldn't quite make out and then she was gone.

Every memory after that was filled with agonizing crying and coughing fits. It felt like days of wondering when she was coming back and why she'd left me. I'd wondered why my father hadn't gone to get her and bring her home.

I saw myself being taken to the same lady as before, my father's face filled with regret and his eyes filled with tears. The lady, Moira, I think her name was, had tears in her eyes as well.

She was gentle with me when she said: *this is only going to hurt for a moment and then it will be over, okay, Nicholas?*

I never understood but I always assumed it was something to get my mother back. I hurt just like she said and then suddenly the memories go blank.

The memories replayed and replayed, forcing their way into my mind so that they would stay. My head throbbed and my eyes were closed so tight I felt tears sting at the corners.

I heard a locking sound as if they had found the places they forever belonged and they planned on staying there.

A light sound, a voice that stilled my heart and repaired a part of the oversized parental hole in my chest whispered across my mind.

I love you so much, Nicholas. One day I hope you will remember that.

Her voice was soothing and wrapped around me like a hug I didn't know I needed.

I pushed away from the chair and landed on the floor, feeling a sense of vertigo when I opened my eyes. I looked around searching for a trash bin. I stalked over to it and emptied the contents of my stomach.

I heaved, seeing from the corner of my eye that Natalia was handing me a washcloth. I wiped my mouth, running the back of my hand along my eyes.

"So, how did it go?" Dani asked, moving around the chair so she could be closer to me.

I let out a shuddered breath. "She really loved me."

Natalia placed the empty sphere in the box. "Your resurrection that your mother had transferred to you, I can remove it if you'd like. I can't say it won't be any less painful," she offered.

I looked down at Dani who shrugged, leaving that decision up to me completely. I was waiting for her to have some sort of input, but this one was all me. I rubbed at my chest, feeling like even with all the memories it wasn't enough. "I think I'll keep it."

"Oh?" Natalia raised her delicate eyebrows.

I nodded swiftly, regretting it instantly when I felt the nausea start again. "My mother gave it to me because she wanted me to hold onto it for her. If I can use it to do something good again even years from now, then I'm satisfied."

Natalia laughed softly. "Your mother would be very proud of you. I know I am."

"Same here." Dani kissed my cheek and I moved to kiss her mouth but she reared her head back. "As much as this moment calls for a passionate kiss, you just threw up in that trash bin, so no thank you."

"Fair enough," I conceded. I looked over at Natalia. "Thank you for not giving up on this."

She smiled at me. "You have got a pretty great crowd around you Nicholas. I don't think you will ever have a chance to falter again."

51
DANI

A MONTH LATER

I dragged Elise down the hall watching as people filtered in through the front doors of the great hall. Enchanters and angels stood at the doors to take their coats and help them in any way they could.

The grumpy demon grumbled but allowed me to continue to pull her forward. Natalia had been in talks with Maurice about hosting a gathering that could be the setting for a new realm. The buzz that it created was massive. The grand hall in The Skies was huge and Natalia had it decorated just for this occasion. Tiny orbs of light were strung on the ceiling. Ivy circled the columns and multicolored lights flickered as if by magic in between the ivy itself. A bar cart was placed at each corner and there were so many dancing bodies, I couldn't even count.

"Dani, I put on a fucking dress for this shit, what more do you want from me?"

I turned around to face her. "You can't just hide in one of their kitchens because you don't want to socialize."

Elise snorted, giving me a lackluster curtsy in her thigh length black strapless dress. "Fine, I'll go socialize by the bar, if I must." She gave me a middle finger before trotting over to one of the bar carts.

I followed her to the one closest to the door. Before I could even sidle up next to her, she had ordered shots. "You are just a ball of sunshine, aren't you?"

She scoffed. "I'm a riot."

I turned to look out at the dance floor seeing Beetee, in her hot pink dress, get low to the ground so she could let Leah's son twirl her. Things were getting a bit easier, Leah was coming around more often and her smile was becoming more genuine.

"Beetee and I are leaving," Elise announced.

I sucked in a breath, confused. "Leaving?"

"Back to Purgatory."

"But wait, you…" I started but Reese came up cutting me off. "Oh, no you're leaving. How sad. If you need help packing, don't ask me because I'm busy."

I shushed the blonde angel. "Slow down. Why?"

Elise slapped the bar, insinuating that she wanted another shot. "Because this isn't my vibe okay. You might enjoy this vomit inducing realm where you get fucked on the regular by a pretty angel but yeah, I do not."

Reese had his drink to his lips right as he sputtered. "I know very well that my friends are fucking but I really don't like to openly talk about it."

Elise rolled her eyes. "You don't have to worry about Dimitri's father or anyone else coming after you. He thought he could promise Lucifer something he couldn't deliver so the big guy isn't about to come here and demand it himself. It wasn't his idea, so he's not going to spare his precious time with ideals from a pretentious prick who got his ass handed to him by a hybrid."

"And you're so sure about this whole we are safe from the likes of Hell because…how?" Reese pressed, looking over his drink at her. His hazel eyes narrowed.

"I just fucking am. And I'll make sure of it."

I clucked my tongue. "How do you plan to do that? You are quite scary, but you aren't *that* scary." I fanned the ends of her hair with my fingers.

She made a shooing motion at me. "I'll run Purgatory."

Reese sputtered into his drink for the second time, placing it on the bar. He opened his mouth to make a joke, but then he stopped. "Actually, I think that's kind of perfect for you. You can just tower over everyone and stomp all over their dreams, like the little menace you are."

"You can just do that? Take over?" I asked, leaning against the bar.

I hadn't realized Beetee was standing in front of us until she spoke, "of course she can, next to you, she was basically next in line to succeed Lilith. Even if that wasn't the case, it's pretty much set in stone by…"

Elise shushed her. I narrowed my eyes at her, wondering what she was being so coy about. "Set in stone by the fact that Purgatory isn't the kind of territory where the residents can vote. Their choices are either me or death so it's probably a really tough call." She grabbed her third shot, downing it.

Beetee shook her head, fanning herself. "I love it here, Dani, but my place is at the hostel. My moms are ready to go home, but Natalia is giving me a key so I can come back." She squealed with joy doing a twirl.

"You all look lovely," Natalia complimented, her hair in a multitude of twists that were piled on top of her in a neat bun. Earrings adorned the outside of her ear and two bangles sat firmly at her biceps.

"I do clean up nice." Reese ran his hands down the lapels of his navy suit jacket.

Natalia raised an eyebrow at him, but didn't give in to his obvious need for more compliments. "I hope you are enjoying yourselves and not fretting about the future. As much as I enjoy a good strategy plan, I like to think some mind numbing fun is always in order."

I laughed. "I'm really sorry, but there is just something stopping me from seeing you have mind numbing fun."

Natalia proceeded to speak but Elise cut her off, "we all know the high witch just needs to get laid. That kind of plan worked for sweet old Nicholas and he is happier than ever, give or take some missteps."

Reese groaned. "Do you just speak to hear yourself talk?"

I drummed my fingers on the bar. "As much as I respect sex as a coping mechanism. That would have to be a very secure woman and I think Natalia has better things to do than find a worthy sex partner."

Natalia nodded. "You would be correct, but I assure you finding them isn't a difficult task." She lifted her shoulder in a simple shrug.

Beetee's lilac eyes widened, as Elise cackled, lifting up her next shot. "I have no doubt they all salivate over that enchanting pussy you're hiding."

Reese slammed his drink down, wiping his mouth. "For fucks sake, I need something stronger if I'm going to stay in this conversation." He motioned to the bartender. "Can I have tequila in the biggest glass you have?"

"What did I just walk into?" A familiar deep voice pulled me out of my laughing fit. Lips kissed the top of my head and I leaned back against the warm body of my angel.

"Uh, nothing just....girl talk."

"Girl talk indeed." Natalia hummed. Zane came up behind her with a drink in his hand.

"Your Highness." He handed her the glass and she smiled at him gratefully.

Beetee cleared her throat. "Ellie, why don't you come dance with me and the kids."

Elise gave her a hard look. "Yeah, hard pass."

"Damn you are heartless," Reese said, waggling his finger at her.

Natalia let out a light laugh, taking a sip of her drink. "Well that can't be true. I heard from Leah that you are leaving Axel here for the children. She actually said that you insisted he stay here with them and that you would come back with Beetee when you could to check up on him." Natalia's honey eyes sparkled with delight. "Or I could be wrong, but I am quite certain that's that truth." Natalia patted Zane's arm and he followed her away from us and in the direction of where Maurice was standing.

"Aw, Elise, that's actually kind of sweet." Nick went to pinch her arm but she swatted him away.

"You shut the fuck up or I will make it so you never wield a sword ever again." Elise let out the loudest groan of annoyance. She was about to turn around and ask for another drink, but Beetee grabbed her hand.

"Come on Ellie, your threats are futile at the moment. Let's dance with the children you pretend not to like even though you have a soft spot for them, just like you do for all of them." The pink haired demon eyed each of us, but Elise refused to look anywhere but straight ahead.

"Fucking fine you insufferable reptile."

Before she could get too far, I ran over to her. "Nick told me that you called me your friend after Dimitri took me. Well, after you handed him his ass about his inner demons."

Elise gave me an unamused look. "Your point?"

"No point just letting *you* know that I know. You don't ever have to say it to my face, but I'm happy you admitted it to someone."

Elise pulled at one of my curls, watching it spring upward when she let it go. "My dog isn't the *only* reason I plan to visit."

My lips lifted into a small smile. "You'll make a cutthroat queen of darkness."

She tapped her index finger to her chin. "Yeah, I think *mistress* is more appropriate." She wiggled her dark eyebrows. Elise looked over my shoulder at where Nicholas and Reese spoke. "Pretty boy hurts you and I'll cut his dick off and feed it to Blondie." With that she turned around and trudged over to where Yuri and Jasmine danced out of rhythm with Beetee and their mom.

Leah looked over at me and gave me a smile that had me returning one back to her.

I made my way back to the bar cart, catching the middle of the two boys' conversation.

"All I'm saying is that your dad is the man in charge now, so I wouldn't mind if he played favorites. I will never say no to nepotism. I'm quite literally like a second son to him."

Nick laughed. "You'll have to take that up with him. He's having a meeting with every angel in the coming months to reevaluate and hopefully get this place to an honorable standard."

I slid my arms around Nick's waist and he pulled me closer to him. "Your father is going to do wonderful things."

"Just because you are dating his son doesn't mean Maurice won't make you work, just like the rest of us." Reese slid my drink over to me and I stuck my tongue out at him. "I'm still the favorite, alright." He smirked over at Nick who gave him a nod as if he agreed completely.

I rolled my eyes."You still need to come by and get your lucky charm."

Reese shrugged. "I'll get it. Since this is your home now, I think I'll know where to find you." He lifted his chin to Nick who kissed the side of my head.

My home. I had felt lighter walking around this place and knowing there wasn't some impending doom I had to wait for. My mind was clearer now that I had a place to be my entire self and someone entertaining the idea that I could cause chaos but that I could also be the glue that holds everything together.

"You look beautiful," Nick whispered against my hair. I spun around to give him the full effect of my dress. The sleeves had tiny specks of sparkle in the thin fabric and the bodice and skirt were black velvet, reaching right at my knees. I pressed my hands to his chest, feeling my palms heat, but not enough to burn his dress shirt.

Daya and Maurice waved at us from their place across the room and a sense of pride filled my chest knowing that I had allies on all fronts. I had come into this entire thing thinking I could flirt my way through a mission and go back to Purgatory, but thinking things are simple in this life seemed to always be a misguided mistake.

Love and an odd type of destiny wasn't what I had in mind, but it's what I got. I wasn't complaining but it had me pondering on the future.

Alex rushed over to us, her long dress showcasing her mid size figure. She had dyed the front pieces of her hair a stark white, making the whiskey color of her eyes pop. "You can't stand here. You have to dance! If I don't make you, my mom sure as hell will. And trust me you do *not* want that."

I giggled watching her grab Reese's hand and pull him to the dance floor where Xander and Natalia were having the time of their lives it seemed. Even Zane was letting loose in the best way he could, his shoulders doing a small shimmy every now and then.

I tugged Nick's hand, but he pulled me back. I gave him a curious look. "Don't tell me that you don't dance, Nicholas. We both know that's a lie."

He shook his head, leaning his face down to kiss me. "No, I'll dance with you. I just like having you to myself every chance I get."

I kissed him back. "I am quite a prize, aren't I?"

"And so modest too."

I pulled back, gripping his hand and pulling him into the circle of our friends.

"Where are we going?" Nick asked, as I pulled him down the hall. We dodged plenty of Enchanters wanting to stop us and talk or angels who wanted to tell him how great it was that his father was at the helm now. He could talk to them later, but right now, he was mine.

"You asked that a few minutes ago and I told you to just wait," I scolded, making a turn and then opening the door to the storage closet.

I tossed him inside, closing the door behind us. String lights were tumbling out of a box on one of the shelves and I pointed my finger at them. A spark of light flew from my fingertip and towards the lights. The moment the light touched them, they flickered on, giving us some dim lighting in the room.

Nick turned on his heels. "You brought me into a closet, because…"

I got up on my tiptoes when I was close enough and nuzzled my nose against his. "Oh, so you don't want to have sex with me in a closet?"

He placed his hands at my sides, squeezing. He moved me so I was flush against him. "No, but a little warning would be nice."

"Not in my nature, plus I like to keep you on your toes, *Nicholas*." I nipped at his lips.

I walked him backwards so that his back hit the wall. My hands worked on his belt, undoing it and shoved his pants and underwear to the ground. I grabbed his cock, stroking it, letting my thumb flick over the head. He let out a hiss of satisfaction.

He hardened quickly in my hand and I dropped to my knees, not giving him a moment to prepare himself before I took him into my mouth. I used my hand to work the parts of him I couldn't reach. I looked up, seeing his eyes hooded and watching me.

I swallowed his cock down, pulling back and licking the underside of his shaft before taking him in my mouth again. His thighs tensed as I scratched my nails down his skin. I bobbed back and forth, swirling my tongue at the head of his dick when I could.

"Fuck, that's so good. That's my girl," he praised, threading his fingers into my hair. He pushed me down further, but then let me up for air.

He let out a choked laugh before stopping me and pushing me lightly back by my shoulders. He bent down, hauling me up by my waist and placed me on the table that seriously needed a good dusting. He leaned down to kiss me, curling his tongue with mine and sliding his hand up my thigh.

"I'm such a good girl that I decided to not wear panties tonight, just so you wouldn't have to work so hard." I blinked innocently at him.

He groaned, leaning into my neck to plant kisses there. Kisses that felt like an inferno against my skin. "Very considerate of you."

"I'm a sweetheart." I reached down between my legs, swiping a finger over my pussy and placing it at his lips.

His tongue came out and savored my taste. "Already so wet, aren't you?"

I bit my bottom lip and nodded. He grabbed my thighs and yanked me to the edge of the table. He bent down, bringing his face around to kiss the healed scar on my thigh. It was a bit worse now that I'd burnt through more layers of skin than I would have liked. He kissed every inch of where the skin was raised, keeping his eyes on me the entire time.

He brought his face to my pussy, after my attempt at pulling his hair to get him where I wanted him. He licked at my core, flicking his tongue over my clit. I let out a relieved moan as I tilted my head back, spreading my legs out more for him. He pressed his face against me harder; I was sure his air supply was low with the way he devoured me. He stuck his tongue in my entrance, taking it out to place his tongue flat and lick me completely. He pushed my thighs up to trace a circle around my tight hole and then back up to my clit making me shiver with need.

Nick stood up, bringing my mouth to his as he pressed his fingers inside of me and curled them. He fucked me with his fingers and his thumb massaged my clit. I whimpered into his mouth as his fingers moved harder, the heel of his hand replacing his thumb as it pressed against my aching clit with each of his movements.

"Let me see how beautiful you are when you come, Dani. I want to see that pretty light of yours."

I moaned, gripping the edge of the table and hearing it whine and sizzle as my light came out, burning the wood. The brightness seeped out between my fingers. "Yes, yes, yes!" I yelled, feeling the wood burn completely and dust particles came off of where the missing piece used to be.

I let the remnants fall away from my hand. I could have chuckled from this incident, but my body was pulled off of the table and turned around. Nick placed a hand at my back pushing me flat against the wood. He kicked my legs apart and I felt his cock slide over where I was wet and needy.

He clucked his tongue. "I think your light can do so much better than that, needy one."

He pressed into me, moving my dress up so he could palm my ass. He thrusted forward, pulling back and then thrusting again. He held my hips tightly as he started to fuck me hard, his pelvis slapping against my ass filled the room and probably any nearby area outside the door.

"Always take my cock so *perfectly*." He groaned, pulling my hips back harder as he pounded into me.

He spanked me, grabbing my arms and crossing them over one another at my back. He held them in place with one of his hands and kept moving inside of me. He reached forward and grabbed my hair, twisting my curls in his fist as he pulled my head back.

My breaths were shallow as I moaned against the table. "Oh god, keep going, please."

"Is this pretty pussy going to come for me?"

He released my hands, spanking me again and reaching around to run his fingers over my clit. "Yes, Nick, please."

He let go of my hair, placing his hand on top of my own on the table. His palm ran over the back of my hand, threading his fingers through mine. He pounded harder, shifting the table as he thrusted. I saw the stars shining behind my eyes and I felt my hand start to heat, along with my shadows that slithered up my legs and around his body, keeping him inside of me as I came. The light from my hand shot out and he quickly let out his own, subduing any major damage. I shivered from the way my shadows caressed his body, as if I could feel everything he was feeling.

He moved inside of me in quick succession before coming, holding onto my hip. My light flickered out and he grazed his hand over my arm and past my shoulders. Nick leaned down kissing my spine. "I am so fucking in love with you."

I giggled, wiggling my ass against him. "I am so fucking in love with you too." He pulled out of me, adjusting the bottom of my dress before turning me around. He made sure his pants were safely secured by his belt before he tucked a piece of my hair behind my ear, twirling one of my curls with his fingers.

I leaned up to kiss him. "I think having a hybrid girlfriend turns you on a little."

"Hmm, I think you just turn me on generally."

I let him twirl me around, bringing me into his chest as I laughed. "You and me, Nicholas."

I let my shadows travel over his neck, but his eyes were set on mine. Nothing about my powers fazed him anymore and he simply accepted what I had to offer him.

He held my hand, bringing it up and letting his light move against my fingertips. "Existing with all the scars. Together."

Dani and Alex had convinced Elise and Beetee to stay a little longer than they intended. Eventually Elise had told Dani it was time and that Heaven's Gate was starting to give her a rash, so going back to Purgatory was happening whether my girlfriend liked it or not.

We all huddled outside my house watching as Elise took the portal key Natalia had made for Beetee and drew a circle in front of her. The portal electrified with light and loomed around us. Beetee and her moms hugged each of us, the snake shifter pulling Daya tight to her chest when they embraced. She gave my father and Alex a hug filled with equal intensity.

They had said their goodbyes to everyone else earlier today, claiming that they didn't want their departure to be a huge ordeal.

Axel barked in Reese's arms, bouncing to get out of his hold. My best friend put him down, letting the hellhound run over to Elise as she bent down to meet him. She scratched the back of his ears and let him roll over so she could do the same to his belly. He would be good for Leah's kids. We were told to never bring up Elise's good deed, but regardless of how much she didn't want to admit it, I knew she would miss her dog.

Elise picked him up and carried him back over to us, dropping Axel in my arms. "Don't let him get into trouble or do…either is fine by me."

"We'll make sure of it," I said, turning around and depositing the dog into Reese's eager arms.

"Later little one. I hope you become the most terrifying leader in Purgatory. I'm sure they'll write songs about how demented you are," Reese said, giving her a tight lipped smile.

A portal opened behind us, telling me that Natalia was here. My father had invited her over for dinner as a friendly gesture but also to throw in some discussion about the future as well.

Elise rolled her eyes at us. "That is probably the nicest thing you've ever said to me. Let it be the last." She raised her middle finger at him before giving her attention to Zane, who kept close to Natalia as they walked up. "Keep my room nice and tidy for me, would you?" She winked at him, giving us a small salute before dragging Beetee towards the portal. Zane grumbled some incoherent words, his face unamused.

Once the portal had closed, I looked up at the sky noticing that the sun had gone down significantly. Reese placed Axel on the ground, the dog following at his feet when he started to walk back to my house. Daya and my father were right behind him. I tucked Dani under my arm, so that we could go in and get some food when Natalia tugged at my arm.

She looked over her shoulder, silently telling Zane to take a few steps back so he wasn't crowding her. He did so without question. "I know with everything that's happened you likely wish for there to be no more secrets lurking around the corner."

"That would be nice," Dani admitted, chuckling.

Natalia ran a finger over her bottom lip. "When I did my check on you both, making sure everything was okay, as I've done before, I wasn't lying when I said you were both in good health. Although, I did find something interesting that I needed to get another opinion on. I trust my healers immensely and I wanted their thoughts before making a bigger deal out of this than it needed to be."

"Natalia, what are you talking about?" I pressed, placing my hand at Dani's hip.

"I did a check on her after the fight with Markus and everything was normal, it was as I suspected. I meant to do one when you came back from Purgatory, but with everything that happened with your father, I forgot. Once I did it now, there was a difference. I had Xander go behind me and discuss his own findings. Despite my role in Oculus, I know when my opinions alone may not be enough."

Dani stiffened beside me.

"You said we were in good health, I don't understand."

Natalia pressed her lips together and furrowed her brow. "You are, you both are. Dani is in a wonderful state of health. The kind of wonderful that has surpassed a certain previous aging curse."

Dani pushed away from me gently. "I'm sorry, what?"

"It's like the aura in your body has movement again. It is no longer stunted. I would like to believe it happened when..."

I swallowed hard. "When I brought her back?" Garrett had said it was like putting the pieces of someone's soul back together. I had removed any remnants of Lilith which I had assumed was just her dagger, but maybe I had restarted her all together.

Natalia nodded softly. "I am deeply sorry, I should have told you this sooner."

Dani shook her head. "No, no. This is...*good*." The way she spoke was slow as if she was trying on the words and seeing how they fit in the current situation.

I smiled at the High Priestess. "On top of everything, I think this is the cherry on top of a perfect night."

Natalia pointed her finger at me. "Quite right, Nicholas. I umm... since we discovered that Lilith's anti-aging no longer applies to Dani, we are still trying to figure out what that means for something *else*." Her eyebrows raised as if she was hoping we would understand what she was trying to say.

Dani rubbed the back of her neck, letting out a deep breath. "The anti-aging wasn't the only thing she bestowed upon her people."

I blinked, confused. I rummaged through my brain trying to remember what Dani had told me that night in my bed. I blinked again.

Good thing I can't get pregnant, because you might be fucked by now

I found myself stuttering. "W-wait, she's not…I mean she couldn't be…I'm not r-ready for…"

Dani placed her hand over my mouth and leaned up to kiss my cheek. "Ha, you think I am? Deep breaths, babe."

"I'd suggest using protection from now on until we can get a solidified answer. Xander makes an excellent contraceptive elixir." Natalia winked at me before laughing softly. 'For now that's the best you can do and just be happy in whatever way you can." The High Priestess motioned for Zane to follow her as she gave Dani a smile and walked past us.

"One step at a time, okay?" Dani brought my face down to look at her. I nodded, knowing this wasn't the worst we'd faced.

She looked up, taking in a deep breath and placing her hands on her hips. "Let's go to Oculus."

"Now?!"

She nodded, her expression serious. "Just you and me."

"But what about…" I pointed towards my house, but she just gave me a smirk. Her look told me she was daring me to say no to spending alone time with her.

I scratched my head, but conceded. I reached into my shirt for my portal key but she stopped me. "No, we are going to fly."

"You just want me to carry you."

Dani squinted at me playfully. "Actually, no. A couple of weeks ago, I was curious about something, especially with the hybrid power stuff. Natalia let me go to a more secluded part of the woods in Oculus and we discovered this." Dani stepped away from me and took in a slow breath.

My eyes widened when her wings emerged but they weren't textured like leather with talons at the tops. They weren't quite angel wings either. The feathers were black, but gold lined each one, shimmering as the moon came from around the trees.

Each feather looked delicate, but there were so many I knew they were sturdy and tough enough to withstand a heavy hit. She curled them inward. "I have no idea if I like them or not."

I pushed my own wings out and stood close to her. "I think they suit you perfectly."

Flying with Dani was a new type of high that I could experience over and over again without getting tired of it. I liked carrying her in my arms, nestling her close to me, but this was something that felt like pure magic without us having to do much at all. She had swooped around me and I'd tackled her before she rolled away, falling a few feet down so I could chase her around in the sky.

We'd landed in Oculus to an almost soothing silence. You could hear people every now and then, but they felt so far away right now. I couldn't wait to spend so much time here with her, with everyone. This was the dawn of a new time, a time where the past didn't need to repeat itself, but we were vigilant that the past was to not be forgotten.

Flowers bloomed around us and the trees swayed with a slight breeze. Dani looked up at the sky and took in a deep breath as if she was letting the silence and whispers of the wind settle on her skin.

"Can I ask you something?"

I crossed my arms over my chest. "Sure."

"Do angels believe in soulmates?"

The question stunned me, but it also wasn't something I hadn't thought about. I'd thought about it a lot more since being with Dani. "Not technically."

"And what *do* you believe?"

I ran my fingers along my chin. "I think I don't believe there is a destiny kind of soulmate, where the realms have chosen who you are going to be with for the rest of your life." I reached out to touch her forearm, watching as her brown eyes bore into my own. "I do believe that we decide who we fall in love with and if someone is willing to hand someone else their heart, allowing them to keep it safe, then I think it's a safe bet to believe that their souls are likely bonded in some way."

"Nicely put, Mr. Cassial."

"Do you remember when you told me how my story would go? You told me that I would fall in love with an everyday angel and tell the world about our story; how I teamed with a living legend and fought the bad guys."

"That sounds familiar."

"I don't think I ever wanted that. I think you were always what I wanted even when you didn't know it. I think I've loved you far longer than I'd like to admit."

She slid her hands up my chest and wrapped them around my neck. Her curls were defined ringlets that shaped around her face, her brown skin seemed to glow from the moon's backlight and the way she looked at me was something I never wanted to end.

Fuck, she was pretty.

"Take what Natalia said as a good thing, Nick. We can look at the future with *all* possibilities in mind." She kissed me, biting my lower lip. "I plan on loving you for a very long time."

I held her tighter. "Sounds like you want forever with me?"

"Maybe." Dani let her fingers trail along the back of my neck. I felt a small amount of heat, letting me know she had ignited her light. "Does forever with me make you nervous?"

I pressed my forehead to hers. "Possibly, but a good nervous. You know how I am without a plan."

Dani's chest vibrated with laughter as her shadows curled around us, making it so I had to remain as close to her as possible until she let me go. "Oh, don't worry Nicholas. I'll take good care of you."

Turn the page to find out what's happening for Elise in 2026

I leaned back, trying to make myself more comfortable on my throne, but the consistent babbling from the man in front of me, made that kind of comfort damn near unachievable. I placed my elbow on the arm, curling my hand into a fist and resting my cheek on it. I tapped my foot on the dark red stone that decorated the floors and walls, impatience getting the better of me.

Tobias, Dimitri's father, thundered in here, seeking an audience with me due to the fact that is his son was dead. I was letting him prattle on about how he shouldn't have let his son do this and how the angels would pay. I pressed my tongue into my cheek, very aware of the fact that I had always presumed his son would die due to his lofty goals. I would have loved to be surprised if Dimitri had come back victorious, but yet again, a let down of the highest degree.

Dimitri was a boy, masquerading as a man. He wanted to fill shoes that weren't quite his size and that cost him his life. I could have chuckled at the thought, well, actually…I had. The moment he left for Heaven's Gate, I was counting down the minutes to his victory or his downfall.

"What are you planning to do, sir? We can't do nothing! Those angelic assholes and that girl need to be dealt with!" Tobias's face was flushed red and his body was shaking. Oh my, was he upset.

"Ah, yes. I have thought of something to do." I brought my head back, flexing my fingers around the arms of the throne.

Tobias nodded, eager to hear my plans.

I waved my hand around, letting out a short laugh. "Nothing."

His eyes went wide, scrunching his mouth up as if he was holding in the words he wanted to say. If he let them out, they may very well be his last. "Nothing, sir?"

"I have thought long and hard about how to avenge your son's death and the best option is absolutely nothing."

He wiped a hand over his mouth. "Is that a ploy for a more devious plan? Are we lying in wait?"

I got up from the throne and walked over to him, stuffing my hands in my pants pockets. "No, no ploy. No devious plan. No waiting. No, nothing. Business as usual."

Tobias ran a hand through his hair. He opened his mouth and then closed it. He carefully spoke his next words, "this is my son, Lucifer. I must do something. *We* must do something."

I ran my tongue over my front teeth. I considered Tobias an ally. He never questioned my judgements and he knew his place more than anything else. He didn't seem to provide that same knowledge to his son or he wouldn't have given him that club so quickly or let him think he needed to prove himself and that would put him in the same league as us, same league as *me*.

"We will do *nothing*. I don't love repeating myself, so let me make this very clear. I will keep doing the things I always do, but you my friend can go mourn your child." I placed a hand on his shoulder and his body stiffened. "I enjoy being very honest with others, so I will give you some truth. Your son was an idiot. He thought highly of himself when he really should have considered his limits. I admit I gave him the tools to fight against Heaven's Gate, but just like the others I put my trust in, he came up empty." I pressed my fingers into his shoulder and saw shadows dusted with red mist climb over my shoulders and whip around. "You both had such a disdain for Lilith when in reality, he was just like her. Fortunately for her, she at least got a taste of what legitimate power could be."

"Sir, I cannot just stand around and…"

"You can! You want to know why?" I let go of him and pushed him back, moving my hands behind my back, grabbing one of my wrists. "Because I told you so. Dimitri wanted to fight this battle himself and I commend him for it. It was a nice plan and it could have been quite spectacular if executed better. I have always told anyone who wishes to fight in the realms that leaving Hell out of the chaos was the only rule and he chose to bring that girl *here*. As a result, all her friends came along as well. Lilith is to blame for creating that girl but Dimitri is also the problem for letting himself get too close. I explained to your son that if things went wrong, I would not be there to help. I am a man of my word, am I not?"

Tobias swallowed, hard. He nodded and then nodded again, running a hand down his button down. "Of course you are, sir."

I let out a small smile. "Your cooperation is delightful. Now please, I am not completely heartless. Go mourn your son, have a drink, do whatever you need." I looked over his shoulder, one of my servants coming through the door in a hurry.

Her heels clicked on the stone. She held a notebook to her chest and stopped the minute she was in between me and Tobias. She looked at each of our faces. "Am I interrupting?"

I laughed. "Oh no. Tobias was just leaving. What is it that you were going to do?"

Tobias blinked. "I am going home to mourn my son and then I'll be right by your side as usual, sir."

"I love to hear it." I gave him a full smile.

The servant cleared her throat. "I spoke to the guards like you asked."

Tobias was about to turn to leave, but stopped. "The guards from the attack at the Hell prison?"

The servant girl nodded but looked back at me. "Luckily there were a few that were coherent enough to answer me. Most of them didn't recognize any of them besides Dimitri and the Soul Seether. There was one though…"

I raised my eyebrows urging her to continue.

"He said he couldn't be completely sure, but would bet an eternity in Limbo that it was her."

I took in a breath and let it out with a huff. "That's all I needed to know."

Tobias stepped closer to me, clearly deciding that leaving wasn't in his best interest. "Who, sir?"

I ran my index finger over my chin, giving Tobias a once over. "Elise."

Tobias narrowed his eyes. "Why would she come back? It was my understanding she chose to go to Lilith and do her bidding."

I glanced over at my servant. She shuffled the papers in her note-book. "The guard said it seems like she was fighting alongside the Soul Seether." She blinked up at me, waiting for my reply.

Lilith truly didn't know what to do with a good thing when she had it. Whether she created it or it showed up at her door wanting to be taken under her wing. I shook my head. "Lilith's throne is empty."

Tobias reared his head back. "You don't think she's going to just waltz in there and claim it."

I shrugged, my mind filling with ideas. "She can and she will. I will need to know when she arrives and I want her brought to me."

"My son stood beside you, he wanted to impress you and you mock his death! Elise chooses to leave and go be with that vile woman, who should have never been given the power over Purgatory in the first place and you want a meeting with her, welcome her with open arms!?"

Tobias opened his mouth to continue but I grabbed his throat, watching his skin turn an ash gray, black decorating his veins. He tried to breath, flailing around.

"If you wanted to join your son, all you had to do was ask. Is that what you want, Tobias?"

His eyes bulged out as black venom dripped from the corners of his eyes. I saw my reflection in his eyes. The black cracked lines that decorated my faces, the red fire that danced in my eyes. I scoffed letting him drop to the ground with a large thud. I pointed a finger at him, letting disappointment wash over my face. "You will hold your tongue next time you wish to spew your opinions or I assure you I will rip it from your mouth and let you choke on your own blood. Are we clear, my friend?"

He nodded quickly, holding his throat. "We will bring her to you. I promise." His voice was shaky. It brought me joy.

"See yourself out." I turned away, motioning for my servant to come closer. "The moment Elise is here, the moment she steps foot into Lilith's castle and claims it as her own, you collect her for me."

"Yes sir. Anything else, sir? Would you like any gifts made up or maybe a dinner?"

"No, she will only see that as trying too hard. I will handle everything else." I gave her a smirk. "Just bring me my daughter."

Acknowledgments

Um…how do I say thank you to the readers who have made this entire series possible. Living Legend wasn't the series I thought I would write, but I'm glad I did. Some days I still feel like I could have changed something or given a little more. Overall, I am happy with Dani and Nick and how I sent them off. This isn't goodbye, it's just a see you later. They deserve all the happiness and I've been waiting for the moment when I could give them what they've been fighting for. Thank you for loving them with the same fierce commitment they have for each other.

The love of my life, Mr. Shante, I love you forever and always. You have stuck by me through my never-ending tears because this author life is hard. You have pushed me since the beginning to see this series through and I probably wouldn't have, if it wasn't for you telling me how much people needed this story and my words. Your love and humor is littered throughout this story and I wouldn't want it any other way.

To my mom, the only person who could sell my book better than me by simply saying "I birthed the author."

To my main squeezes and the OG Living Legend lovers. Kaylah and Brittany. Thank you for being my favorite beta readers! You are stuck with me. Full stop.

To my PA, Ashley, thank you for handling my dramatics and helping make my dreams come true. Thank you for alpha reading and loving this series just as much as I do. You are the best lead demon a girl could ask for.

To my author babies, you know who you are, that have made this author journey bearable.

Shoutout to Halle, my cover designer, who has made every cover in this series a complete banger.

To my arc readers & street team, thank you for making me feel like a rockstar.

About the Author

Allie Shante was born and raised in Georgia and graduated from Georgia State University with a biology degree. While science was fun, books have always been a part of her heart and writing right up there with it. After writing and never finishing any of the books she started, she buckled down years later to finish a novel she never actually expected to write, let alone finish.

When she's not reading and writing confident females and stubborn men, she enjoys being an overprotective dog mom and crushing escape rooms with her husband.

Check her out at:
www.authorallieshante.com
Follow Allie:

instagram.com/allieshantewrites
tiktok.com/@allieshantewrites

www.ingramcontent.com/pod-product-compliance
Lightning Source LLC
Chambersburg PA
CBHW020335010826
48970CB00012B/920